ELIXIR SAVED

KATIE L. CARROLL

Published by Shimmer Publications, LLC

Cover illustration by Sue Tait Porcaro

ISBN: 9780998925448

Visit the author's website at www.katielcarroll.com

For Kylene
Always

Prologue

Odeletta, the Princess of Spring, had been holed up in the frozen wasteland of Blanchardwood for hundreds of years. Her only respite from the cold was the courtyard garden in Kristalis, her ice palace. But there was no respite from a broken heart. Or the bitterness that had turned her more frigid than the coldest of winter days.

Hopes of returning to her former self dwindled with each passing year. Her love, Fyren, had betrayed her, tricked her into loving him so he could steal the power of true love's kiss. He'd taken what he wanted and abandoned her, never having loved her at all. His true love was power, and there was never enough of that to go around for creatures like him.

Odeletta was the Ice Queen now, and would remain so forevermore.

The problem with stealing another's power, though, lay in the bonds that tied the two together. A magic that—unlike hearts —was unbreakable. So when Fyren began using that power to amass magic in the old fort of Drim, Odeletta sensed this. For she didn't know it, but all during her sojourn in Blanchardwood, she had slowly been strengthening. The hurt of a broken heart concealed her growing strength, but it was there. Oh, it was there.

The sensation, a tingling under her skin, a blaze of heat she had felt only one other time in the moment just before Fyren's lips had touched hers, awakened one frozen morning and set it apart from all the thousands of frozen mornings before. And with it, she became aware of her strength, something she had long thought dead and buried beneath the mountains of snow.

All morning it rippled and wrapped around her, growing like poison ivy strangling a tree. She relished the feeling as it replaced the years of heartache, until finally it burst forth in a spark of fire. An arc of lightning surged into the sky and landed far, far away.

With it three messages were sent, irrevocably.

Odeletta, spent of her power, retreated to her garden sanctuary where she would listen, and wait, and feel. For now that she had released her heartache into the world, her insides were no longer frozen. It was exhilarating and terrifying. There was hope once more that spring would return to Blanchardwood, but it would come at a cost. And it was no longer Odeletta who would pay the price.

If the messages were heeded, sacrifices would be made. Lives would be changed. And lost.

Chapter One

The moment lightning cracked from the clear autumn sky and struck the old oak tree overhanging the outdoor stage, a familiar ache returned to Kylene's arm. It was a pain that had nothing to do with magical lightning—or everything to do with it. The voice of a higher being rang in her head with a message, the implications of which rooted her in place as if she suffered from a bad case of stage fright.

A fiery branch crashed down and split the backdrop straight down the middle, barely missing Kylene and the other actors. Sparks shot out toward the crowd. The whole production—written by, directed by, and starring Kylene—flashed to a halt.

Pushing through the shock of the absurd moment, she regained her senses and took a spectacular leap off the stage. She tumbled to the hard ground, the browning grass pricking her palms and staining her pants. She pushed off the ground and dashed away from the carnage.

From a safe distance, she watched the destruction, a tingling numbness overtaking all her feelings, except of course the chronic pain from the old spear wound. The dose of healing Elixir she had stolen from her sister's stores had staved off the throbbing for a paltry two hours. She had hoped for half a day, or at least to make it through the performance. What was a couple hours of relief when she had been suffering for more than two years?

The wooden stage served as kindling and the whole thing billowed with smoke and flames in a matter of minutes. She backed farther away to escape the ash, but acrid smoke curled close and burned her throat. Props of faux golden pillars melted and distorted into shapes reminiscent of grotesque faces. As the stage collapsed in on itself, she sank to her knees and sobbed, fingers digging into the cold dirt.

A strong hand pulled her to her feet. Her younger but much

taller brother, Bhar, grasped her hands. His blue eyes turned hazel as they reflected the orange flames.

He squeezed her shoulders. "You okay?"

Kylene wasn't, not really—she hadn't been okay in a long time—but she nodded, knowing Bhar wasn't asking about her state of being, rather inquiring if she was hurt from the fire. As she searched the frenzied crowd, her stomach twisted in worry. She had been mourning the production when she should have been making sure everyone was safe.

The list of family members tumbled from her dry lips, "Ma, Pop, Lili, Ariana, Katora, the kids? The cast?"

"They're all fine!" Bhar yelled over his shoulder as he ran to the perimeter of the disaster. "Pop says meet at the farmhouse. I'll see you there."

He peered into the flames, presumably searching for anyone trapped in the ruins of the stage, but it seemed everyone had escaped. A crowd of spectators, actors, and crew—many crying—streaked past. An old man fell in the chaos. Bhar lifted him up, offered him a shoulder to lean on, and escorted him to the road, the two of them disappearing into the throng.

Kylene stood, frozen in place, while her dreams of a successful production burned to the ground. The last support beam creaked and groaned, giving itself to the inferno. She fled, the early autumn leaves crackling underfoot in rhythm with her hiccuping sobs. Her white-blond hair flew wildly in her wake and tears flowed from her bright blue eyes, obscuring her vision. Not that seeing mattered; her feet knew the way down the dirt road to home.

It wasn't the failure in front the entire town of Tussar that brought on the tears as much as the message resonating in her head. In the Great Peninsula, higher beings—sometimes even Mother Nature herself—communicated with humans through the weather. The messages were often cryptic, hard to interpret. However, the message brought by the lightning was as clear as the glass bottles that held the essence her family made—a renowned beverage in the Great Peninsula.

Kylene sprinted straight through the front door of her family's wooden farmhouse, up the creaky stairs, and into the room she shared with her sister Katora. She flung herself onto her bed and sucked in heaving breaths. Even with her face buried deep in the freshly laundered pillow slip, all she smelled was fire.

Before long, a warm hand caressed her back accompanied by Katora's soothing voice. "Shhh. It's okay. Don't cry, Ky."

Easy enough for Katora to say. She never cried. She didn't have to worry every minute about her emotions spilling over because they kept a vigilant perch on the edge of a knife. Kylene's emotions had always run deeper than the waters of the West Raur River, but the added strain of chronic pain had pushed her to her limits. She knew her whole family thought she cried too much; they didn't know the wound plagued her. Katora, with her healing Elixir, least of all would understand why Kylene was so quick to shed tears.

Eventually the sobs abated and Kylene's body quieted. She sat and smiled at Katora, one of her three older sisters, the one closest in age to Kylene.

Katora's blue-green eyes sparkled in her flushed faced. "You heard the message too. Sounds like another quest."

Kylene rubbed her eyes and frowned. She shared neither her sister's interpretation of the message nor her enthusiasm for quests. The last and only quest she had been on had nearly killed her. Kylene had gone to support Katora, whose job was to pick the flowers that gave their family's secret Elixir its healing magic, but Kylene had received a deadly wound from a poisoned spear as a souvenir. If not for the Elixir, she probably would have died. As it was, the wound bothered her most of the day and often kept her awake long into the night.

Fresh tears prickled the corners of her eyes. "The message for the last quest, to pick the flowers for the Elixir..." Kylene paused, not sure how to phrase what she wanted to know without giving away her secrets. "Did you hear it?"

"No." Katora's brow furrowed. "I only saw the snow. The message was for Pop—he was guardian of the Elixir then."

5

"Did Pop tell you what he heard?" Kylene asked. "The specific message."

Katora stared past Kylene, not looking at anything in particular. "I don't know if he heard a specific message. What was it he said? Something about how the greater beings aren't always clear on what they mean. He told me the snowstorm came as the Elixir's supply was low, so he took that as a message that we needed to retrieve more of the nectar."

Kylene frowned. The message she heard as the lightning struck held no such ambiguity. "But you heard a specific message this time?"

Katora's eyes sparkled with excitement. "Oh, yes. It was like someone speaking right inside my head. No guessing games this time."

The experience sounded the same as Kylene's. Tears squeaked from her eyes again, blurring Katora's face so much it reminded Kylene of the grotesque shapes of the melting columns. Perhaps she had misinterpreted the message and someone else would be made to fulfill it. She shivered, sending a fresh wave of pain up her arm. She didn't want the message to be true for her or anyone else.

Katora wrapped her up in a hug, which made Kylene think she must really look a mess. Her sister wasn't the hugging type. Kylene breathed in the earthy scent of her sister's clothes and searched deep inside herself for peace. She thought of the neat lines of essenberry vines framed by blue sky and fluffy clouds, and managed to keep the tears from resurfacing.

Her family grew essenberries to make essence, a different beverage than the Elixir. Where the Elixir was a powerful and dangerous healing potion, essence was a regular drink. Delicious, but lacking in any magical properties, and created as a front to hide the fact that the Kase family brewed and guarded the Elixir.

Katora held her at arm's length. "Go clean up. Pop wants us all—Lili and Ariana too—to meet in the dining room."

Lili and Ariana were the oldest and second oldest, respectively, of the five Kase siblings; the only two who no longer lived at home. Although in their primeyears, Kylene, Katora, and Bhar still resided at Kase Farm. Katora would probably live here her whole life as she was in the process of taking over for Pop as head farmer. Kylene couldn't imagine living anywhere else, but she wasn't sure if a future at Kase Farm was hers to dream about.

She feared if she went on this quest, she wouldn't have a future beyond it. She hoped the premonition was like many of her initial reactions, which tended to be overreactions.

In the washroom, Kylene splashed the last of the tears from her face and stared in the mirror above the washbowl. Red lines streaked the whites of her eyes; only time would wash those clean. It took several tries with shaking hands to smooth her hair into a ponytail.

Tranquility eluded her. She sought her special place, the Golden City, to calm her nerves. She had been transported there briefly during the quest for the Elixir's nectar. It was the inspiration behind her now defunct play, and a place with no pain. In her mind, she conjured the gold buildings, which sparkled a rainbow of colors in the sunlight, as easily as if she had seen them yesterday. The city's music and sweet voices singing in an unknown language filled her heart once more. It beat heavy in her chest, and her hands steadied.

With measured breaths, she descended the stairs to face her family and find out whether or not the fated message from the higher beings was her destiny.

Chapter Two

Zelenka sat next to Palafair in special chairs on the Kases' dining room table, waiting for the family meeting to begin. Palafair claimed they were seats of honor, but they only served to remind Zelenka of the fact that she stood a good four feet shorter than Katora, the smallest Kase sibling.

Six months since Zelenka and Palafair had gotten married, and she still didn't feel like part of the family. Perhaps because Palafair wasn't a true member of the Kase family. Zelenka knew demicks, especially tilli demicks, had no business pretending like any human wanted them as more than employees. It was easier for Palafair, being an anni demick, to live with the Kases. Ever since crossing the Narrow Pass to the Great Peninsula, the anni had peacefully existed with humans. Not the case for the tilli, who had chosen to retreat to the wilds of Faway Forest. The Kases were more open-minded than most, but many humans considered the tilli demicks wild creatures.

Zelenka's way out of this bizarre family dynamic came in the form of a lightning bolt and a message from the higher beings. *Go back home.* The message couldn't have been more clear than if it had been etched in the cliffs of the Three River Split, the place she longed to be, the place she would return to even if Palafair argued for her to stay at Kase Farm. The Three River Split. Home.

She doubted she would receive a warm welcome. The last thing she had done before leaving her people was throw their leader, Roodesh, out of a cave window to his death. Roodesh had gone mad searching for immortality the Elixir couldn't provide. He also happened to be her father. By throwing him to his death, Zelenka had released him from the madness, and gained herself and her people independence from his dictatorship. But she had fled before being able to explain all that, and without taking the time to mourn.

She sent a silent prayer to the Great Mother that she could mend her broken relationship with the tilli and that Palafair would be at her side when she returned.

Her leg ached as she sat perched upon the table like a roasted turkey waiting to be consumed on the winter solstice. Immediately after her father's death, Zelenka had joined Palafair and the Kases on Katora's quest for the Elixir's secret ingredient. They had tangled with Yeselda—a higher being and the witch of Faway Forest—and fought her animal army. Zelenka had nearly died. The Elixir had saved her life, but it couldn't fully heal her leg.

Palafair rubbed her thigh and flashed a warm smile, accentuating the wrinkles around his eyes. He always doted on her. She loved him because of—and sometimes in spite of—his devotion.

Kylene, the youngest Kase daughter, floated into the room, all wispy hair and long, thin limbs. Zelenka noticed Kylene's bloodshot eyes, and her stomach knotted with a pang of sympathy for the primeyear girl. Watching months of hard work burn to ashes in mere minutes would take its toll on someone as hard-tempered as Zelenka, never mind on someone with as sensitive a soul as Kylene.

Katora, the current guardian of the Elixir, entered next, followed by Pop, the former guardian. He sat at the head of the table, and Katora sat beside him. Katora's face was flush. Zelenka imagined the excitement Katora was feeling over a new quest was akin to her own. Zelenka supposed she would allow Katora to accompany her to the Three River Split. She had proven her loyalty in many ways and was a fierce fighter.

It was hard to come to terms with the fact that Katora was an ally, not an enemy, as it had felt like for so long on the last quest. The two strong-willed women were too similar and competitive to be easy friends.

The rest of the Kase family trickled in until finally the room burst with people. The fire crackling in the hearth coupled with the body heat created an oppressive atmosphere. All the more reason to go back to the Three River Split and its chilly, drippy caves, away from all these humans and their vast bodies congregating in small spaces.

A seed of a plan had begun to grow in Zelenka's mind. She hoped she could convince Palafair to go along with it. He loved the Kase family in a way Zelenka never would. Not that she hated them; they had treated her well in the two years she had spent with them. It was difficult to find love for a species who had treated her own people so badly. Even if the Kases themselves had not perpetrated the misdeeds, they also did little to correct those who thought poorly of the tilli.

Pop cleared his throat and effectively earned her attention. He stood and gazed on them with downturned lips. "It is a sad day that we were not blessed to see Kylene's wonderful production of the Golden City. It is a happy day that no one was seriously injured in the fire." He raised a glass. "To hard work even if it does not come to fruition. I pray to the Great Mother that one day we will witness Kylene's play in all its glory."

The family raised their glasses. For her part, Zelenka clinked cups with Palafair and offered Kylene a nod.

Pop paced across the hearth, hands behind his back. "Unfortunately it may be some time before we will have that opportunity. All too often I call a family meeting to announce that some of us are to leave. The lightning strike, while unnecessarily jarring, was an obvious enough message from the higher beings."

Zelenka rubbed her hands together, knowing what was coming, as Pop continued, "Katora and I both received the same message. 'The Ice Queen needs you.' We believe it means Katora must travel to Blanchardwood to speak with Odeletta, the Ice Queen and daughter of Mother Nature."

Zelenka scowled; that wasn't the message she had received, and she wasn't the only unhappy one. Kylene's features fell at Pop's announcement and tears shimmered in her light blue eyes.

Before Zelenka could compose her thoughts and announce her own plans, Pop said, "I know it has been all too brief a time since you have returned from your last quest to retrieve the nectar for the Elixir, but I am requesting Bhar, Kylene, Palafair, and Zelenka set off on this new mission as soon as we can make arrangements."

"Hirsten should go, too," Katora added. Hirsten was Katora's boyfriend, and he was a good choice for any journey because he had the ability to create magical maps.

"No!" Zelenka stood and winced when pain shot up her leg. She cleared her throat as the Kase family looked at her quizzically. "I do not protest Hirsten's inclusion. I protest mine." Palafair's eyes narrowed in concern as he squeezed her hand. "I will not—cannot—go with Katora."

Pop rubbed the sparse stubble on his chin. "Zelenka, my dear friend, I would never make you do anything. As I said, it is a request, not a demand. The message was for Katora and does not bind you."

Zelenka stared at Katora, a frown playing at the primeyear girl's lips. She didn't want Katora, or any of the other Kases, to think her a coward. "It is not what you think. I received a different message from the lightning strike."

A murmur of voices blended with the shuffle of clothing and the scrape of a chair. Palafair's hand slipped from hers. Everyone in the room seemed surprised at the news of a second message. Everyone, Zelenka noticed, except for Kylene, who sat perfectly still, a tiny tear slipping down the side of her nose.

Zelenka cleared her throat and the room quieted. "I must return to the Three River Split. The time has come for me to return home and make amends. I only ask for a few provisions for the road."

Her heart pulsed with excitement...and a touch of nerves. She took up Palafair's hand. Her voice cracked at the next request. "Palafair, I want you to come with me."

He knelt at her feet. "I will go anywhere with you, my love."

Zelenka's face warmed, not at the public declaration—she was used to such displays from Palafair—but at the joy filling her heart that her husband would stand by her. It had been silly to doubt him; he was Palafair, her love.

Pop clapped his hands. "The higher beings never cease to surprise me. Very well, Zelenka. I would never keep you, or Palafair, from such an important task. You know you are welcome to anything we can provide. I would send along Katora and the others if they didn't have their own mission."

Zelenka's heartbeat settled into a calmer rhythm as she and Palafair both sat back down in their special chairs. Pop wasn't going to challenge her.

Pop turned to his daughter. "Katora, let's adjourn to my study." He turned to the demicks. "I think you two should come along. We'll discuss your arrangements as well."

Zelenka's heart raced again at the thought of going home. It was really happening. She had always known she would return to the Split, but before today, it had been something for the future.

Ma pushed her chair back, stood, and said in a voice that would have been loud for most people but was normal for her, "Everyone else to the kitchen to help with supper."

Zelenka climbed down the leg of the table on special pegs that had been set up for the demicks. She took Palafair's hand as they headed to the library, her heart a pitter-patter of excitement in her chest.

Chapter Three

As soon as Pop Pop—as all of Pop's grandchildren called him—declared there was to be a private meeting in the study, Devon slipped out of the dining room unnoticed. One advantage to having a large family was that it was easy to get lost in the shuffle. His mother, Ariana, probably wouldn't notice his absence in the kitchen, as she always had her hands full with Devon's younger sister and brother. The disadvantage of a large family was that it was easy to be overlooked. He refused to be overlooked on the matter of this latest quest.

He crept into the dark room before the invited family members arrived. Shadows from the low flames in the fireplace danced along the bookshelves, igniting Devon's imagination. In one corner he saw a hooded spirit of the forest, in another a giant bulbous-nosed face. He shook his head, trying to dislodge the illusions.

Voices from the hallway did what he could not and chased away the shadows. He squeezed behind a high-backed chair and crouched in the corner, hidden from view. Through the slit between the chair and the wall, he watched Pop Pop and Katora enter the study. Palafair, who stood as tall as Pop Pop's knee, and the slightly shorter Zelenka came in next, holding hands. Katora closed the door behind them.

Devon heard the faint pop of a lantern being lit. Brightness filled the room, not quite reaching his corner. He heard the shuffle of bodies settling down. A crinkly squeak of leather told him someone had sat in the seat creating his hiding place.

"The higher beings never cease to amaze me." Devon shrank farther into his corner as Pop Pop's booming voice seemed to vibrate the chair. "Two messages with one lightning strike. Two perfectly clear messages at that."

Devon resisted the urge to peek around the edge of the seat

as Katora asked, "Are they not usually so clear?"

Pop Pop chuckled. "Not in my experience. Then again, times have never been so desperate."

"You mean the rumors of strong magic at Drim," Katora said. "Who—or what—do you think is the source?"

"There are few creatures powerful enough to create magic that strong," Pop Pop said.

"You think it is a greater being," piped in Zelenka.

The chair in front of Devon creaked again, and he imagined Pop Pop nodding. "The question is are they working to help us or harm us."

There was a tense beat of silence before Katora asked, "And if it's to harm us?"

"Then we may be facing a war," Pop Pop said. The tension tightened around the room like a rope on a turnbuckle.

War was a scary word. He had studied wars in school: conflicts between the higher beings and the giants in ancient times, and the more recent, but still long ago, battle between humans and Fyren the Fallen. He knew of it as a rare thing of the past, not here in the present.

Devon clenched his teeth to keep quiet. Now was not the time to reveal himself and declare his intentions of going on a quest. He listened to every sound as Pop Pop stood. He heard the thunk of wood as it was added to the fire, Pop Pop's soft pacing footsteps, and the heavy beat of his own heart. He waited, nearly holding his breath.

Finally, Pop Pop spoke from somewhere near the fireplace, his voice sounding less commanding than before. "Two years ago when I sent you for the nectar, I feared this." Pop Pop sighed long and low.

Devon remembered Katora going on a quest but didn't know it had been for nectar. Before he could wonder about it too long, Pop Pop continued, "That was when I first heard reports of activity in the old fort Drim. Magical activity. And then there was the snowstorm that made you guardian, Katora. The signs are pointing for us to be prepared. How is the supply of Elixir?"

Devon's brain tripped over the word "Elixir," not because he didn't know the word itself, but because the way Pop Pop used it so familiarly. Then the discussion moved on.

"The supply is plentiful," Katora said. "I've been making lots of it since picking the flowers. And with the new formula Bhar and I worked out, what we have is more potent than ever."

Bhar was in the on this Elixir, too. Did everyone know of it but Devon?

A touch of smoke permeated the room from the fresh logs on the fire; a tickle in Devon's throat threatened to turn to a cough. He swallowed repeatedly in an effort to keep his throat clear.

As Pop Pop sat again, the chair slid back, closing in on Devon's hiding spot. "I'll make sure there are supplies here at the farm, so we won't have to suffer if shipments are delayed. We have our own produce and wood. We can get local meat from the market in town, but I'll store extra here just in case. What else?"

Palafair's tinkly voice chimed in, "Flour, soap, blankets, and clothes. You should bottle and store extra water as well."

"It would be wise to be properly outfitted with weapons," said Zelenka.

The tension tightened further, the crackle of the fire the only sound in the room.

Finally Pop Pop sighed. "I suppose you're right."

Devon could feel the reluctance of the words. With all this talk of war, Devon wouldn't mind having a weapon or two at his disposal. He had a small pocketknife, but he doubted that would help much in a battle.

"I'll speak to the Tines about making extra weapons," Pop Pop conceded.

Devon's stomach gave a flutter. The Tines were Tussar's blacksmiths. Their daughter, Emmaline, used to baby-sit his brother and sister when Devon was too old for a baby-sitter himself but not "responsible enough," as his mother used to say, to watch his siblings on his own. Emmaline had become a primeyear two winters past, and Devon had always had a bit of a crush on her. There was a certain poem he had been working on that he would give to her, if he ever got the courage up to do it.

He silently shifted his position and wondered if it was time to reveal himself. His legs were beginning to cramp, the tickle in his throat was worsening, and he was just plain tired of being quiet. He scooted his back along the wall as quietly as he could and managed to maneuver into a sitting position, relieving some of the pain in his legs. He would wait it out a little longer.

"Here's my proposal for the quest," Katora said from much closer than Devon expected.

It seemed in his shuffling, he had missed her coming near, her arm resting across the back of Pop Pop's chair. "Hirsten, Bhar, Kylene, and I travel to Lughorn. We drop off a shipment of essence as cover. From there, it's only a short journey to Blanchardwood and Kristalis, the Ice Queen's palace."

Her arm inched farther down the back of the chair, closer and closer to Devon's head. He quieted his breathing, despite his racing heart.

"You'll need a guide through Blanchardwood." Pop Pop's voice was once again across the room. "I have contacts in Lughorn who can set you up with one."

"I wish I could be two places at once," Palafair said. "I hate to think of you four in Lughorn without me."

Katora's hand hovered inches from Devon's upturned face. "We'll be fine. Your duties lie with Zelenka."

"It's settled then," Pop Pop said, his voice getting closer to Devon with each word. "We'll prepare everything tomorrow, and you can all leave the day after that." Pop Pop's hand appeared on the back of the chair. "The only matter that remains to be settled is a serious one."

"Oh, what is that?" Katora asked in a falsely high voice.

Devon held his breath, anticipating more bad news. Finally Pop Pop let out an exaggerated sigh. "The matter of what to do about eavesdroppers."

Before Devon could react, the chair flew away from him, exposing his hiding spot. His instinct was to back up, and he smacked his head against the wall. Pop Pop and Katora, arms folded across their chests and mouths tight in frowns, stood in front of him, sentries blocking any chance of a quick exit. Devon rubbed his head as he stood. He caught Zelenka smiling from across the room.

Devon pasted a nonchalant grin on his face. "So you've found me."

Even though he was taller than Katora, her glower made him feel demick-sized.

"I can explain," he said as he held his hands out in front of him.

Katora shot a sideways glance to Pop Pop before narrowing her eyes. "Explain? What's there to explain? You snuck in here and have been eavesdropping on our private conversation. I wonder what your mom will think of that."

"I only did it because I want to go with you," he said. "I'm almost a primeyear, and it's time I got to go on a family adventure."

"It's not the winter solstice yet," said Katora, which was when Devon would officially move out of his youngeryears into his primeyears. "Even if it was, this isn't a quest for baby primeyears."

Pop Pop put his arm around Devon's shoulder. "I admire your bravery, but this mission is not for you."

"But—" Devon began.

"No buts," Pop Pop said. "You're not going, and we're not discussing this further. Nor will anything discussed tonight leave this room. Understand?" Devon nodded, knowing for once it was best to keep his mouth shut. "Good. We have much to do before everyone leaves." Pop Pop guided Devon to the door. "Why don't you see how dinner is coming along?"

Despite the pressure of Pop Pop's hand on his back, Devon held his ground. "Can I ask one thing?"

Pop Pop looked down, firelight dancing in his blue eyes. "You already did, but you may ask something else."

"What's the Elixir?" Devon held his breath while he waited for the answer, but had to let it out because Pop Pop just stood there stroking the stubble on his chin.

Finally he answered, "It's a very powerful healing Elixir. And it's important for the safety of all of us that you keep it a secret. Not a word to Skylynn or Landon." Those were Devon's younger siblings. "Certainly not a word to any of your friends. Understood?"

Devon shook his head solemnly, but that wasn't enough for Katora. "You must swear on the Great Mother."

Devon placed his hand on his heart. "I swear on the Great Mother. Just don't tell *my* mother. Okay?"

"Only if you don't tell her either." Katora pushed him over the threshold. "Off you go." She closed the door behind him with a loud bang.

As hard as it was to keep secrets, he knew this one was important to keep. The quest and his exclusion from it was another matter. As he shuffled down the hallway, he decided that no matter what Pop Pop said, he would find a way to be a part of an adventure soon.

Chapter Four

Kylene received the news of her role in the quest with as much grace, and as few tears, as she could manage. She pitched in all the next day and followed orders from Katora on packing the wagon, earning herself a mighty sore arm in the process. Despite the fatigue of a hard day's work, she knew she'd have trouble sleeping. That evening she approached Pop in his study.

The door was open a crack, and she ed in to see Pop sitting at his desk, head bent low over a mess of papers. She knocked quietly on the doorframe. Pop looked up and smiled, accentuating the fine lines of his face. Kylene didn't remember there being so many.

"Have a seat." He indicated the leather chair in the corner and turned his own chair to face it. Kylene obliged his request, the cold leather chilling her bottom. "You look concerned. What's the matter?"

"I…" Kylene trailed off.

She wasn't sure how to ask what she wanted to know without raising Pop's concern. Since she was the only one who had heard her particular message from the Ice Queen, she figured it was her burden to carry. Still, she had questions that needed answers.

Kylene took a deep breath and tried again. "I wanted to know how often you've received messages from the higher beings."

"That's an easy answer," Pop said. "Exactly three times. The first, I was in my primeyears, right after I took over as guardian of the Elixir. The message came in the form of a flash flood, which wiped out an entire crop of essenberries. Not having to worry about the crop that season gave me lots of time to work on a new batch of Elixir. That winter's cold brought with it a nasty illness, but the Elixir never ran low." He paused and studied her face. "You know the other two. The second was when I passed guardianship to Katora, and the third was at your play."

19

"Were you upset with the first message when the crop was ruined?" Kylene asked.

He stared into the fire as if remembering. She shoved her hands under her legs to keep from fidgeting.

"I was angry. We're blessed with wonderful soil here in the south of the Great Peninsula, and the farm has a plentiful water source in the West Raur River, but it takes long days and much effort to grow life. Backaches, sunburn, dry hands. All those pains come with being a farmer, and there are few things worse than a lost crop."

"Do you think you would've had enough Elixir to treat everyone if there had not been a flood?"

"Probably not."

"So the," Kylene thought a moment about the next word before saying it aloud, "sacrifice of the crop was worth it?"

Pop cocked his head the slightest bit. "You certainly know how to ask tough questions. Yes, the sacrifice was worth it. The Elixir saved many lives that winter, and no one was harmed from having to miss a single season's worth of essence."

Her shoulders slumped in sadness. It was the answer Kylene expected but not the one she had hoped for.

What will be my task? And will it be worth it?

Pop's voice pulled her from her thoughts. "You don't have to go with Katora."

Dare she tell him she had heard a different message from the Ice Queen? Could she reveal that it wasn't that she didn't want to go with Katora, but rather she was afraid of what she would have to do while on the quest? She shook her head. No. It was her problem, not Pop's. He already had too many things to worry about.

"I want to go," she said. "To help Katora." *And to help myself figure out what the message really means.*

"I know you do." Pop smiled. "You always want to help others. It's one of the things I love most about you. That and how you always see the good in others."

He stood and pulled her out of the chair, embracing her in a tight hug. Kylene wrapped her arms around his torso and breathed in the fresh-linen scent of his shirt.

He kissed her on the forehead. "Get some sleep. You have a long journey ahead of you."

"Thanks, Pop. I love you."

"I love you too, Kylene."

She closed the door behind her, the quiet click echoing in her head. It felt like she was closing a door on any happy future she had imagined.

* * * *

As the sun rose the next morning, Kylene let the tears slip down her cheeks while she sat in the back of the wagon with Bhar. Her warm breath rose in smoky puffs in the cool autumn air. Up front Katora, with Hirsten beside her, took the reins and urged the horse forward. Palafair and Zelenka traveled in a much smaller wagon, tethered to a pony borrowed from the great-granddaughter of an old family friend.

Through tear-filled vision, Kylene watched a waving Ma and Pop grow smaller. When the wagon turned a corner and her family home vanished from sight, Kylene closed her eyes. She hoped the clip clop of the animals would drown out the dread hanging around her thicker than smoke from green firewood.

A mile north of Tussar, Palafair and Zelenka turned off the east road toward the Three River Split. Kylene waved good-bye as she and the others continued north.

Her tears had run dry; she watched the scenery pass by with clear eyes. Orange and yellow leaves glimmered in the weak morning sun. A single, brown leaf from high up on an oak tree—the same type of tree that had fallen on her stage and burned it—floated down through the air into her blanket-covered lap.

She picked it up by the stem and held it to her nose, inhaling the musty scent. In it she smelled Ma's nut bread baking in the oven, the summer-kissed soil after a long day in the essenberry fields, and one of Pop's dirty shirts before she plunged it into soapy water. She dropped the leaf over the side of the wagon, shedding her sour mood with it. No sense ruining the time with self-pity.

"Let's play a game." Her words sounded melodic in the quiet air.

Bhar opened his eyes, picked his chin up from his chest, and yawned. "That's more like it. Let's liven up this journey. What do you want to play?"

"Hierarchy," Katora piped in from the front. "Tournament style. Ky and Bhar you start."

Hierarchy was a game Katora and Bhar had invented. It involved two players throwing different hand signals and a complicated point system. Kylene had never bothered to learn the intricacies of the scoring and usually lost, but she was willing to try any distraction. She mostly threw water—wiggling fingers splayed out—because it beat all but one other signal, although it was worth the fewest points.

The game wore on, Kylene solidly in last, along with the day. The road north grew busier as the trees grew scarcer. Many of the people in carts or passing by on foot recognized the Kases and offered cheerful greetings.

"Off to sell more essence," one man said with a tip of his hat. "Give my regards to your parents."

A woman in a tattered overcoat came right up to the wagon, forcing Katora to slow it to a stop. She kissed Katora on the hand and smiled to show crooked yellow teeth. "May the Great Mother bless ya for helping an old woman."

Face in a tight frown, Katora patted the woman's hand, before clicking her tongue and urging the horse forward. While passing the woman, Kylene offered the smile her sister refused to give.

The woman waved her arms above her head and shouted at Katora, "Take care, girl! I've never met none with your healing powers!"

The Kases kept the Elixir a secret; it was part of the magic that bound Katora, and Pop before her, to it. Therefore, many who had been treated with the Elixir didn't know it existed. This had given Katora something of a reputation as a healer. All day long, strangers greeted Katora in a similar fashion, Kylene awed by the number of people it had helped.

Before nightfall, the travelers stopped to make camp a ways off the road. They had left behind the outskirts of the forest miles ago. With no trees to block the view, the cerulean sky stretched out in every direction like a massive dome until it met the muted earth tones of the plains.

The sun seemed to take a long time to dip behind the horizon. Campfires from other travelers popped up all along the open countryside, giant stars of the land. Once settled in her bed of blankets near the hot embers of the dying fire, Kylene connected the real stars into shapes, making her own constellations.

First she strung together a rainbow, each segment the same dark blue. Next she formed a unicorn, reworking its posture until it appeared to be jumping over the monotone rainbow. *Is it still a rainbow if it's only one color?* Kylene smiled that she was able to contemplate a thought having nothing to do with the cursed message from the Ice Queen. She sighed, losing her hold on the links she created in the sky.

From down by her feet, Hirsten whispered, "It's always worst the first night."

"What?" Kylene whispered back.

"The homesickness." Hirsten propped himself on his elbows and glanced around. Next to him, Katora was sound asleep, and across the fire from Kylene, so was Bhar. "Katora and I are lucky. We have each other. She would never admit it, but she gets homesick too. She loves Kase Farm more than she'll admit."

"It's the perfect place to call home," Kylene said.

Hirsten nodded, then rested his head on his hands and stared at the fire. Kylene wondered whether he thought of Kase Farm as his home. He didn't live there, but he seemed to spend more time there than anywhere else. She supposed he and Katora would marry one day and live together on the farm.

It was easy to imagine their future but hard to picture her own.

"Hey," Hirsten said, and she realized she was staring at the sharp lines of his jaw. "I know you're practically my sister, but I consider us friends as well."

"Me too." The realization brought a smile to her face. "Goodnight."

"'Night, Ky." He yawned and snuggled up to Katora.

Kylene rolled on her side and stared at the twinkling coals. Everything looked like stars tonight. Maybe that was what happened when people died; they became stars. Spending the afterlife, shimmering up there in the great unknown, might not be so bad. A single tear rolled down her cheek. She caught it and flung it into the fire. Then she tucked the rest of her sadness away for the night.

Chapter Five

The scuffing of an animal in the ashes of the fire woke Kylene. A russet fox paused in its scraping and appraised her with a swift up and down movement of its snout, like it was nodding. Then it returned to its task, digging into the ashes with a paw until it reached deep enough to where the coals burned hot. She wondered how it tolerated the heat, if it possessed magic.

The fox nuzzled the sizzling coals with its snout until it uncovered a faceted gem the same reddish-brown as its fur. A thin, pink tongue lapped up the jewel and then hung out in the open air, a fine mist rising from it. Golden eyes peered at Kylene for a long moment. With a sharp yelp, the fox snapped its mouth shut, and the gem disappeared.

An impulse to reach out and touch its fluffy tail overtook Kylene, but the fox turned and ran away before her hand came out of the blanket. With unnatural speed and grace, the creature dashed across the browning grass of the plains and vanished into the sunrise.

Kylene scooted out of bed, the cold of an autumn morning nipping at her nose and ears. She pulled a hat from the depths of the blanket and tugged it over her head. Squatting at the edge of the fire pit, she touched her finger to where the fox had dug and yanked it away in an instant. The coals sizzled with heat. She slipped the tip of her finger into her mouth to try and stop the burning pain.

The stirring of her companions pushed away the magic spell of the fox. The buzz of morning preparations drowned out the questions that had formulated from observing the fox. She wondered if the incident had been a dream that bled into her waking state.

She paused her packing to find the spot where the ashes had been disturbed and decided she hadn't dreamed the whole thing;

maybe her sleep-addled mind had exaggerated it, and it had simply been a fox digging in the coals.

Katora slapped a plate of veggies into her hands. "Warm it in the coals if you want. Then we need to get moving if we want to reach Skimere on schedule."

Kylene grabbed Katora's elbow to keep her from walking away. "Have you've ever seen foxes in the plains?"

"Sure," Katora said. "From time to time."

"Do they ever act funny?"

"Funny?" Katora raised her right eyebrow in question. "They act like foxes. You might get a glimpse of them at dusk or dawn, but they keep away from people and the road. Why?"

"No reason really." Kylene didn't want to get into it with Katora; it could lead to a whole lot of questions she didn't know how to answer. "I saw one this morning."

She left it at that, and Katora seemed satisfied with the answer, or she was too preoccupied to dwell over it. At least the strange behavior of the fox had taken Kylene's mind off her arm and the message. She'd hardly thought of either as they ate and finished packing.

As they headed back to the road, Kylene took one last look at the fire pit. The morning activities had obscured any evidence of the fox. So much of her current life was consumed by uncertainty, she welcomed the idea of a mystery to solve that didn't focus on her mortality.

* * * *

The fox did not make another appearance for the remainder of their trip to Skimere. The last rays of the setting sun were swallowed by the buildings and cast the streets in an early darkness. Kylene had been there once before with Pop on an essence delivery. He had been guardian of the Elixir then, so perhaps he had been there on Elixir business as well. She remembered thinking the city was very large and very loud, but now she found the mess of building and alleys, the whinny of horses pulling carts, and the shouts of people on the streets a welcome distraction.

This trip to Skimere, her overriding impression was of dirt and noise. Smoke rose out of high chimneys, filling the air with the scent of oak, roasting meat, and spices. No building stood more than five stories, but the Skimere Mountains loomed a few miles north, making the city seem small in comparison, though it was far bigger than Tussar.

Katora navigated the wagon through dusty streets, her deft hand guiding the horse through the narrow spaces. She stopped in front of a two-story building that sprawled over most of one block. The sign read SKY INN and had an image of an open door. By now the streets were dotted with lights, curious lanterns with no flame that Kylene guessed were lit by magic.

Katora offered Bhar a ten-inch dagger sheathed in leather that bore the sunburst symbol of Mother Nature. "Keep an eye out while Hirsten and I make arrangements for the night. If anyone gets too close to the horse, stab 'em."

"Why would you want me to stab the horse?" Bhar asked with a glint in his eye.

Katora muttered a "Great Mother" and pointed the dagger at Kylene. "Stab Bhar and anyone else who messes with the horse."

"Should I be worried?" asked Kylene.

"Probably not, but it can't hurt to be safe."

She accepted the weapon, but disliked the weight of it in her hands, so much heavier than her small pocketknife. She had been forced to kill on the last quest and hoped it wouldn't come to that. She and Bhar settled into the seats at the front of the wagon and waited. Katora's unease had set her on edge.

Instead of quieting down, the city livened up as night fell. Darkness blanketed them in a less dramatic way than it did in the country. Torches stood like sentinels in doorways, their light dancing off storefronts and taverns. The curious, possibly magical, lanterns adorned the many carts and wagons clogging the roadway. Idle chatter blended with the clip clop of hooves on cobblestone. A gust of wind blasted down the street, tossing Kylene's hair about her face.

A deep shout echoed above the other noises, followed by

grunts and more shouting. A crowd gathered at the end of the block, shifting together in a circle with a wavelike motion.

"A fight!" Bhar jumped out of the wagon and ran down the street.

Kylene stood in the wagon and tightened her grip on the dagger. She squinted down the road, but Bhar was nowhere in sight. Dust puffed up where the crowd gathered, further obstructing her vision.

The wagon shook. A blade flashed at Kylene's throat as a hand grasped her ponytail, pinning her head back. Rings with large green gemstones decorated the fingers grasping the knife handle, which also glittered with fat, brightly-colored jewels.

"Drop the weapon," growled a voice in her ear.

The cool touch of a hoop earring bobbed against Kylene's neck. The scent of tobacco and mint reached her nose as she obeyed. The dagger fell from Kylene's hand with a faint thump on the wagon floor.

"I know what goods you carry, Kase daughter," whispered the voice, her captor's throat thrumming against Kylene's neck. "And I'm not talking about essence."

Kylene scanned the constantly moving crowd, hoping to catch a glimpse of Bhar's golden hair. The woman yanked harder on her ponytail, eliciting a quiet cry of pain.

"Don't move." The captor shifted, and Kylene saw a woman with calculating green eyes framed by messy hair tied back in a purple bandanna. "You're going to show me where in this mess the Elixir lies. Or I'll stab you in just the right spot so the last warm thing you'll ever feel is your own blood spilling over your neck."

"I can't help you with a knife to my neck."

Kylene wasn't sure where in the depths of her brain the quick remark came from, but she liked the way it sounded. The comment was effective, too, as the woman let go of her hair and moved the knife from her neck to behind her back. Not much of an improvement, but at least she could move.

With an eye on the crowd, hoping for Bhar's familiar face to surface, Kylene rooted around the back of the wagon to buy time.

Her hands trembled as she shook out a blanket as if searching for the Elixir. Not that she planned on handing it over. Surely one of her companions would show up soon, before the woman grew impatient with Kylene's stalling.

She reached down to open a box, which she knew contained essence, when strong arms encircled her midsection, pinning one arm to her side and the other to her chest. Hot breath misted the back of her neck, and a distinct scent tickled her nose. Then she was twisted around and forced to the floor of the wagon, nose-to-nose with a man on top of her.

Chapter Six

Autumn in Faway Forest smelled like a cold breeze that finished with a hint of rotting earth. Fallen leaves created a symphony of crinkles, rustles, and whispers. The days were growing shorter and the nights colder. The first couple of evenings after leaving Kase Farm, Zelenka and Palafair warmed small rocks in the dying embers of their dinner fire. Then they surrounded themselves with the hot stones and snuggled up under a blanket.

On their third day of travel, the pony, which Zelenka had nicknamed Poky in honor of his slow pace, nickered and shook his head before stopping in the middle of the path. Palafair clicked his tongue and gently flicked the reins, but the pony wouldn't budge. The sudden silence of the forest was a giveaway that something was wrong. Maybe Poky wasn't as slow as Zelenka thought. She reached for the dagger at her belt.

Palafair whispered, "I think we are being watched."

She had anticipated being noticed by the tilli at some point on the path to the Three River Split, but she hadn't expected to be found so soon. Wishful thinking really. Nemez, leader of the tilli army, was the best tactician she knew. He would have the base of tilli operations well guarded.

The question remained whether or not he would treat her as a friend or foe. For years, she had acted as his second in command, but killing Roodesh and deserting the tilli might negate that history.

She had a small supply of Elixir as a bargaining chip. Convincing Pop and Katora she needed some for the journey hadn't been hard, especially with Palafair's help. Pop trusted him, and by extension Zelenka. Katora was new enough as guardian to defer to her father's advice.

"What do you want to do?" Palafair whispered.

"Keep moving forward," Zelenka said.

What else could they do? She was determined to meet her people and face the consequences. The pony, however, wasn't interested in following Palafair's commands or prodding. Zelenka clenched her jaw to keep from spitting on the stubborn beast. Without much choice, she stood to confront the spies.

"You may as well show your faces!" she shouted to the trees lining the path. "You have managed to spook my pony and we would prefer to ride instead of having to pull him along."

No less than thirty tilli demicks showed themselves, stepping out from behind bushes and climbing down from tree branches. One marched right up to the pony. Zelenka and Palafair were average height for demicks, but this demick was not. His head barely reached the top of the wheels of the small wagon. He looked young, too, hardly a wrinkle on his face.

He tapped the butt of his spear on the packed dirt of the path and shouted, "All who pass within the realm of Nemez must be presented to him!"

The corner of Zelenka's mouth twitched with a smile. Replace the name Nemez with Roodesh, and the young tilli had said the same thing Nemez had told the Kases when they had arrived at the Three River Split several years ago. Palafair looked to her.

She opened her arms in what she hoped was a benevolent gesture. "Excellent idea, soldier. Nemez is exactly who we were hoping to meet."

The soldier frowned, clearly not expecting her to agree. Zelenka smiled down at him with a condescending look. He glanced back at several of the other soldiers, who crept closer to the wagon with halting steps. Zelenka wondered what had happened to the fearsome tilli army of which she had been a proud member. Her army would have seized the pony and wagon, confiscated any weapons, and marched Zelenka and Palafair straight to the Split's caves. As it was, it looked as if they couldn't decide between running away or asking Zelenka and Palafair to politely follow them.

"It seems you have spooked our timid pony," Palafair said in a kind voice with no hint of superiority. He was always so much more diplomatic than Zelenka. "I suggest you introduce yourself to him properly, and then you can show us the way."

Palafair offered a few sugar cubes to the soldier, who took them with a sheepish grin. He sidestepped alongside the pony until he reached the muzzle and held out his hands. When the pony went to sniff the cubes, the soldier snapped his hand away. Zelenka's cheeks twitched and she rubbed her lips together to keep from laughing.

"He will not bite," Palafair said. "Talk to him in a soothing voice."

The soldier once again presented the sugar cubes to the pony. "Here, boy," he said in a high-pitched voice. "My name is Ronan. I have a nice treat for you...um..."

"Captain Buttercup," Palafair said. Zelenka couldn't help but snort at the absurd name. She had never seen a flower the dusty gray of the pony's coat, and he was far from a captain of anything, except maybe stubbornness.

Before long Ronan and Poky—Zelenka refused use the name Captain Buttercup—were great friends. Zelenka formally introduced herself and Palafair. She wanted to be frank about who she was. Being honest with them, and Nemez, was the only way to earn back her place among the tilli.

The thirty soldiers surrounded the wagon as they proceeded to the Split, but they did so with a casual air. Zelenka barely contained herself from disciplining one young tilli who whistled a lively tune during the march. Palafair massaged her leg and the tension seeped out. Her shoulders sank in relaxation.

Over the next few days, the tilli treated Zelenka and Palafair more like companions than prisoners. The tilli never bound them, but they did keep a watch, the soldiers alternating nights. And when Palafair offered them provisions, the tilli declined.

At least they have some sense. Far too easy to poison food.

Not that Zelenka would do that. She had come to make amends, not kill them, but they didn't know that. She had been honest about who she was, but she hadn't revealed why she had come there; she wanted Nemez to hear it first.

Their progress proved slow, as demicks could cover only so many miles a day, and Poky seemed to enjoy the leisurely pace. Zelenka swore his horsy lips had fixed themselves into a permanent grin. Then a familiar hum tickled her ears.

Unable to hide her excitement, Zelenka squeezed Palafair's shoulder. "Do you hear it?"

"Hear what, my love?" Palafair asked.

"The falls." She raised her voice. "Ronan! If these soldiers march double-time, we should reach the Split before day's end. Can we pick up the pace?"

Ronan jogged from his place in front of the pony and wagon. "Ma'am—"

She cut him off, "My name is Zelenka. Use it." It wasn't her proper title of Major, but she wasn't about to pull rank yet.

"Zelenka, ma'am, we have had many days of marching and keeping watch. Everyone is tired."

"Tired?" She slapped her hand on the wagon seat. "You are tilli soldiers. Do your job and do not complain. Lead your company."

"Yes, ma'am." He marched to the front of the soldiers and announced, "We are stepping up to double-time. Move out!"

To Zelenka's satisfaction, the tilli soldiers picked up the pace. Palafair flicked the reigns and Poky easily matched their speed.

He leaned in and asked, "Do you have to be so hard on them?"

"I do," she said. "You know I do. Soldiers need discipline."

He kissed her cheek. "Of course. I know so little of army life."

Zelenka squeezed his shoulder and breathed in the forest air, crisp and clear...and familiar. The whoosh of the waterfall, the sound of home, eased her mind. No matter what happened when she met with Nemez, she would have one more opportunity to gaze upon the waterfalls. Tumbling heaps of water. Phantom rainbows in the mist. Thundering noise so cacophonous it drowned out any thought.

The day passed achingly slow. She feared the sun would set before they arrived, and nearly lost hope of catching a glimpse of the falls before dark. All the while, the crash of the water teased her.

Then the tumult reached a deafening level. Poky followed the tilli around a bend in the path. Zelenka sucked in a breath as she witnessed the East Rauor River cascade over the cliff and split into three tributaries. It did this because the cliff's edge snaked in and out in a distinct pattern, as if Mother Nature had carved it in the shape of her initial.

Two branches of the river flowed on either side of the "m" and a third one spilled straight down the middle. Each formed its own churning, bubbling pool, making three new rivers that rippled their way south through Faway Forest, before feeding into the ocean. Hence the name Three River Split.

Zelenka grasped Palafair's hand, sharing this moment with the demick she loved. The reins fell slack in his hands. Poky stopped to graze on the tall grass to the side of the path. Zelenka didn't remember standing, but found she was. Palafair caressed her cheek and his fingers came away wet with tears. A sob caught in her throat, an anemic sound lost to the rushing waters.

Three years gone without having been able to stare at this wonder of nature.

In front of the wagon, Ronan shouted words that had no chance of being heard. Most of the tilli jogged past the Split without a second glance and disappeared into a cave entrance off to the side. A handful stayed behind the wagon and ushered Zelenka, Palafair, and Poky toward the rock. Zelenka's gaze remained fixed on the falls until she rode into the darkness of the cave.

The mouth was large enough for several wagons to fit through. An intense quiet pierced Zelenka's ears as they moved deeper into the cave and crossed the threshold into the main atrium, a steady drip the only indication of the massive amounts of water on the other side of the rock. Poky snorted and it echoed through the cavern. Torches were ensconced into the walls, the light not quite reaching the ceiling, which Zelenka knew sloped a good hundred feet overhead. Black spaces along the far wall indicated the openings to different branches of the complicated cave system. The tilli had not built the structure, but they had inhabited it for many years, adding passages over time.

The tilli company stood in a long line at attention, Ronan in the center. A figure, his back to Zelenka, paced the length of the line, inspecting the soldiers and their equipment.

The figure spoke, the large space making his voice seem louder and deeper than it really was. "I see you have returned with a great catch." The last word bounced all around them until it faded away.

The water trickled as before, unaware of the tension filling the room.

Ronan saluted, his gesture steadier than his voice. "A great catch, sir?"

"Did she not tell you her name?" Ronan's superior kept his back to the wagon.

"She did, sir," Ronan said. "Zelenka is her name. Her companion is Palafair, and the pony is Captain Buttercup, sir."

"She is an honest traitor." General Nemez turned to examine her.

She smiled and saluted. "Nice to see you, General."

"Seize all their possessions, including that ridiculously-named pony," he commanded. Zelenka let out the smallest of sighs. "Bind her and the anni demick and lock them up in the lower dungeons."

Zelenka reached out. "General, please. Let me explain."

Nemez headed to one of the openings on the far wall.

"Nemez!" Zelenka shouted. "Wait!"

She threw one leg over the side of the wagon, but Palafair yanked her back. The soldiers surrounded them. Palafair wrapped his arms around her stiff form.

Her voice broke as she said, "I thought he would give me a chance."

"Give him time," Palafair whispered. He moved her an arm's length away, gripping her elbows. A severe frown etched wrinkles on his forehead. "Let us do as they say for now."

The tilli escorted her off the wagon and bound her arms behind her back. She let them guide her out of the cavern into a dark hall with a stairway at the end. She knew this passage led underground to the dungeons. In all her time at the Split, her work had been in the field and she rarely had cause to take prisoners, so the corridors they took soon became unfamiliar. Ironic that her first trip to the dungeons was as a prisoner.

They removed her bindings and locked her in a cramped rock cell with metals bars as a door and pushed Palafair into one next to her. The soldiers marched away, taking their torches with them. Enveloped by complete blackness, Zelenka thought she could feel its bitter touch on her skin.

She had thought she'd be able to come to the Split and make things right. Now she had dragged Palafair into her mess and didn't know if they would make it out. She backed up until her hands brushed the cold rock, and slumped to the ground, her forehead resting on her knees. Despair, blacker than her prison, shook her body as she waited to find out her fate.

Chapter Seven

A tinny tapping interrupted the monotonous drip of water in Zelenka's cell. Roused from her dozing, she lifted her head from her knees. The absolute darkness made it impossible to tell how much time had passed since the tilli had thrown her and Palafair into the dungeons. Enough for her body to have stiffened in the damp chill.

She stood, her old injury sending an ache up her leg and through her body all the way into her head. With one hand stretched out in front of her and the other rubbing along the rough stone, she moved slowly along the wall until her hand struck the cool metal of the bars. The tapping sounded again, louder this time.

Then she heard a whisper accompanying the percussive din, "Zelenka, can you hear me?"

She clutched the bars with both hands. "Palafair?"

The tapping abruptly stopped. "Yes."

Zelenka fell to her knees and pressed her face as far as she could between two bars, inhaling the rusty scent. With her sight useless, her other senses were on full alert. "I am so sorry I brought you here. I thought Nemez would hear me out before punishing me."

"He may still." His voice echoed down the passageway. "He is angry. We must be patient."

Zelenka groaned. Patience was a virtue that eluded her, and she hated feeling powerless. A flash of anger sent a rush of blood to her ears, drowning out the unending drips. She grabbed the metal rods and tried to shake the door. Rust ground into her hands, but the door refused to budge. She let out a frustrated bellow. Crisp footsteps halted her outburst.

"What is all this racket?" asked a commanding voice.

Torchlight flitted down the wall, the delicate light an assault on eyes used to utter blackness. Zelenka squinted as she retreated to the center of the cell. As her sight adjusted to the light, she got her first good look around. It was about five square feet with uneven slate walls and a smooth rock floor. Stalactites hung overhead, their tips visible in the torchlight. She scanned the cage door and found no trace of a lock. This piqued her curiosity, but she didn't have time to puzzle it out.

Bare hands and her wits were the only weapons at her disposal. She flexed her leg muscles and settled into a slight crouch, resting on the balls of her feet. The light flitted ever closer, the soldiers' treads louder with each step.

Six tilli, one for each bar on the door, pulled on the metal while the torch bearer watched. It slid open, revealing it had never been locked. Even if she had been able to see the door earlier, Zelenka doubted she would have been able to force it open by herself. A clever way to detain prisoners, and Zelenka wished she had taken the time to study the bowels of the caves when she had lived here.

The torch bearer, flanked by his companions, entered. He stood the same height as Zelenka but flabbier of frame. He wore his black hair in a low ponytail. When the torch illuminated his face, Zelenka noted the smooth texture of his skin, betraying his youth.

"General Nemez wishes to speak with the prisoner," the torch bearer said. "On your knees and keep your hands behind your back while we bind you."

Zelenka acquiesced. She would do what she had to in order to speak to Nemez. The torch bearer flicked his head at two of the soldiers, also very young. All men, too, just like all the ones who had escorted them to the Split. In her time with the tilli army, many women had served, but now it seemed all the soldiers were men; another curiosity she had little time to consider.

They approached Zelenka with slow movements, like she was a skittish colt ready to attack. She could probably disarm these men—boys really—but she wouldn't be able to open Palafair's cell on her own.

As the chains locked around her wrists and ankles, she asked, "May my husband come also?" She wanted them to be together in case an opportunity to escape presented itself.

The torch bearer let out a curt laugh. "You mean the anni demick? He is coming, too, on the General's orders."

The soldiers opened Palafair's cell and fettered him. Side-by-side with chains clinking, Zelenka and Palafair followed the torch bearer back into the atrium.

Palafair nudged her with his elbow. "See, you will get to talk to Nemez after all."

"Silence!" yelled a soldier.

Palafair stayed close, bumping her elbow every so often. She knew it was his way of comforting her. She wished she felt reassured, but her heart beat out a nervous, heavy rhythm.

They traveled into a narrow passageway and up a flight of winding stairs. The steps were perfectly sized for tilli feet as this was one of the sections that had been added after the tilli had laid claim over the Split. The stairway spiraled up a narrow circle in a space-saving design that also limited how much rock had to be excavated, one of her father's designs. He had a brilliant mind— until he had gone mad.

After going down several hallways and up another set of stairs, Zelenka knew they were headed to Roodesh's old quarters. She knew of a quicker way but figured they were taking a circuitous route to try and confuse her...as if they could.

At the end of the stairs, the torch bearer stopped on a landing and knocked on a wooden door. Nemez himself opened it and gestured them all in. Zelenka knew this room all too well. She held her breath as she observed the boarded up opening on the opposite side. The wood was not able to contain the sound of the waterfall, which she knew crashed down the cliffs outside. The last time she had been in this room, she had thrown her father out that hole to his death.

Palafair moved close enough to touch her hand. She stared at his wide eyes. He had been there on that fateful day and clearly realized where they were.

He whispered close to her ear, "It will be okay."

Nemez gestured to a demick-sized table and chairs. "Sit!" he yelled over the din of the waterfall. He looked at his men and pointed to the door.

Zelenka slid into a seat, her bound hands hitting the back of the chair. The sound of the waterfall ceased the instant she touched the wood, the work of an enchantment. There was a time when she kept a shard of the enchanted furniture in her pocket so she didn't have to sit in the chairs to hear conversations in the cave, but those days had vanished when she left the Split with the Kases.

It seemed whatever magic Roodesh had acquired to make the furniture had outlasted the demick himself. Ironic, Zelenka thought, since Roodesh had spent the second half of his life in search of an immortality Elixir that didn't exist. The Kases' Elixir was powerful, but it was for healing, not eternal life.

Before he became Roodesh—a name passed down from one tilli leader to the next—he had been called Fanas. Zelenka could picture his brown eyes, the deep color of fertile soil, the way they twinkled when he offered a rare smile. Fanas had been her father, loving even when a disciplinarian. Roodesh had been a madman, obsessed with achieving the impossible. As Roodesh, he had built a strong army, only to use it for self-serving missions. Zelenka still wondered how he had managed to take a proud people, who had survived the treacherous journey from Demick Island to the Great Peninsula and survived on their own for generations, and reduce them to a group whose sole mission was to find the impossible.

She believed she had done a great service to her people by killing Roodesh. Yet here she was, a prisoner of the tilli.

Palafair chose a seat beside her, and Nemez took one directly across the round table from her. The last soldier to leave closed the door behind him with an authoritative bang. For a moment, Zelenka felt as if the stone walls pressed in on her, but she took a deep breath and the pressure in her chest lessened ever so slightly.

Nemez faced revealed no emotion as he spoke, "I will be frank with you, Zelenka. I need information. That is the only reason you and your anni friend are alive."

Zelenka thought her General had grown cruel over the last few years. Of course she knew murder among the tilli was punishable by death, but the accused had always had an opportunity at defense. "Information is all that keeps us alive. Not past service, old loyalties, or honor?"

"What honor is owed a traitor?" Nemez asked, finally revealing a touch of emotion by narrowing his eyes in anger.

"You knew of Roodesh's madness, how deep his desire for the Elixir ran. You read his journals, listened to his obsessive rants. We spoke of it at length. His mind was gone long before I pitched his body into the falls. When he heard the Kases' Elixir could not grant him immortality, his last grasp at sanity broke." She stomped her bound feet. "Mercy, for a man who was once my father and for the people I love and serve, moved me to end the madness."

Her hands were clenched in tight fists behind her back, pressed up against the enchanted chair.

"Enough stalling!" Nemez shouted, his calm demeanor shattering. His bloodshot eyes bulged and his cheeks puffed up. "I want to know what happened to the army I sent after you. What did you and those cursed Kases do with my soldiers?"

Zelenka faltered, confused by the accusation. "What did we do?" Her mouth hung open as she struggled for words. "We did nothing. We never saw the army. I would never..."

Nemez's white-knuckled hands gripped the edge of the table. "You would never? I sent out five hundred soldiers after you. We did not know if you had been kidnapped or brainwashed by magic. I sent them to save you. And not a single one returned. An entire army vanished."

Palafair stood. "No. She would never do that. After we escaped over the bridge and into the forest, we never saw a single tilli soldier after that."

Zelenka remained silent. Suddenly the state of the army made sense. The green recruits patrolling the path to the Split. How they were all so timid and young. Nemez had sent out most of the tilli army after Zelenka, and none of them had returned. Guilt washed over her in waves that manifested themselves in gut-wrenching pain. She gulped in a breath. She was responsible for the demise of the tilli army.

Chapter Eight

Although Devon's mother taught at the same school he attended, he never walked to or from the small brick schoolhouse in the center of town with her. It wasn't that he didn't like his mom or was embarrassed by her—she was pretty cool, for a mom. Rather, he preferred to use the time it took to walk to his house on the edge of town to let his mind wander. He considered himself to be quite the writer and spent his few minutes of alone time contemplating his latest work.

On a crisp autumn afternoon not too long after he had eavesdropped on the conversation about war in Pop Pop's study, Devon burst out of the schoolhouse doors with the rest of his classmates. The cascade of youngeryears pouring down the front stairs was as loud as an actual waterfall. He figured it wasn't as noisy as the Three River Split, but he could only imagine that because he had never actually been there. He had never actually been much of anywhere outside of Tussar. All the more reason to figure out a way to be involved in a quest.

With heavy thuds, Devon's footsteps pounded the well-packed dirt roads as he raced through town, waving good-bye to his friends when they reached their houses. He slowed to a casual stroll, hands in his pockets, a posture he thought worthy of a learned writer gracing the world with his brilliant presence. He flicked his head and brushed his hair out his eyes, only to have it fall right back into place.

Today a particular line of poetry filled his head. He whistled a lilting, romantic tune that complemented the poem, which he was considering anonymously slipping to a particular primeyear.

As he made the turnoff to his street, the grind of wagon wheels and the unhurried clip clop of horse's hooves grabbed his attention. Ms. Pennyfold, a merchant and trader, acknowledged Devon's presence with a nod and steered her wagon full of goods down the road. A blanket covered a lumpy mound reaching higher than the wagon's sides. At the end, Ms. Pennyfold took a left onto the country pathway.

Devon ripped his hands from his pockets and sprinted after the wagon. The only establishment in that direction worthy of a visit from Ms. Pennyfold was Kase Farm. Ms. Pennyfold was probably delivering supplies to the farm, maybe even the ones Pop Pop had discussed in the study that night.

He caught up to the wagon and waved down the merchant, who pulled on the reigns and slowed the horse to a stop. Ms. Pennyfold was older than Pop Pop, but not by much. Her sandy hair was cut short and she had a few wrinkles around her eyes that might have deepened when she smiled, but he had never seen the cantankerous pastyear smile. The old woman's nose bulged in the middle, probably having been broken a time or two. The middle of her body was thick and soft-looking. Her arms were thick, too, but not in a soft way. Her muscles, strong from years of lifting goods, bulged under a faded red button-up shirt.

"You're a Kase, right?" she asked.

"Yup," Devon replied. "You heading to my Pop Pop's farm?"

Ms. Pennyfold peered down at him with squinty brown eyes, adjusting her glasses as she did so. "That's the plan. You need a lift?"

Devon hopped up next to the merchant. "Thanks."

They rode in silence for a few minutes. Devon drummed his fingers on his thigh as he formed questions in his head before asking them, a difficult feat given he often said exactly what he was thinking the moment he thought it. He didn't want Ms. Pennyfold to grow suspicious.

"You delivering or picking up?" he asked.

"Delivering." The merchant stared straight ahead at the dirt path.

"Anything special?"

"No." It seemed Ms. Pennyfold was a woman of few words. "What business is it of yours?"

Devon shrugged, realizing that easing information out of Ms.

Pennyfold was proving to be more difficult than squeezing his whole fist into his mouth, something his best friend had no trouble doing. "Well, Pop Pop is my grandfather. And I work on the farm all the time. So it is kind of my business."

"A pipsqueak of a boy like you." Devon bristled at the implication. "Nothing serious is your business. You're Ariana's oldest, aren't you?" Devon nodded. "I thought so. I remember you when you were a little sprout of a thing."

It figured Ms. Pennyfold decided to be chatty when it came to an embarrassing topic like when Devon was little but wouldn't spill a word about what was in the back of the wagon.

The merchant blathered on. "Sickly boy you were. I'd come and visit your Pop Pop and he'd always be fretting over your health. And he was right to, with your sallow skin and blue marks under your eyes. His worries went on for years. Then one day my family and I come up to Kase Farm for a party at the end of first harvest. And there you were, pink-cheeked and plump, the model of a healthy child. I guess you grew out of it."

Devon didn't remember being sick. He lost his breath easily when he got over-excited or exercised too much, but that was a condition he'd always had, not a childhood sickness that had gone away. Maybe she had mistaken him for someone else. She could have been talking about Bhar for all Devon knew. Still, it piqued his curiosity enough that he would have to ask his mom about it later.

They had just about reached Kase Farm when the wagon hit a rut in the road and pitched to the left. Devon bounced on his seat and grabbed ahold of the railing to keep from falling. The tinkle of shattering glass sounded from the back of the wagon. Ms. Pennyfold muttered a word Devon was not allowed to use in front of his mother and jerked on the reigns to stop the horse.

The merchant dismounted with a lumbering gait, the wagon tipping to the side with her weight, and lifted the blanket

She swore again. "This is going to cost me a fortune." Then she yelled to Devon, "Get down here and help me, kid!"

Devon hopped down and pulled back a corner of the blanket.

Tiny pieces of broken glass glittered in the sunlight. A puddle darkened the floor of the wagon and liquid dripped through cracks in the boards. Wooden barrels stood fat and tall at the front of the wagon, creating the largest lumps. At least half of the contents remained shrouded by the blanket, and Devon could only guess what was under there.

With her head suck under the blanket, Ms. Pennyfold rummaged through the back of the wagon until she produced an empty bucket. She pulled the blanket back far enough to fully reveal the mess without revealing the rest of the contents. Then she pushed the bucket into Devon's chest. "Clean this up, and try not to cut yourself."

The merchant went to inspect the wheel, so she didn't see Devon roll his eyes. She was treating him like a maid. Indignant as he was, Devon did see an opportunity for snooping, so he climbed into the back of the wagon and began carefully picking up the tiny pieces of glass. He dipped his finger into the dripping liquid and sniffed. A subtle floral scent filled his senses, followed by the even fainter aroma of damp soil. It reminded him of picking essenberries under the summer sun, the farm baking in the heat.

Thinking the smell of the liquid seemed innocuous enough, he sucked on the wet finger and tasted...nothing. Less flavor than well water, which always tasted a bit mossy to Devon. Less flavor than water from the West Rauor River, which was fresh and ice cold on the tongue. Disappointed he went back to cleaning, but it wasn't long before a strange sensation hit the back of his throat. The tingling spread to his tongue and mouth, and then up to his brain and down his throat into his belly.

There must be magic in it!

A new squirming sensation filled his stomach as the tingling dissipated. What if the magic was already working and he sprouted a green beard right in front of Ms. Pennyworth? What if it made him sick? Or worse? No matter what, he couldn't let the merchant know he had tasted the liquid.

Feeling slightly nauseated, Devon leaped out of the wagon, escape the only thing on his mind. As he sprinted away, he shouted over his shoulder, "I forgot about something! I have to go!"

When Ms. Pennyfold yelled for him to stop, without missing a stride, Devon pumped his legs as fast as he could and labored down the pathway to town. Just before reaching the turnoff to his road, he collapsed onto the grass and dead leaves in the shade of a tall oak.

His chest heaved as he tried to catch his breath. Sweat glued his shirt to his skin. An uncontrollable coughing fit seized him. He rolled over on his side into the fetal position. What the heck had he tasted? His vision blurred and he closed his eyes, coughs still spouting from his mouth like steam from a boiling pot of water. He thought he might be dying and wished he had gotten to go on at least one grand adventure in his lifetime. Tears squeaked out of his clamped eyelids. He opened his eyes for what he hoped wasn't the last time and watched blurry clouds form pictures in the bright blue sky.

Chapter Nine

Kylene tensed under the weight of the man who had tackled her to the wagon floor. Grunts of a scuffle were muffled and the streetlight was blocked by the body on top of her. The wagon rocked violently. All she could see were dark brown eyes surrounded by exceptionally long lashes.

Only one person had lashes like that. "Hirsten?" she asked, her lips uncomfortably close to his.

He grunted and rolled onto his back. "You're cut."

She touched her neck, and sure enough, felt the warm stickiness of drying blood. She also felt the sting of the wound now that she knew it was there.

"Stay here," Hirsten said. "I'm going to help Katora."

The wagon pitched to the side as he jumped out. Shouts erupted from nearby. Kylene crawled across the floor and peered over the front seat of the wagon, which began to rock harder as the horse danced in irritation.

Katora and the green-eyed woman circled each other in the street. Neither possessed a weapon. The scuffle Bhar had run to a few minutes earlier had ended, the crowd gathered around Katora and her foe.

The woman feinted with her right hand and cocked her left hand back to strike Katora. The arcing hand sparkled with four gem-studded rings, which would make for a terrible blow if it connected. Luckily, Katora ducked.

Catching the woman off balance, Hirsten ran up behind her and grabbed her arms. Katora reached for the dagger she kept at her waist and found only air, clearly forgetting she had lent it to Kylene.

Kylene groped around the wagon floor, and her hand grazed the leather sheath encasing the dagger. She snatched it up and jumped into the street. She offered the dagger to Katora handle first. Katora pulled it from the sheath and pressed it against the woman's throat.

Two men—identical from their massive size right down to their salt-and-pepper beards—emerged from the crowd, each holding one of Bhar's arms.

"Stop!" shouted the one on the left. "Let m'lady go, else I'll break his neck." He jerked his head at Bhar, who winced as the men wrenched his arms awkwardly.

The crowd hushed, the snorts of the agitated horse the only sound in the street. Kylene's body buzzed as she waited to see what her sister would do. Katora's white-knuckled hand gripped the dagger, her face twisted in a fierce scowl. Hirsten tightened his hold on the woman's arms.

Kylene's heart pounded as she held out her arms, as if the simple motion might prevent an act of violence. "Let's be reasonable here. We have someone you care about, and you have our brother, who we most certainly care for. Perhaps we can negotiate."

The man on the left grunted and looked to the woman, who said, "A fair request. Perhaps if your girl," Katora growled at the word, "would lower her dagger, I might be able to talk a little freer."

Instead of obliging the request, Katora pushed the dagger into the woman's flesh just deep enough to draw a trickle of blood. The men shoved Bhar to the ground face first, his cheek pressed against the dusty street. He grunted and his neck reddened to the color of Ma's homemade tomato sauce. Now even the horse had fallen silent.

Kylene walked to the men but kept her eyes on the woman. "Okay, okay. On the count of three, we release you and your men release our brother."

"You seem the honest sort," the woman said. "But I don't trust your girl."

"She'll do it if your men swear on the Great Mother," Kylene said. "Right, Katora?"

"Only if they swear," Katora said.

The woman glared at her men. "Well, do it."

The men mumbled their oaths. Katora's face was shadowed as she cocked it toward the men, so Kylene couldn't read the expression, but she had faith her sister would do the right thing. Kylene crept closer to the men. If they broke their word, she would do what she could to help Bhar.

"Ready?" Kylene said. Katora's hand was steady on the dagger poised against the woman's neck. "One. Two. Three."

Kylene crouched and held her breath. A split second passed and nothing happened. Then the men released Bhar and backed away. Hirsten let go of the woman's arms, and there was only a small hesitation before Katora lowered the dagger. The woman and her men entered the inn, one of them glaring at the Kases as he slammed the door shut.

Kylene's chest deflated with relief. The nighttime sounds of the city street—the staccato clip of horse hooves, a buzzing murmur of people chatting, the hint of music from inside a tavern —resumed.

Several among the dispersing crowd expressed their displeasure over the fight breaking up so quickly. "I mightn't liked to see them break the blond boy's arm. Newcomers tain't got no business stirring up trouble."

She was glad Katora didn't hear the comment; her sister was likely to start another fight the way her blood boiled when it came to threats to the family.

Bhar brushed off his pants the same way he brushed off Kylene's inquiries of whether or not he was okay. She fussed over him as he stretched his shoulders and neck until Katora grabbed her shoulder.

"He's fine." Katora raised her right eyebrow at Bhar. "You should be worried about Ky. Look at her neck." Kylene touched the newly formed scab. "What were you thinking, leaving her alone with the wagon and its contents?" Kylene knew Katora wouldn't dare mention the Elixir out there, but the unsaid words hung heavy in the air all the same.

"I was set up," Bhar argued. "The fight was a diversion. It

was those two goons against each other. As soon as they realized their friend was in trouble, they grabbed me and dragged me over."

"Next time we might not be so lucky." Katora tossed a cloth to Kylene. "Clean up. I don't want to have to treat it if it gets infected." Again, no direct mention of the Elixir, and no mention of how it had saved Kylene once already, but the reminder was there all the same.

Kylene's face burned as red hot as an infected wound. She poured water on the cloth and held it over the cut. It probably wasn't intentional on Katora's part, but Kylene often felt she would never live down being stabbed by the poisoned spear in Faway Forest. Was she living on borrowed time because of it?

Katora put her arm around Kylene's shoulders and steered her to the inn. "Bhar and Hirsten can take care of the horse and wagon. I'm in the mood for a drink."

Boisterous music spilled out the open doorway, wrapped around Kylene, and pulled her inside. It lifted her spirits better than any libation. The sisters found a table in the corner, prime for observing the patrons of the busy pub, which took up the bottom floor of the inn. Candles at every table and in candelabras along the walls created a movement of light that danced with the lively piano player in the opposite corner.

A harried waiter took their drink orders: plain essence for Kylene and the spiked variety for Katora. The piano's song turned softer, darker. Kylene's spine tingled with delight when a low baritone voice accompanied the music. She swayed with the tune, an almost subconscious act. She didn't know the words, so she quietly hummed the melody.

Bhar and Hirsten soon joined them and ordered another round of drinks plus food. When the spicy venison, beans, and root vegetables arrived, delicious scents steamed up from the platters. Kylene tucked into a full plate of beans and vegetables, the food warming her belly and the music tickling her soul.

The piano player switched to a quieter background brand of songs, and conversation picked up once everyone's hunger was sated. Katora and Hirsten discussed the route. They would head east through the plains, staying south of the Skimere mountains all the way to the Eirome River and then follow the river north to Lughorn.

Now with a full stomach, Kylene gained the confidence to order a stronger beverage. She opted for an apple ale like Hirsten's. The first couple of sips started out cloying and ended tart in the back of her throat. Halfway through the drink, though, she was enjoying the balance of sweet apple and bitter hops.

After his fourth drink, a red-faced Bhar pointed to a table of anni demicks. "I'm gonna see if they'll let me join their game."

He pushed his chair back and stood, his hands resting on the tabletop. Katora slammed her hand on his and held him in place. "No cheating. No fighting. Understood?"

Bhar smiled and his eyes glinted in the candlelight. "I'll be on my best behavior."

Katora's hand gripped Hirsten's shoulder, and she gave him a pleading look. "Could you—"

"I'll keep an eye on him," Hirsten finished. "Though I'm not much of a gambler."

Katora's lip quirked. "You can be dealer."

They locked lips, Hirsten grabbed a hold of the back of Katora's head, and they kissed like they were the only two people alive. A blush rose on Kylene's cheeks and she turned her attetion to the far side of the room where Bhar threw down a handful of coins at the anni's table. Hirsten slid out of his seat and walked away. He punched Bhar on the shoulder and pulled up a chair. He smiled and said something, and Kylene could hear the laughter from across the room.

She plopped an elbow on the table and rested her chin on her hand. "You're lucky to have Hirsten."

Katora nodded in agreement. "You know, you could find someone if you put yourself out there."

"You mean ask someone out?" Kylene asked.

"Yeah. Why not?"

Kylene stared at Hirsten, wrinkles of concentration on his forehead as he dealt the cards. "Maybe. When I find the right one."

Katora and Hirsten's feelings were palpable when in their presence, but Ky had never experienced anything like that and wasn't holding out much hope that she would find it one day.

"I'd like to tell you that you'll know when you find the one." Katora laughed. "But it took me awhile to figure that out with Hirsten, almost the whole long journey in Faway Forest in fact."

All thoughts of love vanished when the woman with the green eyes approached. What possible good could come of another encounter with this ruffian? The woman slid into the chair between the sisters and plopped down a tankard of ale. She flashed a quick smile, which Kylene figured was supposed to be friendly, but the itching of the wound on her neck kept her on guard. The twin men stood behind the woman.

"Sorry to interrupt," she said in her gravelly voice, her green eyes piercing. "I think the incident outside got us started on the wrong side of the fence, while I feel we are actually on the same side."

"Same side of what?" Katora's tone was casual, but Kylene recognized a tightness to it. Who *would* be comfortable around this woman and her goons?

"Bear, Wolf." Without taking her eyes off Katora, the woman held out a fistful of coins to her men. "Go relax and have a drink." They grinned, knocking into the growing pub clientele as they lurched to the bar. The woman offered her slender hand—the one that had held a knife to Kylene's throat—to Katora. "I'm Nika, a merchant of all that glitters."

Katora took it, squeezing hard enough that Kylene heard Nika's bones crunch. The bands of Nika's rings must have been digging into Katora, but she showed no sign of discomfort. "Katora Kase, though I'm sure you already know my name and my business. I believe you also know my sister Kylene."

"Kylene, my dear." Nika touched Ky's arm, though she kept her gaze pinned on Katora. "I hope you can forgive me for the way we met."

"Forgiveness must be earned, but I will certainly make considerations." She was surprised by the reply; Nika seemed to evoke her brazen side.

Nika tilted her head back and laughed, her curly, black hair shaking under the bandanna. She took a long draught of ale and wiped her face with her sleeve.

"I'll be frank." Nika leaned in and lowered her voice. "Drim, the great battle fort, is stirring. I think Fyren the Fallen is gathering an army." She paused as her bold declaration sank in, but she wasn't done. "War is coming to the Great Peninsula, and that's where we'll be on the same side. You possess healing power, a prized commodity during such times. And I'd like to come out on the other side of this alive."

Kylene sucked in a breath of surprise. War. Was that where fate led her? Would the Ice Queen's message come true on the battlefield?

Chapter Ten

Katora bent her head toward Nika, the motion pulling at Kylene like iron to a lodestone. The three women hunched in close as if conspirators planning a great crime. The music picked up in tempo, but Kylene barely heard it.

"War may be stirring," Katora's gaze darted around, scanning the room, "but times of uncertainty call for mistrust and discretion. Fyren is a powerful name to bandy about."

"Are you willing to meet up in private?" Nika asked.

"It must be tonight," Katora said. "We leave tomorrow."

Nika conjured a piece of paper from her sleeve, the sleight of hand a neat parlor trick Kylene had seen Bhar perform during his poker games. With a flick of Nika's wrist, the paper landed in front of Katora. "Directions. I think we can agree to leave our men out of this. Women are better with secrets."

"Ky doesn't need to come," Katora said, much to Kylene's relief. Nika's refusal to make eye contact unnerved her.

"I insist she comes," Nika said.

Katora narrowed her eyes but said, "Fine."

The waiter set a plate topped with clouds of whipped cream in the center of the table, bringing the intimate conversation to a close. Kylene leaned back and let out a deep breath, releasing the building tension in her neck.

Nika flipped a coin to the waiter. "Thanks, Morty." As the waiter left to return to the kitchens, Nika said, "Fresh wildberry pie and cream. The berries grow at the base of the Skimere Mountains and are fed fresh spring water." She pushed her chair back with noisy scrape and stood. "Enjoy."

Kylene watched Nika until she exited the pub with her men in tow.

"Portion out four servings." Katora stood. "I'll get Hirsten and Bhar."

"Is it safe to eat?" Kylene asked.

Katora cocked her head and squinted at the pie. "Nika needs to stay in our good favor. I don't think she'll poison us, not tonight anyway." She let out a hard chuckle and with smooth movements, slipped across the pub.

Kylene wasn't sure she agreed with Katora's assessment; it was possible Nika wanted them dead so she could steal the Elixir, but Kylene trusted her sister more than she suspected Nika. She sliced the pie into four big slices and then closed her eyes and listened to the dark melody oozing from the piano until her companions returned.

Bhar's pockets were bulging with winnings. Hirsten was humming, not with the music, but to a tune all his own. Katora eagerly stuck her fork into the pie and ate a big bite. Nothing untoward happened, but Kylene only picked at her own dessert.

Katora explained to Hirsten and Bhar about the meet-up.

Bhar leaned back and balanced his chair on its hind legs. "It could be a trap, another set up. And why insist Ky go?"

"I don't know," Katora admitted.

"There was no lie in Nika's face," Kylene said, and all her companions swiveled their heads to stare at her incredulously.

"No offense, Ky," Bhar said, "but you're not the best judge."

Kylene's chin jutted out stubbornly. She had been too trusting most of her life, but since returning from Faway Forest, she had kept everyone at bay. It had made her more wary of others and their motives.

Katora patted her hand. "It's just that you always strive to see the best in people. And you go out of your way to help them."

Pop had said as much in his study the night before Kylene had left; he and Katora were both right...and wrong. She did see the best in people, but that didn't mean she trusted them.

Across the table, Hirsten winked. "That's not a bad characteristic. Katora, you could stand to be more trusting at times."

Katora gave Hirsten a light punch in the arm. "Well it just so happens in this case, I agree with Kylene. I don't think Nika will try anything shady. I think she really does want to earn our trust and stay on our good side, for her own safety. Besides, it's not like I'm going to bring the Elixir. I'll leave that here with you, except for a small vial...just in case."

"I don't like it." Bhar let his chair slam to the ground.

"We'll be fine," Katora said, and Kylene believed her.

She half listened to the rest of the conversation as it turned to the lighter topic of the poker game with the demicks. The warm food and cold drinks had set her at ease; her arm barely twinged. She took a big bite of pie and choked on a berry. Bhar slapped her on the back and the fruit forced its way down her throat. She drank the last of her apple ale and pushed the plate away, her appetite gone. Suddenly exhausted, her head felt like a lead weight on her shoulders and it was difficult to keep her eyelids open.

"Katora, do you think the rooms are ready?" Kylene asked.

Katora glanced at the clock on the wall behind her. "Should be. The innkeeper said he'd give the room keys to the barkeep. You and Bhar are sharing a room."

"Wouldn't it be easier if we shared a room, since we have to get up to meet Nika?"

Katora slung her arm around Hirsten's shoulders. "I'll come wake you when it's time. Bhar sleeps so soundly he won't even notice."

"That's true," Bhar said, mouth full of the pie Ky had left on her plate.

She didn't care where Katora slept, not really. But thinking about what Katora and Hirsten shared and what Kylene didn't have seemed all the more poignant since receiving the Ice Queen's message. How much time did she have left for all the special things in life she hadn't yet experienced? Her mind kept going places she didn't want it to, and she blinked the tired thoughts out of her head.

"I'm going to bed," she said. "Bhar, will you come up to the room so I don't have to bring the key back down?"

Bhar opened his mouth, probably to protest, but he shut it

after staring at Kylene. "Okay."

She must have looked terrible for Bhar to agree so readily. She trudged through the rowdy patrons to the bar, while Bhar trailed behind her, beer in hand. The lone bartender was a burly man with bushy brown hair and a thick beard. He zipped back and forth behind the bar surprisingly fast for a man of his heft, his belly jiggling under a white apron. Kylene slipped in between a man and a woman sitting on stools and raised an arm to try and get the barkeep's attention.

"You're not going to get anything that way," Bhar said from behind her. "You've got to be more assertive."

"How do I do that?"

Bhar pushed her out of the space and squeezed in. He pounded his now empty beer mug on the counter. "Guy! Another drink!"

The barkeep nodded his head in Bhar's direction, finishing his current order before hustling over. Kylene shook her head; it was amazing how far a little rudeness could go to achieve what you wanted. She just wasn't sure she had it in her to be as impolite as Bhar.

The barkeep asked, "Whatcha drinkin'?"

"Light ale," Bhar said. "And our room keys, under the name Kase."

The barkeep grunted and grabbed the mug, leaving it in a bucket with a pile of dirty ones. While dispensing a drink with one hand, he searched under the countertop with the other, swiping around like a bear trying to catch a fish. He placed the beer and the keys in front of Bhar, who flipped a few coins on the bar with a "thank you." Despite the one-handed pour, the beer had a perfect frothy head on top.

They went into the main entryway and up a wide, wooden staircase that creaked loudly. Words carved into a wooden sign at the top of the stairs directed them to the right, where their room was about halfway down the hall. Bhar unlocked the door and held it open.

"I had the innkeeper bring our backpacks up earlier," he said.

Her small bag sat lopsided on one of the single beds, and Bhar's larger one leaned against a pillow on the other bed. "Goodnight." He turned to leave.

"Bhar," Kylene said, and he faced her. "Don't drink too much, okay?"

"Okay," Bhar paused dramatically, "Ma!"

She knew she sounded like a boring pastyear, but she was too tired to care, and Bhar always drank too much. After washing her face with water from the small washbowl in the corner, she kicked off her boots and lay down. A half thought about the Ice Queen's message formed in her mind and was gone as she fell asleep facedown on the bed.

A shaking awoke her, shattering the peaceful state she had managed to achieve in slumber. She rolled over and rubbed her eyes, trying to massage the drowsiness from them and see into the dark space. Where was she? And why was it so dark?

A whispering voice sliced through the blackness. "It's time to meet Nika."

Then it came to her: the evening in the pub, the meeting with green-eyed Nika, the quest to Kristalis...the message. Kylene shuddered. *Best not to think about that right now.*

Shapes formed as her eyes adjusted to the darkness. Katora was hunched over the lone chair in the room, rummaging through Kylene's bag, her loose hair covering most of her face. Katora yelped "Great Mother" when she accidentally smacked her hand against the arm of the chair. The lumpy outline of Bhar snored away on the bed to her right. The porcelain of the washbowl glinted as it caught the little light sneaking in under the door.

Katora grunted, pulled Kylene's cloak from the pack, and tossed it on the bed. "Put that on. It's cold." Kylene fingered the soft wool, her mind taking its time processing the words. "Let's go," Katora hissed. "Don't forget your dagger."

Kylene slung her feet over the side of the bed and shoved them into her boots. The sheathed dagger was deep in her pack. She hated wearing it but wrapped the holster around her waist before throwing on the cloak and tying the cord. The ponytail she hadn't bothered to take out before she'd fallen asleep sat in a messy heap on the back of her head. She tried to redo her hair while Katora yanked on her elbow, urging her out the door.

A lone lamp burned in the hallway and it created enough light to make Kylene squint. She hustled after Katora, down the stairway, the wood creaking noisily underfoot. Downstairs the pub door stood open, empty except for one man mopping the floor. Kylene turned to go out the main doors, but Katora flitted past them down another corridor, and Kylene followed without question.

They slipped through a side door, Kylene clicking it shut behind them, and onto a dirt road. With quiet steps, she matched her sister's pace. The streets were silent and dark, glowing lanterns casting eerie shadows. They took several turns, Katora sure-footed and Kylene skittering along after her. She lost the thread of the path and trusted her sister to keep them from getting lost.

After zigzagging through the roads long enough that the bite of the night air had chilled Kylene's nose, Katora halted so abruptly that Kylene bumped into her. They were in an alley formed by two brick buildings. Neither moon nor lantern lightened the space, the far end of the alley lost in empty darkness. A cold breeze swept through, rustling unseen leaves. Kylene wrapped her cloak tighter around her shoulders. Katora fingered the dagger at her side.

Side by side they stood, peering out to the main road. The thump of footfalls swung them around. Bandanna-shrouded women—seemingly dropped from the stars—crouched in a row from one side of the alley to the other. Kylene counted seven. The one in the middle held a fireless lantern like the ones lining the main roads of Skimere, so Kylene could now see the alley dead-ended in another brick wall. And all of them held sickles, their curved blades gleaming like grins in the low light.

Katora stepped in front of Kylene, close enough that Katora's hair tickled her face. A glance behind showed Ky a second line of crouching figures, in the center were Nika's twins, Bear and Wolf.

The sisters positioned themselves back-to-back, Kylene facing the dead end and Katora the blocked road. *Burned once again by my trusting nature.* She was surprised Katora had fallen for it as well.

One woman in the line broke rank, her lantern held at an angle so the shadows obscured her features. Nevertheless, Kylene recognized Nika's frizzy hair, barely contained by a red bandanna.

Nika set down her lantern and smacked her gloved hands together, the leather dulling the sound to more of a thump than a clap. "Welcome, my new friends." Her words echoed off the bricks and disappeared into the alley's dim corners.

Katora shifted, keeping the sisters back-to-back but maneuvering them so they could see both threatening rows of adversaries. Tension radiated off Katora and seeped into Kylene, filling her mouth with a metallic taste. She had faith in Katora, in her sister's ability to angle their way out of a tricky situation, but personally she saw no way out.

"Not much of a welcome," Katora said. "Feels more like a trap. What are you playing at, luring us here under the pretense of camaraderie and then surrounding us?"

The lines marched forward, closing in on the sisters. Nika's group rejoined their leader and marched to within a few feet of Kylene and Katora. The group with Bear and Wolf marched in as well, Kylene and Katora a meager serving of meat in a bread of enemies.

Kylene's boots scuffed through the dirt as she pressed her back tight against Katora's. "I thought we agreed to leave our men out of this."

"I had a change of heart," Nika said, her teeth glowing impossibly bright in the dark alleyway as she grinned. "We have no desire to harm you. We only want you to join our sisterhood. Take the vow to serve and protect our members."

Kylene's brain filled in what Nika's words didn't, blood dripping from pierced fingers and more blood spilling over a sacrificial altar. *Sacrifice.* It was too much of a coincidence that it was one of the words from the Ice Queen's message.

Her breath tripped over sobs she desperately tried to hold

back. A sigh seeped out of Katora, and Kylene felt her sister's body sag, sucking the last of her bravery with it. She hoped it wouldn't come to the atrocities her mind conjured. If Kylene had to make a sacrifice, she wished with all her heart it would be for a person worthier than Nika.

Nika's eyes gleamed with dark pleasure over her quarry, and Kylene feared her life would be forfeit to this most unworthy task.

Chapter Eleven

A terrible silence followed Nemez's revelation of the missing tilli army and Palafair's defense of Zelenka. To break it, Zelenka stood, ceasing all contact with the magical chair keeping the din of the waterfall at bay. The tumultuous whoosh of water, so ingrained in her brain as the sound of home, soothed her fraught nerves and heavy heart.

Nemez's glare wasn't tempered by the waterfall, though. His mouth moved, an angry slit forming words Zelenka couldn't hear, but his rage-filled expression said enough. With arms out in a placating manner, Palafair answered, his words also lost in the cacophony. She turned her back on them, seeking a moment before she reacted.

She pictured her father's face as she remembered it from her youngeryears, often stern but never unkind. So much different than his face just before she had thrown him into the falls in this very cave. It had been tired and wrinkled, a berry left out in the sun too long. His mouth had gone slack when he had learned the Elixir wasn't an immortality mixture, and his eyes had taken on a dead, watery look. There had been no reason to mourn him upon the death of his body because she had already lost him years before that.

She never thought the act of mercy—albeit patricide—would destroy an entire army, an institution she had helped build, one she had come back to lead. She had to find out what had happened to her people.

When she turned back to the table, Palafair and Nemez's postures were mirror images of each other. Hands gripping the edge of the table, bodies pressed forward, their heads nearly touching, they were locked in a heated debate. Zelenka remained standing, but placed a hand on her chair. Unintelligible shouts of anger replaced the steady rhythm of the cascade.

"Enough!" Zelenka yelled. The demick men fell silent and stared at her, the intensity in their expressions likely to frighten someone of a fragile constitution. "General, you need not believe my story, but I swear on my father's good name before he became Roodesh that we had nothing to do with the disappearance of the tilli army."

Palafair fell back into his chair, his eyes softening around the edges in an expression more fitting his demeanor. Nemez continued to glower.

"I came here to take back my place in the army, and I hoped to have your blessing." Her eyes prickled as she thought of how much like a father Nemez had been in the years following Roodesh's descent into madness.

"Why come back now?" Nemez asked, his voice as cold as the river in the dead of winter. "Why leave in the first place?"

Zelenka hoped her answers would be good enough for Nemez, even when they didn't feel adequate in her own mind. "I left because of the Elixir and Roodesh's obsession with it. The Kase family walked right into our caves. I had to learn everything I could about it."

"And what did you learn?" Nemez asked.

"I learned that it was never what Roodesh thought it was. That he had been chasing a phantom all those years and nearly destroyed our people because of it. I learned that I had done what needed to be done for the mighty tilli demick, but in doing so, I had lost my place among them." Her voice broke.

She wished it hadn't come to Roodesh's death to free her people. What she said was true, but she also wondered if she had fled in part because she was afraid to face the consequences of her actions. But now she was here, ready for whatever judgment befell her.

Nemez's fierce expression softened for a second, but he wasn't finished interrogating Zelenka. "Why wait two years to come back? Surely you would have realized it would not take so long for wounds to heal. Not unless you did something far worse than put a madman out of his long-suffering misery."

It was the fate of the army that was the sticking point. Nemez wasn't infuriated about Roodesh, but he was furious about the disappearance of the army. As he should be. When Zelenka had decided to return to the Split, she hadn't anticipated being accused of such an egregious crime. This was more than a wrinkle in the sheets keeping her from getting a good night's sleep. This was a valley she had to traverse before reaching the mountain of her problems.

"I should have come back sooner," Zelenka said in a voice deep with emotion. "I suppose I was biding my time, waiting for a sign that the moment was right." She paused and looked to Palafair, who nodded with encouragement. "Then the sign came. A message from the Ice Queen. She told me to come back to the tilli. Until I heard the message, I did not realize how I longed to be home again."

"Home." Nemez spit out the word, like it was dirt in his mouth. "The only home left here is a broken one." The intense glare he had worn since Zelenka's arrival broke and fell into a frown. The general's shoulders sagged.

"Do you not see it?" Zelenka asked. "The Ice Queen sent me back here to find the tilli army. They were lost because of me and I intend to remedy that."

Nemez kicked over his chair and pushed the table hard into Zelenka's chair, so it knocked the breath out of her.

"So you admit you are responsible for the disappearance of the army," he said. "I knew it. Traitor." The last word came in a quiet, intense tone. It would have been better if he had shouted. It said he didn't believe Zelenka, that he never would.

"I am responsible." She looked Nemez right in the eyes, faced the wrath there. "But not in the way you think. Palafair spoke the truth. We never detected a trace of the army once we left the Split. I am only responsible in the sense that they were sent after me, not because I did anything to them. Someone—or something— must have gotten to them, prevented them from coming home."

"Sir," Palafair piped up, "you must see the logic in my wife's words." Nemez's eyebrows rose when Palafair called Zelenka his

65

wife, but he let the anni demick continue. "Including Zelenka, there were only six of us on the quest. What could we have done against an army of five hundred?"

Nemez leaned over the table, staring hard at Zelenka. She detected hope in his eyes, the same deep brown color as her own—as her father's.

"I swear on my father's memory, I had nothing to do with it," she said.

"An oath on your father be damned." He pounded his fists on the table. "You swear to me. You swear on the Great Mother you had nothing to do with their disappearance."

"I swear. To you. On the Great Mother. On anyone and anything that will convince you I speak the truth." The vow was said with a confidence she drew from her heart, from knowing she was innocent—from that one crime at least.

She squeezed Palafair's hand, the only sign of nerves she showed in the intense moments of waiting for Nemez's response.

"Then I give you the army I have assembled in the last two years and any willing demick you choose," he finally said. "You go as deep into the forest as necessary to find our army." Zelenka's heart rose; it was her army again. "You bring them back. And if they are not alive to bring back, you find out who killed them, and you bring me their head."

Zelenka's lips twitched into a wry smile that used to come so easily but had been scarce since she had been injured. The time had come to make amends for her past transgressions and make her general proud.

Chapter Twelve

Nemez himself took Zelenka and Palafair to a small cave with a cheerful fire burning in the large hearth. A hay mattress was in one corner and a washbowl sat next to it. Simple, but as far as caves went, it was cozy, and most importantly dry. Compared to their former accommodations in the dungeons, it was a veritable heaven.

"I will have someone bring up your personal possessions," Nemez said.

Zelenka saluted him as he left. Palafair took her hand and pulled her closer to the fire. He rubbed her back while she let the warmth of the flames lick away the aches left by her time in the damp cells. A knock at the door broke the silent reverie they had fallen into. Palafair retrieved their bags and a supply of wood from a young tilli and thanked her with a coin. She stared as if she didn't recognize it before closing her palm and quietly shutting the door.

After Zelenka washed up and changed into clean clothes, the stinging hurt of the less-than-hospitable homecoming slipped away. As she stoked the fire, she began making plans about where to take the army. She settled into bed with Palafair, tactics on her mind.

He snuggled up to her back and rubbed her bad knee with his foot, a habit she enjoyed but never mentioned; she knew Palafair understood it comforted her. Yearning for warmth, she leaned into Palafair and pulled his arm over her.

They fell asleep that way and didn't move until morning when another knock awoke them. The young tilli who had delivered their bags stood at the door. She was tall and slender, with long legs—unusual for demicks, who tended to be of a stockier build—and dark, piercing eyes that gave her a more mature look than at first glance.

"Good morning," she said in a voice as light as a dandelion wisp. "General Nemez requests your presence in the main atrium."

"Thank you," Palafair said, his short hair standing out in all directions. "It is hard to tell the time of day in these caves."

He reached into his pocket, but Zelenka grabbed his arm before he could give the girl another coin. She hesitated for a slight second, a shy smile blossoming on her face, before leaving.

"You should not do that," Zelenka said.

Palafair gave her a playful peck on the lips. "I was only being polite."

"This is not an inn," Zelenka said, a note of contempt in her voice. "The tilli live here. These caves are our homes."

Palafair kissed her hand in a properly contrite fashion. "My apologies. I will not do it again."

She smacked at his face, missing on purpose, to lighten the mood. "Hurry and get ready. Nemez should not be kept waiting."

They dressed quickly and Zelenka led Palafair to the atrium where they had first entered the caves. Most of the ragtag tilli army had assembled there. Zelenka surveyed the soldiers, her gaze going up and down the lines of the meager one-hundred seventy men gathered in the large cavern. The remaining thirty soldiers were out on patrols and would stay at the Split to protect the rest of the tilli.

Nemez, face graced with an inscrutable expression, appraised the army, his arms folded across his chest. Finding the soldiers wanting in her inspection—they were all too young and inexperienced—Zelenka approached the general.

"You certainly sent the best of the army out after me." Though she was flattered by this, it left little for her to work with. "Were there no women volunteers after the disappearance?"

Nemez cleared his throat and fidgeted, betraying a hint of discomfort. "After your defection, I did not allow women to enlist."

Zelenka's eyes widened as she realized how deeply her perceived betrayal had hurt Nemez. It also helped her to understand the shabby state of the army. If Nemez hadn't allowed women to join, that meant there were able-bodied tilli not enrolled.

With untapped recruits, there was hope for a successful mission. Once again, Zelenka felt the corners of her lips curl into the wry smile she used to wear like a second skin.

"You said I could take any willing demick with me," Zelenka reminded Nemez. "Does that include women?"

Nemez cleared his throat again before shouting to the gathered soldiers, "Major Ronan!"

The young tilli whose battalion had escorted Zelenka and Palafair to the Split marched up. He saluted. "Yes, sir."

Nemez said, "Colonel Zelenka is interested in seeing if any other tilli would like an opportunity to enlist in the army." Zelenka started at the title of colonel; she had been a high-ranking major before leaving the Split. "Organize a party to gather the candidates here in one hour."

"Yes, sir." Ronan saluted again but hesitated to leave, a hint of a blush coloring his cheeks. "Excuse me, sir. You mean *any* other tilli?"

Nemez stared down the young soldier, mouth pressed in a tight frown. Zelenka knew the look well, intimidating on the receiving end, but more of an appraisal than anything else. A slight dimple in Palafair's cheek showed he was trying to keep from smiling.

"Yes," Nemez said. "*All* tilli should be informed of this opportunity. Anyone not in the organizing party should have a nice large breakfast. Send someone to alert the kitchen staff."

"Yes, sir." Ronan returned to the soldiers and began giving orders. The army dispersed in various directions, their crisp movements amplified in the large cave.

Once the space quieted, Zelenka turned to Nemez. "Colonel Zelenka." She liked the way the title sounded, the feel of the strong C in her mouth. "I've been promoted."

"Yes," he replied. "Do not be overly flattered. As you saw, there were few candidates to choose from. You should eat. Once the selections are finalized for the last recruits, I want you to set off right away. Before midday if possible."

Nemez winked, actually winked, and she nearly fell over

from shock. Such a different reaction from when they had arrived.

Once again leading the way, Zelenka showed Palafair to another large cave that served as a dining space. Since the Split hadn't originally been set up as a permanent residence, most of the small rooms did not have the necessities for cooking. When the tilli had settled there, a central dining area had been set up near where they had established a kitchen. Most tilli ate at least one meal a day there.

Breakfast was served buffet style. They retrieved their food and sat at one end of a long table, a few empty seats between them and a handful of tilli. As they tucked into the piping hot herb-seasoned oat cakes and eggs, Palafair poked her in the arm with his bony elbow.

"I am so proud of you." He smiled, a sprig of fresh basil stuck in his front teeth.

Zelenka gestured for him to wipe his teeth and giggled. She couldn't believe how ridiculous it sounded. First Nemez winking, and now she was giggling. Were they so happy to be reconciled that it was making them giddy with joy? Whatever the cause, she could get used to the way her heart swelled with emotions too big for her chest.

Palafair stared at her with earnest green eyes. "You kept your cool and made your point with diplomacy, and Nemez listened to you. Believed you. Forgave you. And now you are back in your rightful place with your people."

"Almost," Zelenka whispered too quietly for him to hear.

Her rightful place, as only heir to the last Roodesh, was leader of the tilli. She had never wanted to take the name of Roodesh, but the title of leader was tempting, though she wasn't convinced she deserved it. And if another tilli wanted to lay claim to the name and the title, it was their right to do that and force a vote on the matter. Though it seemed no one had taken advantage of that right in her absence. Maybe they had all been too worried with finding the army and building a new one.

Zelenka forced the meal down a throat thick with worry.

One step at a time, she told herself. First worry about finding the rest of the army, then concentrate on figuring out if you want to be leader.

Back in the main atrium, Zelenka glanced past lines of the current members of the army and concentrated on the thirty or so potential recruits. Among the volunteers, one head stood out, several inches higher than the next tallest tilli. It belonged to the young tilli who had twice come to their room. Something about her posture, maybe the way her hip stuck out to the right in a slightly defiant pose, made Zelenka think she would have to keep an eye on this particular girl.

The rest of the recruits looked sturdy enough, albeit a little nervous. She noticed several glancing around the room, like they weren't sure they wanted to be there. Overall, though, Zelenka thought they would make a good addition to the army; they certainly couldn't make it worse.

There was something she had to do before asking these soldiers, old and new alike, to join her on this mission. Nemez had admitted earlier in the morning that he hadn't told the rest of the tilli about Zelenka killing Roodesh. He had told them Roodesh had killed himself and Zelenka had run off in despair when she heard about her father. The tilli knew the army had been sent out after her, but not the full reason why.

She inhaled and imagined filling her lungs with courage. She needed all the courage she could get to do what was necessary. Zelenka opened her mouth to tell the truth to the tilli and ask them for forgiveness.

Chapter Thirteen

In the shade of the tree, Devon practiced deep breathing until he no longer felt like he was dying. He continued to stare at the clouds when one shaped like an upside-down chair wafted into view. It reminded him of a certain chair he had recently hidden behind. Like brushing his hand across a coin long forgotten in the depths of his pocket, his mind swept across the memory of the mysterious Elixir mentioned in the study that night. He had kept the secret of it packed so far into the back of his mind he had almost forgotten it entirely.

He swallowed and found his throat no longer felt tight. In fact, it felt as great as the rest of his body. He pulled up his pant leg and examined his knee, skin perfect and intact when he had skinned it playing bagball the day before. He poked the spot where the raw skin should have been, as if that would suddenly make it reappear.

Was the strange substance from the wagon the Elixir? Could it have healed his knee? If it was the Elixir, why had it made him feel so terrible immediately after tasting it? Now that he remembered the secret, it burned to be let out.

Devon shot up from the ground and ran home, letting the wind blow off the leaves and dirt clinging to his clothes. His house stood on a street full of crooked houses, each three-stories high with a deeply pitched roof. His wooden house had been painted over so many times that streaks of red, yellow, and a horrible pink peeked through the cracks in the newer coat of blue paint. Rather than looking like a picturesque rainbow, all the colors smeared together into one blur of brown.

In a blur himself, Devon rushed through the side door and slammed it shut. He found no one inside, so he headed for the back door and out into the small yard, boxed in by a faded wooden fence. His dad was cooking deer steaks over the fire pit, while his mom played with Skylynn and Landon in the patchy grass. A full clothesline created a maze of shadows for the kids to run through.

Devon marched right up to his mom. "I need to ask you something."

His mom paused in chasing Landon long enough to glance at Devon. "So ask."

"No," he said. "In private."

That caught his mother's attention. She stopped running and clapped her hands. "Okay, time to clean up before dinner." She pointed to Skylynn and Landon. "You two, go wash your hands."

His siblings headed to the back door, arguing over who got to open it and pushing their way through together. His mom sat against the fence and patted the ground next to her, indicating for Devon to sit there.

"What's on your mind, my precocious child?" his mom asked.

"I ran into Ms. Pennyfold after school today," Devon began. "She mentioned how she remembered me when I was a baby, how I was sick all the time and then got better fast. Was she talking about my breathing condition?"

His mom folded her arms across her chest, and he wondered what was with the hesitation.

"You got sick a lot as a baby and were a terrible eater and sleeper," his mom said. "Right after your first birthday, we tried a new medicine and you got a lot better. Though you still have your spells of labored breathing. We never found anything to make that go away."

Hands pressed to the dry grass, he asked the big question, the one he hoped would allow him to release the burden of his secret. And maybe one that would help him learn more about it. "What medicine was it?"

"What?" she asked in a casual voice, but her neck muscles tightened and her thumb tapped a rapid beat against her knee as she sat cross-legged on the ground.

He spoke the next words slowly, staring at his mother for any hint of a reaction. "Was it the Elixir?" The word shot out of his mouth like a poisoned dart aimed for his mother's heart.

But a word can't really hurt, can it?

He got the answer to his silent question as her posture stiffened and she stared at him, eyes wide in terror, her mouth poised open in an O.

"Where did you hear about that?" she whispered in a voice as tight as her expression.

Devon wanted to take it all back, undo the conversation and find a better way to reveal he knew about the Elixir. One that didn't make the lines in his mother's face so deep.

"In Pop Pop's study," he said, his stupid voice cracking. "After dinner on the day the lightning destroyed Auntie Ky's play." He told her of the conversation he had overheard, how Katora had made him promise not to tell anyone.

"I can't believe Pop and Katora didn't tell me," she said more to herself than to him.

"I asked them not to—"

She cut him off, "I don't care what you asked them to do. You're a youngeryear. They're grown-ups. Pop's in his pastyears for the Great Mother's sake." She grabbed him by the shoulders and shook him hard enough to rattle his teeth. "You musn't tell anyone about," she lowered her voice to a whisper, "the Elixir. Not anyone at school, not a single friend, not your brother and sister." His mom's gaze cut to the grill across the yard. "Not even your father."

Devon stared in shock at his mother. "You mean Dad doesn't know about the Elixir?"

"Shhh," she hissed. She shook her head. "He doesn't. And we need to keep it that way. Desperate people would kill for it. The fewer people who know of it, the easier it is to keep us safe. I can't believe Pop and Katora let you find out about it."

Unshed tears glistened in her eyes. She pulled him in for a hug. Warm, wet drops moistened his neck. It was the first time he had experienced his mom crying. It almost forced a few of his own tears to squeak out, but he held them in, a lump forming in his throat.

His father, clearly too engrossed in getting the perfect sear on the steaks to pay attention to the tense conversation across the yard, shouted, "Dinner!"

His mom pushed Devon out of the hug and they stood. He caught a glimpse of her wiping her cheek with her sleeve. When she looked at him, the slight reddening of her eyes was the only sign of her distress. He gripped her arm, realizing for the first time he had grown taller than his mother.

"I won't mention it again." He mimed locking an imaginary padlock on his lips and throwing away the key, something he used to do with his brother and sister. It elicited a tiny laugh from his mom. She patted his arm in return and mouthed a "thank you."

Dinner felt a solemn affair to Devon, though Skylynn and Landon filled the air with their chattering and bickering. He couldn't get into the usual banter with his dad about his upcoming bagball game. His mom must have noticed his uncharacteristic quiet because she kept glancing at him with a pinched look of concern. He was all too relieved when dinner ended and he was allowed to retire to his room in the attic, the one sanctuary he had in the small, cramped house.

His attempts to read a book failed miserably, so he took to resting on his bed, staring at the knots in the ceiling beams. He had promised to keep secrets before and not done a good job of it. As it was, he had already broken his promise to Katora that he wouldn't tell his mom about the Elixir. He'd do better this time; he had to do better.

He imagined tucking the knowledge of the Elixir away in the furthest reaches of his head. He laughed as he pictured himself locking it away with a huge lock and key and throwing it in the West Rauor River. His smile faded when the make-believe game did little to banish the Elixir from his thoughts.

In his experience, secrets never lasted long. And a secret as momentous as the Elixir could result in much trouble. No amount of pretend could make him forget a secret like that.

Chapter Fourteen

With her back pressed against Katora's in the dim alley, Kylene's gaze flitted back and forth between the two lines of Nika's cronies. Even if she had wanted to join Nika's sisterhood, how could she take a vow to protect its members when she felt like the fate of her own life was out of her control?

Katora turned her head to whisper in Ky's ear, "Stay calm."

Her heart was skittering around like a nervous colt and Katora was advising her to *stay calm*. Tears squeezed from her eyes. Her blurred vision gave unnatural life to the leaves blowing in the alley. Under the ragged pants of her breathing, she barely felt the subtle rise and fall of Katora's shoulders as her sister took slow, even breaths. Was Katora made of stone?

Nika handed over the lantern to one of her minions. Then she pulled a pocketknife from her pants and flicked open the blade. A sob slipped up Kylene's throat and escaped her mouth as a hiccup. Katora's bony elbow poked her in the side.

"Nika," Katora said, her confident voice echoing off the brick buildings, "you seem to be knowledgeable about my line of work. But perhaps you don't know the full nature of it. If you did, you would know what you ask of me is impossible."

Kylene recognized the vague wording Katora used when speaking of the Elixir. As guardian, Katora was bound to serve it so any vow she took would be null. It was impossible to tell if Nika knew this because all she wore on her face was an unreadable grin. The women and the twins stood at the ready. Their sickles stood tall, mocking Kylene and Katora, so woefully ill-prepared for the ambush.

Yet Katora's voice remained steady. "I can no more take an oath to your sisterhood than I can to that monster raising an army at Drim."

Deep-throated growls came from both lines of enemies.

Kylene's stomach twisted at the mention of Drim, the site of the worst battle in the history of the Great Peninsula and perhaps the site of a future battle. The guttural rumbles from the women and twins continued.

Nika's smile turned to a sneer and she growled, the sound more animal than human. "You can't take the oath, but your sister can."

Keeping her gaze on Katora, Nika grabbed Kylene's wounded arm, sending a jolt of pain through it, and swung her around. Before Katora's hand was halfway to her dagger, Bear and Wolf grabbed her arms and pinned them behind her back. The women fell silent. The wind howled mournful and low, shooting up the alley and rustling Kylene's hair. An owl hooted in the distance, and she wondered why an owl was in the middle of a city. Maybe the rats made for a good midnight snack.

Katora bared her teeth and growled long and loud. It seemed everyone's animal instincts were kicking in, except for Kylene's; she fought her strongest instinct, the only one she seemed to have, which was to cry.

Nika twisted Kylene's hand until it was palm up. She squeezed Kylene's index finger, and it throbbed with pumping blood and flushed red at the tip.

"Reye!" Nika shouted.

A thin woman stepped out of line. She wore a black vest with bulging pockets. From one, she produced a small vial filled with an indigo liquid.

Kylene jumped when hands touched her shoulders. A third woman held a curved blade close to her neck. Where did they think she was going to go?

Nika's knife flashed in the lantern light as she brought it close to Kylene's finger. Reye removed the stopper from the vial and held it under Kylene's hand. The owl hooted again, louder than before. Katora let out a screech and struggled against Bear and Wolf with little effect on the burly men.

"Wait!" Katora shouted. "Let's talk about this."

Nika's smile widened before she began chanting, "Blood by

blood, life by life." The women repeated the words. A chill crept up Kylene's spine, but the tip of her finger burned hot. "Hear ye fire to conspire."

They chanted in unison, their voices rising high above the brick buildings and into the night sky. "A drop runs free, binds eternally. Blood by blood, life by life."

With a wave of panic, Kylene thought of the Golden City and held the gilded buildings in her mind during the desperate moment.

"Great Mother!" Katora yelled, her face an angry crimson. "This isn't right. In the Great Mother's name, let's talk about this first!"

Kylene's eyes met Katora's and she saw a blue pool of deep pain there. All her hope seeped away with the resignation in Katora's eyes. She sucked in a cry when the blade pricked her skin, not from the pain, but from the shock of what was happening.

A bright red drop formed on her finger. The blood that coursed through her veins because the Elixir had saved her back in the forest when she had been stabbed by the poisoned spear. The blood that now betrayed her as it dripped into the vial, its vital color lost in the indigo liquid.

"Your sisters welcome you," Nika and the women recited, their words unnaturally loud in Kylene's ear, "as red turns back to blue. Blood by blood, life by life."

For a second it seemed like the world stopped; everyone froze as the liquid turned to a light blue and then to the same glorious color as the buildings of the Golden City. The world moved again as Reye stoppered the vial and carefully returned it to her chest pocket.

Then to Kylene's horror, Nika licked Kylene's finger, leaving a bead of saliva where the blood had been. She cried out in disgust and pulled her hand away, wiping it again and again on her cloak. Not that any amount of cleansing could cure the binding placed upon her, tainting her blood. She tugged at the ends of her long hair, trying to keep tears from spilling down her face, and failing.

What would she have to endure next? What would she have

to do to honor this abomination of a sisterhood?

Closer than ever, the owl hooted in three quick successions, the sound echoing off the buildings like it was in the alley with them. Kylene started, while Katora stood very still, her arms pinned by Bear and Wolf.

A breath of a second passed, Kylene locked in a stare with her sister. Katora winked, not a friendly "hi" kind of wink, but an intense one in which she closed her right eye tight for longer than necessary. Kylene barely processed it as a sign when Katora kicked Bear in the groin and quickly did the same to Wolf, breaking free. The twin mountains fell to their knees.

A holler came from the main road. The women all turned in its direction. Katora wielded her dagger high above her head, shouted, and ran straight at the line of enemies blocking the exit. Completely forgetting about her own dagger strapped at her waist, Kylene followed in the wake of her sister.

She burst out onto the street. A cool breeze blasted her face and chilled the tears on her cheeks. In the lantern light from the main road, Kylene saw two cloaked figures atop horses. A wave of fear shook her. She had last encountered horsemen in Faway Forest, not really men, but spirits under the power of the great witch Yeselda. They had captured the travelers and had nearly thwarted the whole mission of finding the Elixir's nectar.

One of the figures pulled off the hood to reveal sandy-brown hair and gray-blue eyes. Kylene's heart leaped into her throat as she recognized Bhar. The other rider, who Kylene assumed to be Hirsten, hoisted Katora up behind him.

Bhar offered Kylene his hand and yelled, "Hurry!"

She grabbed it and using Bhar's foot as a stirrup, flung her leg over the saddle. Before she was fully settled, Bhar kicked the horse's sides and it shot off down the dark street after Hirsten and Katora's beast. Sobs wracked Kylene's body, tears wetting the back of Bhar's cloak, as they left behind Nika and her cursed sisterhood.

The horses galloped through the quiet streets, their hooves beating out a funeral march on the cobblestone to honor the death of Kylene's freedom. She pressed her face to Bhar's back, blocking out the buildings rushing by. There was no peace in the blackness, but at least it stemmed the flow of tears. A few minutes later, they made a sharp turn and came to an abrupt stop. The pungent stench of manure filled her nose.

A few horses stuck their heads out of their stalls and nickered at their arrival. Katora and Hirsten had already dismounted and were talking with the stable girl. Her eyes looked heavy from sleep and her hair was tousled with several pieces of hay stuck in it. Katora gave her instructions too quiet for Kylene to hear, and the girl ran down the aisle, stirring up dust on her way out. Bhar let Kylene dismount first and then thudded down next to her.

Katora glared at all of them. "What in the Great Mother happened?" She seemed to be trying to keep her voice down, but the anger in her tone was evident.

Bhar shrugged. "We got a little lost. No big deal."

Katora's face turned an interesting shade of reddish-purple. "No big deal!" she screamed with no pretense of being quiet.

Kylene, still reeling from being forced to join the sisterhood, rubbed her head. She sensed an explosion coming from Katora and tried for a distraction. "Why were you two even there? Only Katora and I were supposed to meet with Nika."

Bhar waved his hand dismissively. "We made other plans after you went to bed. You didn't really think we'd let you go off without backup, did you?"

How thoughtless of them to have left her out of the plan, but she kept her opinion to herself for fear of escalating the argument.

"Some backup you turned out to be." Katora followed that up with a string of expletives, punctuated by several exclamations of "Great Mother."

Hirsten placed his hand on Katora's shoulder, but she glared and yelled, "Don't touch me!"

He pulled his hand away and his face scrunched up in a pained expression. The urge to reach out and comfort him overcame Kylene, but she resisted the temptation. Now was not the time, not with Katora in such a huff.

"What's your problem?" Bhar asked. "We made it there didn't we?"

Kylene flinched as Katora shouted, "Not before Nika made Ky take an oath to the sisterhood!"

As if Kylene wasn't scared enough already, Katora's breath hitched with a sob and she let Hirsten pull her into an embrace. Kylene's mouth hung open in disbelief; this was really bad if Katora was crying.

Bhar wrapped a protective arm around Kylene. "What happened?"

She waited for Katora to respond, but her sister's face was firmly buried in Hirsten's chest. Kylene cleared her throat and told them of the chanting and her blood turning the liquid gold. Her heart pinched in pain over having to relive the experience. When she finished, the boys stared at her with matching expressions of horror.

"But blood oaths aren't real," Bhar finally said.

"The priestesses on Capdon Mountain believe in them," Hirsten said. Katora stared at him incredulously, and he shrugged. "One of my aunts lives at the temple."

"They also believe in elemental magic," Katora said, "so I wouldn't trust them on the matter of bloods oaths."

Elemental magic was an ancient belief that every living mortal could tap into one of the four elements—earth, air, fire, water—as a source of magic and that immortals could wield all four. In the thousands of years of recorded history, no one had been able to prove it, so the idea had fallen out of fashion generations ago. The priestesses of Capdon believed, though, and many thought them crazy for it.

Katora was clearly among the skeptics. "Show me your finger." Kylene obliged and Katora examined it, turning it this way and that. "Not a mark. I don't think there's anything I can do if it's real. Not even the Elixir can fix this." She said it with a quiet finality that made Kylene shiver. When had the night turned so cold? Or was she just frozen from the inside out?

Chapter Fifteen

The barn door banged open, and a bitter breeze whirled through, setting the light flickering in the lanterns, which were the regular kind Kylene was used to. Several horses snorted as a portly man plodded down the main aisle with heavy footsteps. Katora's wide eyes remained fixated on Kylene's finger. The tip was smooth and unmarred, no visible signs of the spot where Nika had pricked it.

"What do we do now?" Bhar asked in a low voice.

Katora shook her head and rubbed her temples, like she was trying to erase the night's events from her memory. "We stick to the plan. Head to Lughorn, get our guide, and then on to Blanchardwood to meet the Ice Queen...and we hope Nika's sisterhood doesn't call on Ky to fulfill her oath."

Kylene had a question, but her tongue stuck to the roof of her mouth, like she had eaten a big glob of honey. The man reached them before she could unstick her jaw. He was the barkeep who had given Bhar their room key.

He yawned, his eyes hooded with sleepiness. "You better have a good reason for waking me after hours, Kase daughter."

"Zed, you know I wouldn't have disturbed your sleep without a good reason." He grunted as Katora explained, "We need to leave the city. I require four horses and four trustworthy people willing to take our horse and wagon on the road back to Tussar."

"Wait," Bhar said. "I thought we were sticking to the plan."

"We are," Kylene said softly. She was amazed at how fast Katora had been able to make adjustments in order to protect her. "Nika will think we went home when the wagon and horse head south, but we'll be heading east to Lughorn on new horses."

Zed grunted again. "I can give you two horses, and I've got a few workers who won't mind a journey on your wagon."

"Two horses?" Katora said. "We need four."

"They're sturdy beasts." The barkeep appraised Kylene and

her companions with a smirk. "They can handle your scrawny bottoms."

Katora put her hands on her hips. "Three horses. And we'll need saddlebags, large ones. You know I'll make it worth your while."

Zed tilted his head in thought before finally agreeing. Kylene wondered if the payment would be with Elixir and how many people knew the Kases' secret.

Too exhausted to think about it and with her arm feeling like it was on fire, Kylene wandered over to a horse stall. She clicked her tongue, and the animal moved nearer. With a shaking hand, she caressed the horse's smooth, warm muzzle. A glance at the placard on the stall told her his name was Jinks. His chestnut coat was marked with sooty dapple that started at his neck and trailed down his back.

"Hey, Jinks," she whispered. She pressed her cheek to his muzzle; breathed in the mixed scent of straw, manure, and horse sweat; and ran her finger through his black mane. "I'm the one who feels like a jinx."

Jinks nipped at her ear, a harmless little bite that left a trail of saliva.

"He's a good boy but a bit mischievous." The barkeep's gruff voice had a hint of softness. "Lives up to his name." Kylene murmured her agreement. "You can take him as one of your horses."

She raised her head. "I'd like that."

"Just don't let him get away with too much. He needs a firm hand to keep him in line."

Doubt twisted her stomach as she took a step away from the horse. "Maybe I shouldn't take him."

Jinks snorted and stretched his neck, inching as close to her as the stall door would allow. Zed's mouth twisted into a lopsided smile and he patted her on the shoulder. "Take him. He likes you. A journey will be good for my mischief-maker."

"Thank you." She offered her hand for a shake, and he took it.

He opened Jinks's stall and showed Ky where the bridle hung. Then he took her to the closet with all the saddles and let her choose one. Figuring she and Bhar would be riding on the same horse, she selected a large one, despite knowing it would mean extra weight. They would have to make sure not to overtax Jinks. She hummed a made-up tune while she brushed his coat.

For the other horses, Zed offered them a large gray mare named Gem and a small bay named Maple. He informed them that Maple was uniquely devoted to Gem and would follow the mare anywhere. Bhar and Hirsten saddled up Gem. Then the stablegirl arrived, laden down with bags and provisions. Katora loaded up Maple with saddlebags of supplies.

As she mounted, Katora reminded Zed to take care of the horse and wagon. Ky hugged the barkeep, and he squeezed her back in a fatherly manner.

"Remember, you're the boss of Jinksy boy, not the other way round."

She nodded and swept a tear from the corner of her eye.

Bhar grabbed Jinks's reins, mounted, and said, "I'm driving this one."

Kylene shrugged and settled in behind her brother. "His name is Jinks. He's a troublemaker like you, so you two should get along fine." She didn't know where the clever retort had come from, but she smiled at her cleverness.

With a wave from Zed and the stablegirl, the four travelers and three horses were off, jogging down the roads of Skimere. Soon they crossed the bridge over the Skimere River and left behind the windy city streets. Then they were back on the plains road, skirting the foot of mountains and heading east.

Ahead of them, Katora urged Gem into a canter and sure enough, Maple matched the pace. Bhar spurred on Jinks. Kylene inhaled the cold air, savoring its freshness. Such a contrast from the stale city air. She peered around Bhar's back and watched the first rays of the rising sun. The horizon turned a deep pink, offset by the dark blue sky. When the sun broke above the horizon, the pink streak changed to orange and the sky lightened.

As fatigue weighed down her eyelids and hunger gnawed her stomach, she rested her head on Bhar's shoulder and let the lull of Jinks's cantor carry her off to sleep.

She was jolted awake to the scream of high winds and shouting. A blast of air whipped her hair about and sent dirt into her eyes. Dark storm clouds covered the sky, making it impossible to pinpoint the time of day, though she figured she'd only slept a little while.

Still mounted on their horse, Katora and Hirsten faced them. Bhar urged Jinks forward until they were next to each other.

"What is it?" shouted Bhar.

Katora yelled back, "A squall! We need to find cover!"

Kylene squinted against the battery of debris swirling around. "Should we head for the mountains?"

"Too far!" Katora pointed to a group of rocks about fifty feet away. "Head there!"

Katora's mount, followed by the pack horse, sprinted for the rocks. Bhar's heels slammed into the sides of Jinks, and the horse took off in the same direction. The boulders were about four feet high and formed a sort of circle with a patch of low grass in the middle.

Hammered by strong gusts on all sides, they dismounted. Kylene slapped Jinks on the rear and sent him running away from the storm with Gem and Maple following. She hoped they would find a safe spot to ride out the weather.

The wind whipped around in circles. The sky was a swirling mass of purple clouds, dangerously close to the ground. Fat raindrops fell, icy pricks on her skin.

The four travelers squished into the circle of boulders and huddled under a deerskin blanket from Bhar's pack. Pressed close to her right side, Hirsten's heartbeat slammed against Kylene's side. He had one arm wrapped around her and the other around Katora. Bhar did the same on her left.

With the boys' holding them tight, Ky and Katora did their best to secure the deerskin, but it was only minutes before the churning air lifted it up and tossed it away. The freezing raindrops fell in a deluge, soaking Kylene straight through her clothing.

They clung together in a tight circle against the relentless wind. The rocks provided little protection from the storm, which advanced on them like a giant lumbering across the plains. The storm filled her ears, louder than the falls of the Three River Split. Warm tears sliced down Kylene's frozen cheeks as she bent her head. She clutched Bhar and Hirsten with hands numb from the cold.

Her lips mumbled a quiet prayer to Mother Nature, asking her to see them through the storm. She doubted her words made it out of their little group, which was now at the mercy of the squall.

Chapter Sixteen

Zelenka opened her mouth to spill the truth about how she had killed Roodesh, but no words came out. Looking out at the young faces of the tilli who were willing to put their lives at risk at her command, she was afraid of losing their allegiance.

A nudge in the back from Palafair spurred her on.

"Fellow tilli," she began, her voice reverberating in the large cave. "I have longed to come home to the Three River Split and make amends with you. You may have heard terrible things about me. Perhaps how I destroyed the entire tilli army, but those claims are untrue. My only burden when it comes to the army is that they met their demise while out searching for me, not that their demise came about by my hand. But I do have a burden, one you deserve to know before you follow me into the forest."

She paused. Now was the time to tell them. Start with a clean slate. Let the words out so the guilt could wash away down the waterfalls as Roodesh's body had done.

The atrium was silent, save for the low incessant drips of water. Palafair's brow was knit with concern. He gave her a slight nod and that was all she needed to make her confession.

"I killed Roodesh." Her words echoed throughout the atrium. A buzz of talk broke out among the soldiers. Most of their faces looked confused, though a few angry ones stood out.

"I thought he killed himself!" a soldier shouted. "Threw himself into the falls in a fit of madness!"

"We have been lied to?" came another shout.

"How can you expect us to follow the killer of our leader?" another soldier demanded.

Nemez took a step forward, hands raised. "Settle down! I did tell you Roodesh killed himself. I lied—"

The buzz of voices turned into cries of outrage. The anger in the room was palpable, an irate energy spewing out from the crowd.

Nemez shouted once again, "Silence! That is an order!"

The ragtag army was green but smart enough to follow a direct order. The room fell quiet. Nemez kept his expression stern, but there was a slight twitch to his eyelid. Zelenka wasn't the only one who had to make amends.

"Now is a time to listen, then you can judge," he continued. "I did not know the whole story then, but I do now. Hear Colonel Zelenka out."

"Thank you, General Nemez." Pleased her voice came out steady and strong, she found the strength to continue. "Before he bore the name of Roodesh, our most recent leader was a strict man with a military background, but a kind man. He used to keep candy in his pocket to sneak to children."

A smile spread across her face as she thought her father. "But that is not the man you all would know. That was Fanas, my father, the man he was before he became Roodesh." A few murmurs rose up from the soldiers. Some of them, the younger ones in particular, probably didn't know that the last Roodesh had been her father; a fact she kept quiet after he had begun to go mad. The noise quickly died down. She had their attention at least, if not their allegiance.

"When Fanas took over as Roodesh, he turned hard and cruel. Only the disciplinarian side remained. Eventually all traces of kindness disappeared. His mind was poisoned by an impossible dream. His predecessor destroyed Hillock in pursuit of this same dream, and my father destroyed his own humanity following the same course."

Hillock, a mountain in the middle of Faway Forest, had been the home to the tilli after they crossed over from Demick Island and broke away from the anni demicks. An intricate of network of tunnels and rooms crisscrossed under the mountain; this was where the tilli lived for hundreds of years...until it was destroyed. Fanas's predecessor had ordered the army to dig deep into Hillock in search of the Elixir's secret ingredient, which he believed was buried under the mountain. Eventually the integrity of the network was compromised. Many tilli died when the tunnels collapsed, and the survivors fled to the Three River Split to build a new home.

With this history heavy in her mind, Zelenka spoke with renewed energy. "Many of you are too young to remember Hillock and the brave tilli we lost when our tunnels collapsed. And what did we lose our home over?" With a prayer to Mother Nature that Palafair would forgive her for revealing the Kases' secret, she reached into her pocket, pulled out the small vial of Elixir she had brought from Kase Farm, and held it up for all to see. "This Elixir, or rather the idea it represents. The thing the Roodeshes searched for was a myth. These madmen believed the Elixir would keep them alive forever. This," she punched the air with the vial, "is only a healing potion, not a path to immortality."

Her voice broke on the last word, the sound echoing in the cavern. She lowered her arms and put the vial back in her pocket. She hated carrying the cursed potion around and couldn't wait to return it to the Kases, though it seemed to have done its job of helping the tilli to understand her actions.

She swallowed past the lump in her throat and plowed through the rest of the story. "For years I watched madness consume our most recent Roodesh, the man who was once my father. I wondered how many lives he would ruin in his quest. When the Kase family showed up at the Three River Split with the Elixir, Roodesh found out the truth. How it has very powerful healing properties, but it will not keep a demick or human alive forever."

She glanced at Palafair, hoping he wasn't mad at her. His eyebrows were raised, but he nodded encouragingly. "His mind had been damaged before, but it was permanently broken after learning this. I had to free the tilli from him before he destroyed us."

As she spoke, she wanted to believe her own words, but a part of her wondered if she had done the right thing, if it had been necessary to throw Roodesh down the falls. She shook her head, knowing she had to convince her people to trust her, despite her doubts. "I have come back here to plead for your forgiveness and to make amends by putting your army back together."

Zelenka braced for a reaction, her toes dancing in her boots anticipating...what? She didn't know. An outcry of rage perhaps. Certainly not the dead silence that greeted her. She looked to Nemez. He stood stock still, staring out at the crowd, his mouth slightly open. Finally someone coughed.

"A new Roodesh has come home to claim her place as leader of the tilli!" a young woman, one of the new recruits, shouted. The women around her clapped and cheered. Several soldiers joined in. As more soldiers took up the cheer, the sound rose and echoed off the cave ceiling. "Hooray for the new Roodesh!"

They cheered for her but for the wrong reason. The name of Roodesh had been ruined, and she had vowed never to take it. She wasn't sure if a name could taint a person's mind, but she wasn't interesting in testing the theory.

Zelenka waved her arms, seeking to stop this nonsense. "No! No, no!" The crowd quieted, but a hum of excitement simmered. "I am humbled by your response. But I do not seek the name of Roodesh. I will lead you as Colonel Zelenka if you will follow me."

They once again grew quiet. Nemez finally spoke up, "This new mission is one of utmost importance. The core of the army was sent out in search of Zelenka when she fled the Three River Split. They never returned. We do not know what fate they met, but Zelenka has been tasked with finding out what happened to them. Because of the dangerous nature of this task and our new army's inexperience, no one is required to participate. If you wish not to go, you may leave the atrium now and resume your normal duties with your tilli honor intact."

A handful of tilli slipped out but most stayed. Zelenka's heart thumped in her chest at witnessing the fortitude of these young soldiers.

"Thank you all for staying," she said. "Pack for a long trip in Faway Forest. I do not know how long we will be gone, so make sure to be prepared for cold weather. Once you are ready, meet in the dining room for lunch. The cooks have prepared a hearty meal."

Her lips rose in her wry smile as she watched the tilli disperse to prepare. Palafair slipped his hand into hers and squeezed. She squeezed back and let the warmth of his hand rise up her arm.

"You are not mad at me for revealing the secret of the Elixir?" she asked.

He let out a little chuckle. "It has proven difficult of late to keep its existence under wraps. Pretty soon it will be the worst-kept secret in all of the Great Peninsula."

She kissed his cheek, hoping it conveyed her gratitude. "We need to find you a proper weapon." She flicked the dagger he carried. "This will not do much against the terrible beasts of the forest."

Palafair laughed louder this time, the sound like water trickling down a rock wall. "I do not need any more weapon than you by my side, my love."

"I have a green army to protect. I would feel better if you had a spear or a sword."

He bent at the waist in a mock bow, pulling her down with him. He raised his head and planted a kiss on her lips. "As you wish. I am yours to command."

She whacked him on the arm. "I will take you to the armory."

As they left the atrium, Zelenka let the high of her victory wash over her. Soon she would be back in the wilds of Faway Forest with a new host of worries plaguing her.

Chapter Seventeen

Less than two hours after Zelenka had addressed the tilli army, she was checking the straps on Palafair's bags to make sure they were tight enough. The army snaked in a long line several tilli deep from the bridge at the top of the Three River Split back to the cliffs on the west side of the river. With a clear blue sky and a bright autumn sun overhead, the orange, yellow, and reds of the forest spread out before them like a vast wildfire.

Zelenka breathed in deep, inhaling the light, misty air of the Split for one last time. It was extra crisp at this elevation and would only grow colder as winter approached. She hoped they would be home—with the missing army—before winter came, but hoping for a thing never made it true.

She adjusted her pack and stretched her legs one last time before giving the command for the march to start. She led the tilli down the far side of the waterfalls and into the wilds of Faway Forest. Leaves crinkled and popped underfoot so the forest not only looked like fire but sounded like it too.

Zelenka had decided to follow the course she, Katora, and the others had taken when the old tilli army had followed them. Faway Forest was vast and wild with few paths beyond the Split to accommodate ponies, not that they hand any except for the now famous Captain Buttercup, who had been left at the Split in the loving care of several enthusiastic youngeryears. So their route was due east on foot. It wasn't a great starting plan, but it was the only one she had.

Palafair strode along beside her with sure-footed steps. Zelenka's leg ached as it often did in the colder weather. It wasn't long before the forest closed in on them, the thickets and brambles a thorny cage. The army marched all afternoon, the scenery changing little. A somber mood permeated the soldiers and they were a quiet group.

Once the sun set, the air turned bitter, their breaths rising in puffs to the starlit sky. Zelenka called a halt to the march and ordered them to set up camp. There were few places in the forest that were open enough to accommodate tents for so many demicks, so they simply spread out over the wooded area haphazardly. Some were in tents, but others opted for blankets and huddled close to small fires.

Zelenka and Palafair warmed rocks in the fire and slipped them into their shared bedroll. They snuggled close to one another. She fell asleep with Palafair's warm head on her chest and the cold, hard ground at her back.

* * * *

Zelenka lead the tilli army east through the increasingly thick brush of Faway Forest for several days. Daylight was a scarce commodity in the forest this time of year, so she made them wake up early each day and pushed them to continue the march until it was too dark to see. The exhaustive pace showed on the glassy-eyed faces of the untested soldiers. Despite the desperate need to train the soldiers, Zelenka refrained from making them do drills at night. They didn't have the energy nor the space for it, and the need to keep moving forward outweighed any others.

One evening, Major Ronan approached Zelenka and Palafair's fire, two bowls in hand. He moved both bowls to his side, awkwardly holding them with one arm, and saluted. "Colonel! Hot soup for you and Sir Palafair." The soldiers had taken to addressing Palafair as sir, though being an anni demick, he held no position in the tilli army.

"At ease, Major," Zelenka said. "Sit with us a minute." Ronan's shoulders fell into a relaxed position as he handed out the bowls. "Did you eat?"

"Yes, ma'am," he said.

Palafair dug into the steaming soup and grinned after his first bite. "This is good. Who made it?"

"Private Laurel," Ronan said.

"The girl who helped Zelenka and I settle into our rooms?" Palafair took another bite.

It was typical for Palafair to be thoughtful enough to remember the girl's name. Zelenka put a spoonful in her mouth—the broth was thick and tasty—and closely watched their exchange. She wasn't sure where Palafair was going with this. It could be friendly chitchat or it could be more.

"I believe so, sir." Ronan shifted and couldn't seem to find a comfortable position. Perhaps he was uncomfortable with being so close to Palafair. Despite the outward politeness of the army around Palafair, she had no idea how they privately felt about an anni marching among them.

"Not that I have any say," Palafair winked, "but if she keeps cooking like this, she may just earn herself a promotion."

She shot Palafair a glare, hands shaking at his audacity.

Instead of yelling at her insubordinate husband, she thanked Ronan for the meal and asked him, "Was there something else you needed?" She had originally planned on chatting with Ronan to get a sense of the army's mood, but now she was anxious to speak to Palafair privately.

Ronan shifted again, so much so that Zelenka wondered if he was sitting on a bed of thistles. "Out with it," she ordered.

"Uh, well, ma'am." He blinked several times in quick succession and cleared his throat. "The soldiers are tired. Uh...well not all of them, not me...but many have told me they are. They would like a day off. And, um, I think it is a good idea...for them to rest, not because I need it."

Zelenka stood and approached Ronan, who quickly scrambled to his feet. She leaned into his face so they were eye to eye.

"The soldiers want a day off." Her voice was a low grunt. She turned it to an artificially nonchalant tone. "How long have we been on the march, Major?"

Ronan's shoulders stiffened and his posture went back to attention. "Five days, ma'am."

Noticing they had gained the interest of those around them, Zelenka turned and raised her voice a notch higher. "And how many more days will we be on the march?"

"Uh..." Ronan spluttered. His eyes blinked as fast as the

wings of a hovering dragonfly.

"Major Ronan," Zelenka boomed, "I asked you a question."

He saluted and seemed to regain his composure. "Yes, ma'am, um Colonel. We will be on the march as long as it takes to complete the mission."

"And how much longer will it take to complete the mission if we rest tomorrow?" Zelenka paced the length of the fire, arms tucked behind her back and chest puffed out.

Ronan frantically glanced around. "Oh, um—"

"Major!" Zelenka shouted. "Do you have an answer?"

"Yes, Colonel. One day longer than it should."

Palafair rested a hand on her shoulder. Already furious with him, she snapped her head around and fixed a harsh stare on him, not that it would work to intimidate him. He wasn't a green private who quivered under her orders.

At least this time he had the decency to whisper in her ear while being contrary. "Zelenka love, give them a day off. Who knows how long we will be out here."

"All the more reason not to waste a day," she quietly argued.

"They are tired. I know I am. And they are scared. They would never tell you, but they are." The way his breath tickled her ear as he whispered felt too intimate for the topic at hand. "And I would not mind a day off. We could take a walk through the woods together."

Her anger melted away at the pleading innocence on his face. "Fine, you win on this point." She raised her voice and said, "Major, we will not be marching tomorrow, but I want you to continue with a full weapons training regimen. We need all the practice we can get."

A wide grin broke out on his face and without so much as a salute, he rushed off to tell those not within earshot. She sighed. Her army was hopelessly inexperienced, and Palafair was turning her soft.

She swatted him on the shoulder. "Do not ever suggest giving any of my soldiers a promotion. You will not gain any favor by making promises that you cannot keep."

"Aye aye, Colonel," he said with a poorly executed salute. Then he raised his eyebrows suggestively at the tent, which they had found enough space to set up among the trees. "Shall we retire for the night?"

Holding open the tent door, she ushered him in before he embarrassed her in front of the whole army. Their shared bedroll was cold when they got in. Despite his ineptitude at being a soldier, she loved him and never shied away from showing him that in private. It wasn't long before they grew warm.

Chapter Eighteen

Devon jogged down the path to the farmhouse, his belly grumbling in anticipation of dinner. He didn't know what his grammy was cooking, but everything she cooked was delicious. The late afternoon sun was warm for this time of year and beads of sweat dripped down the side of his face.

The path narrowed and darkened, shaded by trees. He ran faster and replayed his latest bagball game in his mind. A grin crept across his face when he remembered a hard play he had made that had kept the game locked in a tie. The smile grew wider as he pictured the ball soaring through the air after he had whacked it clear out of the field to score the game winner.

As the trees thinned, Devon caught site of the big wooden farmhouse. He slowed to a walk. Four large barrels stood there, two stacked on each side of the front door. His breath caught as he wondered if they held Elixir. He kicked the doorframe; so much for going even a single day without thinking about it.

He should have never mentioned it to his mom. Ever since he'd learned how important it was, Devon had done all he could not to think about it, with little success. During his game, he had found himself pondering what enemies might want to steal it. Whenever he tried to write, all his words left him and were replaced with one word: Elixir. He wanted to stand on the roof of his house and shout it over and over to get it out of his system.

Grammy startled him when she opened the door, hands covered in flour. "Since when do you knock?"

"Oh." He held his hands behind his back and struggled for an explanation that didn't reveal he had kicked his grandmother's house. "I was thinking about my bagball game."

"You think too much about that sport," she said with a shake of her finger, but she wore a smile. "You did have a good game."

Devon shuffled his feet, having a hard time concentrating on the present. "Thanks."

"Come in, come in. Dinner's almost ready." She ushered him in, leaving a white handprint on his shoulder. "Your mom and brother and sister are helping me in the kitchen. You can set the table."

He grabbed dishes and utensils from the cupboards and set to work arranging them on the large dining room table. It only reminded him of the night after the lightning had burned Kylene's stage when the whole family had dined there and he had learned of the Elixir. A plate cracked down the middle as he accidentally slammed it down.

His mom tutted when he returned to the kitchen with a piece of it in each hand. She handed him an intact. "A little less force this time perhaps."

"Sorry," he muttered.

"Are you feeling okay?"

"Yes," he nearly shouted. The last thing he needed was for his mom to think he was sick.

"When you're done, go find Pop Pop out in the fields. Tell him it's time to come in." She pursed her lips. "And that I want to speak with him after dinner."

He figured she wanted to tell off Pop Pop for not telling her about Devon being in on the family secret. He finished setting the table without breaking any more dishes and slipped outside to find his grandfather.

Big, purple essenberries hung from the vines, ripe for the picking. He plucked one and popped it in his mouth, a burst of sweet followed by a tart flavor tickling his taste buds. Essence was a safe beverage to think about, and any made from these succulent berries would be strong. He eyed the long rows of vines and wondered who would help harvest all the fruit since Katora, Ky, Bhar, and Hirsten were all off on their adventure.

He let the idea of finding his own adventure simmer while he scanned the fields. Pop Pop was on the far end of the farm, near where the landscape turned woody and lead to the river. A bucketful of essenberries hung from Pop Pop's arm. His grandfather straightened up and smiled.

"Dinnertime?" he asked, and Devon nodded. "I hear your mother isn't happy with me."

"Furious." Devon noticed how low the sun hung in the sky, the wooded area near them darkening with each passing minute. Could something evil be hiding among the vines, listening and waiting to pounce on them? "No," he amended, his voice a croak that he cleared with a cough. "She's scared for me."

"It is a serious matter. Has it been hard not to talk about it?" Pop Pop's lips were tight, but his eyes glinted in the low sunlight.

"Yes, sir," Devon admitted as he shuffled his feet in the soil. "I try not to think about it, and I know not to say anything, but I'm afraid the word Elixir will pop out of my mouth."

"Maybe if you know more about it, you might find it easier to keep it from popping out of your mouth. Why don't we talk about it after dinner?"

Devon remembered what his mother had said about speaking to Pop Pop. "Mom wants to talk to you, too."

"I figured she would. The three of us can discuss it. Hopefully you'll both feel better then." Pop Pop pointed at the two buckets of berries at his feet. "Why don't you help an old man carry these?"

Devon stared at this grandfather's dark hair and mostly unwrinkled face; he hadn't really thought of him as old. He'd known Pop Pop to carry three heaping buckets on each arm with little effort. Then he noticed the glint in Pop Pop's eyes was a full-on twinkle. He lightly punched his grandfather on the shoulder and picked up the buckets, groaning like they were too heavy. Pop Pop ruffled his hair and followed him down the line to the house.

With the prospect of learning more about the Elixir on the horizon, Devon felt less twitchy. He dropped the buckets at the back door and hustled to the dining room, stomach grumbling with renewed hunger.

Chapter Nineteen

Stomach near bursting from Grammy's cooking, Devon grunted as he bent over to fill the fireplace in the study with logs and kindling. The match hissed and lit as he struck it against the brick. He touched the tiny flame to the paper underneath the logs, tossed the match in, and watched the flames spread as they blazed into a fire big enough to warm his cheeks.

He straightened when his mom and Pop Pop entered. His mouth fell open as they argued like a couple of hens clucking over the last specks of cracked corn.

"You shouldn't have let him find out," his mom was saying.

"I didn't mean for it to happen this way, but it did. He was probably going to find out eventually, Ariana," Pop Pop said.

"At this rate, the whole of the Great Peninsula is going to know about it, and I still haven't been allowed to tell my own husband."

Pop Pop calmly set three glasses on his big desk and poured essence into them. The liquid was a dark amber and almost as thick as syrup. Devon had never seen essence so thick. "It has been more difficult since Katora took over as guardian to be discreet about the Elixir. There have been many sicknesses and injuries these last few years, the demand for it is unprecedented."

"We've all heard of Katora's growing reputation as a healer, but I don't want Devon to get dragged into it, or into these rumors of war."

Pop Pop offered her a drink, which she accepted with a steely glare. Then he gave one to Devon.

"Instead of scaring him half to death, why don't we educate him?" Pop Pop said, misinterpreting Devon's open-mouthed stare as one of fear when it was actually one of shock at his mother's outburst.

"Shut your mouth and sit down," his mom said.

Devon's mouth dropped lower until he realized she was talking to him, not Pop Pop. He clamped his lips tight and chose a seat near the fire, while Pop Pop sat at the desk.

His mom sat in the leather chair Devon had previously hidden behind, crossed her legs, and wagged her foot in irritation. "Where would you like to start, Pop?"

Pop Pop sighed. "I know you're not happy, Ariana. I'm doing my best to remedy the situation." He turned to Devon. "I think it would help if you knew the history of the Elixir."

He explained how many years ago an ancestor by the name of Luths Wharrel was captured by Yeselda, the witch of Faway Forest. Devon shivered at the sound of Yeselda's name; he had grown up hearing about her wicked horseman spirits who stole children that wandered too close to the forest. He had always thought it a fiction, but since finding out about the Elixir, he had wondered how many crazy tales were actually true.

Devon shuffled his chair closer to the fire and forced himself to pay attention to Pop Pop, who was talking about how Luths stole a potion from Yeselda. He sent it down the river and eventually it found its way to the farm and Luths's long-suffering wife. She and her sons experimented with the contents of the vial until they had created an early version of the Elixir.

"Our family," Pop Pop said, "has been the guardians of it ever since, making its healing properties stronger with each generation. We get a finite supply of the magical nectar when a new guardian takes over, and try to use it as sparingly as possible. It's been kept a secret all these years because it's only the guardian that is bound to use it as Mother Nature sees fit. If someone were to steal it, they would be able to use it without limits. A power like that is not to be taken lightly. It's also a great burden to bear, and keeping it a secret lessens that burden. If everyone knew of the Elixir, the requests would be overwhelming and would quickly deplete what we can supply."

Pop Pop paused to take a long drink of essence, which made Devon realize how dry his throat was. He took sip of his own essence and nearly spit it back into the glass at the bitter taste.

Pop Pop had given him spiked essence. No one objected when Devon sipped again, and he took it as a sign that Pop Pop had intentionally given him a beverage that was usually off-limits to youngeryears. Maybe someone was finally respecting Devon's almost-primeyear status.

"Katora has tried to reserve use of the Elixir for dire cases, but it's been hard to keep up with those," Pop Pop admitted.

"And it was dire in my case," Devon said. "When you used it on me as a baby."

The leather creaked as Pop Pop shifted and glanced at Devon's mom, whose face remained impassive. "We believe so."

"Wow" was all Devon could manage. He stared at the fire and thought about how he might have died all those years ago. How fate was a curious beast. He also thought about the current state of his breathing condition. "How does it work?"

"The magic or the guardianship?" Pop Pop asked.

"Both." He wanted to know as much as Pop Pop would tell him.

"The guardian is held under certain restrictions."

"What kind of restrictions?" Devon asked when his grandfather paused yet again.

Pop Pop seemed to struggle with what to say until he finally spit out, "Those set forth by its magic."

The explanation sounded too simple to mean anything significant. "Where does the magic come from?"

"The nectar gives the Elixir its magic." Pop Pop spoke slowly as if measuring each word. "The nectar comes from flowers that grow on The Sleeping Giant mountain in Faway Forest. And Mother Nature is responsible for all that grows in the natural world. So it's really her, the Great Mother, who controls the magic."

"Wow," Devon repeated. Usually he prided himself on being eloquent but found he failed to possess the words to articulate his feelings at the moment. "So what you do is controlled by Mother Nature?"

He glanced at his mother, who stared into the fire with pursed lips, and then turned his attention back to his grandfather.

"I am bound for life, though it is to a lesser degree than it once was," Pop Pop said. "I was the guardian until Katora went on her quest and picked the flowers. Now she is the guardian and bound to serve Mother Nature."

"But you were guardian when you gave me the Elixir as a baby, and Mother Nature was okay with that?"

Pop Pop leaned forward in his chair. "I wouldn't have been able to do it if she wasn't."

The pop of burning wood was the only sound until Devon's mother finally spoke, "Pop, you know it's not that simple."

"I know." He was still speaking in a slow, stilted manner uncharacteristic of his speeches. "It's not simply a matter of a single act with the Elixir being okay or not okay with Mother Nature. She sees and understands things we don't. A perk of being the mother of all things I suppose. Think of it like a mess of vines, twining all around each other." He wove his fingers together in a two-handed fist and held it out as if in offering. "It's much more complicated than you can imagine. Some vines began growing a long time ago and have an end; others are just beginning and won't stop for some time. The Great Mother sees the connections of all things past, present, and future. One simple act affects all others that come after it."

"Like everyone's fate is dependent on everyone else's," Devon piped in, beginning to understand.

"Yes," Pop Pop agreed. "You can look at it that way. So when Mother Nature allowed me to save you, she was saying it wasn't time for your vine to end."

It didn't feel like they were talking about Devon and how his life had almost ended all those years ago, more like they were discussing someone from a story. He was glad for the detachment; it made the heavy thoughts easier to process.

"So the Great Mother sees something important in my future? An important journey or task." Devon's toes wiggled in his boots with excitement. Maybe he was destined for an adventure after all.

"We can't know what she sees," his mother said. "As Pop

said, the threads are complicated. Perhaps you are not meant to go on a journey but to help someone in Tussar."

His hopes seeped out of him like the juice being squeezed from an essenberry. He had always thought his mother wanted the best for him, but perhaps he had been wrong. She seemed to expect very little of his life's journey. He sunk into the chair, his shoulders sagging in defeat.

In a very small voice, he said, "I only hope to make a difference one day, like Pop Pop and Katora are doing."

His mother sat up straighter and reached across the space between them, though she was too far away to reach him. "That isn't what I meant. You will make a difference one day. I only meant that not everyone must go on risky tasks to serve Mother Nature. Some of us are perfectly happy to live quiet lives, raising our children to be good people. Risking life and limb isn't the only way to live a good life."

Pop Pop grunted in agreement and rubbed the stubble on his chin. "Your mother is right. You needn't risk your life to live a worthy one. You're young, Devon. Your youngeryears aren't a time for big adventures. They are a time for growing, learning, and the small adventures of growing up, which are only small to those who have already experienced them."

Devon refrained from rolling his eyes. So much for Pop Pop thinking of him as a primeyear. He wasn't interested in having small adventures; he was ready for a big one. But he knew his opinions would be met with protests, so he simply said, "Yes, sir."

Pop Pop smiled and raised his glass. "A toast to the enthusiasm and spirit of youth."

"Here, here," said his mother. She lifted her cup.

Devon repeated the words and followed suit, hiding a grimace at the bitter taste in his mouth. He would show them he was not content to spending his life doing small acts. One day soon he would find his opportunity to go on a quest, even if he had to risk life and limb—to use his mom's words. What good were life and limbs if you didn't do anything with them?

Chapter Twenty

The squall bore down on the tight circle of Kylene, Bhar, Katora, and Hirsten huddled among the rocks. The cold rain turned to hail that beat down upon the back of Kylene's head, and she shut her eyes tight to block out the wind and prairie dirt.

Nothing could block out the storm, which sounded like the stampede of a hundred horses. Wind flew into every seam of her clothing, sucked away her breath, and tried to rip her from the warm embraces of Hirsten and Bhar. Her shirt ballooned out and then whipped back into place, stinging her skin. The wind yanked at her hair until it felt like it would pull clean out of her skull.

A gust swirled up under her and finally succeeded in tearing her away from her companions. It took her airborne and her silent prayers turned to frantic pleas. Eyes clamped shut, she gulped in the panic and tried to scream, but the wind forced the air back down her throat. She choked on debris, and her limbs flapped uselessly about.

A force greater than the storm thumped into her side and tackled her to the ground. A heavy body wrapped her up and buffeted her from the squall.

And then the roar lessened until it was only an echo in her ears. Kylene peeked out from her human cocoon and watched the storm fizzle out mere feet away from them. The plains fell eerily silent. The strange color of the now dormant clouds tinged everything a sickly green.

The arms of Kylene's savior released her. He was so close to Kylene that she could feel the heat radiating off his body. Her stomach somersaulted. His eyelashes, eyebrows, and hair were covered in dust that made them look blond instead of dark brown. She almost didn't recognize him, but the serious brown eyes gave him away.

"Hirsten?" she squeaked out. She wished he would stop

saving her because it elicited all kinds of strange feelings. "I thought it was Bhar that grabbed me."

"Are you okay?" he asked, his focus completely on her.

She swallowed, her mouth dry from more than the dust of the storm. "I think so." She took stock of her body. The usual pain in her arm and a few other sore spots, but nothing major. "Yes, I'm okay."

He stood and offered her a hand, which she accepted so as not to seem ungrateful. Once she was steady on her feet, she quickly released it, missing the sturdy feel of his touch as soon as it was gone.

They were a few feet from the stones, though it had felt like she had flown a hundred miles in those few seconds she was off the ground. Katora and Bhar brushed off the dirt and dry grass that clung to them, looking dazed but okay. Bhar's hand had a nasty gash that was bleeding freely, but he took no notice of it.

Her siblings rushed over and embraced her. Tears streaked the dirt on Katora's face, but Kylene said nothing about it, knowing her sister would hate to have them pointed out. A warmth settled in her stomach from the outpouring of emotion. Oddly, Kylene wasn't crying.

A bead of sweat slipped down her spine and she shivered uncontrollably. A wave of lightheadedness washed over her. She nearly fainted and would have hit the ground hard if it weren't for the close proximity of her siblings. Bhar guided her to the ground. Katora sat next to her and wrapped an arm around her shoulders, providing Ky with a steady body to lean against.

"Get her some water," Katora demanded. "And a blanket." Despite being so close to her sister, the commands sounded faraway. Kylene shook fiercely and sweat drenched her forehead.

Bhar searched the circle of rocks and shook his head. "My blanket blew away." He took the canteen from his pack and forced her to take a sip.

Hirsten wrapped his blanket around her shoulders and studied her face. His image swam in her vision and she swallowed several times in an attempt to keep the nausea at bay. "I guess you're not okay after all," he said.

Her ears popped with a swallow and the world came back into focus, but the shivers refused to die down. "J-just in shock," she said through chattering teeth.

"Hush, Ky." Katora squeezed her arm tighter around Kylene. "Support her," she said to Hirsten.

Kylene was too out of it to protest Hirsten taking Katora's place or to feel the usual pang of regretful longing at his closeness. She rested her head on his shoulder and closed her eyes against the dizziness. The earthy scent from both Hirsten and his blanket soothed her. The next thing she knew, a wet drop hit her tongue and tingled in the familiar way of the Elixir.

The dizziness and nausea immediately abated, as did the shivers. The warmth spread back into her body and she was all too aware of her sister's boyfriend right next to her. Feeling okay enough to lift her head and open her eyes, she scooted away from Hirsten. She wasn't sure how much longer she could keep her feelings about him inside before they bubbled up and burst out of her. The tears finally came.

Katora was back at her side in an instant. "Why don't you two go look for the horses?" she said to the boys. "It'll be dark soon and it'll be a painfully slow journey to Lughorn without them. I'll start a fire and see if I can find something for us to eat. Be back by dark."

"What if we don't find the horses by then?" asked Bhar.

"Be back by dark," Katora repeated darkly. "We don't need anyone getting lost. Or worse. Hopefully they'll find us by morning if we don't find them."

Kylene glanced around the vast plains nervously. The sun was low in the western sky and it wouldn't be long before night fell. There was barely a cloud in the sky, all traces of the storm erased. Hirsten and Bhar set off north in the direction of the mountains, whistling and calling for the horses. Soon their forms were lost in the great shadows of the peaks.

Katora sat with her until the boys' cries faded away. "Will you be okay while I scrounge up some firewood?"

Feeling like a burden, Kylene nodded. She shivered again as Katora stood and the chill of the late-day plains seeped through the blanket and into her bones.

"Stay here inside the rocks, and yell loud enough for the Great Mother to hear if anything comes near you, even if it doesn't look threatening." Katora headed off in the opposite direction of the boys where there was a copse of bushes that would make for good kindling.

While everyone else made themselves useful, Kylene tucked up her legs and rested her head on her knees. She watched the sun turn the sky a calming lavender, but it failed to offer any peace. A movement that she sensed more than saw directed her attention to a crack in the rock beside her. As she watched in the fading light, a tiny blue flower sprouted and bloomed to reveal a yellow center.

She reached out to touch it, and a charge of energy zapped her finger. She sucked on it until the burning sensation ceased. When she looked back at the crack, the flower was gone, a thin, wilted stem left behind. Standing and looking out beyond the rocks, all she saw was a small cloud of dust to the west, as if something was running across the plains. Perhaps the horses, she thought, and hoped they would find their way back.

She tucked into herself again to worry and wait, thoughts of the Ice Queen's message creeping in, as well as the old familiar pain in her arm as the Elixir wore off. She couldn't fathom why she —clearly the weakest in the group—had been asked to perform such a task, whatever that task ended up entailing. She had no more details than the message the lightning had brought, and the thousands of questions that had surfaced since then.

Chapter Twenty-One

A change in weather ushered in the morning after the storm. Overnight, the cool autumn air shifted to a winter chill. Frost painted the dormant grasses of the plains a sparkly white that shone in the rising sun. The horses, who had managed to elude Bhar and Hirsten the evening before, had returned in the night. They nickered and stamped the frozen ground, mist rising from their warm bodies.

Autumn was barely halfway through, but it already felt like the winter solstice. Kylene wondered if the early cold was a sign, but of what, only the greater beings could know for sure.

If the frantic pace Katora set as they left was any indication of her mood, she was taking the premature winter as a bad omen. It would be at least a few weeks before they would reach the city of Lughorn, even with pushing the horses each day, and the weather remained wintry.

Kylene woke up one particularly freezing morning with her eyelashes covered in frosty tears. She had been dreaming, about what she couldn't remember, but it hadn't been anything pleasant with the way her heart was racing in her chest. She huddled close to the fire during breakfast and was eager to get moving. The horses' breath misted as Kylene and Bhar saddled them up for the long ride. The awkward jog jostled Kylene in the saddle behind her brother, and her bottom was sore by midday.

They stopped to camp as the day waned. Kylene had watched many beautiful sunsets on Kase Farm, and a stunner on a beach along the southern border Faway Forest, but none of them compared to sunsets on the plains. The sky cast out in every direction, except north where the high peaks of the Skimere Mountains obscured the view. In the west, the sun burst into a fiery ball of orange and yellow as it dipped below the horizon. In the south and east, the sky faded to muted shades of pink and lavender, the colors of the hydrangea bushes dotting the farm in summer. She could almost smell the sweet blossoms. The burst of color was gone too soon, and she was left staring at the darkening vastness, brightened only by the twinkling specks of the stars—the moon late to the party, or perhaps absent all together tonight.

"Do you know what it means?" Kylene quietly asked her sister as they huddled close to the fire, tucked tightly into blankets to keep out the deep freeze. "The cold coming so early?"

Katora rubbed her chin, a gesture reminiscent of Pop. "I don't, but I don't like it. This isn't like the snowstorm that blasted in and out of Tussar so quickly, sending us off to Faway Forest for the nectar. And it's certainly not like the lightning strike when I heard the Ice Queen's message in my head. If this cold is a message, I'm not getting it."

A shiver shot up Kylene's spine. She was constantly trying not to think of the message she had received, those words she would never forget, nor would she forget how the bolt had destroyed her play. She hoped this weather wasn't personal.

Katora tended the fire, and Kylene sipped her tea—that's what they called the boiled water seasoned with rosemary and lavender. It helped warm the chill away, at least until Katora settled down next to her and spoke again. "I think it's Fyren."

Kylene choked on the tea. "What?"

"I think he's the one making it so cold. It might be a message or maybe a rallying call to our enemies. Whatever it is, it's tainted with dark magic. I can feel it to my core."

"All the more reason to get to Lughorn and then on to Kristalis as fast as we can," Bhar said from across the fire, startling Kylene, who hadn't realized he had returned from gathering wood.

He dumped a pile of sticks on the ground near the fire. Hirsten followed shortly after with his own armload.

"Katora," Kylene asked thoughtfully, "you can feel magic?"

Katora shrugged. "Yeah. Sometimes, but mostly only magic that has to do with the Elixir."

"Have you always been able to do that?" How was it that her

sister possessed so many talents when Kylene lacked so many?

"I think so, but I don't think I knew it until I became guardian of the Elixir. Or maybe being guardian brought out the magic in me."

Hirsten interrupted them, "I'm going to bed. Katora, you joining me?"

"Yeah," she said. "Bhar, you're on first watch. Ky, you look terrible. Get some sleep."

Kylene stuck out her tongue, and Katora returned the gesture. Kylene's thoughts turned more serious as she hunkered down deep into the bedroll and blankets in an attempt to keep out the magical cold—as Katora claimed it was. She wondered if maybe she did have a special power and it hadn't shown itself yet. But what good was hoping for such a thing when she had the Ice Queen's message hanging over her? Perhaps it was best not to think of it, as she had tried—and failed—to do with her injury for the last two years. Kylene tossed and turned for hours until it was her watch.

She shifted into a sitting position, but nothing made the thoughts in her head or the stiff ache in her arm any better. Eying Katora's pack, Kylene considered asking for a dose of Elixir. She could claim a sore back from sleeping on the ground; she didn't have to fake a sore bottom from so much riding. But Kylene was anything but selfish, and it would be very selfish to use the Elixir to soothe her pain when it could be used to save lives instead. Even a small dose for a few hours' relief wouldn't be worth the guilt of knowing someone else might need it. She sighed, something she was doing a lot now, and counted the stars as a distraction.

They sparkled from high above, her fogging breath obscuring them as she tried to stay alert. There was not much to see at night on the plains, only the faint shadow of the tall grass dancing in the breeze and the dark silhouette of the mountains. She wondered if Fyren was really responsible for the early winter. Now that Katora had said it, the weather felt like dark magic.

She could almost hear it crackle with danger, like thin ice on the river back in Tussar, which Bhar would dare her to walk across. Ky usually refused, but Katora never backed down from a dare. Once Katora was halfway across when the ice broke with a loud pop. Kylene had watched from the riverbank as her sister disappeared into the frigid water, her brain slowing the action down as if happening in slow motion. Luckily the water wasn't too deep and Katora managed to keep herself afloat until Bhar grabbed a branch and fetched her out.

Katora had tested fate and made it out alive, but Kylene didn't have her luck when it came to matters of destiny. This whole journey felt like a rigged test that she was doomed to fail.

Before she had thought it was nothing personal, this strange weather, but as the icy air sucked away her breath, it felt very personal.

Chapter Twenty-Two

Zelenka slipped away from a snoring Palafair to her pack. She tore through it and found the small leather pouch she desired, pulling it open only to discover it was empty. Then she remembered using the last of the baileaf root just before leaving for the Three River Split.

No, no, no, she thought. Her stomach gurgled with rising panic, but she pushed it down and forced herself to think. The med kit must have some.

Keeping to the dark pockets among the trees, Zelenka made her way to the infirmary tent. It was empty except for the one army doctor.

"Colonel Zelenka," the doctor nearly shouted as she jumped up from her pile of pine needles and leaves. She pulled pieces of the forest bed from her hair and her voice came out at a normal level when she next spoke. "Excuse me for my appearance. I was not expecting anyone, especially not you. I mean, uh..." She cleared her throat and rocked from one foot to the other. "How may I help you, Colonel?" The she stiffened and gave a sloppy salute, clearly a new recruit who had joined the army for this mission.

"At ease, soldier." Zelenka tried for a soft tone, but it wasn't in her nature, and it came out brusque. The doctor went back to rocking side to side nervously. "What is your name?"

"Doctor, uh, Private Horne. Are you ill or injured? Do you need a cot?" The cots were thin foldable mattresses that were strictly reserved for the infirm.

"No, I am well." Now it was Zelenka's turn to clear her throat. "I would like to check the med kits...to see how our supplies are faring."

Dr. Horne led her to the bags of medical supplies and stood there bouncing, seemingly not finding it strange that Zelenka's request to check the supplies had come in the middle of the night.

"You may rest, doctor," Zelenka said. "I do not need any further assistance."

As soon as the doctor settled down, Zelenka began methodically searching bag after bag, placing each item back into its proper place once checked. She came across every sort of remedy short of the Kase's healing Elixir itself: ginger for upset stomachs, salves for every kind of skin ailment you could imagine, and a curious blue stone of which Zelenka could only guess at its purpose. But not a single trace of baileaf root.

"May I help you find something, Colonel?" came the soft voice of Private Laurel.

Zelenka took a quick breath to slow her heart and tried not to show her surprise at being found practically buried in medicines. "No. I was doing inventory." With a glance at the napping Dr. Horne, Zelenka led Laurel out into the night. "Why are you out so late?"

Laurel's breath puffed in the cool air as she explained, "Sir Palafair woke and you were not in your tent. I was on watch and he asked me to keep an eye out for you. I think he was worried. Though there really is no need for him to worry about you. Is there, Colonel?"

Zelenka let out a laugh. "Certainly not, but Palafair is a worrier." She shot an appraising look at Laurel as they walked through the camp. "Private, can I count on your discretion on a certain pressing matter?"

"Without a doubt."

"I seem to have neglected to refill my supply of baileaf root. I was not able to find any in the medical supplies, but perhaps you have some I may use." It wasn't the fact that she used baileaf root that caused the awkwardness, rather the implications of what could happen if she didn't find any.

"Oh," Laurel said, followed by a more high-pitched, "Oh! I see." A very pregnant pause passed. "Do you need it for future use or right now?"

"It would be most prudent of me to use it now." The possibilities rolled around in her head, making her stomach turn.

"That *is* a pressing matter. The problem is that we have had a male-only army for several years now, which means there has been no need to stock baileaf root."

Zelenka could have easily made some if she had baileaf, but the plant grew in the plains and there was no chance she'd find it in Faway Forest. She held onto Laurel's arm to stop her, as they were approaching Zelenka and Palafair's tent. She didn't want Palafair worrying.

She dropped her voice to a whisper. "And your personal supply? Only if you could spare some."

Laurel matched her quiet tone. "I am sorry, Colonel. I have no need for it."

"Of course," Zelenka said quickly, her distress making her lazy in her assumption about Laurel. "I apologize for intruding into your personal life." She rubbed her forehead at the headache that was forming there.

"Perhaps someone else would have it. Would you like me to ask around?"

"Great Mother, no!" Zelenka practically shouted, before lowering her voice. "I can handle it." The last thing she needed was to give the army an excuse to question her competence.

Laurel placed a comforting hand on Zelenka's. "Let me know if you change your mind, Colonel." With a crisp salute, one not at all typical of a new recruit, Laurel continued on her patrol of the camp.

Chapter Twenty-Three

The tilli march continued with no sign of the missing army or any clue as to what they should be looking for. Zelenka had veered their course in a southerly direction, a great looming hill of bad memories within their path.

The army dragged along behind Zelenka with Palafair at her side. No one dared utter a complaint about the long days of marching through the deep underbrush of Faway Forest, but it was easy to read their tired postures and see the bags under their eyes.

According to the maps she had borrowed from Hirsten, they were approaching Hillock, the former home of the tilli demicks that had been destroyed.

She had no desire to return there and relive the floods that had been unleashed when Roodesh dug too deep into the mountain. Most of the current soldiers were too young to remember the tragedy, but Zelenka recalled it all too well. Given the importance of the landmark, Hillock nevertheless was a logical place to search for the missing army.

There were a few hours left until sunset, but Zelenka was about to call a halt to the day's march, hoping the extra rest time would give them a fresh outlook in the morning. Then she felt a prickling on the back of her neck, like someone was watching her. She held up a hand for quiet. The order moved back the line of soldiers quickly, and soon silence descended.

A bird squawked and took flight into the cerulean sky. Zelenka ordered the army to stay put and followed the tiny bluebird, dodging low branches and brush, until she saw it land on a woman's shoulder. Zelenka halted. The woman was tall, even by human standards, with lush black hair and pale, almost white, skin. Her lips were blood red, as were her fingernails. She was not, in fact, a woman at all but a greater being.

The sharp stomp of boots accompanied Palafair as he emerged from behind a tree, followed by a group of twenty tilli soldiers, Private Laurel among them. While Palafair stood next to Zelenka, most of the soldiers formed a tight circle around the couple, spears at the ready. The remaining soldiers placed themselves at strategic locations outside the circle, bows drawn and pointed at the witch of Faway Forest. Zelenka noticed they were all women.

Not wanting to tip off the witch, Zelenka struggled to keep her face impassive as she wondered where this group of female soldiers had learned to do such a thing.

"Yeselda." Palafair politely nodded to the witch.

Zelenka bit her tongue and clutched her spear tight. Yeselda might have been a daughter of Mother Nature, but she was also a power-seeking sorceress with questionable morals when it came to the treatment of what she believed to be lesser creatures—namely demicks and humans. And she was the reason Zelenka walked with a limp, an injury incurred when a pack of animals had attacked them during Katora's quest. Zelenka's injuries in that battle had been so severe she would have died if not for the Elixir, but not all wounds could be healed by magic. Zelenka had endured pain and resentment every day since then.

The calming touch of Palafair's hand on her shoulder allowed her to loosen her grip on the spear. Yeselda's magic was strong enough that the most accurate pitch of steel would prove futile.

"What business do you have here?" Zelenka asked loud enough that the words echoed through the trees.

"The Watcher and I have heard of dark tidings in the west." Yeselda examined her nails as if the news meant nothing to her, but the fact that the bird, who Zelenka noted was in fact the Watcher, was also there meant the tidings were far from benign. The Watcher was an even more elusive greater being than Yeselda, and in some ways a more powerful creature. Though he looked rather weak as a tiny bluebird, Zelenka knew he could take different forms.

"As have we," Zelenka said and offered nothing more.

More soldiers had filled in the empty spaces between the trees to listen to the exchange. Mercifully they remained silent as Zelenka stared down the witch. She would not bow to the tyrant of Faway Forest any more than she would let Private Laurel take over the army, nor would she be the first one to get to the point of this meeting that was not of her design.

"The time for rumors and riddles is past," spoke a baritone voice.

Zelenka looked around and, unable to find the source, her gaze settled back on Yeselda and the little bird resting on her shoulder. Then the bird's beak moved in time with the deep tones. "My brother Fyren has fallen far and seeks to assuage his damaged pride by waging war on humans and demicks alike. He will not dare venture into our territory." With a wing, it gestured out toward the trees. "Nor will he enter any of the other greater beings' realms."

Yeselda made a scoffing noise and flicked a finger at the little bird. The Watcher jumped from her shoulder, and in an impressive feat, transformed midair into its griffin form. The back half of its lion body was a rich caramel color that gradually darkened to match the brown feathers of its wings. The beady eyes were the same fathomless black as the bluebird's, only larger in the eagle head. The griffin stretched its wings and Zelenka was pleased to see they reached higher than the witch's head. To the soldiers' credit, they remained steady in the face of the impressive creature.

A shaky, sweaty hand found its way into Zelenka's dry, steady one. Yet Palafair appeared calm as he asked, "So what will Fyren do?"

The griffin settled its wings to the sides. "He will remain in his fortress at Drim and continue to build an army until he is ready to attack."

Zelenka offered a squeeze of Palafair's hand before pulling it away and addressing not only the witch and the Watcher but also her soldiers. "Then we must not let him strengthen his army. We will fortify our army by finding our lost comrades. We will rally the humans and whoever else will help us. Then we will go to Fyren at

Drim and attack."

One of the soldiers from the circle raised her spear and shouted, "To Drim! To Drim!" The words echoed through the trees as the rest of the nearby army took up the call.

"Silence!" screeched Yeselda, the whites of her eyes streaking red. She smoothed her hair back with both hands and her eyes returned to normal. "It is a lovely sentiment, my dear demicks. But how do you expect your," she cleared her throat pointedly, "*little* efforts to make a difference in a war against a greater being?"

"Little," said Zelenka in a deadly serious voice. "Little."

Palafair's grip on her elbow kept her temper in check, but barely. It would be very unwise to provoke the witch of Faway, but it was hard to keep that in mind when Zelenka's blood boiled in fury.

"Perhaps I can help your campaign," the Watcher said. "Follow your ears, they hear what the eyes cannot believe."

With that, the Watcher turned and flew into the sky, turning back into the little bluebird before disappearing into the distance. Yeselda let out a loud "Ha" and disappeared without so much as a puff of smoke.

"I thought the time for rumors and riddles was past," Palafair quipped.

Zelenka frowned. "Apparently not."

The breeze picked up, whipping leaves off the trees and adding them to the piles that already blanketed the forest floor. The sun was below the canopy and darkness would soon be upon them. The witch of Faway had three woodland spirits that patrolled the forest on horseback at different points of the day. Zelenka had encountered the white horseman, Ivory Star, and the red one, Crimson Fire, and came out the other end intact. The memory of her one glimpse of the black horseman, Ebony Knight, and the shiny midnight coat of his horse made her shudder even now, several years removed from it. He would take over patrolling duties at midnight and ride through the forest until sunrise. Zelenka shuddered to think of meeting him in the dead of night and sought out Palafair's hand once more.

"Find Ronan," she told him. "Tell him we camp here for the night."

The circle parted to allow him through. Then the women soldiers broke formation and stood around their colonel, looking awkward—all but the one who had started the chant. She wore an expression as sharp as the tip of her spear; it was almost a challenge. Zelenka shot Laurel a look, but she refused to make eye contact.

"Your name, soldier," Zelenka said to the chanter.

"Private Sherav at your service." She executed a perfect salute, and the other soldiers did the same.

"I have seen you practice." Zelenka slowly approached Private Sherav until she was face-to-face with her, but it didn't seem to intimidate the soldier. "I was not impressed. Which makes me wonder where you learned a protective formation and why I am only learning about this skill now."

Sherav's lip twitched in what looked like a half smile, but before she could speak, Laurel stepped forward. "Colonel, forgive us—"

"I will tell her," broke in Sherav. "I have long admired your career, Colonel. When you left us and General Nemez banned women from the army, I was devastated. I learned all I could from the moldy books saved from Hillock and began training myself in secret. Private Laurel stumbled upon me in the forest one day, and then we began to train together. As word spread, we added more to our group. We call ourselves Sisters in Arms."

She gestured to her companions, who were looking less awkward and more empowered as her speech went on. "When you returned to the Three River Split and we were allowed to join the army, we were cautiously optimistic about our futures for the first time in years."

"Cautious, indeed," said Zelenka. "So much so that you decided to hide your talents from me...until there was a need for them."

"And now you know what we are capable of." Sherav took a

knee, quickly followed by the other soldiers.

"And now I know," Zelenka whispered, heart in her throat and eyes prickling with tears of pride. She swallowed and said, "Stand. Private Sherav, I promote you to captain and request you dine at my tent tonight. You come too, Private Laurel. The rest of you should eat and rest. I will be demanding a lot more of you in the future."

Sherav and Laurel followed Zelenka to where Palafair had set up their tent. A few officers were sitting around the fire as dinner cooked. Palafair was regaling them with one his adventures in his time with the Kase family, who in many ways were his only family. Palafair rarely spoke of his anni demick parents. They had died when he was a youngyear from a sweeping illness that had nearly wiped out their entire demick community.

When he saw her, Palafair gave Zelenka a questioning look, but she shook her head to indicate she'd tell him all about the Sisters in Arms later. For now, she settled for introducing the new captain to her fellow officers, and then everyone tucked into the meal. Zelenka wolfed down a large portion of the freshly caught rabbit meat, but a gnaw of hunger remained. Palafair caught her eyeing his plate and offered the rest to her. She ate that and felt a little more satiated.

The sun had long set and the stars were out in full force. Zelenka decided it was time for some much-needed rest. Her leg ached with the many days of marching, more so than usual. She pushed off the ground, only to find her hip wouldn't bend correctly. She tipped sideways and Palafair caught her.

"Are you okay?" Laurel asked with a piercing look that said she knew too much already.

Zelenka pushed away from Palafair and regained her balance, shame stinging her cheeks. "I am fine." The words came out gruff, so she softened them for a quick "thank you" before heading into the tent.

She claimed fatigue in order to justify not wanting to share a bedroll with Palafair. Soon he was snoring the night away, but Zelenka lay awake. Her leg ached, and dinner, which she hadn't been able to get enough of earlier, churned in her stomach. Even the discovery of the Sisters in Arms couldn't keep Zelenka from tossing and turning late into the night.

Chapter Twenty-Four

With his head full of visions of the quest Mother Nature had seen for him when he was a baby and his stomach full of spiked essence, Devon fell into a fitful sleep. He tossed and turned, his feet sweating under the thick covers. He pulled off his socks and threw them against the opposite wall. Just when he was about to nod off, a buzzing noise had him up and at his window. There was nothing to be seen outside except for the shadowy houses of the neighborhood and the silhouette of the big tree in his yard framed by the star-streaked sky.

The buzzing stopped and he fell back on top of his covers... only to be roused again by the noise. It buzzed on and off for several minutes. He squeezed his eyes shut, rolled on his side, and put the pillow over his ear, but still the noise chirped. It sounded like a cricket, but it was far too deep into autumn for their to be any crickets around. Maybe one had gotten into his room and had managed to stay alive all this time, which didn't explain why he had never heard it before tonight, but his sleep-deprived brain wasn't working at its best.

On hands and knees, Devon searched under his bed, in every corner of the room, and in the darkest recesses of the compartments under the eaves. But he found nothing.

He threw open the window, exposing the room to the frosty air in hopes that the insect would find its way out and leave him in peace. A gust of wind sucked at his nightclothes and pulled him precariously close to the window sash. Curiously, the yellow-leafed tree outside was motionless, not a single leaf blowing. Yet the wind tugged at him harder. He stuck his head out of the window—in an admittedly ill-advised move—and his entire body was pulled clear through it.

He soared on the breeze, which seemed to exist solely for the purpose of transporting him, through town, past his grandfather's farm, and across the countryside to Capdon Mountain. His formerly sweaty feet were still bare and should have been freezing, but he found himself perfectly comfortable. The wind zoomed him up the side of the mountain to the top where a sprawling stone building matched the granite rock of the precipice it overlooked. The wind shuddered and he dropped several feet before it picked him up again. He hovered over the yawning gap on the steep side of the cliff. The wind died down completely, and he plummeted to the rocky ground below. A scream tore from his lips just before he fell upon the sharp stones.

With a gasp, Devon woke up in a sweaty tangle of limbs and blankets. His breaths were short and ragged, and it took him several minutes to be able to breathe normally. A buzzing—the same one from his dream—had him untangling himself. The window stood wide open, though Devon only remembered opening it in his dream turned nightmare. A flutter of shimmery wings on the sash caught his attention. There was little light as the moon was nowhere to be found in the night sky, but the wings were a bright gold as if reflecting the sun. They belonged to the smallest dragonfly Devon had ever seen; its entire body and wings together were no larger than his pinkie nail. It flew at his face and he swore he saw it blink all its thousands of tiny eyes at him, but it could have been a trick of the light, though there was little light for a trick.

Was he still dreaming?

He blinked back at the creature, and in that brief moment, it disappeared into the night. He stuck his head out the window once more, though doing so in his dream had turned out to be a bad idea, and searched the sky for the dragonfly. It was gone, the night was quiet, and Devon was fully awake. He crept down to the kitchen, avoiding two flights worth of creaks on the stairs, and helped himself to a glass of milk. He would have warmed it but didn't want to risk waking anyone. There was something about the dream that had felt urgent, beyond that it had felt completely real and had retained that feeling into wakefulness.

Maybe he *had* gone up Capdon Mountain and his mind was

processing it as a dream. Was that possible? Before learning of the existence of the Elixir, he would have said no, but now his mind had been opened to new possibilities, and what once seemed far-fetched was within reach. All the more clear was that he was destined for more than a simple life in the small town of Tussar. Perhaps this dream was Mother Nature's way of communicating that he was to go on a quest. He placed his glass silently in the sink and went back to bed, not to sleep, but to plan. He was going to journey to the temple of Capdon Mountain—for he was sure that was what he had seen when he flew up the mountain—whether his parents and grandparents wanted him to or not.

* * * *

Now that Devon had a plan, he felt like he could do anything. And he needed to feel that way in order to execute the slightly impossible task of climbing Capdon Mountain. It wasn't that the mountain was that tall or far away—it was neither of these things —more that the air on Capdon Mountain was particularly thin. So thin that a healthy primeyear could easily pass out, never mind a person with Devon's breathing difficulties. Not that he ever let that get in the way of him doing anything; it simply forced him to be more creative from time to time. He was willing to get really creative in order to reach the top of the mountain because he was determined to visit the temple he had dreamed about, or visited in his sleep if that was the case.

Water and a slow pace were his weapons; there wasn't much else he could do, save stopping at the farm and stealing the Elixir. He didn't know where it was kept, and he was sure it wasn't just lying around, so he wasn't going to waste his time, or his breath, trying to find it.

He figured if he visited the temple and left an offering, the Great Mother would hear him. If she did, then Devon was sure she would find a way to help him be included in the next quest. Maybe he would even hear one of those legendary messages from the greater beings; then there was no way his mother and Pop Pop could refuse him.

The trickiest part would be sneaking out of the house

without anyone noticing. Leaving his carefully penned note on the kitchen table, Devon flipped the hood up on his cloak, slung his pack over both shoulders, and slowly, slowly, slowly opened up the back door. Normally it was creakier than an elderyear's knees, but he had offered to do chores around the house earlier in the day, including—he thought very cleverly—oiling the hinges on the door.

He slipped into the night, his breath hitching with the cold. It took a few minutes of walking and steady breathing, but he soon adjusted to the late autumn air. He was able to jog out of town and into the sparsely wooded countryside that ran along the northern border of Faway Forest. As the sun rose, Capdon loomed a grayish-blue in the distance, growing larger as he jogged. His lungs had that pinched feeling and his head a lightness that signaled he was close to an attack. He stopped for a sip of water and resumed at a walking pace.

It was a long day of walking and stopping to catch his breath. The air on top of Capdon Mountain was icy cold and impossibly thin. Or maybe the problem wasn't with the air but with Devon's lungs. Every breath was like needles pricking him from the inside. His body felt heavier with each step, but his head felt lighter and lighter. He stumbled on a rock and fell to his knees. It had taken him so long to scale the sloped, southern side of the mountain that the sun had set long ago, but the moon was on the rise. It blurred and winked on and off as Devon's vision faded in and out. He sucked in as much of the air as he could and heaved himself up. He slowly forced his legs forward.

The temple of the priestesses was in sight, torches blazing in the night air to welcome Devon. He was relieved it wasn't the side of the temple that faced the cliff because he could have easily stumbled over the edge given the poor state he was in. Before he made it to the long stairs, his lungs seized and his vision blinked all the way out. He landed in a heap on the cold, hard ground.

Chapter Twenty-Five

Every day grew colder than the last as Kylene and her companions skirted the southern edge of the Skimere Mountain Range. They hadn't expected to face this kind of weather until Blanchardwood and their plan to buy warmer clothes in Lughorn didn't help them now. They had to settle for wrapping themselves up under their cloaks and extra blankets. Around midday, the wind swept in from the west and brought along with it snowflakes.

Kylene's hood flew off and threatened to unhorse her. With one hand holding tight to Bhar, who sat in front of her in the saddle, she used her other hand to pull the scarf from her neck and secure the hood. Then she took the loose end of the scarf and wrapped it around her mouth and nose to try and keep out the cold. It didn't work, and she began to shiver uncontrollably.

Bhar pulled Jinks to stop. Kylene peered around her brother and saw Katora slow Gem and motion for them to follow her to spot near a large rock that looked like it might offer some relief from the wind. Maple dutifully followed behind Gem.

The wind whipped around from all directions, so it didn't matter where they stood, the rock could not block it out. It was cold, cold, cold. Kylene dismounted and stomped her feet to try and get feeling back in them but only succeeded in making them sting with the impact.

"Lovely day," Bhar said as he slapped his gloved hands together. His mouth was hidden behind a scarf, but Kylene saw his eyes crinkle in a smile.

Katora rolled her eyes, the only part of her visible underneath the blanket she had wrapped around her head and body. "Ha ha," came her muffled voice. "This weather is bad news, and we're not even halfway to Lughorn. Once we're past the mountains, it's all open plains with no cover." She was shouting to be heard through the layers and over the wind.

"Maybe we should find somewhere to camp near the base of the mountain where it isn't so exposed," Hirsten suggested. "We can wait out the weather."

"I don't think this is a regular storm," Katora said. Kylene wrapped her arms around herself as she recalled her sister's assertion that Fyren was manipulating the weather with magic. "You know snow isn't just snow in the Great Peninsula. I say we press on as fast as we dare."

Bhar leaned against the rock like he hadn't a care in the world. "For once, I agree with Katora. Let's get to Lughorn already!"

Hirsten wrapped an arm around Katora and kissed the tiny part of her cheek that was exposed. "I say there's merit to waiting a day or two to see if this will blow over. What do you think, Ky?"

A blush crept up Kylene's cheeks and warmed that part of her body, even if the rest of it felt as cold as ice. She looked up at the gray sky. The flakes were few and far between…but for how long? If this snow was magical—and that was generally the only kind of snow they got around here—surely it would be wise to move on as quickly as possible.

"Sorry, Hirsten, but I'm with Katora and Bhar. The quicker we get to Lughorn the better."

"Fair enough," said Hirsten. He turned to Katora. "Shall we eat or move on?"

A fresh gust of wind blasted them. "It's too windy to bother with a fire!" Katora shouted. "We'll eat on the move and hopefully find a better place to stop before dark. Let's push the horses, see how far we can get."

Kylene stretched and rubbed her muscles underneath the many, but nonetheless inadequate, layers before mounting. The one good thing about the bone-jarring cold was that her arm was too numb to be bothersome. Jinks pranced nervously as the intensity of the snow increased.

Bhar grabbed the saddle and was about to launch himself up, but Ky placed a hand on his shoulder. "I'll lead for the rest of the day."

"You sure?" asked Bhar. "Jinksy seems kind of jittery."

"I can handle him." She mounted and scooted to the front of the saddle, making room for Bhar in the back. She was tired of taking a backseat, and maybe taking the reins would help warm her up.

Katora and Hirsten galloped off on Gem with Maple following. Kylene urged Jinks into a jog. She wasn't sure what fate she was riding into, but she wasn't going to let it hold her back, not in this moment anyway. She let out a whoop that got lost on the wind and urged Jinks up to full speed, the cold invigorating her spirits.

* * * *

The snow and wind doggedly chased the group as they moved out of the shadow of the Skimere Mountain Range. The overcast sky subdued the colors of the browning grasses and packed down dirt to a depressing gray. The snow remained light but steady, with little sticking to the ground.

They pushed the horses to their limits each day and made better time than ever. Kylene continued to relegate Bhar to the back, which he claimed allowed him to be lazy. She had grown accustomed to the sting of the air in her eyes and the rush of adrenaline when Jinks galloped to his fullest speed. It kept her distracted from the pain and worry. The days shortened as the winter solstice approached, and they had to be diligent at night about keeping the fire ablaze.

When they reached the Eirome River, the snow turned to flurries before fading entirely. The air took on a milder feel—not warm, but not the biting cold they had been experiencing. Kylene took a deep breath and was amazed at how nuanced the scents were after days of numbing cold in her nose. She guided the horse after Katora's on a northward path along the river. The sun burst through the gray sky and a light wind swept the clouds away. They found a spot to settle for the night among a thicket of small trees with tufts of vivid red leaves that made it look like they were ablaze.

Kylene offered to fetch fresh water. She walked upstream to

where a line of giant fir trees stood along the opposite bank. Against the darkening sky, they looked like sentinels guarding the water. The green needles filtered the last of the fading sun, dappling the river in dancing strips of light. Standing in the shade of trees after so many days along the flat plains, listening to the gurgle of the rushing water, Kylene had a taste of home. She imagined standing by the river at Kase farm, the outskirts of Faway Forest reaching out a friendly greeting. It filled her heart to the brim with homesickness, a fresh pang that overshadowed the aches of riding and the hurt of her old wound.

Two tears dropped off her nose and fell into the water. She was overdue for a good cry. She inhaled deeply, taking in the spicy pine scent, and returned to the moment, her mind, if not her heart, back at the place where she stood along the Eirome River. The prickling sensation behind her eyes subsided.

She dipped a bucket in the biting cold water, careful not to wet her sleeves, then set it aside to scoop up a drink. There were few things more refreshing than water straight from a cold river. Kylene was rubbing her hands dry on her cloak when a ripple in the middle of the river caught her attention. A dark brown snout popped out of the water, followed by the head of a fox, its fur matted down by the water, making it look narrow and diminished. Golden eyes met hers as the fox yelped what sounded like a greeting. Its front paws paddled toward Kylene for a few strokes before the fox was dragged back down into the depths.

With a gasp, Kylene stripped off her boots and cloak, ready to dive in after it. The cold would be a shock, but she couldn't let the poor thing drown. Before she had a chance to dive in, the fox resurfaced a few feet from the edge and swam to her. Its tongue was out, wagging with panting breaths. Two pinks jewels sat on it. The fox jumped up onto the riverbank a few paces away from Kylene, its tongue lolling out, and she realized the jewels were clear and only appeared pink because of the fox's tongue.

The fox shook off the water, fur puffing up and lightening with each shudder. It now stood before her, mist rising from its chestnut fur in the last beams of sunlight. She'd seen this fox before; it was the same one who had unearthed a red gem from the fire coals. No one else had seen it then, and no one was here to see it now. Was it following her? And what was it doing with the gems? The fox slipped its tongue and the jewels back into its mouth and bounded away before Kylene could voice her questions. It seemed like the kind of creature who might be able to answer.

Shaking her head, Kylene picked up the bucket and headed back to the fiery trees where the others had set up camp. Darkness was quickly approaching, but a fire had already been lit to show her the way. Her arm ached under the weight of the bucket and with the cold of the night, but she did her best to ignore it. The reappearance of the fox had given her plenty to think about, and she kept quiet over dinner. The mystery of the gem-loving fox she wanted to keep to herself.

Chapter Twenty-Six

The respite from the bitter cold was brief as Kylene and her companions traveled north up the river to Lughorn, but it wasn't the same unnatural cold they had felt on the journey across the plains. And the snow stayed away. It was a good omen, and the group's spirits reflected that. There was more joking and lighthearted talk in the evenings, and the calm babble of the river lulled them to sleep each night.

Before this leg of the journey became tedious, the sight of the Lughorn bridge greeted them. The three stone archways had massive towers at either end that served as lookout points, though they usually didn't have anyone on them. Lughorn had adopted a casual approach to safety, a luxury of a long peace. The three horses clip-clopped their way across the stones, past the second empty watchtower, and onto a street made up of paving stones of all sizes and shapes that fit together like a haphazard puzzle.

As she rode behind Bhar on horseback, Kylene's first impression of Lughorn was of a man's naked form as he lay prone in the gutter of the road. It was a fitting introduction to a place that was known for a good time. Lughorn was settled by a young consort of Great Peninsula citizens who loved to have fun. Several hundred years since being founded, it attracted the rowdiest people south of the Appachian Mountains. It was also the largest importer of essence in the Great Peninsula. Everyone except for Kylene had been there before, and none of them seemed to bat an eye at the naked bottom sticking up for all to see.

The man groaned and rolled over. Kylene averted her eyes and asked Bhar, "Should we help him?"

A line of shirtless men riding bareback galloped past, the resulting whoosh of wind nearly unseating her. She grabbed on tighter to Bhar, and her arm twitched with the familiar pain.

"Who?" he asked.

She pointed to the man in the gutter. "Him!"

"What?" he yelled over the noise.

She muttered, "Never mind." Bhar was already following Katora and Hirsten into the city.

Kylene possessed a deep-seeded desire to help those in need but never felt she was in a position to do it. Katora had the power of the Elixir, but either she hadn't noticed the man or she didn't want to bother with him. Kylene was tired of her sister explaining that there was a limited supply of Elixir and she couldn't possibly help everyone.

"It's the toughest decision I make," Katora had once said, "deciding who not to help."

As the man disappeared from sight, Kylene sank a little lower in the saddle and distracted herself with the sights of the city. The soft light of twilight brought a buzzing energy; Lughorn came alive at night. Shopkeepers were bringing out displays of goods to the streets. A slight woman struggled with a tall rack of brightly colored shawls and scarves. She nearly caught her wares on fire when she brushed past a man setting a torch out on his steps. The flames illuminated a sign for a pub and inn, a pint glass and a bed carved into the wood. In Lughorn, there were no words on the signs, only pictures.

They dismounted and Bhar went to find a stable for the horses, while Kylene, Katora, and Hirsten entered the pub. They were greeted with raucous laughter and shouting that demanded to be heard over the booming music. The band, made up of a group of demicks, played in a dark corner of the room. Their miniature instruments certainly didn't hamper how loudly they could play. The low ceiling and dim lights made the room feel claustrophobic. A bar spanned the entire length of the back wall. Tables of all shapes, sizes, and heights were arranged in no discernible pattern, some with cushioned stools, other with rickety chairs, and a few with no seats at all where people simply stood. Patrons danced in the spaces between the tables, and there were even a few couples intimately embracing in dark niches cut into the walls.

Kylene's face would have been an inferno even if they had

been in the middle of frozen Blanchardwood. It wasn't that she disapproved of the Lughorn lifestyle; it was a matter of not having been exposed to it. A flutter of nerves—or maybe excitement—rumbled her stomach.

"We're going to try and find a table!" Katora shouted as she pulled Hirsten into the crowd.

Kylene nodded and tried to find a non-voyeuristic spot to look. She settled on a painting hanging on the wall to her right and studied the rounded shapes, trying to figure out what they were.

"You like it?" asked a waifish man who stood entirely too close. A piece of his shaggy hair brushed Kylene's cheek, and she shuddered. "It's one of mine." His breath smelled of ale and, oddly, like the essenberry fields on a damp morning, sour with a hint of spice. "I call it *Ode to the Breast.*"

She backed all the way up to the door just as it swung inward. It jostled her forward, right into the artist's arms.

Bhar washed in with a burst of fresh air. "Hands off, buddy." His tone was friendly, but there was a warning in his eyes that said he was liable to do some serious damage if he wasn't heeded. It didn't hurt that he was twice as wide and a head taller than the artist, who winked at Kylene before slipping away. She swallowed back the sourness in her throat.

"Where are Hirsten and Katora?" Bhar asked. "They shouldn't have left you alone."

"I can take care of myself," she said, not remotely convincing herself or her brother.

He rolled his eyes. "Sure you can. C'mon, I see them." He pulled her toward the side of the pub opposite the band. All the furniture and tables and bodies buffered the music and they no longer needed to shout to be heard.

Bhar ordered a round of spiked essence for the table and four dishes of exotic sounding food, none of which Kylene had heard of. The most bizarre was a bright red creature about a foot in length with giant pincers protruding from its front end. It was served on a bed of greens, the beady eyes sparkling despite the very dead state of it. The strange dish convinced Kylene she was right in her choice to abstain from eating meat. She indulged on essence instead. Of the other dishes, her favorite was a slightly chewy, salty bite of vegetable that had a smoky flavor from the grill.

By the time dinner was over, a light tingling had replaced the usual throb in Kylene's arm. Bhar ordered another round of essence, and Ky found herself swept up in the excitement of being in a new city. She grabbed Hirsten's hand and pulled him to a spot just big enough to engage in a lively dance. The music grew impossibly louder, and pretty soon all the spaces between the tables were filled with dancers.

They all went to bed very late that first night in Lughorn.

Chapter Twenty-Seven

The scouting party marched in a single file close behind Zelenka as they crept closer to the strange sound. The Watcher's riddle, *follow your ears*, was what they were doing.

The throaty thrumming was coming from the other side of a thicket. It was like cicadas on a summer night, only more robust. Was it a swarm of insects lying in wait? It certainly wasn't summer, as fall leaves crunched under Zelenka's boots.

She halted in front of the thick brush and signaled for silence. Everyone in the scouting group—made primarily of members of the Sisters in Arms—stilled. She crouched low on her belly and forced her way through the underbrush. Sticks scratched her skin and clothes as if warning her to keep out. She crawled her way through until she had a view of what lay beyond.

She gasped as she drank in the wondrous sight before her. Insects like giant dragonflies fluttered around a clearing, darting from flower to flower and over a large pond. There were hundreds of them, the combined beating of their wings so loud it was like being inside a bee's nest at peak honey season.

It was the mythical sciathilte.

The sciathiltes' shiny insect bodies, twice as long as Zelenka and as wide as her body in the thickest part, glinted in the sunlight. Each had a pair of wings that flapped as fast as a hummingbird's. They shown in iridescent shades ranging from a pale summer-sky blue to a purple so deep it was almost ebony. Most were single-colored, but a few sported a rainbow of blue, purple, and green or red, orange, and yellow. Bulbous eyes bulged from the sides of their rounded heads.

Zelenka ducked back into the bushes to hide from their keen sight. The sciathilte were creatures of legends, ridden by demick heroes in bedtime stories. And apparently they were real, living right here in Faway Forest.

She was afraid if she left them, they would disappear, but she had to tell the others, if only to confirm they weren't conjured by her imagination. She scurried backward through the thicket. The scouts stared at her disheveled form, twigs sticking out of her hair, and waited for an explanation.

Looking each of them in the eye, she whispered out of both fear and awe, "It is the sciathilte. They are real and we have found them."

A hushed, yet decidedly excited, murmur went through the group. The repeated whispers of "sciathilte" wafted through the forest on a clandestine breeze.

"What do we do now?" asked Private Laurel.

"We ask them for help," replied Zelenka. "But first we go back to camp." She knew just the person for a diplomatic job dealing with wild creatures.

With superstitions running high in her mind, Zelenka instructed Laurel to sneak through the underbrush and keep watch over the sciathilte. She wasn't taking any chances that they would disappear.

"We keep this on a need-to-know basis," Zelenka instructed the others, who complied with a salute and a chorus of "yes, Colonel."

While the rest of the scouting party waited outside the entrance to the sciathilte cluster, she marched straight into camp to her tent. It was empty. Refusing to let her aching leg slow her down, Zelenka zigzagged her way around tents and dormant campfires until she came to the officers' quarters. Palafair sat on a blanket, dealing cards to a group of officers.

"You need to come with me now," Zelenka said. One look at her face and Palafair dropped the cards and jumped up. The officers peered at her curiously, but she remained tight-lipped.

She pointed to one of them. "Tell Major Ronan I am on an important diplomatic mission, and I will debrief him when I come back tonight." She anticipated that it would take at least a few hours to negotiate with the sciathilte, provided they could find a means of communication. "He is in charge while I am gone." They captain stood, waiting for more orders. "You are dismissed."

"What is this about, Zelenka?" asked Palafair as they headed out of the camp. "What kind of mission could you possibly need me for?"

"You have to see for yourself. It is a miracle, a true miracle."

A crisp breeze blew leaves about as they hurried through the forest. Palafair kept quiet, but she could practically hear the curiosity of his silence. She couldn't remember the last time she had been so excited, her skin tingled with anticipation.

When they reached the scouting party, Zelenka ignored their whispers, and left them outside the thicket with a reminder not to speak to anyone of what she had seen. She guided Palafair to the small break in the brush and motioned for him to follow. They scooted through the underbrush. Upon reaching Laurel's outstretched legs as the soldier spied on the sciathilte, Zelenka silently instructed her to push aside. She reached a hand out to Palafair, and he squeezed up next to her. She studied his face as he took in the mythical creatures for the first time. He opened his mouth in a silent exclamation of awe. The sciathilte buzzed around, unaware of the interloper demicks.

"Is that...?" he whispered.

Zelenka nodded and brought his hand to her mouth and kissed it; she could barely contain herself. Her face felt like it was splitting in two, her smile was so big.

He leaned in and whispered in her ear, "I do not understand what you need me for."

In addition to his diplomatic nature, Palafair had an uncanny talent for putting people and animals at ease. Zelenka had once watched him single-handedly soothe a flock of runaway sheep for a neighbor back in Tussar. No small feat for a one-foot tall demick who was too small to ride a horse on his own.

She rested the side of her head against his and stared at the wonder before them. "To convince them to align with us. To help us find the missing tilli army, and ultimately fight a war against Fyren."

He kissed her, hands tangled in her hair, as they lay next to each other, and Zelenka didn't even care that Laurel was almost as close on the other side.

"One thing at a time, my dear," he said. "Let us start by introducing ourselves." He gave her one more kiss. "You ready?" he asked, and Zelenka nodded. He squeezed out of the brush, raised his hands, and waved his arms. "Most ancient creatures!" he shouted as Zelenka and Laurel emerged from the brush.

As one, the entire cluster of sciathilte halted their flight in midair and turned to face the demicks. Their wings were frantically beating, but their bodies were still as they hovered. Hundreds of bulbous eyes stared back at them, reflecting a rainbow of colors, impossible to read.

Staring down the unnerving sight of hundreds of sciathilte, Zelenka watched as Palafair pointed at himself and said, "Palafair of Tussar." Then he introduced Zelenka and Laurel in like manner. "Colonel Zelenka of the Three River Split tilli demicks and Private Laurel, also of the Three River Split tilli demicks. We are humbled and charmed by your presence. We bring tidings from outside of the forest and request an audience with your esteemed queen and drake."

Zelenka elbowed Palafair in the side. "You know what language they speak?"

"No," he whispered out of the side of his mouth. "But I figured I would start with the language I know."

Whether they understood or not, the sciathilte responded by gathering in the center of the clearing. They formed a circle and flew around in a synchronized dance. The buzzing of their wings grew louder and louder until Zelenka could feel a vibration in her chest. When three of the mythical creatures broke formation and zipped toward the demicks, Zelenka realized that was how they communicated with each other. The humming died down and the other sciathilte resumed their various activities.

The three who were headed to the demicks all had deep indigo wings, almost black, though when they caught the sunlight, it reflected in a blinding flash. Pointy black stingers protruded from the back end of their bodies.

Each stopped and hovered right in front a different one of the demicks. The one opposite Palafair spoke in a thrumming voice, "The royal dyad has been awaiting you."

The creature's eyes took up so much of its face that it was hard to tell where its mouth was. Zelenka wondered if it had a mouth at all. It was curious that the sciathilte had been expecting them, but that could work in their favor. Or it could mean the sciathilte were prepared to eliminate them. Her army training had taught Zelenka to consider all possibilities, from the most optimistic to the bleakest. She chose to focus on optimism; whatever language they spoke among themselves, they also spoke the same language as the demicks. And that was proving to be a good start to the relationship. She nudged Palafair to reply.

"Thank you," he said, a smile plastered on his face that would look sincere to anyone but Zelenka. She saw the uncertainty behind it. "We are eager to meet them."

He bowed, and Zelenka followed suit, pleased to see that Laurel did as well. She hadn't necessarily planned on bringing a green member of the army along, but as things were playing out, Laurel was a good choice. She was intelligent, accommodating, and polite to a fault...and a member of the Sisters. In fact, she would make an excellent asset as a diplomatic soldier once she had some proper training. Zelenka tucked that thought away for when the mission was complete—and probably not until the war was over either. Fyren would not likely wait until the young tilli army was trained to strike. But she was getting ahead of herself; first they had to see if they could convince the sciathilte to work with them.

On foot, the demicks followed the three indigo-colored sciathilte deeper into the clearing. They came to the edge of the pond and stopped. The sciathilte who had spoken earlier turned and regarded them with its many bug eyes.

"You must ride us to see the royal dyad," its voice thrummed.

The indigos dipped the back end of their long bodies low so their stingers touched the ground. Zelenka and Palafair exchanged a glance, and it seemed he wanted to approach the stinger as much as she did, which was not at all. Her face paler than usual, Laurel glanced back and forth from the sciathilte and Zelenka, seemingly waiting for an order.

"Climb on," the sciathilte urged. "The point of our stingers will poison you only if we want them to." Its eyes narrowed and its head shook as a buzz emitted from it. The other guards were doing the same thing, and Zelenka realized they were laughing. Had the sciathilte made a joke?

It worked to set Zelenka at ease. She took a step toward the middle one and glanced beside her to see Palafair and Laurel also inching closer. She hesitated at the foot of the stinger, and the sciathilte said, "Do not worry, climb up. Your bodies can do us no harm."

She bristled—she'd like to see how it would fare at the sharp end of her spear—but swallowed her pride and reached for the stinger. It was rigid and smooth under her hands, but easy enough to climb hand-over-hand and foot-over-foot at the angle at which it was tilted. She reached the body and mindful of the tiny hairs all over it, scooted up in between the creature's two sets of wings.

Chapter Twenty-Eight

It wasn't so much the speed with which the sciathilte flew over the pond that was dizzying but the motion of its wings. With one set fluttering in front of Zelenka and a second fluttering behind, she was in a sea of motion. There was nothing to do but hold on, so she rested her hands on the sciathilte's smooth indigo back and tightened the hold her legs had around its middle. Her leg ached in protest, but Zelenka wasn't about to let herself fall into the murky water below.

In the middle of the pond lay an island that was covered in tall reeds. All three sciathilte dove abruptly. Laurel let out a shriek, and Palafair grunted. As it was, Zelenka had to bite her tongue to keep from grunting in surprise herself. The sciathilte were quick and nimble, and Zelenka never wanted to find herself on the pointy end of their stingers.

The sciathilte ended its dive a breath away from the ground and hovered among the grass for a moment before landing. Zelenka scooted off its back end with a sigh of relief. Palafair and Laurel found their way off, both looking slightly green.

A touch dizzy herself, it took Zelenka by surprise when a buzzing voice spoke from the reeds. "Why do you seek us Roodesh of the tilli demick?" It was a rough voice with an echo-like effect.

Heat spread across Zelenka's neck as she thought of her mad father falling to his death. "I am not Roodesh but Zelenka of the tilli demick."

The reeds shook with the buzzing of a sciathilte laugh. "You may not go by the name, but we have known you to be heir to it."

Zelenka squinted as she peered into the grass, but there was no sign of the creature. It was unnerving talking to someone she couldn't see, especially about such a sensitive topic as Roodesh and all that went along with the name. She looked to Palafair. He nodded, encouraging her to speak.

With a deep breath, Zelenka summoned her most patient, diplomatic tone. "I do not go by that name, though I do speak for the tilli demick in my capacity as Colonel of their army."

"So Zelenka, Colonel of the tilli army, why is it you have come here?" came the echoing voice.

"The sciathilte are legends of Faway Forest, some would say a myth. You are a being I never thought I would have in my humble presence. Our meeting feels serendipitous, yet we all know," she included the indigo sciathilte, the reeds, and her companions in a sweeping gesture, "Mother Nature does not deal in coincidence. We—the tilli—have lost...something dear to us." These mythical creatures turned real were still very much an unknown, and Zelenka hoped her wording didn't make the tilli sound weak or give away too much. Though how could they not be considered weak when losing their own army?

"Lost something indeed," said the hidden sciathilte. "We know the missing to be someones."

Zelenka's heart skipped a beat. Did they know where the army was? Palafair subtly nudged her elbow. Her hope was mirrored in Palafair's twitch of a smile. It was time to be frank, even if she disliked being open with the mysterious sciathilte.

"Do you know where the missing tilli army is?" she asked.

Two identical sciathilte with bodies the same exact spring-green shade as the reeds seemed to appear from nowhere. Zelenka blinked, half expecting them to disappear, but they remained corporeal. Antennae curved above their beady eyes in the shape of a crown. They blinked and moved in unison.

"The royal dyad," one of the indigo sciathilte announced.

Palafair bowed his head in respect, as did Laurel. Zelenka knew it had been the right decision to bring Palafair along and hesitated only a moment before dipping her head.

"To know seems simple enough, until you consider having known," the dyads spoke together almost as one, the echo effect from one trailing off before the other. "We have known the way the harvest moon softly reflects off the water. We have known the crunch of a beetle between our mandibles. We have known the soft flesh of our enemies pierced by our stingers. What we know is the cool, soft mud beneath our legs. We know the whistle of the wind between the reeds. We know the brown depths of your eyes as you stare at us."

Riddles, always riddles with these magical beings. To know and to have known sounded like utter nonsense.

As if sensing Zelenka's growing frustration, Palafair intervened. "You have known and know a great many things. Perhaps you have known or know of our comrades' whereabouts."

"We have known of a place in the forest where things disappear and are left to wander places unknown to those that see," the dyad said.

"You do!" Zelenka exclaimed. "Where is it?" Palafair's fingers on her forearm reminded her to calm down.

The dyad ignored her inquiry. "We also know you desire more than your lost army."

At the risk of asking for too much, Zelenka ventured, "War is coming. Is this among the things you know or have known? Yeselda knows this, as does the Watcher. We seek to align allies. Will you stand with us in battle?"

"Us?" the dyad questioned. "We know nothing of this *us* you speak of."

"Us, the tilli demicks...and anni demicks," said Zelenka. "Us, the humans who will fight alongside the demicks. Us, the greater beings who wish to stamp out evil before it rises. All of us together make up this *us.* Will you stand among us?"

"That is a great *us.*" The dyad's front legs twitched in unison, their heads turned toward each other. Their wings buzzed but not together, first one, then the other. They were conversing.

Zelenka reached for Palafair's hand and found it cold. His skin looked pale in the waning light. She had not realized how late it had become; the sun had dipped below the forest trees, and darkness would come quickly.

The buzzing ceased, and the dyad turned back to the demicks. "We have known of this rising threat. We will help find your lost army. We will help fight your battle."

The sciathilte seemed to know—or have known as they were prone to saying—a lot more than they originally let on. Despite their isolation, they clearly had ways to gather information about activities outside the forest.

Zelenka remained wary of these mysterious creatures, but an alliance with them would benefit not only the tilli but also all of the Great Peninsula.

She squeezed some warmth back into Palafair's hand. Then she offered her hand to the dyad, not at all sure what they would do with it. The dyad nodded their heads in unison.

"When do we get started?" Zelenka asked.

* * * *

The indigo sciathilte flew Zelenka, Palafair, and Laurel back to their camp. The dyad had assured Zelenka that they would return with a retinue of sciathilte to take the tilli to the place where they believed the lost tilli army was.

As Zelenka settled into her bedroll, it was the first night since they had set off that she felt comfortable. Her leg felt more tired than sore and Palafair's snores were a familiar comfort. Then she felt a gurgle in her stomach that brought back all sorts of unpleasant thoughts. She pushed them down to the depths of her mind; she didn't have time to worry about anything other than the mission. But the thoughts refused to be ignored. The bizarre sciathilte concept of knowing versus having known took on new meaning in light of what she didn't know and what she might know in the future. Eventually she fell asleep, but not until the darkest part of the night had already come and gone.

Chapter Twenty-Nine

Devon woke to a faint chanting, a deep resonate sound that emanated from faraway. Great, wheezy coughs wracked his body and drowned out the lovely tune.

When Devon recovered, he found himself in a stone chamber not much larger than his attic bedroom but with much taller ceilings. Small torches sat in iron sconces in each of the corners, lighting the room quite effectively. He was covered in a thick quilt and fully dressed underneath, except for his boots and cloak, which hung from the back of a chair at a small, wooden desk. The chair also housed a hooded figure cloaked in an emerald robe. The scratchings of pen on parchment paused.

Without turning around, the figure spoke in a smooth voice, like honey dripping from the comb. "Welcome to the temple on Capdon Mountain. Are you feeling better, Kase son."

"How..." the word came out rough and quiet. He forced a shallow cough to clear his throat and tried again. "How do you know who I am?"

The priestess swung out of the chair and picked up Devon's cloak in one graceful motion. She held it up between two fingers as if that provided the answers to all his questions, both the one he had voiced and others that only swirled inside his head. When he remembered that his grammy had embroidered his name on the inside of the garment to keep it from getting mixed up with all the other cloaks, he realized the gesture did in fact answer the question he had asked...supposing the priestess had actually looked there. She had an aura about her that said she might know these types of things without proof.

"You should put this on," the priestess recommended. "Your boots, too. The temple gets drafty, especially at night."

In the hallway, the echoing of the vast, stone floors and the solemnness of the temple struck Devon quiet. The usual witty repartee that constantly went from his brain straight to his mouth stayed silent. The chanting had ceased and his footsteps were loud, especially compared to the lights steps of the priestess. She held up a lantern that lit the spaces between torches. Devon trailed slightly behind, a slightly shorter shadow to the holy woman. She walked at a swift pace, her robes shuffling slightly, but Devon had no trouble keeping up. His lungs didn't feel so pinched and his throat was less raw than when he had first awoken. His breath rose in mist as he walked, proving the priestess right about the drafty conditions.

"Are you planning on making a pledge to the Great Mother and joining our order?" The priestess remained facing forward, her posture stoic, but Devon detected a weightiness to the question.

"Can men join the order?" he deflected.

"Of course," the priestess answered. "The order is open to sentient creatures of any gender."

They reached a staircase that went up and spiraled before disappearing around a curve.

"I've only met women priestesses." He stayed a step behind to avoid stepping on the holy woman's robes.

"Humans identifying as women are the largest number of our order here on Capdon. We are a devout group and not suited for all temperaments." Her voice curved around the twists of the staircase and echoed eerily from several directions. "There is a large order of priestesses on Demick Island comprised entirely of demicks. Near the Appachain Mountain Range, there is an order of humans, most of whom identify as men. They are each devout in their own way. We govern only those of our order and leave others to worship the Great Mother as they see fit. Here we study elemental magic."

"I see." That was a lot to take in. Despite being so close to Capdon Mountain, there wasn't much talk in Tussar about the priestesses and their order. He had heard of elemental magic, primarily that each creature had one dominant element that tapped into their personal magic, and that some individuals were inherently more in tune to their magic than others. This was a viewpoint from older times and had fallen out of common belief.

The Kase family made the usual offerings at the summer and winter solstices, but that was about the extent of how they formally honored Mother Nature. Pop Pop and his Aunt Katora—though she wasn't shy about using the Great Mother's name as an expletive now and then—certainly showed a great deal of respect for Mother Nature in the way they treated the land, and in their guardianship of the Elixir as Devon was coming to realize, but there was nothing formal about it.

Though an offering to the Great Mother in the temple could go a long way to communicating his readiness for a quest, and ideas about what to leave churned in his mind. Despite being curious about other ways to worship, he felt the need to be honest with the priestess. "I am not here to join your order."

Never pausing in her ascent, she finally took a glance back at him. "No. I do not suppose you are."

"Where are you taking me?"

"To the head priestess. She would very much like to meet you."

Devon wasn't sure he liked the sound of that, but it was too late to turn back as they had reached the end of the stairs. An arched wooden door stood open at the end of the landing. A roaring fire blazed in a stone fireplace that was as wide as the chamber he had slept in earlier. Standing in front of the fireplace, their backs to the door, were a hooded priestess and two people he very much did not want to see. His mother and Pop Pop caught sight of him before he could turn and run down the long staircase, through the corridors, and straight down the mountain. He'd much rather face the possibility of another episode than the stern faces of his mother and grandfather. His breath hitched uncomfortably as he stepped over the threshold into the heated room.

Chapter Thirty

The morning after arriving in Lughorn, Kylene met her companions for breakfast in the pub, all looking bleary-eyed from the late night. The rowdy room from yesterday had a diminished feel in the light of morning. The scuffs and imperfections were evident without the mass of bodies and dim lighting to hide them.

Kylene took a sip of burning hot coffee, which helped to stave off the headache she felt building at her temples. She nibbled on toast and slightly congealed oatmeal. Oh how she missed Ma's home cooking. On Sunday mornings after all the chores were done, Ma would have breakfast sandwiches and biscuits with piping hot gravy on the table. On hot summer days, she would served it with iced tea, and when the days turned cold, she would make hot chocolate that warmed the belly. Kylene prodded the sad excuse for a meal and took another sip of coffee to burn away the taste.

Across the table, Katora took one mouthful of runny eggs and her eyes bulged. She spit the bite into a napkin and rapped her knuckles on the table as if calling a meeting to order. "Our mission today is to find our guide. His name is Tarq and he's the best—and by best, I mean only—person who has successfully navigated their way through Blanchardwood."

Bhar shoveled food into his mouth as if he had no qualms about its quality and nodded along. Hirsten drank his coffee and munched on a croissant that looked halfway appetizing. Kylene wondered where he had gotten it and stared at his mouth until he caught her looking.

She turned her gaze to her hands while Katora continued, "He's reclusive and might prove tricky to find...if he's even in Lughorn right now. One of my business contacts saw him in Lughorn a few days ago, so hopefully he hasn't been hired since then." She pulled a paper from her pocket. "I've got a list of places he hangs out, so I thought we'd split into two groups and meet back here for dinner...with Tarq if you find him."

Bhar finished his last bite and snatched the list from Katora. Next to him, Kylene peered over his shoulder and saw the paper was covered with symbols she figured matched up to the picture signs on storefronts. He ripped the paper down the middle, kept the side that had a lot of food-related pictures on it, and slipped the other half across the table to Katora. "I know a bunch of these places. Kylene and I will take a look at these, and you and Hirsten can do those."

"Figures you'd take all the pubs," Katora teased. She handed Bhar a pile of coins. "Consider this a business expense. That means no getting drunk, got it?"

"Sure, sure." With a mischievous glint in his eyes, Bhar asked Ky, "You ready?"

She took one last look at the cold food and downed the rest of the coffee. Hopefully one of the establishments on the list would have something more appetizing.

Outside the pub, Bhar waved down a cabbie wagon and they jumped on top with the driver. Bhar slipped him a coin. "To the harbor."

The wind whipped Kylene's hair in all directions and she hastily tied it back as they lurched through the cobblestone streets. The stench of briny ocean grew stronger as they rode. She had smelled the ocean one other time, while in the southernmost part of Faway Forest on the quest for the Elixir's nectar. They had been brought there by Yeselda. One of Yeselda's terrifying horsemen, who had struck Bhar unconscious with its magic, had whisked them there. Kylene shivered at the memory.

The wagon crested a hill, revealing the full glory of the harbor. The morning sun was at their backs and threw the scene into colors so vivid they seemed impossible. The water sparkled bright enough that it was hard to look at. The ships' sails puffed out in the breeze, whiter than freshly fallen snow. The yellow, blues, and reds of the dockworkers' clothing, which matched the Lughorn flag that flapped on a pole at the center of the docks, popped against the faded gray wood of the jetties. The wind picked up as they descended the hilly road to the harbor, and Kylene was glad for the warmth of her cloak.

"You can leave us at the Poisoned Pig!" Bhar shouted to the driver.

The wagon slowed in front of a waterfront building three stories high whose stone foundation was partly covered by water. The tide was low and barnacles spotted the side of the building up to the high-tide mark. Dockworkers, humans and anni demicks alike, bustled about the wharf.

"We'll start here and work our way back to the inn." Bhar led her into the alleyway leading to the waterfront building. "These are mostly houses for the dockworkers, but they have to eat, too. And they have a healthy appetite for strong beverages. Lughorn imports more spiked essence than any other city in the Great Peninsula." He winked as he pointed to a sign. Carved into the green wood was a pig with an apple in its mouth, each of its eyes replaced by a large x. Bhar grinned and held open the door. "After you."

The door jangled shut and they found themselves shrouded in a dim, filtered light. Once her eyes adjusted, Kylene noted the bar was surprisingly busy given the early hour of the day. The air had a foggy, heavy quality as many of the patrons were smoking. The bitter, herbal fragrance tickled her throat. She coughed into her sleeve and gave Bhar a pleading look.

"One drink," he said. "Plenty of time to inquire about our guide, and then we'll go." They made their way to two empty stools. Bhar placed a few coins on the counter and waved the bartender over. "Two distilled apples."

"Katora said not to get drunk," Kylene said quietly.

Bhar shrugged. "We won't."

The drinks arrived in small glasses more fit for a newly born youngeryear than a couple of full-grown primeyears. Bhar pushed one to Kylene and downed the contents of the other in one large gulp. She sniffed hers and was pleasantly surprised to find it smelled of freshly sliced apples. Mimicking her brother, she tipped the tiny glass and imbibed the drink in one go. It burned a little on the way down but tasted good enough.

"Eh, barkeep!" Bhar yelled. He placed two more coins on the table and pointedly added a third. "One more round and a question."

The bartender swiped the glasses off the countertop, grunted, and said, "Go on."

"We're in the market for a guide. You know any?"

"I know a few." The bartender poured two more shots, offering Kylene a smile as he leaned in conspiratorially. She refrained from leaning back and endured the stench of his stale breath; it wasn't any worse than the rest of the air in the place. "Anyone in particular?"

"Who do you recommend?" asked Bhar.

The bartender rattled off a list of names, none of which was the one they sought. In a moment of boldness, Kylene tipped back her drink, slammed the glass onto the bar, and batted her eyelashes in what she hoped wasn't too obvious an attempt at flirting. The alcohol sat like a rock in her empty stomach and her heart beat fast in her chest. "What my brother means to say is that we're looking for a particular guide. His name's Tarq. You know him?"

He grunted again and nodded, his eyes slightly narrowed. "I know the guy. Haven't seen him around in a couple of weeks." Then he muttered under his breath, "Good riddance."

"Thank you. You've been most helpful." Kylene stood to go, and Bhar hastily downed his shot.

Once they were back out in the alleyway, Bhar high-fived her. "Nice way to charm the bartender."

"I don't get why you didn't just come out and ask about Tarq," Kylene said as they walked to the next place on the list.

"I don't like to play my hand too early."

Kylene shook her head at the poker reference. "Not everything is a card game."

"Look, don't get me wrong, Lughorn is a fun place, and I'm all about having a good time, but it can be dangerous. There are lots of loose lips with all the alcohol flowing through these streets. The right information in the wrong ears can be disastrous. Tarq is known for navigating impossible terrain. If people know we're looking for him in Lughorn, so close to the borders of Blanchardwood—the Ice Queen's domain—someone might put those things together and figure out what we're up to."

They arrived at their second location a few blocks removed from the docks. Hanging above the door was a big red sign with a fish on it. Kylene's stomach felt a little queasy after keeping up with Bhar's brisk pace and she hoped they would be able to order food. Not surprisingly the inside smelled fishy, but in a fried delicacies kind of way, not in a rotting fish kind of way. Bhar ordered spiked essence and fried potatoes and anchovies.

They were the only ones at the bar, so Kylene felt comfortable quietly continuing the conversation. "So I shouldn't have said Tarq's name?"

"No. It was fine for you to say it after you flirted with the guy."

Remembering the troubled expression on the bartender's face, Kylene wasn't so sure it had worked out as well as Bhar thought.

"I don't know." Kylene eyed this bartender as she deposited their drinks on the counter. She had a pinched face and an unpleasant tilt to her mouth, like she was sucking on a lemon. "You can handle this one."

The bartender dropped off their plates, one piled high with small, steaming pieces of breaded anchovies and the other a basket of crunchy wedged potatoes covered with a spicy seasoning. Her hair was as greasy as the food, but her smile erased the pinched look. Her gaze lingered on Kylene while she asked if they needed anything else.

Bhar offered up a toothy smile. "Another round of spiked essence, please." Kylene had never heard him be so polite, and she certainly didn't need another drink, but the woman disappeared behind a door before Kylene could change the order.

Bhar said, "Don't worry. I've got this one under control."

Chapter Thirty-One

The essence was delicious, of course, as was the food, though it sat heavy in Kylene's stomach. While the bartender cleared the dishes, she accidentally brushed Kylene's shoulder with her bare arm. It was near Ky's injury, but she barely felt it. She excused herself and felt their gazes on her back as she wobbled to the washroom. How many drinks had she had?

After taking care of the necessities, she stumbled her way back to the bar. Bhar and the server were engaged in an intimate conversation, so Kylene hovered a few paces away. The server's eyes met hers and drew Ky back to her seat.

"Ciselle, meet my sister, Kylene," said Bhar.

Ciselle poured two more spiked essences. "These are on me. If you don't find what you're looking for, there's more where that came from." She winked at Kylene and went back to the kitchen.

"What was that about?" Kylene asked as she held in another burp. "I don't think I should have another drink."

"Turns out I should have let you take this one," Bhar said. "Ciselle has eyes only for you, dear sister."

"Oh!" Kylene's cheeks blazed with heat. She wasn't used to people being so openly interested in her.

Bhar chuckled. "Don't worry, I still got a lead. One more stop ought to bring us right to our elusive guide."

"That's it, one more stop." Kylene yawned, the idea of having time for an afternoon nap was quite appealing.

Bhar put an arm around her shoulders. "C'mon. We'll take a cabbie wagon to the Snog Taigh and then walk back to the inn."

"The what?"

"The Snog Taigh. It's a...well, you'll see when we get there."

The alcohol induced sleepiness muted any sense of foreboding Kylene might have had at Bhar's vagueness, and she gladly took a seat on the cabbie wagon he flagged down for them.

The breeze refreshed Kylene as they rode through the bright streets, which grew busier as they approached the center of Lughorn. It was after midday and the city was wide awake. Vendors moved their most enticing wares outside the buildings and called to potential patrons as they moved passed. Small fire pits along the side of the road attracted groups exchanging the latest gossip. The people, the cabbie wagons, the horses and ponies all culminated in a rush of colors, noise, and scents. Kylene was overwhelmed; the busiest festivals in Tussar were no match for the everyday chaos of Lughorn.

They arrived at the Snog Taigh to be greeted by a shirtless man with flowing gold pants that tapered in at his shins. His features were nothing short of perfect. Kylene tried not to stare at his sculpted muscles and wondered how in the Great Mother's name he wasn't freezing with the crisp breeze that blew in when the door was open. He ushered them though a beaded curtain into the main room. Quiet music filtered up from the back and the combined light of hundreds of flickering candles created a warm atmosphere. There were no windows, so it was impossible to tell what time of day it was from inside. There was a stage in front, currently concealed by a red velvet curtain, and a bar in back with small tables filling the space between.

"What exactly is this place?" Kylene whispered as Bhar paid the entrance fee.

"A performance space," he said. "I would think a woman of the theater like yourself would recognize a stage."

Kylene huffed. "I know it's a stage. What kind of performances does it host?"

"Dances, of a sort." Bhar led her to an empty table.

Shirtless men and women wearing little more than underclothes brought food and drinks to the patrons.

"Do they keep their clothes on?" She didn't object to whatever kind of dancing they did here—art was art—she just wanted to be prepared.

"Some of them."

The curtain opened and fully dressed dancers stood onstage.

A piano played a lively tune and the dancers spun and leaped and lifted each other in a dizzying set of movements; all their clothes remained firmly in place. The music stopped, the audience clapped wildly, and the dancers disappeared backstage.

Kylene elbowed Bhar. "Why do you do things like that to me?"

"To see the horrified expression on your face." Bhar stood. "Enjoy the show. I'm going to make some inquiries."

Kylene rolled her eyes and waited as the next performers walked onstage. The music started in low and somber, as did the dancing, before kicking it up to another level. The dancers were performing feats Ky had never imagined possible. The acts continued, one more dazzling than the next. Then the curtain closed and the bustle of servers began again. When one came to her table, she ordered a water and tried to keep her focus on his face, not his bare chest. Her brain felt fuzzy from the earlier drinking and her mouth was as dry as a thistle plant during a drought. The candlelight made her dizzy. She closed her eyes and dosed off to the lilting background music.

A poke to the shoulder, followed by an impatient "excuse me" woke her. She jerked up and wiped away a bead of drool in the corner of her mouth.

"Ah, yes?" she croaked out.

A primeyear man with black hair and startling gray eyes stared at her with an intensity that made her toes squirm in her boots.

"Are you okay?" His words came with the clipped accent of someone from near the Appachian Mountain Range.

"Yes, I'm fine." She stared at those unnerving eyes as she waited for him to respond.

"Do you mind if I sit here?" He gestured at the seat across from her, and Kylene let out a breath at the innocent request. All the others tables had filled up while Kylene had slumbered.

"That would be fine."

He wore traveling clothes much like hers. He took his time removing his gloves and cloak. A woman server came by and asked him what he'd like, and he also ordered a water.

"Nothing stronger?" she asked. "Or perhaps something sweet?" She fingered the scarf at her waist.

"Water is fine, thank you," he insisted. His gaze grazed every corner of the room as if scouring it for something—or someone—until the server came back.

Kylene took a gulp of water and managed to slosh it down the front of her shirt. She cleared her throat. "I'm Kylene...well, Ky, to most people." She offered her hand across the table and waited for him to introduce himself. He reached for his drink instead and glared at her. She pulled her hand in toward her chest and fiddled with a button, unnerved by his open hostility.

Despite that, she babbled on, "I'm not here alone. I'm waiting for my brother." The man continued to glare at her with more intensity as each minute passed. "We're looking for—" she cut herself off. "We heard a friend might be here, and my brother went to find out if he was." She bit her lip but then rushed on, "You look like you've been traveling. Have you come from anywhere interesting?"

Great Mother, why was she still talking?

His glare turned slightly less disapproving and more appraising, though he didn't appear friendly. "I have been traveling. I just came back from taking a group of demicks to Hirithor Woods." He took a long drink of his water, effectively halting his end of the conversation.

That didn't deter Kylene from making more of a fool of herself. "I've never been to Hirithor Woods. I hear the trees talk to one another. Now Faway Forest, I've spent far more time there than I care to. Don't mistake me, it's beautiful in its own way, especially the Three River Split, but it's dangerous and terrible, too."

The man raised his eyebrows. "You don't care for dangerous places?"

"Well, no, who does really? But sometimes you must go where you don't want to. Duty demands this of us...well, maybe not you, but it does of me." It had been a pleasantly long amount of time since she had thought of the Ice Queen's message, but there it was, almost corporeal, taking up space at the table.

"We all have our obligations. My work as a guide comes with those as well." He said this almost absentmindedly as his gaze surveyed the room again.

"Wait!" Kylene couldn't believe she hadn't thought of this earlier. "Do you know a guide named Tarq?"

He whipped his head around and pinned her once again with those gray eyes. "What do you know of Tarq?"

"Um, not much really," she stammered. "We—my family and I—are looking to hire him, that's all."

"Hmmm…" Now silent, he stared at her for so long she wondered if he would ever stop. "I'm Tarq, but I don't work for cheap."

"Oh!" Kylene jumped up and knocked into the table, which sent the glasses rolling to the ground and water flying everywhere. "You're Tarq?" She moved as if to dash away, but came back and put a hand on his shoulder, which made him wince. "Don't move. I have to find my brother."

She confronted the nearest server and asked, "Have you seen a primeyear man named Bhar. Blond, blue eyes." She held her hand several inches above her head. "About this tall." Without waiting for an answer, she ran off in the direction Bhar had gone earlier.

* * * *

After some smooth talking from Bhar and the promise of a free meal—not necessarily a good one, given the sad state of breakfast that morning—Tarq agreed to meet with Katora.

They spent the last of the business money to take yet another cabbie wagon back to the inn. Bhar insisted Tarq sit up front with him and ushered Ky into the coach. Her head was pounding from all the drinks, and the ever-present ache had returned to her arm. The latch on the window was broken, so she couldn't open it, and the air became stifling. Between that and the constant bumping and swaying, Kylene's stomach churned. When the wagon pulled up in front of the inn, she burst out and ran up to her room where she struggled to get to the bathroom in time.

The liquor and potato wedges did not taste nearly as well coming up as they had going down. She rinsed out her mouth, straightened her wild hair, and did her best to look presentable. Sighing because there wasn't much she could do about her bloodshot eyes, Kylene headed downstairs to the pub.

Katora was deep in conversation with Tarq at a back table. Hirsten and Bhar sat there as well, but they seemed more interested in the food. It was early enough that the dining room wasn't busy, and the only entertainment was a soft melody played by a single anni demick on her lute.

As soon as Ky sat, Bhar pushed a fresh pint of ale her way. She was about to send it back but shrugged and took a gulp. She couldn't feel much worse than she already did. A few gulps later, a small burp bubbled up her throat and escaped her lips. A giggly sensation replaced the headache and muted her pain. She slapped the drink down on the table and was surprised to find it almost empty. More food arrived and she picked at a few of the offerings, but it was as bad as breakfast. Across the table, Katora refused Hirsten's offering of a plate and continued her hushed discussion with Tarq. Kylene paid them little attention and ordered another ale. She stared at the lute player and allowed herself to get lost in the music.

"Then it's settled!" Katora shouted as she slapped the table, startling Kylene.

Bhar hurrahed in triumph and raised his pint. Hirsten did the same and gave Katora one of his close-mouthed smiles. Tarq merely nodded. When he glanced Kylene's way and caught her taking another gulp of ale, his stoic expression turned dark. She set down the drink and wiped her mouth.

Katora outlined their plans for traveling through Blanchardwood to Kristalis. Kylene half listened; she figured she'd be assigned her role and follow orders accordingly. Meanwhile, she ordered another drink, sinking into the numbness of the alcohol.

Tarq's glare deepened each time he looked at her. Something about him, other than the glaring, unsettled her, though everyone else seemed at ease.

He smiled at Katora when they shook to seal the deal and she slipped him a bag of coins. He joined in on Bhar and Hirsten's card game once the food was cleared and yet more drinks were ordered. Kylene wondered what she had done to earn such a callous reaction, but brushed it away as her headache returned. Playing it off as fatigue—she *was* tired—she excused herself from the table and returned to her room.

As she settled into bed, the room seemed to spin. She closed her eyes and took deep, calming breaths. She rolled on her side and caught a glimpse of Katora's pack in the far corner of the room among Ky's belongings. Somehow it had ended up in the wrong room and Katora must not have noticed. Moving faster than she should have, Ky got out of the bed, swayed, and then steadied herself on the wall. Sitting cross-legged on floor, eyes darting around as if she expected someone to jump out and catch her, she rooted around until her hand closed over the cool, smooth vial of Elixir.

She held it up to eye level. The faint light of the candle glinted in the blue glass, like the vial was winking at her. She popped the top and took a whiff. It was the same nothingness as always—where Katora could fully smell the nectar and Bhar faintly smell it, Kylene had never been able to detect any scent. It wasn't hers to smell, and it wasn't hers to decide who needed it. Nevertheless, Kylene placed the cool lip of the vial to her mouth and took the smallest sip. Instantly, her headache abated and the queasiness in her stomach vanished.

As sat on the floor, a nagging sensation tugged at her consciousness. It wasn't until she rolled her shoulder and pain lanced up her arm that she realized the Elixir had done nothing for the chronic ache.

Chapter Thirty-Two

Dawn brought the stirrings of the tilli camp, the young soldiers finally adjusting to the rigors and early hours of army life. Zelenka stretched out her stiff legs over a cup of weak rosemary tea that Palafair had brought to their tent. It settled the butterflies in her stomach as the army awaited the arrival of the famed sciathilte.

Zelenka joined Ronan and the other officers around the fire. Arriving back to camp last night on the indigo escorts had caused quite a stir. The excitement of not only their existence but their willingness to help the tilli had carried over to the cold morning, and the air snapped with anticipation.

The buzz turned palpable as an actual sound came from beyond the trees. The sciathilte were coming! Led by the indigo escorts, the first group zoomed into the tilli camp, gracefully landing in the spaces between trees, fires, tents. A few overexcited tilli reached out to touch them, only to be frightened back when the sciathilte turned their stingers. Perhaps Zelenka should have included a lecture on interacting with the mythical creatures when she had announced they were coming.

Soon a rainbow of sciathilte were taking up all the spare spaces in the camp. Their iridescent bodies and wings shone in the rising sun. Zelenka wasn't sure whether she was relieved or disappointed that the dyad weren't among them. A part of her wanted to learn more about them, while another part could go forever without hearing their unsettling echoing voices.

Ronan's mouth hung open rather indelicately. Private Laurel, in her infinite wisdom of having seen them once before, smirked and elbowed him.

"You are practically drooling," Laurel said, while Sherav looked at them rather intently rather than at the sciathilte. Ronan clamped his mouth shut, but his eyes remained wide open.

Zelenka turned her attention to the sciathilte. "Thank you all for coming." The buzzing went silent. "I will be selecting a small team to accompany me and the sciathilte to find our missing comrades." A cheer went up from the tilli, many of whom had missing family members.

Zelenka had debated whether or not to once again leave behind Ronan to have someone she trusted in charge of the tilli, but in the end she decided he had to come along on this mission. Instead she had asked Sherav to stay and take charge. Laurel proved to be a valuable asset time and again, so she was among the group to go, along with a few other privates that Palafair had gotten to know.

Looking over the army, Zelenka realized she was woefully ignorant about what kind of soldiers each of these tilli were. Her mind had been full of the task of navigating them through Faway Forest. She had been reluctant to promote too many of the youngsters in deference to the senior members of the army she hoped would return. She didn't want to start the melding of the two by having to resolve conflicts over rank, but that left them with very few leaders.

And what if they didn't find the missing soldiers? Or what if they found them, but they were in no condition to return to the army? She dared not give too much weight to the nagging voice in her head that argued they could all be dead. Now that she had a solid lead on where they might be, she feared more than ever what she would find.

Palafair, Ronan, Laurel, and the chosen tilli privates gathered around the indigo sciathilte who had been the escorts to the dyad.

"You know the protocol for if anything should happen here at camp?" Zelenka asked Captain Sherav.

"Yes, Colonel." Sherav saluted. Zelenka noted she had the good sense not to say more; the trees surrounding camp could be hiding any number of creatures who would love to know what the tilli would do in an emergency. Not to mention, the higher beings had ways of finding out information without directly overhearing.

She mounted one of the indigo sciathilte and hoped this

would be the day they put the full army back together. The sciathilte took off in a controlled flurry of beating wings. They flew in perfect formation, and Zelenka was almost jealous of her fellow tilli who got to watch from the ground. *Almost* because she wouldn't trade anything for the feeling of riding these flawless fliers. The crisp air pressed against her face, blowing her hair behind her recklessly. If she focused on the horizon where the treetops met the clear blue sky, she barely felt the movement beneath her. She held on tight with her legs and let the cold blast away the slight nausea that had bubbled up in her stomach.

Who knew what the future held, so for now she chose to live in the moment. Her immediate goal was to find the missing army and not worry about how she hadn't been able to obtain any baileaf root. Her focus needed to be on her army first, and then on defeating Fyren.

In the clear autumn air, a plan formed in her mind. It would require a huge coordination of efforts across the Great Peninsula of demicks, humans, and greater beings, and much effort on her part. Effort that would demand energy she might not be able to spare.

Stop it, she told herself, be in the moment.

The swarm of sciathilte and the tilli on their backs skimmed the treetops for hours. Zelenka tried to ignore the tumble of her stomach and the ache in her leg by focusing on her plan and all the elements that had to come together for it to succeed. The distraction worked...for the most part.

The sun had reached its apex in the sky when a single, round mountain rose in the distance. With a shudder, Zelenka recognized Hillock, the former tilli domain. Many generations ago, a group of ambitious demicks left Demick Island and sailed across the treacherous Narrow Pass to the mainland of the Great Peninsula. The anni remained in human cities and countryside, choosing to build their new lives among the humans. The tilli chose to travel into the depths of Faway Forest and make their home at Hillock. Over many years of hard work, they carved paths, homes, and an irrigation system. For generations, they thrived.

Most of Zelenka's memories of Hillock were the stuff of nightmares. When her father's predecessor ordered the tilli to dig all over Hillock, they dug too much. Their homes and systems collapsed, killing many of their own, including their leader. That was when Zelenka's father became Roodesh and moved them to the Three River Split. Zelenka sometimes dreamed of Hillock's idyllic setting, but the night visions always turned to nightmares, the screams from her memory seeming to emanate from the mountain itself. A tear squeezed out of her eye, and Zelenka told herself it was from the cold air pressing against her face as she flew, not the memories.

As the mountain loomed larger, Zelenka felt in her heart that this was where the missing army would be found. They were among the buried bones of her people, but would they be more than bones themselves? Her stomach twisted in fear; they were nearly there.

The sciathilte buzzed a warning before it dipped back under the canopy of trees. In the sea of red and gold leaves, the air took on an earthy scent. The sciathilte darted in between branches. Palafair leaned over the body of the one who bore him, his knuckles white from holding on and a tight frown on his face. Zelenka's stomach took another flipflop as the sciathilte tipped sideways to dodge a particularly large tree.

The swarm halted at the base of the mountain and landed. The sun was too low to reach the east side of the mountain, and it already felt like night, cold and dark and bleak. Or maybe that was just how it always felt in the shadow of Hillock. It was the one place in the forest she had never wanted to return to.

Zelenka and the other tilli dismounted, and they all looked to her. She brushed them off and pulled Palafair aside.

"Of all the places, why would the tilli army come here?" he asked in a whisper.

Despite her gut feeling pushing her to look for them at Hillock, Zelenka had wondered the same thing time and time again. "I do not know. Nemez said he sent them out to look for us after we fled the Three River Split. Maybe they thought we would come here, though many of them knew me well enough to know I loathed this place."

"Perhaps they thought under our influence," Palafair said, meaning his and the Kases' influence, "you would follow us here."

"But why would they think the Kases would go to Hillock?"

Palafair stared at the mountain and offered up a very sciathilte answer, "That I cannot know."

"It was not by choice," buzzed the indigo sciathilte who had flown her here. She was beginning to notice the subtle differences of the similarly colored sciathilte, and this one had slightly darker eyes than the other indigo ones. "Your comrades were bewitched."

"Who would do that?" asked Palafair. "Yeselda?" Everyone who had been on the quest with had a healthy dose of suspicion when it came to the witch of Faway.

"I would think she would have told us before when she and the Watcher talked to us," Zelenka said. "This does not feel like her brand of magic." She turned to the sciathilte. "I should have inquired earlier, but do you have a name?"

"We do not require such designations within our swarm." The buzz of the sciathilte went through the ones present as they communicated. "Yet we are knowing a need for such things for your species. You may name us as you see fit."

She looked to Palafair, who shrugged. "How about Indy?" she asked the indigo sciathilte.

"Let us thus be known as Indy."

The use of "us" threw her off and she clarified, "The name is just for you, not all the others."

The sciathilte around her buzzed with their strange laughter. Indy said, "This we know."

"Private Laurel may name the others," Zelenka said loud enough for Laurel to hear. As much as she wouldn't have minded putting off the task at hand, it was time to get to it.

"Are you sure the missing army is here?" she asked.

"We have known they were here," Indy said.

Zelenka blew out a frustrated breath, resigned that she wasn't going to get a straight answer. She supposed it was their way, and there was nothing she could do to change that.

"How do we get in?" she asked. The main pass had caved in when the tilli had fled Hillock all those years ago. There were other ways that were all likely to be blocked, and Zelenka has been young enough when the mountain tunnels collapsed that she wasn't privy to all its secrets entrances, though she suspected there were a fair few.

"We knew of a way in here." The sciathilte fluttered its wings at a rockface in front of them. It was one giant slab of rock that stretched far to the sides and went straight up seemingly to the top of the mountain. There was no evidence of it having been anything other than solid rock for all of eternity.

"Are you sure?" asked Laurel, squinting in disbelief.

"Do you doubt what we knew?" asked Indy. One of its beady eyes turned independently of the rest of its head to size her up. Zelenka waited with interest to see what Laurel's reaction would be.

Laurel shook her head, her eyes wide. "Of course not. I am sorry for questioning you." Then she bowed.

Pleased with the young private's correction of behavior, Zelenka said, "The question remains how we get in."

For an answer, Indy raised its wings and the other sciathilte followed suit. The wings buzzed up and down in unison. A humming chant rose from their legs, their mouths remaining silent. The sound rose above the mountain, growing louder as it climbed like ivy up the rockface. It vibrated around them, raising goose bumps on the back Zelenka's neck. The mountain stirred and small rocks fell down from high above. A section of the smooth rockface crumbled to dust and a gap the size of a large cave opened. The chant faded away as the sciathilte stilled, the gaping maw left open.

Zelenka crept to the opening and breathed in the stale air. It stank of earth and mold and death. Laurel walked up next to her, a torch in hand. She lit it and dipped the flame into the darkness. It lit the few inches around it and nothing more. There was nothing to see without going in. Laurel dared to crane her neck a little closer to the blackness and opened her mouth as if to yell. Zelenka stemmed the unuttered shout by grasping the young tilli's arm in a tight grip.

"Best not to waken any beasts that may lie sleeping under the mountain," Zelenka cautioned.

Laurel nodded and said in a quiet voice, "Are we going in now?"

"We?" Zelenka reached for the torch and Laurel handed it over, along with a flint. "Not *we*, I am afraid. Only me."

Palafair scuttled up, put his arm around her shoulder, and whispered up close to her ear, "If you think I am not going in there with you, love, you are sadly mistaken. Give the order for the others to stay, but please do not give me that order. I do not want to break my promise and disobey you in front of your army."

Zelenka broke away from his hold and nodded once before addressing the others, "Palafair and I will go in alone."

Laurel and Ronan had the good sense not to argue, though Laurel's pursed lips showed it was taking some restraint.

"Make camp here for two nights. If we do not return by sunrise on the morning of the third day, head back to the tilli camp. Ronan, once you return, you are in charge. If Sherav has done a good job, you may promote her to major. Understand?"

Ronan saluted. "Yes, Colonel."

"I am promoting you to lieutenant colonel and Private Laurel to captain."

Now Ronan and Laurel both saluted her.

"At ease," Zelenka said. "Captain Laurel, gather up enough food and water for me and Palafair for two days."

Laurel scurried off. Ronan called out commands to the other tilli to set up camp. As for the sciathilte, all but Indy had wandered off into the trees.

"I can count on you to return my soldiers safely back to their camp?" she asked.

The sciathilte's voice thrummed, "We will return them as promised. This we know."

"Very well." Zelenka knew she could trust the creature on

those words. It was clear enough what they meant, riddle or not.

Laurel returned with the supplies. Palafair took them in his pack. It was time to head into the mountain, the place Zelenka had never wanted to set foot in again. Terror rooted her in place.

"I...I..." she stammered, "I do not think I can go in there."

Her stomach lurched. Palafair grabbed her hand and looked her right in the eyes. "You can. You will. We will do it together."

With a deep breath, she stepped right up to the opening. One hand kept a sweaty grip on the torch, and the other held tight to Palafair. His hand was also slick with sweat. Together, they stepped into the darkness.

Chapter Thirty-Three

A few steps into the opening in the mountain, and the darkness seemed to swallow Zelenka and Palafair whole. It was like a physical presence pressing in on them. A whooshing sound swept Zelenka around. A rush of air swooped in, threatened to blow out the torch, and died down as rock sealed the opening. The torch blinked out.

"There goes that way out," whispered Palafair with a quiet chuckle that fell flat.

Zelenka took slow steps forward, her free arm reaching out until her fingertips brushed a rough surface. She retrieved the flint from her pocket and struck it against the rock that had just been open air. It flashed bright for a second before blinking out. Palafair found his way to her side and squeezed her arm.

"Strike it again," he said.

She put the flint to the rock a second time. In the flash of light, she saw Palafair holding the torch right near the flint. Then it went dark again. She struck a third time, and this time the spark caught the torch's tinder. It flamed up blindingly bright before settling into a smaller, steadier light.

Zelenka held the torch up high to illuminate the back end of the cave. It showed a small passageway to the left and a larger one to the right. Palafair pointed in the direction of the larger one. "Shall we?"

His guess as to which the correct way to go was as good as anyone's. She took the torch and led the way down the larger path, larger being relative as it was only wide enough to fit one demick at a time.

This must have been a minor tunnel. Before Roodesh had destroyed the mountain, the main tunnels had high ceilings and wide passages lit by torches in the walls. They were well ventilated and felt downright airy compared to this cramped, tiny tunnel that was only a few feet taller than Zelenka.

Water dripped on their heads. The drips grew more constant as the tunnel turned down in a slow sloping way. Zelenka, with Palafair close behind, crept deeper into the bowels of Hillock. The drips became more persistent, sizzling when they hit the torch. Pretty soon, an uncomfortable dampness settled in Zelenka's hair and clothes.

As the path curved steeper downward, the ominous sound of rushing water rose up from deeper into the passageway. Perhaps they had chosen wrong by taking the bigger path. But there was only one way forward.

For his part, Palafair kept silent and dutifully followed Zelenka.

The rushing water continued to grow louder and the drips continued to steadily rain down on them. Zelenka was about to suggest they turn around and try the other way when the path opened up before them. One moment they were in the cramped tunnel, and the next they were in a large cavern with light streaming in on either side. A rushing river of rapids split the cave right down the middle, blocking the far side.

The cavern was bright but not from sunlight, not this deep in the mountain. The light came from the rock itself. Palafair ran his finger along the bright rocks and then put in in his mouth.

"Salty," he said.

"Lughite," Zelenka said. "It has a natural glow. We used to mine and sell it. Well, not me personally, but it was one of our major exports. It was hard to transport out of the forest but fetched a big price in the cities. I have only ever seen it in large piles as it was brought out of the mountain."

"I have seen it, lighting the city streets," said Palafair. "I had no idea it came from the tilli."

Zelenka let out a hard laugh. "We did not want the people of the Great Peninsula to know where it came from. Only the traders who picked it up on the border of the forest knew the tilli supplied it."

"So the tilli were not as isolated as everyone thought." There was no judgment in Palafair's tone, but she felt it coming from herself.

"We traded lughite for the few things we could not find in the forest." Baileaf root was among those things, but she didn't mention that. "Only a very few met with the humans, so in most ways, we were isolated. I certainly never met any humans until the Kases came to the Split."

She ran her hand along the translucent substance. It was much brighter than she remembered. The pile of rocks the workers brought up had seemed dirty and unimpressive in comparison. It was a wonder that she had never seen it in its natural state.

"Where do we go now?" asked Palafair.

Zelenka would have liked to linger in the cool brightness of the cave, but they had two days and counting before the others would leave them. Palafair took out a nut and fruit bar and they munched on it while they kept to their side of the river. The rapids were too violent for them to swim across, so they found another tunnel on their side of the cavern to continue their journey.

"I suppose not having any other options makes it easy to choose which way we go." Palafair let out a short laugh. She appreciated his attempt at humor, but it didn't help her feel any less trapped. This tunnel was smaller than the previous one and dipped deeper into the mountain.

The whole right side was lughite, so it was bright, but it was also loud as it seemed the underground river flowed just on the other side of the wall. She could feel the energy of the rushing water when she pressed her hand against the glowing rock. At least this tunnel remained dry...for now. The rock had presumably held up to the pressure of the river for many years, and she hoped it had a little more time left in it.

They walked along this path for what felt like a very long time, though time was tricky in this underground place. It was too easy to be inside her own head, worrying. Would she find the tilli army? Would she regret not stocking her own supply of baileaf? What was she going to do if she didn't find the tilli army? How long could she wait before talking to Palafair? Would they waste hours traveling this tunnel only to find a dead end? The questions seemed to echo around as she led the way through the long tunnel.

Her only comfort was knowing Palafair was right behind her. She should trust in him being there for her, no matter what; yet she found she couldn't bring herself to discuss her worries with him. It was a strange thing to remember that she wasn't alone in this world, to allow herself to rely on someone else. It was hard, and yet too easy at the same time. It was love. And it terrified her.

The path took a sharp turn to the right and the light of the lughite abruptly cut off. The sound of the rapids muted as well. Were the only surviving tunnels of Hillock unfamiliar or were there ones to be found that she knew? So far they had only revealed secrets she hadn't known they were keeping.

The air thickened as they walked into the darkness. The torch was holding strong, but it was no match for the dark depths of the tunnel. Zelenka's chest felt constricted and her breathing labored. Sweat dripped down the side of her neck and coated her chest and back.

A hand on her shoulder startled her, but, of course, it was only Palafair.

"We should rest." His eyes betrayed his concern for her, as his own breathing was slow and steady and his brow was dry.

Zelenka popped the torch into a holder ensconced in the wall. They sat with their backs against the rough rock. She took a long drink from the canteen. They shared a snack.

"I would like to keep moving," Zelenka said, now that her breathing had slowed. "We have less than two days."

Palafair lightly touched the back of her hand. "We will find a way home, even if our friends have to return before we leave."

Yet again it felt like a very long time before they reached another cave. The rush of the river had long silenced, leaving a heavy quiet. This cave roof was lower than the one with the lughite, and bone dry, not a drop of water to be seen or heard. It was too dark to see the far end, and a weariness overtook Zelenka.

She dropped the torch and it rolled before snuffing out. The memory of the flame left a redness in Zelenka's eyes before turning black.

"It was a fool's errand." Zelenka's words echoed back to her.

"We will search this cave for another tunnel," said Palafair. "If there is none, we turn back and retrace our steps until we find another way." She heard him searching around in the dark for the torch.

"And then what?"

"We take it to where it leads us. And if we hit a dead end, we try another way, and another if we must. Until we find the tilli army."

"And if we do not find them?" Zelenka whispered, afraid to put a voice to this one fear of many.

"Then we find a way out and go home."

"Where is home?"

The question hung in the air for a long spell. Palafair was silent and still, having ended his search for the torch.

He sighed. "Wherever we want it to be. Kase Farm has been my home for a long time, but it does not have to be *our* home. We can settle at the Three River Split. We can venture to Demick Island." He found her in the dark and wrapped his arms around her body. "Home is me and you together."

Zelenka settled into his embrace; Palafair was such a romantic. She loved him for being a soft counterpoint to her sharp, cynical edges. She turned and kissed him hard. They stayed in each other's arms for some time before breaking apart to find and relight the torch.

They searched the cave wall and much to Zelenka's relief, found another tunnel, one that was wide enough for the two of them to walk side-by-side. She held out her free hand and said, "Shall we?"

He took her hand. "I am with you."

It will be okay, she told herself. Palafair was here in her former home, and he would follow her to wherever their new home would be. She found that this was enough to keep moving forward.

* * * *

They traversed tunnel after tunnel in search of the missing

tilli army. It wasn't so much like being lost in a maze, more like a difficult puzzle with limited choices. They would come to a cave at the end of a path with only one option at the other end. Zelenka kept telling herself that as long as they moved forward, they were making progress, but it was hard to tell if that was true. For all she could tell, they were moving in circles, going through the same caves and tunnels over and over again.

As much as she dreaded finding something that would bring up a bad memory or the remains of all those who had been lost in the collapse of Hillock, she nearly screamed in frustration when they yet again came to a small cave leading to a single tunnel. She leaned her head up against the same gray rock they'd been seeing for hours on end and took several deep breaths. The air was stale, her sinuses dry from breathing it for so long.

"I think it is time to rest," suggested Palafair.

She conceded and propped the torch into one of the holders in the walls. The caves had been long abandoned, but the presence of those torch holders reminded her that they hadn't been like that forever. Zelenka couldn't understand why she didn't recognize any of it. It all looked vaguely the same—except for the cavern with the river and the lughite—but she thought that by now, she would have come across a place that would have sparked some sort of recognition.

As if sensing her frustration, Palafair scooted close and rubbed her sore leg. She had been trying to ignore the sharp ache that arose from walking so much, and the contact was soothing.

"It is like this is a totally different place from where I grew up," she said. "Why do I not recognize any of it?"

"I suspect we are deeper in the mountain than most of the tilli went," Palafair said. "These tunnels are in good shape, so they were clearly used. Perhaps only for access to the lughite."

"Yes, that must be it. I would have had no cause to go here as a youngeryear." She paused and picked at the rough material of her dirty pants. They were sturdy, good for travel and the life of a soldier, but they could chaff, especially when in need of a good wash.

The she dared to ask, "Do you think the missing army is really here?"

Palafair sighed. "I believe they were here. It is so hard to tell with the sciathilte and their knowing and have known."

"It almost makes me miss Pop's long-winded stories about his ancestors."

That made Palafair chuckle. "I love those stories. And the home-cooked meals with a cold glass of essence on the side. Most of all, though, I miss the laughter. The Kases know how to laugh."

"They sure do, loud enough to burst my eardrums." Zelenka rested her head on Palafair's shoulder. "Will you miss them terribly if we settle somewhere else?"

"I will miss them," he admitted, his shoulder shrugging underneath her head. "But as long I have you, I will be okay."

"Sleep, my dear," she said. "I will keep watch."

Palafair settled his head into her lap and promptly fell asleep, his snores echoing in the cave. Zelenka stayed awake and stared at the dull, gray rock. It did nothing to keep her worries at bay, and after awhile, she roused Palafair to continue on.

They traveled through the snaking tunnels for hours more. They reached caves, both large and small, that finally showed signs of the tilli who had once called Hillock home. Many were partitioned out into rooms. One held a wooden bed strewn with the remains of a straw mattress. It now housed a family of mice, plenty of droppings left as evidence of the new residents. Another room held a table and chairs, moldy and rotting from water damage. The air was thick with moisture.

Water had flooded many of the caves when the tilli fled the damaged tunnels all those years ago. Now, Zelenka and Palafair passed many collapsed tunnels. They spent hours walking down a large one, only to come to a place that was blocked by rocks. They had no choice but to turn around and head back to where they could choose a new direction. With her spear, Zelenka scraped an X in the rock next to the cave that dead-ended, should they happen upon it again.

It had started to all look vaguely familiar, but none of it had the character and charm that Zelenka remembered. Large pieces of furniture had been left behind, but all the thousands of small things that made up a home—the dishes, the tapestries, the toys and books—had all been taken or more likely washed away. There hadn't been much time to grab anything before the tilli had fled.

Zelenka's stomach churned with heartache over the memories. The torch shook in her hand as they came upon another cave that had once been someone's home.

Palafair took the torch. "Let me lead for awhile." He handed her the canteen and some provisions.

She took a bite despite a rising nausea. The water proved more refreshing than the snack and helped her keep the meager portion of food down. She clutched her stomach and followed.

This tunnel was taller and wider than most of the others. Many smaller paths veered off along the way, but Palafair kept to the main one. A rush of water filled their ears as they passed more offshoots. An inkling of hope prickled under Zelenka's skin. She peered down a small path, longing to recognize something— anything—and found only darkness. Then she ran straight into Palafair. He let out an "ooomph" but kept a hold of the torch, which was now illuminating a mess of rocks that proved to be another dead end.

"This is madness." Zelenka slumped to the hard, dusty ground.

Palafair placed the torch in a sconce and knocked on the pile of rocks. A few small rocks and dust fell from the top of the pile. A shaft of light shown through. Zelenka gasped and scrambled to her feet. Her heart, which a minute ago had felt heavy, leaped at the slit of light showing through.

Together they climbed to the top of the rock pile and peered through the hole just below the ceiling of the cave. It was the brightest cave they had yet seen, but Zelenka couldn't angle herself to see more than a wall of rock on the far side.

"We will have to dig our way through," she said.

They wasted no time, picking away at the hole one rock at a time. They started with the small ones, so as not to send the whole pile crashing down below them. Before long, Zelenka was able to poke her head and shoulders through to the other side.

The cavern was high and open at the top. Sunlight poured in, momentarily blinding Zelenka. She squinted until her eyes adjusted.

The entire floor was covered in bodies. Underneath the dust covering their armor, Zelenka was able to make out the tilli crest of a serpent swallowing its own tail to form a circle. It was a symbol of eternal life, which the tilli had used long before the last Roodeshes had become obsessed with the Elixir and ruined all the symbol stood for.

Zelenka had found the missing army.

Chapter Thirty-Four

In the temple on Capdon Mountain, Devon's mother rushed to hug him. Then she smacked him on the side of his head. "What were you thinking, coming up here?"

Before Devon could answer, Pop Pop said, "Ariana, give the boy a minute to recover."

Devon realized his breath was tight and he was getting the light-headed feeling again. He forced himself to take a few slow, deep breaths. Only then was he able to be annoyed by Pop Pop calling him a boy, followed by being annoyed with himself for being on the cusp of an episode when he was trying so hard to show them he was strong.

"You stay out of this, Pop." His mother handed Devon a cup of tea. "Drink this."

He did as he was told. The hot liquid was sweeter than he expected. It had the earthy flavor of black tea but with something added to it. Perhaps a drop or two of Elixir, which for some reason irked him even more as the pressure on his lungs eased. He wasn't an ailing child anymore, breathing problems or not, and he wanted everyone to stop treating him like one.

"I'm not a boy," Devon said, sounding very much like a petulant child. "I'll be a primeyear at the winter solstice."

"So you keep telling us," his mother said. "For now you're still a youngeryear, and you're acting like one for sure."

The two priestess stood off to the side, quietly sipping tea. Their hoods concealed their eyes, but Devon could feel their gazes on him.

"I had a dream about coming here," he tried to explain. "It felt like a sign—like one of those messages Katora is always getting—and so I listened."

Pop Pop stroked his chin, which was bare of any stubble. "Did you get a direct message, like Katora and Zelenka received with the lightning strike, or was it more of a feeling?"

Ariana threw her hands up in the air. "I can't believe you're encouraging this."

"It was more of a feeling," Devon piped in before his mother diverted the conversation away from his quest.

"There was no message." Ariana turned on Pop Pop and pointed a finger at him. "Stop filling my child's head with ideas. You may be his grandfather, but I'm his mother, and this has gone too far."

The head priestess pulled off her hood to reveal a head full of short hair that was an orange so bright it couldn't have been natural. "Message or not, your arrival here is fortuitous. There are many things I would like to discuss with you, Popadoro Kase. Are you hungry, Kase daughter and son?"

"Yes," his mother said.

"No," Devon countered. Didn't she realize the priestess was trying to leave them out of the conversation?

"Excellent. Take them to the dining room," the head priestess said to the priestess who had brought Devon here.

"I want to stay," Devon said.

"Go and eat." Pop Pop's blue eyes shown nothing but sincerity when he said, "I will do my best to keep you informed... with your mother's permission."

Devon turned to his mother, who said, "I'm willing to discuss this matter further. You're certainly old enough to be informed, though I'm not convinced you're mature enough for any kind of quest. For now you can eat."

It was a start, and Devon was willing to bend a little if it meant he might get something out of it.

His stomach rumbled as they made the long trek down the stone staircase and through a series of corridors to the dining room. It was larger than any room Devon had been in, though his experience was limited as he had never been beyond the border of Tussar. The largest building there was the meetinghouse, which was used for community gatherings in the colder months. The temple's dining room had v-shaped ceilings that reached at least thirty feet at the highest point. One side was lined with windows that reflected the many torches along the walls and candles on the table.

Beyond the reflection of light, Devon could see it was snowing outside. He wasn't sure about the normal climate of the mountain, but snow in Tussar was very rare, a portent or message usually coming with it. He had only ever seen snow one other time in his life, a couple of years ago. And that had heralded the departure of his mother, all his aunts, Bhar, Hirsten, and Palafair into Faway Forest. His mother and Aunt Lili had returned a few weeks later. He'd heard the stories of the others being held captive by the tilli at the Three River Split, of how Zelenka had helped them escape, and their encounter with the witch of Faway Forest, Yeselda. He had been told Katora had gone to the forest to retrieve ingredients to make a special essence, but now he knew she had gone for the Elixir's secret ingredient.

Plates of venison and roasted carrots and potatoes, all smothered in a delicious-smelling brown sauce, were brought out. Never one to turn down a meal, Devon dug in, only stopping for a sip of essence once he began to feel full.

He held up the metal tankard. "This is good. Too bad it's only made to protect the Elixir."

Ariana gave him a piercing look. "Watch your tongue. You can be sure the head priestess knows of such things, but not the others."

Devon looked around at the empty room. "There's no one else here."

She took a bite of meat and chewed thoughtfully before swallowing. "You know, my son, erring on the side of discretion would go a long way to convincing me you possess the maturity for quests."

Before Devon could open his mouth, his mother cut him off, "Just don't, Devon. Learn when to keep your mouth shut. Now, let's talk of more pleasant things. Your father was very happy with your hitting in the last bagball game."

They talked of bagball and school, both about Devon's lessons and what Ariana was teaching the littlest youngeryears, until Pop Pop joined them. Devon was eager to hear any news, but Pop Pop gave a small shake of his head to indicate that now wasn't the time.

When Pop Pop was done eating, he pushed away his plate. "The priestesses have arranged for a special cart to bring you back down the mountain."

"For all of us?" Devon asked.

"Only for you," Pop Pop said. "Your mother and I will walk alongside."

"What?" Devon's face blazed hot, despite the chill in the air. "Like I'm some kind of baby!"

"The priestesses will be carrying it themselves. Think of it as an honor."

"But—"

His mother cut him off, "Enough! You did this to yourself, coming up here unprepared and having an episode. You act like a child and get sick, you get treated like one."

Devon slouched in his chair, prepared to have a good pout, when two priestesses approached their table. Their hoods were up, their hands clasped together and concealed behind long sleeves. Devon thought the smaller of the two was the same one who had been in his chamber when he had woken up, but it was hard to tell with so little of her features exposed. The other priestess was tall and stout. "Your rooms have been prepared," said a deep voice that suggested this priestess was a man. "Are you ready to go to them?"

"Yes. Thank you." Pop Pop stood. "It's very late and we leave after breakfast tomorrow. Let's all get some sleep."

Devon's inclination was to protest that he didn't need sleep because he was being carried down the mountain, but for once he kept his mouth shut. He stifled a yawn, his throat still scratchy and sore from coughing.

The smaller priestess gestured for Ariana to follow her, while the larger one led Devon and Pop Pop to a small wing not far from the dining area. "This is the wind wing. You each have your own room as there are only a few of us currently in residence." He pointed to two rooms next to each other.

"Thank you." Pop Pop waited for the priestess to retire to his own room before turning to Devon. "You go to your room and sleep. No sneaking out, no wandering around. I'll come and get you in the morning before breakfast. Understand?"

"Yes, sir," Devon said, and he managed to make it sound contrite. "There's one thing I want to do before we leave."

"What's that?"

"Make an offering." So long as his grandfather didn't ask what the offering was for, Devon wouldn't have to lie.

Pop Pop let a hiss of air out between his teeth, a narrow bent to his eyebrows. "I doubt your mother will object to that. We'll find time for it in the morning. Goodnight, Devon."

"Goodnight."

In the deep quiet of the middle of the night, Devon would have loved to explore and learn more about elemental magic, but he figured it wasn't worth the risk of getting caught. So long as he got to make his offering to the Great Mother tomorrow. He fell asleep with a smile on his lips as his brain continued scheming. He dreamed of bold quests and the sweet accolades that followed.

Chapter Thirty-Five

The day after Tarq agreed to be their guide through Blanchardwood, preparations for their departure were underway. The pilfered Elixir had kept Kylene's hangover at bay, which was a mercy because she was in charge of making sure everyone was properly outfitted for the wood's treacherous weather. She knew everyone's size except for Tarq's. Over an unappetizing breakfast of wrinkly tomatoes and toast, Kylene made the mistake of asking about his clothing needs.

"Nothing," he said in a clipped tone. "What kind of guide would I be if I didn't have my own gear?"

Katora raised her right eyebrow, as if to ask what Ky had done to elicit such a response from their all-important guide. For her part, Kylene blew out a breath of frustration and shrugged. If she knew what she had done, she could remedy it, but she still had no clue why Tarq disliked her.

Kylene pushed her plate away and started on the errand. The innkeeper had given her directions to a shop that would have what she needed. It was a brisk but sunny morning, so she decided to walk. It would save her a little money, and she would need to take a cabbie wagon back to the inn with the supplies. Her coin supply was low after last night's drinking, and she didn't want to ask Katora for more money and risk having to admit where all hers had gone.

The innkeeper's directions led her to a desolate and cramped cobblestone street. The buildings were several stories high with commerce on the first floors and apartments above, though many appeared abandoned with shuttered windows and ivy growing up their fronts. They were a hodgepodge of brick, stone, and wood and seemed to get wider toward the top, giving the road a closed-in feeling. Leaves skittered down the road in a cool breeze, but there were no humans or demicks anywhere. Kylene wrapped her cloak tight around her midsection and flipped up her hood. Winter was certainly on the horizon.

As she walked by yet another empty storefront, she considered abandoning this shop and looking elsewhere, until a warm glow greeted her from an open doorway. The scent of spicy cinnamon and sweet apples enticed her closer. The sign above the door was a beaver head carved out of dark wood. The figure had bared teeth in an angry expression. This was the shop she sought out, and she probably would have gone in even if it wasn't because the delicious scent and warm glow were a welcome reprieve from the biting cold and lonely road.

Dozens of candles hung in chandeliers made of large antlers. Most of the floor space was taken up with racks and racks of fur pelts. The walls were a dark evergreen color, giving the whole place a deep woods feel. The chandelier swayed in a gust of cold air from the open doorway. She worried that a single errant candle would send the whole place up in flames.

A wrinkled, gray-haired man and an equally wrinkled, gray-haired woman stood at—or more accurately were hunched over—a counter at the back of the shop. They looked even older than Anos, the oldest of the elderyear members back home in Tussar. The man's hands shook as he served up steaming pieces of apple pie, the source of the aroma that had called to Kylene from the street. Heedless of a customer at the door, he dug into the pie, slurping with a toothless mouth.

The old woman was about to take her first bite when she looked up and noticed their customer. She smiled, showing off her own toothless state. With the fork halfway to her lips, she elbowed the old man. "Eh, Wendell, we have a customer."

Wendell grunted and continued eating, lips smacking loudly.

"Come have a slice with us, dearie," the woman said.

Kylene unconsciously took a step backward toward the door. The old woman elbowed Wendell again. "Stop being a pig. Yer scaring the poor girl."

It wasn't that Kylene was afraid, more that she was uncertain. They seemed harmless enough, stooped over and

184

advanced in age as they were, but the air had a crackly feeling that stank of magic. It left a bitter taste in the back of her throat. She cleared it and stood, undecided, on the threshold.

"I won't bite you," Wendell said through a mouthful of pie. "I've got no teeth!" He opened his mouth wide to show her what was already painfully obvious.

The old woman hauled off and whacked him on the shoulder. "Ignore my witch of a husband," she said and beckoned Kylene over.

Wendell laughed. "Don't let her fool you. She's the witch, not me."

Kylene's last encounter with a witch had landed her in a battle against ensorcelled animals, and she had been forced to kill a great number of them to defend herself. Every so often she got a phantom whiff of the blood and dirt of the battlefield.

"Winnie the Witch, nice to meet you." The old woman held out her hand and cackled.

The urge to be polite was enough to propel Kylene into the shop to shake Winnie's hand. She wasn't sure if the old couple was joking about Winnie being a witch, but Kylene took their sense of humor as a good sign.

She cleared her throat. "I'm here for—"

"Yes, yes," Winnie interrupted. "Yer here for coats warm enough to keep you from death in the bone chill of Blanchardwood. We know, we know."

Witch indeed, Kylene thought with a shiver that had nothing to do with the promise of Blanchardwood's chill.

"Wendell, cut the poor girl a slice," said Winnie.

He took a break from his lip-smacking to cut two slices of pie, one he plopped on his nearly empty plate and the other on a fresh plate for Kylene. Steam rose from the apples sluicing out the sides, emitting a mouth-watering perfume. A welcome treat that reminded Kylene of the inadequate tomato breakfast. Her stomach rumbled loudly enough to elicit a glance from Winnie. "Eat up, dearie."

With a shrug, Kylene picked up the fork and cut into the

piece. The pie threatened to fall off the fork, so she had to lean in to get it to her mouth in time. Apple and lemon and cinnamon flavors burst in her mouth. She sighed. With a clear understanding of all the lip-smacking, she sunk into the pie with gusto.

Winnie stared at her with a wry smile until Kylene finished. "Feeling better?"

"Yes, thank you," Kylene said. And it was true. The pie had left a comfortable fullness in her stomach. Kylene absentmindedly rubbed her injured arm.

"But still not good, eh?" The old witch was sly indeed.

As if on cue, Kylene's arm throbbed under the hand that rubbed it. She smoothed her face into a mask of indifference. "About those furs..."

"Yes, yes, the furs," Winnie said. "We will get to those. Tell me, dearie, what ails you?"

"Nothing." She fought to keep the mask in place.

Winnie leaned over the counter and peered into Kylene's face. "Hmmm, I think not." She disappeared through a door behind the counter. Wendell offered a toothless smile and helped himself to another piece of pie. Kylene began to wonder if she'd ever get out of there with the supplies she needed.

The witch returned with a steaming mug of milk. If Kylene had been able to raise one eyebrow like Katora—and she had wished for this many times—she would have quirked one right then. Instead, she settled for a furrowed brow.

"Not as obvious a choice as hot tea or cocoa, but it goes great with the pie." Winnie sliced yet another slice and slid it across the table. "Two is better than one when it comes to pie."

"Or four," Wendell said through a full mouth.

Kylene sniffed the milk as Winnie watched expectantly. It smelled like...milk, and nothing else. She took a sip and found it was the perfect complement to the spice of the pie. It was so good in comparison to the thrown-together meals on the journey and the lackluster food from the inn. The treat put her at ease and she relaxed, taking off her cloak and hanging it from an empty rack.

"What sizes do yeh need?" Winnie asked.

"Mmmm," Ky said as much in response to the food as to the question. She handed over a paper listing the sizes, took a long gulp of warm milk, and wiped her upper lip.

"Wendell," Winnie interrupted his latest slice, "whites if we have them and grays if not."

With a grunt, Wendell shuffled off and rummaged through the racks of furs. Kylene slurped down the last of the milk and pie. A heady sleepiness overcame her—probably from the rich food. She watched Wendell search for the right furs, while Winnie cleaned up. For a moment her vision blurred, but she blinked and all was fine. The wavering candlelight must have been messing with her head. Despite the open door, it was getting very warm in the shop and beads of sweat formed on the back of her neck.

Wendell flung a huge pile of furs onto the counter. It looked like a heap of dead animals, and Kylene was once again reminded of the battle with the animal army. Her stomach roiled. Wearing animal furs didn't sit well with her, but she had been told it was that or freeze to death in Blanchardwood. Wendell laid the hides out one by one until it was clear there were four different coats. Three were comprised of snowy white hair with gray streaks. The smallest—for Katora—was a bright white that took on a yellow hue in the lighting.

"Pity there is only one white," Winnie said.

Somehow, Kylene thought with more than a little bitterness, Katora always managed to have the best of the bunch. She brushed the thought away; resentment was not a good look on anyone.

Winnie selected the smallest gray fur. "Here, dearie, try it on."

Kylene wavered under the weight of it and immediately began to sweat profusely. It curved around her arms in wide sleeves and the front fastened with large wooden buttons. It was a little loose around the middle but a perfect length, hanging down to just above her ankles.

"Should we bring it in in the middle for you?" asked Winnie.

"No, it's fine." Kylene sloughed off the coat but continued to sweat. A tingling sensation all throughout her body turned to numbness. "I..."

The room spun, and she sagged against the counter. She grabbed at anything to hold herself upright but only managed to pull down the furs as she collapsed. A strange silliness washed over Kylene, and she contented herself with lying on the floor, staring up at the antler chandeliers that appeared to dance on the ceiling.

"Oh, dear," Winnie's voice came from above. "I think I used too much."

Wendell lifted Kylene to her feet and placed her cloak over her shoulders, placing her money pouch back into her pocket. She hadn't even noticed he'd taken it.

"I only took what yeh owe me, nothin' extra," he assured her.

Kylene nodded and allowed herself to be steered out the door and into the back of a waiting cabbie wagon. Winnie and Wendell together tossed the furs next to her on the seat. Kylene's head felt heavy and it lolled to the side. She flapped her hands in front of her face with only partial control.

"What's wrong with me?" Kylene slurred.

"I was only trying to help," Winnie said. "Seems I gave you a little too much of a good thing. But I bet that old wound feels better, eh?"

Of course it did, Kylene wanted to say—her whole body was numb and nothing hurt—but her mouth was too uncooperative to form the words.

Wendell waved from the open door of the shop. Winnie said, "Come back if you want more of that. I will dose you better next time now that I know how much is too much." Then she slammed shut the wagon's door.

Kylene slumped sideways on the soft furs and nestled into them as the cabbie wagon bumped down the road.

* * * *

"What in the Great Mother's name happened?" Bhar shouted as he leaned into the cabbie wagon, waking Kylene.

She was snuggled up among the furs in the back of the

wagon. A blurriness hung around the edges of her vision and her mind felt equally as fuzzy.

"Milk," she managed to reply. Her tongue felt too big in her mouth.

"Milk?" He leaned in farther, right in front of her face. "How did milk do this?" He stared at her face for a minute. Kylene's eyelids felt so heavy, it took all her energy to keep them open. "Never mind. Let's get you inside."

He pulled her out of the wagon and propped her up on the side of it. She slumped against it and struggled not to slide down into the street.

What had that witch done to her?

"Don't go anywhere," he joked, as if she was in any condition to move. He heaved the furs onto his shoulder and held her tight to his side. "Can you walk?"

Her head lolled up and down in her best approximation of a nod. Grunting under the weight of the furs, Bhar guided her to their room, dumping the coats on the ground as soon they entered. Kylene barely made it to the nearest bed before collapsing.

"Are you going to be okay?" Bhar asked.

She shrugged. Through all the fuzziness, a pleasant lightness had filled her. It went straight into her bones, nothing hurt or ached. The tunnel vision and jelly legs were a problem, but she couldn't muster the energy to care.

"These things always happen to you, don't they?" he said. "The poisoned spear, the blood oath to Nika, and now this milk thing. Whatever it is."

"Mmmm," she murmured. It did seem strange that things kept happening to her, like she had been born under an unlucky star, if she believed in that kind of thing, which she didn't. Her brain was too fuzzy to make a coherent thought, so she let the darkness take her and that was all she knew.

Chapter Thirty-Six

The fog held fast to Kylene's mind throughout the night, holding her in a deep sleep well into morning. When she woke, light streamed in through the sides of the window coverings, creating a halo effect, or perhaps that was the lingering effects of the witch's milk.

Mind suddenly clear, Kylene shot up in bed. What had that witch given her? She did a quick assessment of her body. Her toes and fingers worked, her legs moved under the blankets, and she felt fine...good even. She had grown accustomed to waking with a sore arm, stiffness settling in during sleep. An experimental roll of her shoulder revealed something was still keeping the chronic pain at bay.

The bed next to her was empty, the blankets creased and sloppily pulled up over the pillows in a semblance of being made. All of Bhar's belongings were gone, too. Kylene splashed water on her face from the washbowl on the end table and tried to remember what had happened. There was pie and milk and Winnie and Wendell, but the details remained fuzzy.

Kylene remembered Winnie said to come back if she wanted more, probably the witch having a bit of fun with her.

With her belongings hastily packed up and her new furs in her arms, Kylene headed down to the pub. She found her siblings, Hirsten, and Tarq at one of the only occupied tables. All their supplies and backpacks were piled on the floor. Dishes clinked and voices echoed from the open kitchen door. Breakfast—muffins and soggy eggs—was almost over. Kylene grabbed a handful of stale nuts leftover from the night before and poured a cup of lukewarm tea.

"Nice of you to join us." Katora didn't bother looking up from the map she, Hirsten, and Tarq were poring over.

Kylene cleared her throat, ready to launch into the whole

story of visiting the fur shop and what she remembered of Winnie and Wendell, but Bhar narrowed his eyes and gave her a subtle shake of the head. She bit her lower lip instead and sipped tea to buy time to figure out what to say.

"Have a little too much *milk* last night, Ky?" Bhar gave her a pointed look, but she wasn't sure why there was a need to keep the fact that she was drugged—or whatever had happened—a secret.

Tarq perked up at Bhar's words and stared at Kylene with suspicion, but Katora remained focused on the map as Hirsten spoke quietly to it, working his mapmaking magic on it. Lines of roads and landforms spread out across the parchment, like an irregular web forming under the care of an invisible spider. Katora's hand rested on top of Hirsten's, her touch an amplifier to his magic. It was an oddly intimate thing, observing them create a map memory together.

"Something like that," Kylene said slowly.

Hirsten's murmurings trailed off, and Katora finally looked up.

"Well, hungover or not," her sister said, "you did a good job with the furs. Eat something because we leave in an hour and we're not stopping until nightfall. Meet us outside when you're done."

Hirsten patted her hand. "Don't worry about it. Lughorn can do that to the best of us."

Katora, Hirsten, and Tarq gathered up their luggage and headed out of the pub. Kylene took a bite of muffin and found it too dry to swallow. She coughed it into a napkin.

"Next time we come to Lughorn, I pick where we stay," Bhar said. "Katora managed to find the only place here with bad food."

He was trying to distract her out of a bad mood, but Kylene had questions. She picked at the muffin. "Why didn't you tell Katora what happened?"

"What *did* happen last night?" Bhar poured himself a cup of tea and grabbed another plateful of food as if he planned on staying until he had his fill of the terrible food.

"Great Mother, I wish I knew," confessed Kylene. "I went to

the fur shop and the owner offered me pie and milk."

Bhar's eyes opened wide in accusation. "And you ate it?"

"I didn't want to be rude. It smelled so good, and it tasted even better."

"I bet it did...until you couldn't stand upright," Bhar said through a mouthful of food. "You can't be so trusting. This isn't Tussar."

"I think she was trying to help me." Kylene closed her eyes and tried to remember exactly what Winnie had said.

"How do you feel now?" Bhar peered at her, his head dipped in toward her face.

She felt good, except for the prick of pain near her shoulder that she guessed would soon be shooting down her arm in its usual way.

She shrugged. "As fine as ever."

"Are you sure?"

"Yes!" Ky shouted, and then lowered her voice, though they were the only ones in the pub. "Why do you keep asking? And why didn't you tell Katora?"

"I thought you were drunk," Bhar retorted. "You show up in a cabbie wagon draped in furs and half-conscious, babbling something about milk. So I put you to bed."

"But why all the secrecy?" Kylene crumbled her muffin, in full-on pout mode. "I was drugged or something. What if I had died in my sleep?"

"I thought of that," Bhar admitted. "It's not like you to get drunk. So I kept an eye on you all night...hardly got any sleep myself." His eyes did look bloodshot and his body sagged in a tired way.

Sensing more to the story, Kylene prompted, "And?"

"And what?" Bhar wouldn't meet her eyes. "Fine." He threw his hands up in exasperation. "I nicked the Elixir from Katora and gave you some. That way if it was more than being drunk, you'd be okay. And no hangover if you were drunk." His wry smile was back. "Not that I know from personal experience."

"Katora could've given me the Elixir herself."

"She gets so uptight about it, and I wasn't sure if you really needed it, so I did it myself. No big deal, okay?" It was Bhar's turn to shrug. "I helped her brew it, I should get to decide how it's used once in awhile."

Kylene rapped her finger on the back of his hand. "Thanks, Bhar."

"I got your back, sis. Just be careful. I'd rather have to cover for you being drunk than poisoned."

Kylene's arm stung at the mention of being poisoned. The last thing she wanted to experience was anything like being stabbed by the tilli spear; she'd much rather be drunk.

* * * *

The line between where the plains of the Great Peninsula ended and where Blanchardwood started was as distinct as a border on a map. On one side, tall grass swayed in the cold breeze that marked autumn soon yielding to winter. On the other, a line of dark evergreens covered in white blocked any view of the interior of the woods.

The travelers bundled up in their furs and strapped their supplies on their backs. They had sold the horses to a nice family who owned a farm a few miles south. Blanchardwood, with its deep snow and frigid conditions, was no place for horses.

"You're sure Jinks will be okay?" Kylene missed the mischievous horse already.

Hirsten offered a comforting pat on the shoulder, though she couldn't really feel it through all the layers. "A farm's the best place for him. Lots of room to run around."

"C'mom!" Katora yelled. She, Bhar, and Tarq were standing just outside the trees, ready to enter the woods.

Kylene and Hirsten hurried as fast as their bulky attire allowed them. Tarq was the first one to slip in between two trees and disappear, followed by Katora, Hirsten, and Bhar. Kylene took a big gulp of frozen air, pushed her way past the low branches of evergreens, and earned her first look at the frozen tundra of Blanchardwood. The trees and deep snow would be difficult to navigate, but the elements were by far the worst foe.

Kylene wrapped a scarf around her mouth and nose. The wind and snow stung her eyes. They travelers pushed against the wind and trudged along in a single file. It was going to be a long journey to the Ice Queen's palace.

Chapter Thirty-Seven

Though Zelenka had finally made her way through the defunct tunnels of Hillock and found the missing tilli army, they appeared lifeless from her view peeking out of the hole in the rocks.

She came back to the other side to the expectant face of Palafair. "They are here, right on the other side." She gasped. She was having trouble catching her panicked breath. "Keep pulling out rocks. I have to find out if they are alive."

They dislodged a few more rocks until Zelenka was able to squeeze her way through the opening. Palafair was close behind as she scrambled to the bottom layer of rock. Zelenka halted there because if she were to go any farther, she would tread on her comrades.

She dropped down to her knees next to the nearest fallen soldier.

"Do not," Palafair whispered urgently. He grabbed her shoulder and held her back from touching the soldier. "There is powerful magic here. I can feel it in my bones."

"I have to see if they are alive." Please let them be alive, thought Zelenka.

"They are. See how their chests rise and fall."

In her haste, Zelenka had failed to notice the subtle movement of the soldiers' chests. They were in fact alive. She let out a long breath, her body sagging against the rocks behind her. Tears swam in her eyes, but she refused to give in to her emotions. She was a soldier, not a silly child upset over a lost toy. She swiped the tears away with the back of her hand.

A snap of energy swept across the cave and brought her to her feet. A whiff of sulfur permeated the stale air. The unmistakable figure of Yeselda stood in the middle of all the bodies. She was flanked by two of her henchmen, the Red Horseman on his scarlet steed and the White Horseman atop his ivory one. Thankfully, the Black Horseman hadn't accompanied his witch mistress; to lay eyes on him and his ebony horse chilled the soul. As it was, Zelenka suppressed a shiver at the sight of her nemesis. Palafair stiffened beside her.

"You," Zelenka accused. She would never forgive the witch of Faway for her leg injury; nor had she quite forgiven Katora for saving her with the Elixir without her permission. "Why am I not surprised to see you here, among my fallen army? I presume you had something to do with their state."

"Now, now, my little demick." Yeselda stalked toward them, her horsemen following a step behind. "No need to be so accusatory. They came here all on their own. I merely kept them occupied so they would not find you and the Kase daughter while searching for the Elixir's nectar."

"That mission was over long ago," Zelenka reminded her.

"Yes. Tis a pity I forgot about them until our most recent encounter. I could have found some use for them." Yeselda glanced around at the soldiers with a certain gleaming menace in her eyes. "No matter. They have been preserved in their natural state thanks to me."

"And they have lost years of the their lives for it. They had families back home that have mourned them. Their absence left the tilli vulnerable. You have torn apart a people. On what? A whim. And then you forgot about them!" Zelenka's shouts echoed across the cave, though Yeselda was close now.

"A few years is a grain of sand on a vast beach to me. You humans and demicks are so hot-tempered. So much to worry about in your short life spans."

Palafair puffed out his chest. "You will fix this. You will wake the soldiers and stay out of our lives."

"What do I receive in return?" asked Yeselda.

"Nothing." Zelenka refused to negotiate with the witch. "You have taken enough from me, and from my people. You will wake them up and let us go home."

The silence that followed stretched out for an uncomfortable length of time. Yeselda stood high above them, a condescending smile on her face, as she considered the bodies littering the cave. Zelenka expected her to refuse, to ask for something Zelenka could not give in return. She would fight the witch if need be, though a demick against a higher being wouldn't be a fair fight. Palafair squeezed Zelenka's hand and nodded, there with her to the end if it came to that.

A light flashed high above them where the cave opened to the sky and a rumble of thunder followed. Yeselda's gaze went unfocused, as if her mind strayed, and her horsemen closed the distance between them. After a moment, her eyes refocused and she shifted her attention back to the cave.

"Very well," Yeselda said. "I have other matters to attend to." With a wave of her hand, she and her horseman disappeared, leaving behind the stench of rotten eggs.

Zelenka let out an angry half-sob, half-moan and buried her face in her hands. It was her fault she had run away with Katora because she had wanted answers about the Elixir. Her selfishness had led the army here, only to be trapped. Yeselda may have done the deed, but the cause was firmly on Zelenka.

Palafair was comforting her, telling her they would find someone to wake them, when the clink of metal brought her attention back to the soldiers. Several in the middle were sitting up, looking dazed but otherwise unharmed. Their armor and spears clanked as more stirred. The nearest soldier sat up and looked straight at them. His eyes grew wide and urgent. He pointed his spear right at Zelenka's heart and yelled, "Traitor! She is here, the traitor!"

The entire enchanted army stood at the ready, weapons pointed squarely at Zelenka and Palafair.

In all her time looking for the lost tilli army, Zelenka had failed to think about what their reaction would be when she found them. They had been sent to go after her, believing she was a traitor. The events of late—her explanation of why she had thrown Roodesh to his death, the other tilli forgiving her and sending her to find the army—didn't exist in their minds. Thank the Great Mother their orders had been to capture, not kill her, otherwise she and Palafair would surely have been dead already. In hindsight, she realized she should have brought someone who could vouch for them. By not wanting to risk any other tilli, she had put hers and Palafair's lives at risk.

She raised her arms, and a single, pointed look prompted Palafair to do the same. "Peace," she said. "We have come to bring you home to the Three River Split. On General Nemez's orders."

The soldiers parted to allow one particularly short tilli to make her way to the so-called traitor. She pulled off her helmet and light brown hair cascaded past her shoulders. Her piercing brown eyes stared down Zelenka and completely ignored Palafair. She thrust the tip of her spear inches from Zelenka's neck. It was Major Gainsley, who had come up the ranks of the army along with Zelenka. They had both been appointed the title of major around the same time.

At first there had been a good-natured rivalry among the two, but now it was only hard bitterness there. With Zelenka gone, Gainsley would have been a leader in the charge to capture her.

"Peace?" Gainsley said. "Last I heard our leader was dead and you, the next Roodesh, had run off with an anni and a bunch of humans. *Our* orders from the general were to take you in alive. As for your companions," the soldier finally spared a glance for Palafair, one filled with contempt, "well, there was no mention of keeping them alive. Whatever did happen to the humans?"

Zelenka's stomach churned and saliva filled her mouth. She swallowed back the nausea. "Major Gainsley, I will gladly leave this place without a fight and explain everything, if, and only if, you do no harm to me or my husband."

"Your husband!" Gainsley let out a derisive laugh. Many soldiers joined in, the laughter amplified by the cave walls. "My, how far the great Zelenka has fallen. Once slated to be the next Roodesh, now a lowly wife to an anni demick. Tell me, do you work for the humans, cooking their food and wiping their baby's bums?" The laughter grew to new heights, as high as the opening far above their heads.

The major, who had always been jealous of Zelenka's

birthright, had hit more than one sore spot with the insult. If not for the spear at her throat, Zelenka might have done something rash and punched the smug look off Gainsley's face. But she could practically feel the calming vibes being sent by Palafair and swallowed down her pride...for now.

"Years have passed since I left the Three River Split," Zelenka explained. "You have been in an enchanted sleep and much has happened since you were last awake. Do you recognize where you are? Do you remember how you got here?"

Gainsley kept a firm hold on the spear but looked around the cave at her fellow soldiers as if just now realizing how strange it was to have awoken in a cave in Hillock with the subject of their search there waiting for them. Zelenka saw confusion on the other tilli's faces. All Zelenka needed was to connect enough with her former comrades to get them out of Hillock alive; then there would others, people they trusted, to explain what had happened.

"Believe me when I say Palafair and I are here peacefully," Zelenka continued in an earnest voice that addressed more than Gainsley, though Zelenka kept careful eye contact with the major. "We are not threatening you with our weapons." Her arms ached from holding them up for so long, her spear tucked away in its scabbard on her back. "There is war on the horizon, one that will affect all of the Great Peninsula. It is time to come together. Let us leave here and you will find the truth you seek."

The one favor Yeselda had done for Zelenka was to leave the enchanted tilli in a major cave. Zelenka finally had her bearings and knew how to get out of Hillock.

"Private!" Gainsley addressed the soldier who had called Zelenka a traitor, and his spear replaced the major's. "Make sure these two do not move." Gainsley raised her voice to the whole army. "I call an officer's meeting in the southeast corner."

Zelenka knew every officer who gathered in the corner to quietly converse. It had been years since she had seen or talked to any of them, but at one time in her life, they had been as much her family as Palafair was now. She had the advantage of time and perspective to reconcile the hostile feelings they shot at her, but to them, Zelenka's betrayal was a fresh wound that hadn't had time to heal before she waltzed in here and opened it up again. A sideways glance at Palafair told her he was holding up okay under the watchful gaze of the tilli.

The meeting finished and Gainsley, with the other officers behind her, stalked up to Zelenka.

"We have decided your story may have some merit to it. It would certainly explain a few things we ourselves cannot explain." Gainsley's eyebrows were pulled in and she actually appeared slightly sheepish. Zelenka almost felt smug…almost, as there was still a spear pointed at her and her only leverage was that the army was confused about what had happened. "Bind them, and we will see if your claims are true."

The smug expression was reserved for Gainsley now as she barked orders at the soldiers. They dusted themselves off and prepared to leave the ruins of Hillock. Zelenka and Palafair's hands were bound, and their right legs were tied to each other with enough slack so they could walk, as was the tilli way of traveling with prisoners. It was a humiliation Zelenka could stomach, so long as it got them to the green tilli army and the sciathilte, and eventually back to the Three River Split.

As Zelenka shuffled through the cave, tethered to Palafair and surrounded by the very soldiers she used to command, she smiled to herself that Gainsley would soon learn of Zelenka's promotion to colonel. That would surely cure the major of her smug attitude. Once she was no longer being treated as a criminal, Zelenka would make sure Gainsley knew where they both ranked.

Chapter Thirty-Eight

The word of Ronan and Laurel was enough for Major Gainsley to allow Zelenka and Palafair to be untied, either that or the sight of sciathilte convinced her. Their iridescent wings and many glittering eyes were something to behold. Zelenka didn't think she would ever get used to the mythical creatures come to life.

The sciathilte numbered enough to bring the newly revived army and the small retinue of Zelenka's charges back to the tilli camp. The speed with which the sciathilte could fly was awe-inspiring. As far-fetched as it might have seemed to imagine these creatures giving up their elusive stature, she already had ideas of aligning with them in post-war endeavors.

Though it had seemed much longer, Zelenka and Palafair had wandered one day and one night in the bowels of Hillock before stumbling upon the lost army. The sciathilte had them all back to the tilli camp by nightfall of the second day. Explanations from the green tilli army turned the tide of the lost army's opinion in favor of Zelenka. Major Gainsley offered a reluctant handshake to Zelenka with a terse, "Colonel."

There would be no more bindings for Zelenka, and that was a relief. She had enough to worry about without the charge of treason hanging over her head. She took the time to wash the dust and bad memories of Hillock off before practically falling into her bedroll next to Palafair. The fatigue was so complete, she slept the deep slumber of someone not burdened by the heavy weights she carried inside her heart and woke only when Palafair gently rubbed her aching leg to rouse her.

The ride back to the Three River Split was invigorating with the late autumn chill assaulting her senses as she rode in front of Palafair on Indy.

The forest was going out in a blaze of color before settling in for the winter dormancy. As they approached the Split, Zelenka noticed how small the falls looked from up high. And how quiet they were. They seemed tame, instead of the rowdy tumult she was used to. They churned in triplicate into their respective rivers, the mist shooting up and forming small rainbows. The swarm of flying sciathilte formed their own rainbow in the sky, their wings and thoraxes shining in the afternoon sun.

They landed at the base of the cliffs near the largest opening. The strip of land next to the falls wasn't large enough for all the sciathilte to land at one time, so they came in shifts of ten. It was a coordinated effort that required no input from the tilli other than disembarking as quickly as possible. Zelenka watched as wave after wave landed and then took off to a spot above the waterfalls.

Of all the places Zelenka had lived—Hillock and Kase Farm among them—the Three River Split felt the most like home. As with all the demicks, her ancestors hailed from Demick Island, and although she had always envisioned visiting it, she couldn't imagine it as home. Home would always be the Three River Split, and she hoped to settle there with Palafair one day, which was a possibility now that she had reconciled with the tilli. But not until the matter of Fyren was dealt with.

Zelenka, with Palafair beside her, waited until the last group of sciathilte landed before entering the main chamber along with Indy. The mass of demicks moved about the space in unbridled chaos. No one seemed to want to leave and more demicks piled in as word got out that the missing soldiers had returned. There were joyful shouts, tears, and hugs as loved ones reunited. Babies cried, children shrieked, and parents held the daughters and sons they thought they had lost. The story of the army's enchantment and Zelenka's rescue circulated, bits and pieces reaching her as she stood off to the side.

It was nice to have a moment to gaze upon the joy in the room and to know that she played a role in making this happen, not enough to erase the role she had played in causing the heartache in the first place, but it was something. It chipped away at the guilt she had harbored since finding out about the missing army.

General Nemez slowly made his way across the chamber, shaking hands and patting backs along the way.

"Colonel Zelenka," he said when he reached her, "you have brought our people together. It is a banner day for the tilli." His brown eyes shone in the torchlight that lit up the chamber, and he uncharacteristically pulled Zelenka in for a hug. Her cheeks warmed but not in embarrassment; the moment was too sweet to feel anything but joy. She would allow herself to fully feel it because with war on the horizon, joy would be in short supply.

Nemez cleared his throat and stared at Indy, who looked larger than life in the confined space of the chamber. "I see you have brought more than just our lost brethren. Noble creature, welcome to the Three River Split, the home of the tilli demicks." He bowed, though in a rather awkward way as he couldn't tear his gaze from the sciathilte. "We have much to discuss." He turned back to Zelenka. "Gather all the officers for a meeting. We will meet in Roodesh's old cave, so the sciathilte can fly in through the opening over the falls. I am afraid we will have to limit the number of sciathilte who can attend, as we do not have space for more than a few."

Indy did the sciathilte thrumming means of communication before saying, "That exceeds our requirements. We need only one to extend what we will know."

"Okay," Nemez said, brow wrinkled in puzzlement, probably with the whole "will know" comment. "We meet in an hour."

He began to stride off when Zelenka said, "Wait! Palafair is not an officer, but I think he should be there."

Nemez waved dismissively. "Yes, of course, he can come too… as a liaison for the anni demicks."

Though it was difficult to ask the officers who had just returned home to leave their families for a meeting, Zelenka proceeded to do just that. On instructions from Zelenka, Palafair rounded up Ronan, Sherav, and the other new officers. Zelenka insisted Laurel join them, even though she wasn't an officer…not yet anyway. Then she and Palafair rode Indy, directing it to the opening for Roodesh's cave. Zelenka suppressed a shudder as she dismounted. Just cause didn't absolve her of guilt, even while she maintained that what she had done was the best thing for the tilli and ultimately saved lives.

Most of the officers had already arrived. Their lingering smiles from seeing their families had not been erased by having to come to a military meeting.

Nemez strode in, waved his hand, and asked in a loud voice, "Can everyone hear me?"

All the older tilli officers were already in the possession of a shard of enchanted wood that blocked the cacophony of the falls. Zelenka and Palafair had kept theirs from the recent meeting with Nemez, so it was only the new officers who required one, which Nemez promptly passed out. Indy buzzed that it could hear Nemez, whether because of its magic or as part of its anatomy, Indy did not divulge.

"Welcome to all of you who are returning and to our special guests the sciathilte of Faway Forest," Nemez began. For the benefit of those who had been asleep, he launched into the story of Zelenka's return. He detailed how she was tasked with returning the tilli army with the help of the new soldiers. Then he turned to Zelenka and allowed her to explain how they had discovered the sciathilte, how Yeselda and the Watcher had pointed them in the direction of Hillock, and then how Yeselda had admitted her guilt in enchanting the army before waking them.

"And now we are all here, united." She purposely left out being tied up with the intent of mending fences.

Nemez said, "I am relieved and overjoyed that our army has returned and that Colonel Zelenka has been cleared of all charges." Zelenka peeked at Major Gainsley and was pleased to see a scowl on her face. "Zelenka will brief us on the Fyren situation."

Zelenka recounted her conversation with Yeselda and the Watcher as best she could with all their vagueness.

"It is our duty to join in the fight against him," Nemez agreed. "I sent scouts out to Tussar and they spoke with Popadoro Kase. He has heard the rumors of war and has been preparing but had no immediate plans to mobilize. With the higher beings' warning and our full tilli army available, I believe it is time for action. Dare I beseech the sciathilte for help in our campaign?"

Indy said, "We have known our pledge to you. Do you require us to pledge again?" It turned piercing eyes to Zelenka.

"No," Zelenka said. And then to Nemez, "When we first met the sciathilte, we informed them of Fyren's threat and they agreed to fight on our side. Nearly the entire colony has come."

It was only now that she wondered if she should have consulted with Nemez before making such alliances, but he clapped his hands, seemingly pleased, and said. "We will establish a new hierarchy among our old and new officers and set out as soon as we can gather supplies. With the help of the sciathilte, we will stop by Tussar and form a plan to coordinate with the humans and anni demicks. Then it will be off to Bad Beach, which is directly across the inlet from the fort of Drim, to launch our offensive."

"Might I propose a second stop along the way?" Zelenka suggested, ignoring the glares being shot at her from Gainsley.

"To where?" asked Nemez.

"Demick Island." The room seemed to take a collective intake of air and fell completely silent, save for the falls outside. "I know we have lost ties with our native island, but they are a part of the Great Peninsula. They are isolated and may not know of the pending war, but they will suffer if Fyren wins, just as we will. They have a stake in the matter and perhaps they will fight along with us and bolster our numbers."

Gainsley piped up, "So not only are you proposing teaming up with anni demicks and humans, you also want us to ask the demicks we left generations ago to fight with us in a war?" It wasn't so much a question as an accusation of absurdity. "Has anyone had any communication with them? Do we know if they still exist?"

"There is no reason the believe they have gone extinct," Zelenka insisted. "They have a stake in what happens. I think they will want to help once we explain the threat of Fyren, if they do not already know about it."

"This whole thing is absurd." Gainsley stomped her foot like a youngeryear having a tantrum. "Us being asleep for years and expected to join with all these green soldiers as if they had earned their ranks. You," she pointed at Zelenka, "showing up to save us. You are being treated like a hero instead of the traitor you are. And now we ride off to war on the backs of creatures who are not even supposed to exist. I am not okay with any of this."

Nemez opened his mouth to speak, but another voice beat him to it. "With all due respect, Major Gainsley," Captain Laurel said, "you were asleep a long time. Many things have changed. But one thing that has not changed is respect for the army. I am proud to have been afforded the opportunity to join. I will follow my superior's orders, no matter if that superior has been in the army five days or five decades. General Nemez, Colonel Zelenka," she performed a perfect salute, "I am here to serve the army in any way you see fit. I am sure my fellow *green* soldiers will agree."

To emphasize Laurel's point, Ronan and the other new officers saluted. This brave and loyal gesture kept Zelenka from acting out on her desire to challenge Gainsley to a fistfight.

"But to go back to Demick Island when they refused to support our ancestors' departure?" For her part, Gainsley seemed determined to be justifiably indignant. "They cut us off all those years ago. To ask for help would prove that we were wrong to leave."

"It proves nothing," Zelenka said. There was a lot more she wanted to argue, but Nemez cut her off.

"Enough!" he yelled. "I have come to a decision. We will accept all the help we can get. With their permission, the sciathilte will fly us to Tussar where we will consult with the humans and anni demicks. Then we will proceed to Demick Island where we will try to persuade the island demicks to fight with us. So long as Fyren has not made a move in that time, our final destination is Bad Beach."

He gave Gainsley a pointed look. "Anyone who does not wish to come with us may elect to stay here with a small retinue of soldiers to protect the Three River Split." Gainsley turned a dark shade of red and looked about to burst. "I am opening up our ranks yet again for anyone who wishes to join in the fight against Fyren. I truly believe this battle is that important."

Zelenka wasn't sure there was anyone left to recruit after her efforts to bolster the new army, but she was all for her fellow tilli stepping up and joining in this fight. She just hoped she wouldn't have to train any more green soldiers, the thought of such a task suddenly exhausting her. She sought out the sturdiness of the table to keep her legs from shaking.

"We leave for Tussar at first light tomorrow," Nemez said.

Indy's wings twitched at a fast pace, drawing attention to the sciathilte. "Let it be known that we travel at night as well as we do during the daylight."

"Noted. Thank you," said Nemez. "We need time to regroup and rest. You may leave and prepare with your fellow sciathilte as need be." Indy zipped out the cave opening, which had been unboarded, and disappeared over the falls. "Senior officers are to stay here. The rest of you go get some rest."

Zelenka reluctantly sent away all the new soldiers except for Ronan. She didn't bother asking permission for Palafair to stay; he merely stood by her side as he always did.

Under Nemez's strict guidance, the senior officers spent long hours restructuring the tilli army. At the end of it, Zelenka was placed in a leading role with the green soldiers. She was assigned a major from the old army to assist her and to take Ronan under her tutelage. Major Gainsley decided to go along with the army on their journey and was charged with training any new volunteers. She was sent from the meeting with an order to put out the call for new soldiers and prepare them for travel the next day.

The old army's structure was largely kept the same, but it was agreed that after the war, an effort would be made to better integrate the two groups. Zelenka hoped there would be enough of them left after fighting Fyren for this to come to fruition.

Chapter Thirty-Nine

Once Devon arrived safely down the mountain, his backside sore and his ego bruised, he was confined to his house except for school and chores at the farm. He had been allowed to leave his offering, a poem he wrote specifically for Mother Nature, and the prospect of a response to it kept him sane during his punishment.

A week later, he was released for his last bagball game, probably because his mother was tired of him moping around the house like a cranky bear, grumbling and eating and sleeping all day long. Despite the rainy weather and the nip in the air, nearly the whole town showed up to cheer on the teams. One notable exception was Pop Pop, who rarely missed a game, but wasn't there. It was a tight match that came down to the very last pitch. The pitcher heaved the round bean bag at Devon. He whacked it with the wooden paddle and sent it soaring deep into the outfield. Cheers of excitement egged him around the bases. Near the final bag, his teammate waved her arm in a wide circle to tell him to keep running. Devon slid as the bean bag was thrown to the opponent. It seemed like time stood still as he waited for the call from the umpire.

"Safe!"

They had won the game! Devon pumped his fist in the air as his teammates descended upon him in a heap of shouts and back slaps. They hoisted him in the air and chanted, "Champions! Champions!"

The adrenaline rush of being the hero of the game compensated for the lack of air to his lungs and he barely felt the tightness in his chest. It was times like this when his condition didn't matter, where it hadn't held him back. Emmaline Tine, his siblings' old baby-sitter, joined the fans rushing the field. His heart beat double-time as she slapped him on the back in congratulations.

As the excitement faded and his teammates dispersed, Devon wondered when he'd get that feeling back. This had been his last bagball game. What would he do now for a rush? He couldn't bear the thought of having days full of nothing but primeyear work ahead of him. He wanted to travel, to feel the rush of a hard-fought battle won.

The feeling of loss and emptiness followed him to Kase Farm where his family had gathered to celebrate the game. His sour mood painted everything a muted gray, keeping him on the outskirts of the laughter and revelry. The congratulations and handshakes barely registered. When Pop Pop finally showed up, it was with a pinched face as he searched the crowded house. Devon thought he had come looking for him, to offer up congratulations and an apology for missing the game, but Pop Pop's gaze found Grammy's from across the room and the two of them convened in a corner of the kitchen over a letter.

Devon huffily grabbed a plate of food and confined himself to Pop Pop's study. Old ash was all that remained in the fireplace and the room held a bitterness that matched Devon's mood. He lit one candle and fit himself into the high-backed chair in the corner farthest from the door. When his food was finished, he pulled the bean bag from his pocket, the one he had smashed into the outfield to win the game. He tossed it up in the air and caught it, a mindless game that kept him occupied enough not to dwell on the feelings rising up in his chest and threatening to come out as tears. Devon had always been so eager to make it to his primeyears that he hadn't taken much time to consider what it meant to move past his youngeryears.

The bean bag glanced off his hand and rolled behind the chair. He squeezed behind to retrieve it as the study door burst open. Devon gathered in his limbs and attempted to hide himself. He didn't really feel like talking to anyone and he might hear something to cheer his dreary mood if he stayed and silently listened.

"Shut the door, Ariana," came Pop Pop's voice. He continued only when the click of the door signaled a perceived privacy in the room, which was false because of Devon's hunkered form behind the chair. All the lectures from the last time he had been caught eavesdropping rang in Devon's head, and he considered showing himself, but he quickly reconsidered at Pop Pop's next words. "The news from Drim is bad. Anyone else need a drink?"

Devon heard murmurs, followed by a drawer sliding open, then the clink of glasses, and finally the popping of a cork.

Grammy gasped. "The seventy-four bubbly?"

"I'm tired of waiting to drink this, and I need something strong," said Pop Pop. Then came the sound of liquid pouring and the clink of glasses coming together.

The toast of "here, here" was said in somber voices, his mother's and Aunt Lili's among them.

"I've received bad news," Pop Pop said after a moment.

"It's not Katora, is it?" asked Ariana.

"Thank the Great Mother, no," said Pop Pop. Chairs squeaked and creaked as the others settled into seats. Someone sat in the high-back Devon hid behind, pushing it back ever so slightly so that it pressed against his chest uncomfortably. "It's from one of my contacts in Skimere," Pop Pop continued. "She's a brigha."

It was a word Devon had never heard, but the gasps that echoed around the room told him it was something special.

"You know a brigha?" Lili asked. She sounded near but not so close as to be the one in the high-back.

"Yes," Pop Pop said, likely from his desk chair. "But her magic is only known to a few."

"Does Katora know her?" Lili asked.

"No until recently," Pop Pop said. "Though maybe I should have introduced them sooner, as they seemed to have a run-in while Katora and the others were in Skimere. Nika—the brigha—didn't go into details, but it sounded harmless enough. A minor misunderstanding is how she categorized it."

"Did Katora mention it in any of her letters?" asked Grammy, who sounded like she was on the other side of the room. So that left Devon's mother as the one in the high-back.

"Last I heard from Katora, they were in Lughorn," said Pop Pop. "Well past Skimere and no mention of Nika."

Devon's mother cleared her throat loudly, confirming she was in the chair right in front of him. He practically held his breath trying to stay still. "Pop, what exactly is the news?"

"Right," said Pop Pop. "After sensing a large surge in magic from Drim, Nika sent out scouts to explore. She waited a fortnight plus a few extra days in case her scouts had been held up before writing to me. She fears the scouts are dead and something sinister is taking place at Drim."

The fire popped, otherwise the room was silent. Devon's breath shuddered and the air tickled his throat. He held back a cough. It seemed Nika had a means of sensing magic. Was that what a brigha did?

"What does that mean for us?" asked Grammy, her voice thick with concern. "And for Katora, Kylene, and Bhar?"

"I don't know," Pop Pop said. There was a long pause and the thud of a glass being set down, probably from Pop Pop taking another drink of the '74 bubbly. Devon's throat was dry, and he almost slipped out from behind the chair to get his own drink.

"There's more," Pop Pop continued. If Devon had thought the tension couldn't get any tighter, he had been wrong; the room felt ready to shatter with it. "Two tilli demicks stopped by the farm a few weeks ago to meet with me privately. They have been reading the signs as well, and their general wanted to know what we knew. The scouts said the main part of their army went missing after Katora and the others left the Three River Split with Zelenka and haven't been heard from since. The general sent Zelenka and Palafair out to find the army, and they haven't returned yet." Pop Pop fell silent, and Devon imagined him rubbing his chin as he did when troubled. "All these signs and reports are pointing to war... for all of us."

"What do we need to do?" asked his mother.

"We continue stockpiling supplies," said Pop Pop. His voice changed volume slightly as he spoke, as if he were pacing across the hearth. "And we prepare for whatever comes. The strength of the magic Nika sensed says that whoever—whatever—is at Drim is a formidable opponent. I'll send letters to all my contacts throughout the Great Peninsula." Pop Pop's voice continued to waver in volume. "I wish there was a way to get in touch with Palafair and Zelenka, but finding them deep in Faway Forest is beyond my reach. The best I can do is send a message to the tilli general at the Split."

"I'll go to Drim if it comes to war," said Devon's mother.

Devon's heart pounded in his chest as he forced his imaginative brain *not* to think of what could happen to his mother in war.

"Me too," declared Lili.

With clenched fists, Devon added his own silent vow to be among those who marched to war.

"All too many of us will," said Grammy in a very quiet voice. "But who will we be fighting?"

Pop Pop sighed and the whole room felt like it deflated. "All signs point to Fyren the Fallen."

A smack, like a loud clap, issued from the spot where Devon's mother sat. "That sorry excuse for a greater being. I'll be ready for him."

"We all need to be ready," Pop Pop said. "I have letters to write. You should all go back to the guests and celebrate Devon's win while we still have something to celebrate."

The three women shuffled out of the study, while Pop Pop— and the hidden Devon—remained. A shiver of excitement mixed with a tingle of fear ran through Devon. Squished and uncomfortable as he was, he was willing to make that sacrifice a little longer in order to keep his secret and scheme his way to glory.

* * * *

The first morning post being grounded, Devon woke to a whispered hush of a world. He couldn't explain why it felt so quiet; all he knew was that an eerie calm surrounded his warm bed and no one else in the house seemed to be awake. He rolled over and without getting out of bed, glanced out the window to see a world of white. A thick layer of snow blanketed every surface, and it was still coming down hard.

Devon sighed. So much for finally getting out. It was how his luck always seemed to play out; the weather didn't care that he had finally been granted his freedom. All the weather cared about was whether it was sending a message from the higher beings. Devon shot out of bed, nearly banging his head on the sloped ceiling.

The higher beings. The snow. It must be a message.

In socks, he darted down two flights of stairs and slammed out the front door. He cocked his head in the direction of Capdon Mountain and listened hard. The quiet kiss of tiny flakes was all that greeted him. The snow melted under him, soaking his socks and feet, as he stood outside and listened for many minutes.

"Devon!" his sister yelled from the threshold. "What are you doing out there? You're letting all the snow in." Skylynn grabbed him by the shirt, pulled him inside, and slammed the door shut. Wrapping her woolly robe tight around her midsection, she headed into the kitchen and muttered, "Idiot."

Devon shook himself out of the snowy trance and ran up to his room to change into dry clothes. When he got back downstairs, his father and brother had joined Skylynn and the teakettle was on the stove.

The front door banged open and his mother came into the kitchen, her arms full of logs for the fireplace. As she brushed snow from her hair and cloak, she said, "Why was it all wet by the front door?"

"That was Devon," Skylynn tattled. "I found him standing on the front porch in his jammies with his mouth hanging open." She giggled. "The door was wide open. Were you trying to catch snowflakes in your mouth?" She batted her eyelashes innocently, but Devon knew better than to fall for the act.

"More like trying to catch your death," his mother said. "Put your cloak on and bring in more wood. Then you can mop up the mess you made."

He grumbled all the way to the woodpile, but then he

stopped and listened again. A slight breeze kicked up and brought with it a hissing. His heart leaped into his throat and he stood perfectly still, straining his ears for whatever quest the higher beings saw for him. The noise intensified to a high-pitched whistle. A deep blush crept up his neck when he realized it was the teakettle boiling inside his own kitchen. He swept snow off the woodpile with angry swats and carried a big pile into the house. After drying the floor by the door, Devon grabbed some toast and a mug of tepid tea and stomped up to his room to brood.

The last time it had snowed in Tussar, Katora, Kylene, Bhar, Palafair, and Hirsten had gone on a quest. Before that it hadn't snowed in Tussar for hundreds of years. Devon slammed a fist into the opposite hand and growled. This snow *had* to mean something. He hoped that something was for him.

He hid out in his room all morning, pretending to read for school, but his mind kept wandering out the window to the snow. Just in case the higher beings were having trouble finding him, he popped open the window an inch. It was almost lunchtime before anything other than the soft fall of snowflakes reached his ears. A jingle of bells roused Devon from his pretend studying and had him flying down the stairs once more.

But it was only Pop Pop arriving in the wagon that was outfitted with runners instead of wheels. "I could use some help at the farm today," he said to his three grandchildren. "Who wants to come back with me? Grammy's making her famous hot chocolate."

No one could resist the chocolate brew, not even a primeyear. Everyone but his father bundled up and piled into the wagon. The clop of the horse's feet and the slosh of snow under the runners made it impossible for Devon to keep an ear out for a message, but the higher beings knew Kase Farm well, having delivered messages there before. It was with hope in his heart that he sank back into the wagon seat and allowed himself to catch a snowflake in his mouth. It was nearly impossible to be in a bad mood when he was headed for the rich taste of Grammy's hot chocolate.

Chapter Forty

The bickering between Katora and Tarq began not long after they entered Blanchardwood. Tarq refused to give them a timeline on when they should expect to arrive at Kristalis, and Katora claimed Tarq was a fraud who didn't know what he was doing. It got worse as the days wore on and the cold pushed everyone to their breaking points.

This latest fight culminated in a shouting match where Katora gave Kylene, Bhar, and Hirsten an ultimatum. "I'm going this way. Come with me or go with Tarq, but I'm leaving." She squeezed between two evergreens, leaving behind only footprints.

Kylene was now faced with choosing between Tarq, the navigation expert on Blanchardwood, and her sister, who had never set foot in the foreboding forest before this journey. She chose her sister.

With a desperate pinch in her eyes, Kylene took a look back at Tarq. Under a thick layer of wool, his face was impossible to read, but he shrugged as if to say, "It's your ticket to the afterlife."

The dogged snow turned heavy as night fell. Kylene, Bhar, Hirsten, and Katora huddled around a wet pile of sticks while Bhar fruitlessly tried to light them.

Katora grabbed the box of matches from Bhar. "Let me try." Like all the other attempts, this one failed. She threw the box of matches and the whole pile spilled out onto the wet snow. Kylene fell to her knees and picked up every single one, but they were all too wet to bother trying again. Usually her sister's bouts of reckless anger didn't bother Kylene because they usually only hurt Katora. But to go the whole night without a fire in this miserably cold woods was a daunting—maybe deadly—prospect.

"Great job," said Bhar, his tone laced with sarcasm. "Now what do we do?"

"We try and get some sleep, that's what," Katora snapped

back.

"Is it safe without a fire?" Kylene asked. The heavy snow and the darkness made it hard to see each other within their own little circle of people, never mind outside of it.

"We haven't seen a single threat since we entered the forest. We'll be fine." Katora had a quick answer for everything. It could be tiresome in the best of times, and this was anything but the best of times.

Bhar once again beat Kylene to replying, "Great Mother, you're insufferable! First, you make us leave our guide, and now you're forcing us to go all night without a fire."

"The weather's not *my* fault," Katora said. "And Tarq's the one who is insufferable."

Hirsten's head bounced back and forth, watching the two argue, while Kylene waited with bated breath. Any word from her and it would seem like she was taking sides.

"What's next, Katora?" Bhar pointed a finger right at her face. "You gonna summon Fyren here to take us out of our misery?"

"Enough!" yelled Kylene, her fists balled tight underneath her gloves. She grew colder by the minute, and her siblings' bickering was giving her a headache that rivaled the pain in her arm. "We'll find a tree to shelter under." It was hard to detect in the rapidly falling snow, but Kylene spied the dark outline of a large evergreen against the slate night sky. "Bhar, carry the sticks we gathered to that tree over there."

She was surprised when he immediately followed her orders. The bottom branches of the tree were so low, they had to crawl to get underneath, but the branches proved a nice cover from the snow and radiated their body heat back at them.

Bhar cut a few large boughs for them to lay on. Kylene was sandwiched in between her brother and Hirsten. It would have been almost comfortable if it hadn't been freezing.

"I'll take first watch," Katora volunteered.

"You bet you will," Kylene said. "And you'll try lighting the fire again until it's time to wake Bhar up for next watch." Hirsten shot her a wink, and a blush warmed her neck, though her face was too numb from the cold to feel much of anything. As Kylene drifted off to an uneasy sleep, she wondered vaguely if she should take charge more often.

* * * *

Kylene was woken up by Hirsten a few hours before dawn. There was a small fire outside of their burrow under the evergreen tree.

"Katora got it going last night," Hirsten explained.

"She has a long way to go to make up for leaving Tarq." Kylene huddled up as close to the fire as she could without singing the furs and let out a contented sigh as the warmth hit her freezing bones.

"She shouldn't have made us choose," Hirsten said, "but we could've stayed with Tarq."

"Could we have?" Ky gave him a pointed look.

"I guess not. Us Kases stick together, even when it means following someone so hardheaded."

She laughed out loud and wasn't sure whether she was more surprised about Hirsten calling himself a Kase or about him calling Katora hardheaded. "Get some sleep, Hirsten. We've got a long day ahead of us."

She snuggled into her furs and waited for light to reach the woods. It finally did a few tired hours later, muted behind a wall of high clouds. As dim as the sky was, the snow felt too bright, casting everything in a surreal glow. A shadow darted out from beneath a nearby tree. Kylene clutched the handle of her sheathed dagger while the nondescript grayness crept closer. The shadow stepped close enough to be illuminated by the firelight, and Kylene recognized the sleek, auburn body of a fox—the very one who had visited her several times on this journey.

Its eyes met hers, and it beckoned her with a flick of its head. Then it bound off. It left no footprints, as if it were flying over the snow rather than running through it. Kylene cast one glance at her sleeping companions before leaping up and chasing after the fox, sending off a silent prayer to Mother Nature that she wouldn't regret the rash moment.

Tears from the cold clung in Kylene's eyes as she ran, blurring her vision. A few leaked from her face faster than they could freeze and flew behind her as the fox picked up the pace. Abruptly it ran behind a particularly large pine tree. Kylene followed, but it was gone by the time she reached the other side. She circled the large expanse of the pine tree's low branches until she met back up with her own footprints.

A leaden weight filled her chest at having lost the fox. A light panting turned her around, and her chest lightened at the sight of the fox. Its auburn eyes burned with an intense gaze. There was sentience behind them, that was for sure, but the creature offered no sign of emotion. Kylene wished it would speak and let her know why in the Great Mother's name it kept popping up in the strangest of places, and only when she was alone. She blew a raspberry, tears clinging to her eyelashes, threatening to freeze. Then she laughed at the absurdity of the situation. The fox's face turned down into a frown and that only made her laugh harder.

It showed a bejeweled tongue, adorned with smooth, round pearls this time. Then the fox slipped its tongue back into its mouth and bounded away. And still it left no footprints in the snow.

"Bye, you mangy beast!" Kylene called after it.

"Is that any way to talk to the guide you abandoned and who is now here to put you back on track?" came a voice from behind.

Kylene jumped and whirled around to find Tarq glaring at her. "Great Mother!" she yelled. "You scared me." Somewhere along this journey she had stopped caring about using Mother Nature's name as a curse.

"Not as badly as you scared the whole of Blanchardwood with your shouting." The words had a hint of teasing to them, even as his face stayed serious, though Kylene knew better than to think Tarq was actually teasing her.

"There's nothing in this wood to scare, save Katora, Hirsten, and Bhar...and you," she added. She didn't dare mention the fox. She wasn't entirely sure she wasn't hallucinating these encounters with the strange creature, perhaps as a side effect of having been poisoned. If her arm hurt all this time later, what was to say the poison wasn't affecting her mind as well? "Why are you here? I thought you were leaving the woods."

"I decided to stick around. I was hired to do a job, and I'm ready to do it once Katora is ready to accept my help." Tarq looked around at the frozen wasteland of nothing but snow and trees. "Where are the others? You shouldn't be out here alone."

She would have been touched by his concern if she thought it extended beyond him earning his wage.

"They're not far." She followed her single set of footprints back toward their shared bed under the evergreen. Tarq followed silently, walking slightly behind rather than at her side, which she found incredibly irritating.

Snow began to fall again, a light shower, the tiny flakes replacing the tears on her eyelashes. Her face felt raw and frozen, a feeling that extended to her fingers and toes. Kylene didn't hate many things, but Blanchardwood was finding its way to the top of that list.

"What were you yelling at?" Tarq broke the silence, proving not talking had been better.

"None of your business," Kylene said.

"Seriously, what were you yelling at?" he persisted.

Breathing in the frigid air in attempt to calm herself, Kylene shook her head and refused to answer.

He grabbed her and spun her around to face him, which he wouldn't have had to do if he had been walking next to her in the first place. She sucked in a breath to keep from yelping out in pain and resisted the urge to rub her arm. He may not have known about her injury, but that didn't excuse his actions.

"Don't touch me." Her voice was low, dangerous.

"Sorry." Tarq held up his hands in apology, backing up to give her space. His eyes crinkled in concern, and Kylene was pleased to see she had unnerved him for once. "I...uh..."

"What?" Kylene kept the edge to her voice.

"I shouldn't have grabbed you." Underneath his many layers of clothing, Kylene saw his chest rise in a deep breath, the air puffing out in a cloud of smoke. "Blanchardwood isn't a place to be messing around in. It's dangerous, full of magic. I need to know everything if we're going to make it to the Ice Queen safely."

The wind blew and the snow swirled up from the ground in soft eddies. It reminded Kylene of the plains, right before the magical storm struck. She shivered, wondering if magic was stirring now.

"I thought I saw something, but it turned out to be nothing." Kylene's stomach twisted with the lie. "You should worry about Katora, not me. She's the one who will decide whether or not to follow you...and whether or not to pay you."

"I think she'll have realized she's let all of you suffer enough." Tarq was back to being full of himself. At least he seemed to also have forgotten about interrogating Kylene.

They had reached the spot where the others were burrowed under the evergreen branches. Kylene was relieved to see they were asleep and she hadn't been caught wandering off.

"I guess we'll find out." Kylene slipped under the branches and shook Katora awake. She didn't care much for Tarq and his attitude, but she would do her best to convince Katora to let him guide them. The quicker they were out of Blanchardwood, the better.

Chapter Forty-One

Kristalis seemed to appear out of nowhere. One minute Kylene and her companions were trudging through deep snow, surrounded by evergreens and swirling snowflakes. The next minute the trees parted and the snowfall cleared just enough for the sun to peek through the clouds. Light bounced off crystal towers in the distance, a shower of prisms glittering from the turrets. Kylene's breath caught. Her heart ached for the one other place where the buildings shone like a riot of rainbows—a place not of this world. The Golden City.

Thick clouds rolled back over the sun and the kaleidoscope of colors disappeared. The palace was gorgeous, but it no longer reminded Kylene of the otherworldly city, and her lungs once more filled with cold air.

A wide, frozen river stood between them and Kristalis. The initial freeze must have occurred quickly because the ice had captured the waves mid-undulation. It was a treacherous crossing, but they arrived unscathed at an expanse of crunchy snow that led to the palace grounds.

An icy pathway went around either side of a fountain, the ice cascading down in jagged formations. A handful of steps led up to a translucent double-door shining from the inside out with cold white light. The walls of the palace were covered in frost, and it was hard to tell if there was stone underneath or more ice. The windows were made of the same foggy glass as the doors, and although light seeped through, it was impossible to see what lay beyond. Tall towers spiked up high toward the sky in an impressive manner that was not the least bit inviting.

"It's smaller than I thought it would be," Bhar quipped, his breath puffing out with the words. "Shall we knock? I hope I don't break the ice." He chuckled and held up a gloved fist.

"As if you could," Katora remarked. She marched around the

fountain to the entrance, her sure-footed steps showing no indication that the ground was a sheet of ice. Kylene followed at more of a glide than a walk, and the boys slip-slid their way to the stairs.

They crowded in around Katora, who removed a glove and rapped on the door with bare knuckles. The dull thud of flesh and bone on ice was barely loud enough to be heard over the whipping wind, but the side-by-side doors creaked open to reveal a grand entryway.

"I guess the Ice Queen was expecting us," said Bhar, and he walked right in. The others followed, Kylene tentatively bringing up the rear as the Ice Queen's message echoed in her head.

Despite the large size of the room, they stay huddled close together. The inside of the palace was slightly more inviting than the outside, but mostly because it provided shelter from the elements. The floor was made of rippled stone slabs that were so massive they looked like they were ripped off a mountain and plopped down by giants. The walls were a light gray stone on the inside. An arched double staircase, made of the same gray stone as the floor, climbed up on either side of the entryway, giving access to an open balcony on the second floor. Wide fireplaces were built directly into the stone walls on both sides of the room. It was all very bleak and drab, which made what was underneath the open arch of the staircases all the more spectacular.

Brilliant green vines curled out from the open archway, invading the somber space. Flowers the size of Kylene's head were in full bloom, bursting in rich crimsons, dark violets, and delicate periwinkles. Behind those was an array of other flowers—irises, daisies, essenberry vines, honeysuckle, calla lilies, asters, and a host of other plants Kylene couldn't name. They were from all different growing seasons and blossomed in colors too vibrant to feel real. It was the natural beauty of spring, summer, and fall in one garden, plunked right down in the middle of the forest of perpetual winter.

A soft breeze blew across the room, and with it came a banquet of scents, sweet and succulent. Drawn to the heavenly garden, Kylene found herself walking toward it. She reached the entryway to find not a covered courtyard as she had expected but one open to the elements. By some magic, it wasn't the frigid air and snow of Blanchardwood that greeted her. The atmosphere was thick and humid, and a bright sun shone down out of a clear blue sky. Kylene stepped out and pulled the heavy fur-lined hood from her head. She let the warmth hit her wind-burned face; it was glorious after so many days in the relentless snow and wind. She closed her eyes and breathed in the tapestry of scents.

It was impossible to pick out once among the many, and they came together to assault her nose with an overwhelming bouquet of woody soil and sweet honey. A trickle from a nearby water feature added a musical quality. A breeze blew through the courtyard and brought with it the rustle of flower petals, leaves, and vines. Kylene's hair danced around her face, tickling her cheeks.

A gentle touch that she barely felt through her thick coat startled her, and she yelped like a dog whose tail had been stepped on. Kylene blinked in the sunlight. The form of an ethereal woman coalesced in front of her. No, not a woman. The Ice Queen herself.

The greater being was dressed in a long-sleeved white gown embellished with diamonds. Kylene stared past the glare of jewels and realized they weren't diamonds at all but snowflakes that adorned not only the queen's dress, but her dark hair and skin so that she glittered. A fuzzy white muff hung from her neck. Bare toes poked out from underneath the floor-length dress.

"Your Greatness." Kylene did an awkward curtsy underneath her many layers of clothing.

"I see you are enjoying my garden, Kase daughter. It is called Last Spring."

Not sure of the proper protocol when meeting the Queen of Blanchardwood, Kylene cast her gaze to the lush grass that blanketed the ground. "It is a wonder, Your Greatness."

The queen lifted Kylene's chin. "You may call me Odeletta, so long as I may call you by your given name." Odeletta paused, waiting for Kylene to share her name.

She cleared her throat. "Kylene is my name." As an afterthought she added, "Though my family calls me Ky."

The queen smiled. "Ky it is." The simple nickname sounded special in Odeletta's resonant, yet kind, voice.

Catching a glimpse of movement in the corner of her eye, Kylene saw her companions standing on threshold of the garden. Katora's right eyebrow was raised so high it was practically jumping off her forehead. Hirsten sported his closed-mouth grin. Bhar's jaw hung open, his mouth a gaping hole of disbelief. The three of them were amazed, and perhaps a little impressed, with Kylene. But Tarq was another story. His mouth was pressed together in a grim line, and his eyes were narrowed in suspicion.

Kylene wondered what she had done wrong this time. Had she broken some etiquette rule for meeting a greater being? Did she have snow in her hair? Bird poop? What was it about Kylene that no matter what she did, it sent Tarq into a fit of moodiness?

Odeletta turned to the others. "There will be ample time to admire my garden. You are cold and tired. Your rooms are up the stairs and to the right. A hot meal will be in the dining room when you are ready."

Then she walked deeper into the garden, slipped behind a bush, and left not a single bent blade of grass behind to mark her presence.

Chapter Forty-Two

When the meeting to restructure the tilli army ended, Zelenka asked Nemez for a word as everyone else trickled out of the cave for their various duties. She waved to Palafair to let him know she needed a few minutes.

"General," she said, "I hope it was not insubordinate of me to make a deal with the sciathilte without your permission."

"You were in the field and the ranking officer, it was within your rights to make such a call." Zelenka would have been relieved at his answer if it hadn't been for the contemplative look Nemez gave her. "I have had some time to think about your place among the tilli. By rights, the role of Roodesh is yours."

"I never—" she began before being cut off.

"I know you are not fond of the name, but the right to lead remains yours." He pinned her with a piercing gaze. "Our people have had a chance to understand what you did, and those who have not yet forgiven you will with time."

"It is not a matter of forgiveness." Zelenka found she could not meet his eyes.

"No? Then what is it a matter of?"

"I cannot help but wonder if the role of Roodesh corrupts the mind." She shuffled her feet on the cave floor and glanced out the opening, the falls shining in the moonlight. "Both of the most recent Roodeshes went mad. I do not want to tempt fate."

"A name does not make one go mad," Nemez said with a rare softness to his voice.

"But power can." That was the root of her worry. What if it was in her blood to go mad with power? With so much power in their hands, it was the one thing the Roodeshes couldn't control—their mortality—and that helplessness had driven them over the edge. Zelenka was afraid she would do the same if she became leader of the tilli, under the name of Roodesh or not.

"It can." Nemez placed a hand on her shoulder, and she met his eyes. "But that does not mean it has to."

"No," she said softly.

"There is no law that says you have to take over as leader." Nemez was back to his usual stoic self. "We can hold an election for a new leader once this all settles down if that is what you wish."

If that was what *she* wished, so he was putting it in her hands. What would she do with that kind of power? The answer to that question had left her awake many nights. She nodded to Nemez and headed off to find Palafair.

* * * *

The flight over Faway Forest to Tussar proved quicker than Zelenka could ever have imagined before meeting the sciathilte. The cool autumn wind slapped her in the face as they neared the town where Palafair had lived with the Kases for most of his life. While the forest was painted with the vibrant golds and scarlets of fall, Tussar was covered in a deep layer of bright white snow. The forest and town were divided by a distinct line, separating autumn from winter—or rather false winter, probably caused by a greater being. The breeze turned frigid as Indy carried Zelenka and Palafair across the border.

The tilli numbers had swelled by about twenty of very old and very young volunteers who hadn't joined in the previous round of recruitment. Among them were several seasoned veterans that would be great assets for their experience, if not for their aging bodies. The very young would be taught to do things like resupply the weapons, cook the meals, and set up camp, and hopefully wouldn't end up as liabilities on the actual battlefield—should they be allowed there when the time came to fight. Zelenka was glad those decisions were Gainsley's to make and not hers.

Aside from a few soldiers who had been left behind to guard the Three River Split, the entire tilli army, plus Palafair, swooped into Tussar on the shining backs of the mythical sciathilte, now honorary members of the army. The colorful swarm brightened the bleak winter landscape.

As word of the sciathilte's arrival swept across town, humans and anni demicks alike stopped their work to gape wide-mouthed at the brilliant sight, their awe evident from Zelenka's view from above. Indy landed in a foot of snow on a field at Kase Farm. It was large enough for the whole swarm to land. The sciathiltes' bodies, wings, and heads were well above the snow. However, it was a different story for Zelenka and Palafair when they slid off the creature. The snow was up to their faces and they had to quickly push their way through and stand in a space Indy had cleared for them. Zelenka hadn't counted on there being snow, never mind a foot of it.

"Stay mounted!" she yelled, hoping her words made it out of the mound and up to her comrades. Murmuring came from above and it seemed word was getting around as no other tilli attempted to tackle the snow.

Huddled close together in the tiny carving in the snow, Palafair asked Zelenka, "What now?"

Then they heard a familiar voice shout, "Palafair? Zelenka? Are you out there?"

Palafair climbed up the back of Indy, expertly navigating his way around the stinger. "Pop! Over here!" He waved his arms as his legs clung to the body. From her vantage point below, it looked to Zelenka that Palafair was an extra set of wings.

Zelenka heard the muffled shuffle of Pop making his way from the farmhouse through the field, a much easier feat for a human than a demick in the current conditions.

"Great Mother," said Pop. "Where did you all come from?" Zelenka had a feeling that he was referring to the creatures making up half their group and not the sheer size of it. Then his gaze fell on Zelenka, who was shivering in the snow, despite her best efforts not to. "Never mind that. I'll make a path to one of the barns. It should fit all the demicks, though perhaps not your friends."

"Sciathilte," Zelenka supplied.

"Indeed they are." For his part, Pop was doing a better job than most at hiding his shock. Zelenka supposed he had seen a lot of amazing things in his former role as guardian of the Elixir.

"We require no roof above our wings," Indy buzzed. "We will wait here."

Pop returned with a wide shovel and swept a path to a faded red barn on the west side of the farm.

"Follow me!" Zelenka shouted to the army. Her leg was particularly stiff, and she limped her way to the sanctuary of the barn, hoping it was a little warmer than outside.

Chapter Forty-Three

Inside the faded red barn, the air was crisp and had a faint hint of rotted fruit. Other than a few barrels in the corner, it was empty. Shafts of light shone through the cracks in between the wooden siding, illuminating the tiny dust motes that were disturbed as the tilli demicks filled the barn. Much to Zelenka's disappointment, it was not much warmer than outside.

Pop waited by the sliding door until the last of the demicks entered. "I'll be right back," he said before dashing off to the farmhouse.

General Nemez found his way to Zelenka. He blew into his hands before slapping them together several times. "Snow in Tussar, and it is not even the winter solstice yet."

"It is a bad omen," Major Gainsley said.

"Or a message from the greater beings," said Palafair. "The last time it snowed here, it was a message for Popadoro Kase."

"I am telling you," Gainsley insisted, "snow before the winter solstice is a bad omen."

Nemez rubbed his hands together vigorously, distractedly. "Enough prognosticating. The snow is of no concern to us, so long as it does not slow us down. And it should not with the aid of the sciathilte."

Perhaps one day Zelenka wouldn't feel a rush of glee in her stomach when Gainsley was dismissed by Nemez, but today was not that day. There were far too many things to worry about to bother with gloating.

Pop returned with a tray of food and tea and set it on the floor. "There's more coming. I'm sorry we don't have better accommodations. We'll figure something out if you plan on staying the night."

"No need," Nemez said. "We do not plan on being here long. What we do need is to discuss our plans regarding this threat at

Drim."

Nemez then looked to Zelenka to explain the nature of her conversation with Yeselda and the Watcher and how they believed Fyren was building an army at Drim. She concluded by saying, "We feel it is time to go on the offensive against Fyren."

"I agree," said Pop, surprising her with his quick response. She had expected more resistance to the idea of calling out their foe. Then Pop explained about the information from his brigha contact and his quick agreement made sense.

Farmhands, including a few of the Kase grandchildren, arrived with more food and beverages, effectively halting the conversation.

"Eat up," Nemez told the tilli. "We will be leaving soon."

Ma joined Pop and the tilli leaders that had gathered around Nemez. She swept Palafair up in a hug and shook Zelenka's hand.

While the tilli ate, Zelenka took the opportunity to discreetly return the small vial of Elixir to Pop. She understood its usefulness, but that didn't make her comfortable with having it, and she felt better as soon as Pop slipped it into his pocket out of sight.

"Thank you for your help, Devon," Pop said to his grandson, who had been lurking within earshot. "Go check on the sciathilte to make sure they don't need anything." He waited for Devon to leave before saying, "Such a meddler that one. He'd be storming Drim if I let him, and his mother would have my head for it." He sat next to the tray he had brought and offered tea around before pouring a cup for himself. "You must tell me where you ran into the sciathilte."

Everyone looked to Zelenka. As the tilli enjoyed their meal, she regaled Ma and Pop with her tale of the Watcher's riddle of following her ears and how she had done just that to discover the swarm. At Palafair's insistence, she also told the story of how they had found the missing army. Suddenly ravenous, Zelenka swiped an essenberry muffin from the tray.

Pop stroked his chin, his blue eyes alight. "Amazing! And to think the sciathilte have been in Faway Forest all this time, and the lost tilli army asleep in Hillock, by Yeselda's magic nonetheless." His expression turned dark with his next words. "I'm afraid we must turn our attention back to the matter of Fyren. The trick will be to convince everyone of the threat. There have been rumors circulating across the land, but nothing so concrete as to convince others to take up arms. And there is the matter of getting word out to all the cities of the Great Peninsula. It is no small feat to gather an army of people." He seemed lost in thought for a moment. "And what of your plans on Demick Island?"

Nemez finished chewing a bite of his muffin and took a sip of tea. "We hope to gather more allies in our campaign against Fyren."

"Has anyone been in contact with them since coming here?" Pop asked. When Nemez shook his head no, all Pop gave was a thoughtful "hmmm" before pivoting to the next topic. "Did Yeselda or the Watcher mention their plans?"

"Nothing useful aside from the warning about Fyren," Zelenka said. "I am sure you know how they like to talk in circles. They seemed worried, right Palafair?" He was such a good study on how others' were behaving, though the greater beings were difficult to read.

"As worried as a greater being can seem," Palafair agreed. "I think they have plans to act against Fyren, but what those are is a mystery to me."

Pop nodded as Zelenka dug into a second muffin. They were delicious, setting her taste buds salivating with every bite. Pop looked to Ma, and they had a silent conversation with their eyes. Ma finally nodded, her mouth set in a grim line.

"While you rally the demicks, we will work on rallying the humans," Pop said. "I'll try to send word to Katora, and I'll contact all my associates in Skimere, Lughorn, and the smaller towns. We won't wait for answers. We'll leave as soon as we can gather our supplies."

"How is Katora faring?" Palafair asked.

"We last heard that they were leaving Lughorn with a guide and heading to Blanchardwood to seek out the Ice Queen," Pop said. "I hope they found her..."

The sentiment hung heavy in the dusty air, and Zelenka was glad to have the last of the muffin to distract her from thinking too hard about what was happening with Katora, Kylene, Bhar, and Hirsten. She had a complicated relationship with the Kases and their role with the Elixir, but she also had a great deal of respect and admiration for them; dare she admit she cared for them. "We should meet near Drim with our armies, and convey that plan to Katora."

"Yes," agreed Pop. "I imagine you and the sciathilte will travel faster than us, especially with this snow. I hope I can get a message to Katora."

A small rush of wind swept by the group, turning heads to see where it had come from. Nothing looked amiss, so they continued with their planning. They hashed out a timeline for how long it would take Pop and company to travel north through Skimere, recruiting along the way. They built in extra time for others to come from all over the Great Peninsula. Then they would all meet on Bad Beach, the peninsula across from Drim, to launch their attack on Fyren. How many would come was a big question mark of worry. But all that worry shifted when the barn doors flew open.

A larger than life figure was silhouetted in the fading sunlight. A ripple of fear went through Zelenka as she couldn't make sense of what she was seeing. Then the figure took a step into the barn and revealed itself to be two different creatures, one large and one small. The larger figure was Indy, and the smaller one was Devon Kase, Pop's lurking grandson who had been dismissed from the barn.

The youngeryear cleared his throat. "Uh, I couldn't help but overhear that you need to send a message to Katora quickly."

"Couldn't help but overhear?" Pop's knowing tone indicated he knew exactly what Devon had been up to.

"We tilli do not take kindly to eavesdroppers," Zelenka said in a serious voice as she took a step toward the boy, forcing him back into the barn wall. He was much taller than she was, but

Zelenka knew how to intimidate. Not that she would ever actually do anything beyond scare him.

"I'm sorry Miss Zelenka." He took in a wheezy breath and coughed. He appeared sufficiently upset, so Zelenka backed off.

The sciathilte took another step into the barn. "I fail to see how the young human erred if he has a solution to your problem."

Pop opened his mouth to explain, but Zelenka cut him off with a tug on his sleeve. He nodded and acquiesced the floor to her. "Never mind that. What solution has Devon offered?"

"The young human pointed out what we know," said Indy. "We can take the required messages faster than any human means."

"Yes, that would give us the best chance of getting it there in time," Pop said. "Of course, as long as that works for you, General Nemez."

"It does," Nemez agreed. "Let us all move forward with our plans."

"I'll prepare the letters," Pop said. "My invitation to stay the night stands as it seems we've run out of daylight." While they had strategized, the sun had set and the world outside had begun to darken. "The sciathilte are welcome to the cleared fields on the west of the property."

"Thank you," said Nemez. "I was hoping to leave today, but it would not be wise to attempt a crossing of the Narrow Pass during the night."

"I agree, General," said Zelenka. He hadn't specifically asked for her opinion, but he had looked to her when he said it. She had become accustomed to being his second and agreeing or challenging him as necessary, and Nemez's assertion that Zelenka was entitled to be the next tilli leader had only bolstered this thought. Nemez simply nodded in acknowledgment.

Indy departed, and Nemez sent the officers to organize the army for the night.

"As for you, my dear grandson." Pop put his arm around Devon. "You can come back to the house and we can discuss privacy."

Palafair chuckled as Pop, Ma, and Devon left the barn. "I do not envy the lad. I hope Pop remembers what it was like to be an eager youngeryear."

Zelenka narrowed her eyes at the impending darkness outside the barn. "War is no place for a child, especially one who cannot follow orders." She clamped her mouth shut as she thought about how that statement could apply to her own affairs.

"It certainly is not," Palafair said quietly, but Zelenka barely heard as she moved away to help the rest of the tilli prepare for the night.

Chapter Forty-Four

Devon couldn't believe his eyes as he watched the tilli fly into Tussar on the sciathilte. He would have been less surprised if they had ridden on dragons. At least there had been rumors of dragon sightings north of the Appachian Mountain Range centuries ago. Sciathilte were a myth, never before seen, not even a rumor of their existence passed down from the previous generations.

Standing next to one was like being in a dream, and having one offer to help him convey his brilliant plan to Pop Pop would have bordered on delusional if it hadn't actually been the truth. Not that it helped much.

Pop Pop liked the idea of the sciathilte taking the messages to Katora and to the towns and cities of the Great Peninsula, but instead of pat on the back, all he earned was a lecture on eavesdropping and an order to return to the farm in the morning to help make breakfast for the tilli army. On the wagon ride home, his mom picked up where Pop Pop had left off. While Skylynn and Landon tittered in the back, Devon sat up front and endured his second lecture of the day, his mom's voice never wavering, not even when they hit a giant hole in the road, lurching forward in their seats.

When two iridescent green sciathilte rose out from the trees and into the sky, that finally quieted his mom. A hush fell over the road—probably the whole town. The sunset tinged the sky a light pink, offsetting the magnificent creatures' sparkling forms. They twinkled in the waning light, like stars popping up in the evening sky, as they flew north. The wind stilled as if mesmerized by the sight. Devon's breaths came in shallow puffs as he watched the sciathilte turn smaller and smaller until they finally disappeared completely. His mom let out a long sigh, and he heard her whisper, "Wow."

Then his brother and sister were elbowing each other for

space, his mom was telling him once again that it was not appropriate to eavesdrop, and the enchantment of the moment was squashed like an essenberry in the juice extractor.

"You can go right to your room," she told him as they pulled up to the house. "And I'm not bringing you to the farm in the morning. You can get up early and walk there."

Devon knew he should say "yes, ma'am" or stay silent, but he couldn't help himself. He hopped off the wagon and slipped in a few last words. "Good. It'll be fun."

Not his most eloquent response, but he slammed the door shut before his mom could respond...or punish him further. Too bad his dad was sitting in the living room reading by the fire. "Don't slam the door!" he yelled. "And take off your shoes!"

Devon flipped his shoes toward the front door and thundered up the stairs to the sanctuary of his bedroom. He hated how the low ceilings forced him to duck his head to slide into bed, but the space was all his. He stared at the wall as the world darkened outside and the sounds of the house drifted through the floors up to his room. He didn't bother to light a lantern or candle and let the darkness heighten his other senses. His pillow was warm against his head. His breathing was calm and clear. A muffled shout from Landon and his mother's angry response wafted up. There was the clink of dishes and the smell of ham cooking for dinner. He lay on his bed and let it all wash over him.

And in his head he schemed. Tomorrow he would convince Pop Pop to let him travel to Bad Beach and fight in the war against Fyren. He would do more than convince him, he would make Pop Pop see how his unique perspective was necessary for victory.

* * * *

The next morning Devon's mom banged on his bedroom door as the sun rose. "It's time to get up!" she yelled in a sing-songy voice.

"Ugh," he groaned. The argument he had so meticulously practiced last night was caught in the cobwebs of grogginess. He rolled out of bed and stomped down the two flights of stairs, not caring if he woke his siblings. Why should they get to sleep when he couldn't? He grabbed a leftover slice of ham and headed out the door without a word to his mom, wrapping his cloak around him and pulling the hood up against the frosty morning.

The fresh air cleared his head, and he went over the speech he had prepared to give Pop Pop as he jogged to the farm. The road was slushy with melting snow and the bottom of his cloak was soaked by the time he reached the farmhouse. With little sympathy for his soggy state, Grammy greeted him at the door and sent him right to the kitchen. Devon was soaked in sweat by the time he had finished scrambling up dozens of eggs, buttering mounds of toast, and hustling out to the barn where the tilli had slept. He never even saw Pop Pop. After more trips to the barn than he cared to count, the tilli finally seemed satiated and were ready to leave.

Everyone who was at the farm that morning—the numbers of which had been swelling with townsfolk eager to see the sciathilte up close—stood in the fields to watch the spectacle of the mythical creatures flying off into the bright blue sky in a spectrum of sparkling exoskeletons. Devon hugged Palafair and shook hands with Zelenka before they climbed up the back of an inky blue sciathilte and were gone from view.

Pop Pop made his way through the crowd to stand next to Devon, who was nearly as tall as his grandfather. "Don't blink," Pop Pop said. "We may never see such a beautiful sight in our lifetimes again."

Devon squinted up at the bright sky. "Surely you've seen many things this magnificent." His grandfather had traveled to so many places in the Great Peninsula, Devon could hardly believe Pop Pop hadn't witnessed beauty of this magnitude.

"A precious few." Pop Pop patted him on the head, and Devon kind of liked it, even though he was too old for such things. They stared in silence until the very last sciathilte, a burnt orange one that matched the trees cloaked in their autumn leaves, headed west to the Narrow Pass. "Safe travels," Pop Pop whispered.

The crowd around them began to form smaller pockets, some

leaving the farm and others hanging around. The silent reverence had turned to an excited buzz. Pop Pop headed off to the house.

"Wait!" Devon yelled. "I wanted to talk to you."

Pop Pop glanced at his grandson as if considering him anew. "Come to my study. I have work to do." Then he hustled on without waiting for Devon to catch up.

They passed by Grammy, who was in the kitchen with several farmhands cleaning up the mess from the massive breakfast. "Bagging off clean-up duty?" she yelled after them.

"I'll help after," Devon said, hoping they'd be done by the time he finished talking to Pop Pop. Wasn't it enough that he had spent hours cooking?

He entered the office on Pop Pop's heels. The fire was down to ashes, so Devon took it upon himself to add a few logs and get it blazing back up. He wiped his hands in satisfaction and turned to find Pop Pop reading correspondence at his desk, which was decidedly not waiting with baited breath for Devon to speak.

Undeterred, Devon cleared his throat and said, "I think I have proven how valuable I can be." He waited for Pop Pop to confirm, but all that could be heard was the shuffling of papers. Devon opened his mouth to launch into his prepared speech when he blurted out, "I want to go to war."

It wasn't eloquent, but it caught Pop Pop's attention. He set his reading glasses on top of his papers and gave Devon his full attention.

"What does your mother have to say about this?"

"She doesn't know. It's my business, not hers."

"I'd say it's very much your mother's business. Your father's as well." Pop Pop gave Devon a piercing look. "The last we spoke, your mother was very clear about where she stood on the matter."

Devon remembered. His ears still hurt from yesterday's lectures. With everyone against him, all his carefully thought-out arguments were leaking from his head. He turned away from Pop Pop to hide the tears that were threatening to fall.

"You have to remember your limitations, Devon." Pop Pop's earnest voice cut right to his heart. Devon was so tired of being reminded of his failures and of what he couldn't do.

He swallowed though a thick throat before whispering, "I just want a chance to prove myself."

In a moment, Pop Pop's arm was around his shoulder. "Fighting isn't the only way to prove your worth. You show it here when you come to work on the farm. You show it in your schoolwork. You show it on the bagball field. Today you showed your worth by cooking meal after meal for the tilli. These contributions are as important as the ones made by those in the thick of the battle. Maybe we don't do enough to recognize the quieter deeds." He grasped Devon by the shoulders and looked him straight in the eyes. "I am proud of you, my grandson. You don't need to fight a war to prove your worth to me...or to your mother. I'll work harder to make sure you know how proud I am of you."

Now there were tears falling down Pop Pop's cheeks, and Devon's finally broke loose. He was relieved when Pop Pop pulled him in for a hug; it lessened the tightness in his chest. It also made him realize he would never have his family's approval, and despite Pop Pop's declaration of the importance of "quieter deeds," it wasn't enough for Devon. He would prove himself on the battlefield one way or another.

Chapter Forty-Five

Their first evening in Kristalis, Kylene and her companions gathered in the dining room, the entire length of which was made of glass and overlooked the courtyard. A door was open to the garden, the heady scents wafting in on the breeze.

Though there were only five of them around the vast table, the room was warm and dinner felt intimate. They were served by a seemingly endless number of tall and beautiful women, whom Kylene suspected weren't women at all but the fallen queens of stories who had made Kristalis their home. It was unnerving to have higher beings serving dinner as if they were common waiters.

Enjoying the warm quarters after their inhospitable days in Blanchardwood, the travelers ate and drank long into the night. Lights twinkled all around the garden, flitting around like fairies. Kylene was quiet and indulged in too much spiked essence while listening to her companions chatter. She was waiting for Odeletta to appear and enlighten them as to why she had summoned them here, but the Ice Queen remained absent. The only news they received was from one of the women Ky suspected was a queen of Blanchardwood, who announced that a blizzard had come to Blanchardwood and they would be staying at Kristalis until it blew through.

"How long will that be?" asked Katora.

"As long as it needs to be," said the queen, her vague answer erasing any doubt that she was a higher being.

"Let's go to bed," Katora said to Hirsten, and they left.

With Bhar and Tarq engaged in a lively card game, Kylene felt like a third wheel and decided to retire to her room where she promptly passed out.

* * * *

The next morning, Kylene fairly stumbled down to breakfast at a very late hour. She had a headache and was relieved no one else was there, though there was a tableful of food for the taking.

For once the ache in her arm was a distant hurt to the pounding of her head. The smell of eggs and ham sent her stomach roiling, and she opted for toast and tea. The toast was topped with marmalade and was warm and crisp, and the tea was the perfect temperature.

She slipped a generous helping of spiked essence into her tea and gulped down half the cup. Then she filled it up to the top again with essence. Her head felt immediately better and she paid no mind to her arm. With her stomach feeling better, she heaped jam on a crumbly biscuit and filled her plate with fresh fruit.

Tarq burst in from the garden entrance, interrupting her peaceful meal. With him, he brought the cloying scent of flowers and sweat. Kylene set down a slice of pear mid-bite and swallowed back a burp.

With one long look of disapproval, Tarq took in her disheveled hair and wrinkled clothing. One day she might get used to his condescending expression, but today was not that day. He set down his bow and quiver along the wall and took just about one of everything from the spread. Looking very put together despite having been up later than Kylene had, he sat down and began shoveling food into his mouth, much the way Bhar did after a long day on the farm. Tarq didn't so much as look up from his plate.

Kylene sipped her tea, which was mostly essence by now. She couldn't bear the silence. "Have you been hunting? I didn't expect that to be allowed in the garden."

He paused in his ravaging of a biscuit with sausage and gravy, raising only his eyes to stare at her. "People have to eat. It was only a few rabbits. I imagine they'll make an appearance at this table tonight." He rapped his knuckle on the wooden top and went back to his biscuit.

She took another drink and nibbled a blueberry, having lost her appetite. "Are you going back out?"

"No," he grunted in between bites.

She nodded, though Tarq couldn't be bothered to look up. Lacking anything else to chat about, Kylene excused herself and hurried from the table. Behind her, Tarq's chair squeaked back and his heavy booted steps followed her. She rushed through the door to the hallway, not possibly being able to imagine what he'd want with her and not wanting to find out.

"Wait!" he called after her.

She ignored him and walked faster.

"Ky!" he shouted.

His use of the nickname caught her off guard and she faced him. "Yes?" she said cautiously.

He squinted, but it was impossible to tell what he was thinking. He almost looked sad, but why would anything about her make him sad? When he leaned in close to her face, she thought for one insane moment that he was going to kiss her, but thankfully he stopped short of her lips. Kylene's heart quickened and her hands were slick with sweat as she leaned back away from him.

"Ky," he said again, this time quietly, his voice hoarse and gruff, almost as if he cared. His hot breath blew in her face, like a humid gust on a scorching day. It smelled of sausage and gravy and made her stomach turn.

"What?" she whispered, her throat dry. She swallowed and waited, wondering if his answer would finally give some insight into why he always treated her with disdain.

Tarq's face darkened into his condescending expression, much more familiar than the concerned look he had worn a moment ago. He went back to his glowering self, only this time much too close for comfort.

"That's what I thought." He glared. "You've been drinking, and it's not even midday. How long has this been going on?"

Kylene held in a gasp. "You're wrong," she said, but there was no force behind the words. She had been caught, and by Tarq of all people. Humiliation burned from her sour stomach to the tips of her ears. To think a moment ago she had imagined he was concerned, but he so clearly loathed her. What a fool she was.

"I know the stench of alcohol, and you reek of it." A flash of something—perhaps a painful memory—drew across his face, but it passed as quickly as it came. Any chance of feeling sorry for him was wiped away when he leaned in toward her again. "How often do you do this?" He was practically shouting, and a bead of spit hit her cheek.

She took several steps back for some breathing room. She longed to tell someone her secret, the constant battle of keeping a smile on her face when all she wanted to do was lay down and cry because she was so tired of pretending she didn't hurt all the time. It was exhausting and demoralizing. But her confession would not be to Tarq, never to someone who harbored so much hatred toward her.

All she said was "it's none of your business" and fled up the stairs to the safety of her room.

A little while later Bhar knocked and asked if she wanted lunch. She yelled "no" through the doorway and spent the entire afternoon sobbing into her pillow until she fell asleep.

She woke to a dark room, a headache, and a heavy heart. As much as she hated being called out by Tarq, there was a ring of truth to his inquiry. What was she doing drinking with breakfast, albeit a late one? What had become of her that she had to drink in order to make it through the day? She washed up, changed into fresh clothes, and headed down to dinner with her head as full of confusion as it was the pounding headache. With a new resolve not to imbibe any alcohol, she entered the dining room to find Katora surrounded by Hirsten, Bhar, and Tarq.

A giant, glittering insect took up one end of the room. It nodded at her and her automatic response was a friendly wave; she couldn't quite process what was in front of her eyes.

"It's a sciathilte," said Bhar. "Can you believe it?"

She could hardly believe the giant glittering creature was a mythical sciathilte, but the thing that stole Ky's attention from that wonder was the letter in Katora's hand.

"It's from Pop," Katora said.

Swallowing through a dry throat, Kylene rushed over. Bhar held up a glass of essence. Not caring that it was spiked, she gulped down two big draughts and pretended not to notice Tarq's accusing glare. She peered over Katora's shoulder to find out what news awaited them from home.

The familiar scrawl of Pop's handwriting stared up at Kylene; it brought up so many thoughts of home. She missed the simple, hard labor of making her way through the essenberry vines and plucking the ripe fruit, the sun warming the neck beneath her ponytail. At one time, she had considered the work boring and her mind would wander to far-off places of adventures. Now that she had been on several real adventures, she was beginning to realize she preferred the safety of home and the imagined threats of stories.

Her own story was turning out nothing like the ones in books or in her imagination. There was no love to sweep her off her feet or innocent lives for her to save from the villain. She wasn't even sure who the villain was. Was it Odeletta, the Ice Queen herself, who had cursed her to this fate of sacrifice? Kylene doubted it. Odeletta was no villain; she was a higher being. Was it Tarq who despised her for unknown reasons? No. There was no evil intent behind his hatred, that much she could tell. Perhaps it was Fyren the Fallen, who had earned his reputation in the infamous battle at Drim and was possibly preparing for a new war. He was certainly a worthy villain, but she wasn't important enough to be his adversary. She was merely a cog in the wheel in the war against evil, a soft undefined cog at that.

No, Kylene was not even the hero of the story of her own life. She was just along for the painful ride. She gulped down the rest of the spiked essence and set her cup on the table.

She followed along silently as Katora read aloud from Pop's letter. "I hope this letter finds my loves…and Hirsten…well. I hope it finds you at all. We face dangerous times here in the Great Peninsula. Palafair and Zelenka have discovered powerful allies in the bearer of this letter," they all glanced at the sciathilte waiting patiently, "and grim tidings from the witch of Faway and the Watcher. War is indeed on the horizon.

"I dare not go into details in case this letter should be intercepted. I've enclosed a map for Hirsten and Katora. May they have much to add to it with their light touch. In the name of the 'Great Mother,' as Katora likes to say, and with her will, our paths shall cross again soon." He signed off with hugs and kisses from him and Ma.

From Kylene's vantage point behind her sister's shoulder, she watched Katora flip to the second page, which was, as Pop had stated, a map of the Great Peninsula, though nothing appeared to be special about it.

Bhar snatched it from Katora's hand. "Why would Pop send this? We have plenty of maps, and Hirsten's are much more detailed."

"That's it?" Katora unceremoniously tossed the letter onto the table. "An ambiguous letter and a useless map." She grabbed the map back from Bhar, crunched it up, and launched it across the room. "How am I supposed to figure out what to do with that?"

Though Kylene felt much the same way, she said, "Perhaps there's more to it than we think."

"Don't." Katora held up a hand. "This whole thing has been a big waste of time. We should have stayed at the farm instead of coming on this ill-conceived quest to a frozen wasteland. At least then I would be able to talk to Pop. Instead we're stuck here until the storm clears, without a plan and without a clue. And Queen Odeletta has been useless."

"Katora!" Kylene admonished. "You don't mean that." Katora had always been flippant about using Mother Nature's name as a curse but saying such a thing about a greater being outright was an entirely different matter.

"I don't need a lecture, Kylene. I'm done with the greater beings and their messages." Katora stomped her way out of the room, leaving everyone else in the wake of her tantrum. Hirsten followed shortly after saying he wanted to check on her.

"She's right," Bhar said. "I think maybe we shouldn't have come here. It seems to be playing right into our enemy's hand now that we're stuck." He glanced at the table of food. "I'm not feeling very hungry." He, too, left the dining room.

Kylene had never known Bhar to turn down a meal. She

barely noticed Tarq make an excuse and quietly quit the room. Sitting down at the table, she found herself without an appetite as well. The sciathilte startled her when it buzzed, and she found it had silently moved right next to her. It held the balled up map in its front legs.

"We know there is more to it," the sciathilte said in a deep, throaty voice, surprising her once again because she had no idea it could speak. "We will stay in the garden until a reply is provided."

"Thank you," Kylene said tentatively, and the sciathilte retreated through the glass doors to the courtyard.

She clutched the crumpled map and stared down at the letter from Pop, tears poised on her lashes. Through blurry vision, Pop's use of quotation marks caught her attention. She reread the letter, pausing on the phrasing in the second paragraph. Pop wrote that Katora and Hirsten's light touch might add to the map, followed by the "Great Mother" remark. It was curious of him to quote Katora, as Pop usually scolded her for such use of Mother Nature's name. She smoothed out the map and studied it, but it proved to be as simple as the first glance suggested. Unless...

Map and letter in hand, Kylene flew from the dining room up to her sister's room. Not bothering to knock, she burst through the door.

Chapter Forty-Six

The pair of Katora and Hirsten lay on the bed, and Kylene feared she had interrupted a private moment. Katora's eyes were closed and her head was nestled into Hirsten's chest.

She glanced up, a challenge in her expression. "What do you want, Kylene?"

"There is more to Pop's letter than what he wrote," Ky said.

"I don't want to talk about it. I thought I made that clear."

Determined not to be bowled over, Kylene joined them on the bed and shoved the papers at Katora. "Think about it. What does Hirsten do with maps?"

Hirsten's eyes widened and he stared at the letter. After a moment, he said, "Great Mother, Kylene is right."

He winked at her, and she had a hard time keeping a proud smile off her face. For once, Ky had something meaningful to contribute to the quest. Katora bolted upright, her right eyebrow raised. She spread out the map on the bed, smoothing down the center crease so it lay flat.

Hirsten placed his fingertips over Tussar and traced a path up to the city of Skimere, then east to the Eirome River, and finally north up to Lughorn where he paused. When nothing happened to the map, he moved his finger north once more into Blanchardwood where the river split into two, the place where they now knew as the location of Kristalis. It was the story of their journey, but no mind images appeared as Kylene had expected. Hirsten's brow creased in concentration, but still nothing appeared on the map.

Kylene began to doubt her idea; she had been reading something into Pop's words that wasn't there. Katora blew out an exasperated sigh.

"Katora!" Kylene said.

"What?" Katora's tone matched her glare.

"Pop's letter said 'their light touch.' Both of you need to do it," Kylene clarified.

"Yes." Hirsten placed Katora's hand on top of his. Their hands zoomed southwest clear across the Great Peninsula to Bad Beach, right across the inlet from Drim, Fyren's old stronghold.

"Now you have to say it, Katora." Ky liked telling her sister what to do for a change.

The words came slowly, not in Katora's usual cursing way. "Great Mother."

Scrolling letters formed underneath their fingers.

We March North Immediately

Meet Us When You Are Able

Kylene gasped. Katora's mouth hung open, and Hirsten's eyes were big, shining orbs of surprise.

"Let me see the letter," Katora demanded. Kylene quickly handed it over, hands shaking slightly. "This was written only days ago."

"The sciathilte is waiting for a reply," Kylene said. "What will you write?"

Katora rubbed her chin, clearly thinking. "I don't know. We can't go anywhere with the weather like this."

The snow outside the palace was so thick, they could hardly take a dozen steps outside the front door without seeing anything but blinding whiteness. Who knew when it would let up enough to allow them to leave?

"Remember when I thought the snow out on the plains had a magic to it?" Katora asked.

Kylene nodded, wondering what was going on up in her sister's brain, and hoping it was something brilliant. "You think this snowstorm is laced with magic as well, and not Odeletta's."

"Yes. Our foe's magic. We need to fight its dark magic with our light magic. All of us. Odeletta, all of the queens, the Watcher...if we can get a message to him."

"And others," piped in Kylene.

All eyes turned to her. "Who are you thinking of?" asked Katora, suspicion in her narrowed eyes.

"Yeselda." The witch of Faway Forest had questionable motives the last time the Kases had journeyed into the forest, but she was powerful and cunning.

"So you think the sciathilte will travel to Faway Forest?" Katora asked.

"Does anyone know what a sciathilte will do?" quipped Kylene, eliciting a laugh from Hirsten that was contagious, even though the remark wasn't really that funny. Pretty soon all three of them were laughing so hard they were gasping for air. The surreal nature of their situation was a heady reality, and Kylene found the fit of laughter to be a much-needed release.

"I suppose it can't hurt to ask." Katora paused and then very abruptly said, "You should go talk to Odeletta, Ky."

"Me?" she was sure she had misheard.

"Of course. From the moment you two met in the courtyard, you've had a connection. If anyone can convince the Ice Queen to leave her palace to fight Fyren, it's you."

Hirsten was nodding along in agreement.

"Scoot." Katora shooed her off the bed.

Much to her amazement, she agreed with Katora. She scurried out into the hallway to figure out a way to convince the heartbroken queen to remember back to when she had been Princess of Spring and wielded a power like no other. Could she do that in order to help them defeat their foe, who may have been they very being who had broken her heart?

Kylene couldn't know unless she asked, so she wandered the corridors and stairways until she found herself at an entrance to the garden, which was the only place she had actually seen Odeletta. Where the inside of the palace had a constant chill, the garden greeted Kylene with balmy air. Even at night, the magic of the warm oasis amid the frozen wasteland of Blanchardwood was a wonder. Tiny lanterns floated along the paths. One floated right up to Ky, and she saw it was a flower. She removed her boots and headed down a small dirt path in bare feet. Her tread was light and her footfalls made no sound. She could lose herself in the sweet scents and bright colors, but she was on a mission, finally a useful cog in the gears of the greater world. She quickened her pace, determined to search every inch of the garden.

As she walked farther, the garden seemed to have no end. There was always another bend in the path, another spectacular patch of flowers around the corner. She had no idea how long she had been wandering when she came across a fountain with benches facing the water. She paused to rest her feet. It was clear that she would never find Odeletta this way. It occurred to her that the Ice Queen might not be in the palace; she could be anywhere within the borders of Blanchardwood.

Sweat prickled her brow and dripped down her back. She dipped her hands into the cool water and splashed her face. Her stomach grumbled. She was tired and could've lain right there on the bench and slept. As it was, she rested her head on the back of the bench, not to sleep, but to rest and think. With all that had happened that day and her recent sense of purpose, Kylene's arm had hardly bothered her since the morning, but now it ached. She let out a long sigh.

"That is a sound I am not used to hearing here in my garden." Odeletta had taken a seat next to Ky in the silent way of greater beings. The queen's fingers trailed a lazy path in the water as she peered at her.

Kylene shot up. "My Queen...Odeletta, forgive me. It is a peaceful place. I do not mean to bring discontent to it."

Odeletta smiled, her face radiant and youthful, but her eyes held the ancient wisdom of the greater beings. "What brings you here at such a late hour?"

"You," Kylene said and then thought better of her bluntness. "I mean to say, I was seeking to ask something of you."

Kylene fiddled with her hair, wild from not having been brushed since morning. She must have looked a sight with her sweaty face and dirty feet. Nonetheless, Odeletta placed a hand on Kylene's. The queen's skin was smooth, her fingers long, and the nails perfectly trimmed. Her hand was also ice cold.

"What troubles you, Ky?" Odeletta asked.

The familiarity of the nickname set Kylene at ease, and she

answered in an unexpected way, "So many things. The talk of war, Tarq's attitude toward me, this long journey, and you—" She bit her lower lip.

"Yes, of course you have been troubled by my message."

Kylene hadn't spoken of it to anyone, had barely allowed herself to think of it since arriving at Kristalis. It was hard to reconcile Odeletta's calm demeanor with the words that had been delivered with a lightning strike.

"If only I could understand what it means." She couldn't bring herself to say the message out loud, to even repeat it in her own head. To say it—to think it—made it real. Though maybe if she confronted it directly, and with its sender right here, she might find a way to avoid fulfilling it. Kylene swallowed and spit out the words before she lost her nerve, "'You will make the ultimate sacrifice.' That's what you said in my head that day. Does that mean with my life?"

Odeletta peered down at Kylene with a faint, mysterious smile. "Who is to know for sure?"

It was a typical answer from a higher being. Kylene almost let it go, but she deserved to know, especially if it meant sacrificing her life. Didn't she? "But you must know something of it?"

"My confidence lies in what I told you, not in how it will come to be. Such is the way of these messages. We send them, but it is a narrow focal point, a starting and ending, with many different possibilities in between."

Kylene blew out a frustrated breath, and then reddened in embarrassment.

Odeletta patted her hand. "It is like with your blood oath—"

"My blood oath," Kylene interrupted. "What do you know of that?" In all the madness of the journey and the day-to-day of managing life, she had nearly forgotten about the oath to Nika in that alley in Skimere. Was that how she would make the sacrifice? Her life for Nika's?

"I know it was not taken in good faith," said Odeletta.

"So I won't have to honor it?"

"An oath coerced is an oath."

The tiny petal of hope that had begun to blossom in Kylene quickly withered. "So I will fulfill both the oath and your message."

"No sense lingering on the way it will be." She smiled in a knowing way and caressed Kylene's cheek in a warm manner, albeit with cold hands. "I do not often interfere in the short lives of humans. In this case, I felt in you a kindred spirit and passed along the message as a warning. It was not meant to distress you, seeing as you cannot control the outcome, only the path you take to it. I see that I was wrong, and it has troubled you. Let me advise you to think little on it and make your choices with a strong heart. For that is what we all do, Mother Nature's offspring and humans alike."

It was not the answer Kylene had hoped for, but it was a small comfort all the same. She couldn't control the future any more than she could control the weather, and even the higher beings only had control of one of those things. She would heed Odeletta's words and not linger on the message any longer, not if she could help it. She stared into the clear waters of the fountain and sought to clear her mind, but the swirling waters failed to soothe her.

"What else troubles you, my dear?" asked Odeletta.

She looked into Odeletta's divine eyes and almost said, "Nothing." Then she remembered the letter and map from Pop.

"Oh!" she nearly shouted. "I came to ask something of you."

"Of me?" Odeletta leaned back, appearing surprised.

Now that it was time to ask the queen to join the cause, Kylene had no idea how to broach the topic. In the silence, Odeletta held her hand palm up. A perky daisy sprouted from the center of it, its petals the purest white and the center a yellow that glowed like the sun.

Kylene said in a breathy voice, "It's beautiful." It was an understatement; it was the most beautiful thing she had ever seen.

"I was the Princess of Spring," Odeletta whispered. "Growing things has always been easy...natural. It takes far more energy to maintain all this snow around my castle."

"So why do it?"

"To protect myself, and my queens. They are my family. I will never see them hurt again."

Kylene felt an opening into a delicate topic. "My Queen, there is magic stirring at Drim. Do you know what's happening there?"

Odeletta pursed her lips, which were slightly drained of their vibrant red color. "It is Fyren."

"Are you sure?" Kylene dared to question.

"He bound himself to me when he stole my power." Odeletta's face was as white as the snow that surrounded her palace. "I feel the magic growing in his old stronghold. I do not know what he plans, but I fear he seeks to destroy you mortals."

Kylene pressed on. "We mortals, both humans and demicks, are gathering. There is a plan to meet at Bad Beach. My sister, Hirsten, and I were talking and decided we need to counter whatever is going on at Drim with as much magic as we can muster. Katora is attempting to contact Yeselda and the Watcher to ask them to fight along with us. Would you consent to us asking your queen's to do the same?" Cold permeated the humid air of the garden, seeming to emanate from Odeletta herself. Kylene was the one who reached out this time. Odeletta's hand was ice under hers, but she kept a firm hold of it. "Will you fight alongside us?"

Odeletta's chest rose and fell, and the air puffed from her mouth as if it were the middle of winter. A lone tear slipped down the Ice Queen's cheek, glittering in the light of the floating flowers. She snapped a hand out and caught the tear as it dropped off her chin, but not before Kylene got a good look at it. At first she thought it was made of ice, the way it caught the light and reflected little rainbows into Odeletta's hand. But a second glimpse of it, when Odeletta did the strangest thing and popped it into her mouth, revealed to Kylene that it was not a tear nor was it made of ice—it was a diamond. Kylene watched Odeletta swallow the gemstone and quickly glanced away, not wanting to be caught staring at this curiously intimate act. It reminded Kylene of the fox, how it always showed up when she had been crying.

Kylene stared into the fountain, her brain working on an important connection that hadn't quite formed, but she lost the thread when Odeletta finally spoke, "I will tell my queens of the situation, and they may do as they wish. They are bound to me out of loyalty but are free to chose their own causes."

"And you?"

"I—I do not know if I have the power to go against my old... foe."

Biting the inside of her lip, Ky decided to voice her opinion and risk the wrath of a greater being. "Maybe it's time to stop using your power to protect those you love behind a forest of snow. You can hide in the heart of Blanchardwood and be safe, but your unused power puts others—my family among them—at risk. Your inaction is an act against those who are vulnerable."

Fear for her family spurred Kylene to say such things, and she waited for the avalanche of anger to fall, but all that came was a loud sob.

"I do not know if I can leave and survive," Odeletta admitted.

"I believe you will, but it is not in my nature to judge you, whatever your decision may be." Feeling she should leave Odeletta alone, Kylene rose. "We will leave as soon as the weather outside of Blanchardwood permits us to."

"I will gather my queens at dinner tomorrow, and you may state your case to them."

"Thank you, my Queen." Kylene bowed and padded off back down the dirt path, her troubles both lighter and bigger than they had been before she entered the garden.

Chapter Forty-Seven

The main port city of Demick Island came into view as the sciathilte and tilli swept across the Narrow Pass, the strip of ocean between the Great Peninsula and the island. All the stories that told of the days-long passage from the island to the mainland were of a harrowing journey on tiny boats through choppy seas. Many demicks had perished. This time around it had taken a few hours to cross.

From this high up, the tall waves were small, jagged lines of white on the blue-green of the water and the treacherous current was ripples on the surface.

As they reached the coastline, the sciathilte flew in lower out of the stream of faster, colder air high above. Their bodies cast long shadows over the dunes that gave way to sand-colored roads and buildings with thatched roofs. The demicks below craned their necks to stare up at the sky, their faces giving way to looks of wonderment as they watched the sciathilte carry the tilli over the city. Zelenka imagined her face matched that of the island demicks. She had never seen so many demicks in one place in her entire life. They milled about on the streets, buying and selling wares from tented shops. They lounged on city benches and in shaded parks. They rode in carriages pulled by pygmy goats.

The city itself was a marvel, built by and for demicks. No need to retrofit furniture that was too large or rig up special apparatus on a door that was too heavy, as was the case for the anni demick living in a human-sized world. Zelenka was sure no one had to sit at a table atop a larger table as she and Palafair had to do at Kase Farm. Even at the Three River Split, the tilli had to make everything themselves from materials they found in Faway Forest, often improvising when no one in the community excelled at creating a particular item. Growing up at Hillock, sharp knives were in large supply as the tilli were skilled weapons-makers, but the forks and spoons were a mishmash of different sizes, shapes, and configurations because there were no metal workers among them who cared to learn the art of making proper utensils.

Here was a whole city where a demick could simply buy whatever they needed, and everything was fabricated by someone who specialized in that item. From her bird's-eye view, Zelenka spotted shops for candles, shoes, clothing, furniture, and, yes, there was one for dishes and utensils. All the perfect fit for a demick.

Of course, Zelenka had known all along that such a place existed. Anyone who had survived the crossing and chose the tilli side of the demick split had long been dead, but their stories lived on. Yet it was one thing to hear of a place and to imagine it, and another to see it for herself. How much simpler would her life have been if her ancestors had stayed on the island? The ancient rift that had compelled them to travel to the Great Peninsula seemed a small thing compared to what they had given up. Their homeland.

Now that she saw it with her own eyes, she realized she had missed it, if it was possible to miss a place she had never been to. The empty, yearning feeling she had never really allowed herself to process as a real feeling was suddenly so obvious. Homesickness. She was homesick for the land she had come from. A land she had longed for without knowing it. It was the true land of her people, much more so than Hillock or the Three River Split. Those had only been borrowed, claimed for a time in the name of the tilli. An ache burned in her chest as the longing swept through her, so much more real now that she knew what to call it.

Behind her, Palafair squeezed her tight around the waist. "Home," came his breathy whisper-shout in her ear, confirming that he felt it too.

Indy led the other sciathilte past the city to a hill with tall reeds dotted with wildflowers. Beyond that, lay more rolling hills, full of the same grass and flowers. The air on this side of the Narrow Pass was balmy and sweet-smelling, much like early summer in Tussar—a stark contrast to the crisp fall air of Faway

Forest and the snowy Tussar that felt like the dead of winter. The demicks who had crossed all those years ago had forsaken the ways of the island demicks and adopted their own ways on the Great Peninsula.

Her life had always been entrenched in Faway Forest, her time and energy occupied by the tilli way of life—the military in particular. She had barely given a thought to the world her ancestors had left behind; it had felt a part of the past that was irrelevant to her current life. She had not anticipated this well of emotions, the way tears sprang to her eyes at the sight of the demick city.

Indy made a smooth landing, but Zelenka's stomach lurched as they touched down. She practically pushed Palafair off the back of the sciathilte in order to run into the deep grass to be sick. Someone rushed to her side to pull back her hair as she fell on her knees and emptied her stomach. Wiping her mouth, she stood and expected to find Palafair standing next to her, but instead it was Nemez, whose face was pinched in concern. As if having the general of the tilli army witness her vomiting all over the ground wasn't embarrassing enough, Zelenka noted a group that included Palafair, Laurel, and Gainsley watching on from the edge of the tall grass.

Palafair, mouth hanging open in stunned silence, recovered himself and rushed over. "Are you okay?"

She pushed him away and mumbled, "Fine." It felt like the reeds were closing in, holding in the stale air. Zelenka's stomach squeezed, but she managed to keep down the bile. Leaving all those who were witnesses to her humiliation, Zelenka stalked out into the open air where the rest of the tilli and the sciathilte awaited those who had disappeared into the grass.

Laurel was close on her heels and leaned in to ask quietly, "Do you often experience sickness from motion?"

"No," barked Zelenka distractedly.

"Is it the heights or flying?" Laurel persisted.

Zelenka wheeled around. "I do not know. It has never happened before." She shot a vicious glare at Laurel and hoped

257

that would be enough to close the matter.

Laurel gave a little nod and whispered a "sorry" before heading off into the crowd of tilli who stared at Zelenka curiously. Mercifully the sciathilte were their usual standoffish selves.

The reeds parted and Nemez, Palafair, and Gainsley—who wore a smug smile—emerged.

"Set up camp," Nemez ordered, and Palafair followed the order like the rest of the soldiers and began to unpack supplies. To Zelenka, Nemez said, "We will need to seek out the priestesses. They are the ones who will decide whether or not to go to war against Fyren."

Pleased to be back to business, Zelenka asked, "What do you know about the priestesses?"

"Quite a lot actually. My many times great grandmother, who came over from Demick Island, was a priestess before leaving." His face relaxed into a rare smile. "Most who left the island never spoke much of their life before coming to the Great Peninsula. Once they declared themselves the tilli and broke off from the anni demicks, they wanted to start fresh in Faway Forest. As you know, the old traditions were never followed and new ones were established. But my priestess ancestor was particularly proud of her position, despite having left the island, and her stories were passed down for generations in my family."

"So what is our plan to approach them?" Zelenka asked as they looked out beyond the camp to the city below.

"Not my plan." Nemez winked. "Your plan. You will be the one to convince the priestesses to send the demicks to war."

"Me?" Zelenka failed to keep the surprise out of her voice. She knew so little of the priestesses.

Nemez chuckled, a deep rumbling sound. "I think they will take a liking to you. Tomorrow we will go to their meetinghouse and see."

Chapter Forty-Eight

As they traveled through the demick city on the way to the priestesses' meetinghouse, the retinue of Zelenka, Palafair, Nemez, Gainsley, and Laurel attracted curious stares that gave way to polite smiles when one of them smiled first, usually Palafair in his genial way. Zelenka expected Nemez to turn into one of modest wooden buildings with thatched roofing, but they continued on through the heart of the city and out the other side where the streets gave way to grassy dunes.

Zelenka had imagined the meetinghouse would be a simple structure, not unlike the modest, two-story wooden house at Kase farm, but the only building on the dunes was a formidable stone one with triangular turrets on all four corners. It was visible from most of the city, and Zelenka had never guessed it was their destination.

The sand up the path was deep and loose underfoot, and Zelenka had to constantly check her balance. Her injured leg was often stiff, but lately it had seemed less stable as well. The path steepened as they trudged their way up, Zelenka using her hands for purchase. The sand gave way to sturdier ground as they climbed and eventually turned to stone covered with slick moss. By the time they reached the top, Zelenka's chest pinched uncomfortably and she was out of breath. She had always been in top shape while active in the tilli army and figured she must have gone a little soft in her time at Kase Farm, ignoring the fact that she had hiked the tunnels of Hillock not too long before with not nearly as much trouble.

She chalked it up to the unusual terrain and thought of it no more.

For they had reached the meetinghouse and as impressive as it was from afar, up close it was a sight to behold. The peaked roof was not the thatched reeds of the city roofs but a variegated tile made of rust colored clay. The stone walls of the main structure and the turrets matched the sand. On either side of tall double doors, stained glass windows in rich hues sparkled in the sunlight. Zelenka shielded her eyes and even then couldn't make out what scenes they depicted. Nemez led them through the doors and Zelenka blinked to adjust to the muted light inside.

The main room ran the entire length of the building, rows and rows of wooden benches leading up to an altar with a bough of golden dahlias arching above it. More stained glass windows alternated with plain glass ones along the side walls. It smelled of freshly cut wood punctuated by pungent incense. As they made their way down the central aisle, their footsteps echoed loudly in the otherwise quiet space—the kind of reverent quiet that caused goose bumps to raise on Zelenka's arms. Rope ladders at the corners rose up to whitewashed beams that ran the width of the ceiling and led to doors to the turrets. Zelenka hadn't noticed any doors on the outside of the turrets and thought it was a very smart security feature to have access to the turrets via the ceiling beams. But why would priestesses need to fortify their meetinghouse?

A female demick walked from the altar to meet them, her long, white robes made of a light material that clung to her petite frame and fanned out behind her as she walked. She held out a hand. Nemez reached out and they touched the tips of their pointer and middle fingers together and they both said "blessing" before breaking contact. Nemez's proper greeting saved Zelenka the embarrassment of attempting to shake hands, which clearly would have been the wrong thing to do.

"I am Priestess Maran," the robed demick said. "Welcome to our house of worship. Have you come to make the weekly offering?"

"Weekly offering?" Zelenka asked. In their own way, the people of the Great Peninsula regularly paid tribute to Mother Nature. The Kases worked the soil, tending delicate shoots and harvesting crops. The blacksmiths did so by melting and shaping the raw materials the Great Mother provided into something useful: a plow to work the land, a knife to prepare the food, a sword to defend. That was the way of worship on the mainland, a daily practice of usefulness and survival; rituals were saved for the solstices and even those were not so formal. Zelenka always got the impression that Mother Nature had more important things to concern herself with than the trinkets and victuals demicks and humans presented twice a year. For her, it was the intent behind the offering that was more important than the actual items being offered.

Apparently that did not hold true for the demick worship of the greater beings.

"Forgive me." The priestess gave a slight bow. "Are you a priestess and wish to make the daily offering?"

Gainsley let out a loud cackle but quickly covered her mouth. Zelenka glared at the officer, taking a menacing step toward her. Before the situation could escalate, Palafair stepped between the two and said, "We apologize for not understanding your devout ways. We have come from across the Narrow Pass and before yesterday, have never set foot on our ancestors' homeland of Demick Island." He introduced each one of their party, ending with a blush as he said, "Zelenka, fierce leader in the tilli demick army, and, I am proud to say, my wife."

The priestess inhaled sharply, pressed her hands to her flushed cheeks, and felt her way to the nearest bench before practically collapsing into it. "Oh my! We have always hoped our wandering kin would return to us one day, but to have you here in front of me in this very moment...it is a miracle." Her hands remained on her cheeks as she took several deep breaths.

Palafair stood next to the bench and asked, "Priestess, are you okay?"

Her eyes widened and she apologized, "Yes, forgive me. And Maran is fine, no need for formalities."

Nemez fidgeted and cleared his throat, gaining the doe-eyed gaze of Maran. "I, uh, am afraid we have dire news from the Great Peninsula. Is it safe to speak freely here?"

"A dire matter...from the Great Peninsula." Maran held the back of her hand to her forehead, in a rather dramatic fashion

Zelenka thought. "This is a matter for the high priestesses. I will ring the bells and call them." Halfway down the aisle she turned and added, "Please make yourself comfortable. It should not take more than an hour for them to gather." She nimbly climbed a ladder up to the rafters and disappeared through a door in the corner of the ceiling.

Zelenka sat down on a bench next to Nemez. "General, you seem nervous." She kept her voice low in case her observation came off as insubordinate. "Which I do not understand because you said it would be I who would be convincing them to help our cause."

Bells tolled out a solemn tune that echoed from wall to wall. Nemez waited for them to end before speaking in a hushed, broken tone, "Being here in a demick meetinghouse makes me think of my grandmother. As I mentioned, my family remained devout to the demick ways long after any of the other tilli. It would have meant a great deal for her to see this place of worship...to speak to the priestesses as I have the opportunity to do so now."

"All the more reason for you to do it."

"No," Nemez said with authority, sounding more like himself. "They do not want to hear from me. You are the one to do it, Colonel."

It wasn't an order, not a direct one, but the use of her title made it feel like one. "As you wish, General."

A little while later, Maran emerged from the rafter door and beckoned them to join her. "The high priestesses have arrived."

Zelenka followed Nemez up the rope ladder, with Palafair, Gainsley, and Laurel behind. The rafters were high, even by human standards. Zelenka silently chided herself for the tendency to judge things by human standards—a bad habit from living in a human-sized world for so long, one that was more noticeable since arriving on Demick Island where there was no need for such comparisons.

Halfway up the ladder, her injured leg gave way and both feet slipped off the rung. She grasped the rope tighter, the fibers burning her palms until she was able to catch a lower rung with her feet. The whole ladder jerked.

"Watch it!" Gainsley shouted from below.

A reassuring pat on her ankle came from Palafair. "Up you go." His forehead crinkled in concern even as he smiled at her. Zelenka took the time to wipe each sweaty palm on her shirt before making it to the top without further incident. Palafair placed his hands on her hips as they made their way across the rafter to the doorway, as a show of affection or to keep her steady, Zelenka wasn't sure. She didn't like the implications of either. His soft whisper tickled her ear. "Are you okay? Usually you are so sure-footed."

"I am fine." But was she? All day she had been feeling unsteady on her feet in a way she hadn't experienced since first recovering from her injury in Faway Forest.

There was no time to linger over the thought as she went through the door to find a formidable group of robed priestesses standing behind a table curved like a crescent moon. The priestess in the middle had a wrinkled face and flaxen hair that stuck out of her hood at all angles. Zelenka tried to hide the shake of her knees as she stepped forward and Maran introduced her.

Zelenka's voice shook over her first few words, but leveled out as she related the story that had become so familiar to her. The message to return home, the plight of the missing tilli army, and the news of Fyren the Fallen. She relayed the cooperative plan of all the different species to meet at Bad Beach and launch an attack before Fyren could. Her speech was impassioned and eloquent...until her stomach lurched and she vomited all over the floor.

Chapter Forty-Nine

Devon waited until the wagons were fully packed and a stream of Tussarians were hanging around waiting to say good-bye to their loved ones before he settled into a hiding spot on a supply wagon. He had cleverly offered to help Ms. Pennyfold pack her wagon and left a perfect Devon-sized space amid the food supplies. He tucked himself under the wagon seat out of view and pulled a blanket around him.

The brilliance of his plan—other than hiding with the food and insuring that he wouldn't go hungry—was in the timing. He had already hugged Pop Pop and his mother good-bye. Their wagon was at the front and was already heading down the path. The food wagon he had chosen was one of the very last to leave, so he had been able to slip in while Ms. Pennyfold was checking the horse's harness. Of those who stayed behind to watch the procession of wagons head north on the trail out of Tussar toward Skimere, no one seemed to notice Devon's absence.

Ms. Pennyfold gave a "giddy-up" and the wagon lurched to a start. Devon was finally off on an adventure worthy of all the storybooks he had read.

The farewell cries and hubbub of departing quieted, leaving the clop of hooves and the wagon wheels slushing through the melting snow. The biggest flaw in his plan was failing to take into account how boring the trip would be. That and the blanket covering him. It was coated in a layer of dust that rained down on Devon with every bump in the road. Before long he was covered in it. His eyes watered and itched, and his throat tickled ominously. He felt a coughing spell coming on and dared to pull the blanket down below his chin. He spied Ms. Pennyfold's bottom through the cracks between the wooden slats of the seat, but the fresh air was worth the view. He quietly sipped from his canteen, grateful for the noise of the creaky wagon, until the coughing sensation passed.

Unfortunately he ended up drinking his entire day's supply of water to avoid the spell. He decided keeping his head out of the blanket was worth the risk of Ms. Pennyfold looking directly below her seat and discovering him.

Devon rested his head on a carton, affording him a better view of the tops of the trees and the clear, blue sky. Ms. Pennyfold whistled loudly from above and provided a little bit of entertainment on the first day's ride. The sun was barely at its apex and he thought he might die of boredom, but eventually the rocking of the wagon lulled him to sleep.

A sky painted with stars greeted him when he woke. He was only half-covered in the blanket, and his stomach grumbled loud enough that he worried Ms. Pennyfold would hear it. The wagon lumbered along, hitting more ruts the farther they traveled from Tussar. Devon knew the convoy was to travel through the day and into the night as it was almost the winter solstice. It was with all haste they moved, for Mother Nature only knew when Fyren would attack—and maybe even she wasn't privy to such information. Devon crunched a raw carrot. Vegetables kept best when they were not cleaned in advance, so it was a dirty bite. It was too loud anyway, so he slipped it into his pocket, along with several more carrots and two potatoes. He'd figure out a way to clean and cook them once the wagon stopped for the night. He would sleep away the days and eat and exercise at night when everyone else slept.

It felt like a very long time—his empty stomach gnawing away at his patience—before the wagon jerked to a stop. Devon covered himself with the blanket until he heard Ms. Pennyfold climb off with a groan, followed by the utterance of a choice word. Murmured voices and bangs of camp being set up wafted their way to Devon, but no one came near the supply wagon. He had done well to choose this one, which had food that kept well and would be eaten after the perishable goods. A melancholic strumming of a guitar filled the night air, seemingly playing the travelers to sleep. Devon wondered if Pop Pop was playing, but he didn't dare peek out to look. After the last note rang out, Devon waited as long as his bladder would allow before slipping out of the wagon, the blanket folded up under his arm and the food weighing down his pockets. He steered clear of the several fires cheerily crackling among the wagons and tents. Only a few Tussarians were awake on watch, and not very alert at that, as Devon spied a few chins tucked in slumber.

He found a deserted spot among the trees to take care of his business. High above the treeline to the east loomed Mount Capdon. He muttered a quiet prayer in the hopes that his offering was doing its job as he moved farther into the copse of trees. He hung the blanket from a branch and stretched all his muscles, sore from disuse. Then he found a stream to refill his canteen. He drank long and hard and then filled it up again, this time tucking it back into his pocket. After cleaning the vegetables, he set them on a rock. He splashed cold water on his face, the cold bite of it crisp and refreshing. The freezing night air invigorated him.

An attempt to start a fire by rubbing the pointy end of a stick on a piece of flat bark proved unsuccessful. Despite growing up next to the wild Faway Forest, Devon had never been allowed to venture beyond its borders. This first day of the trip was exposing his lack of wilderness expertise. For all his days spent working on the farm, he had always come home to a hot meal and a warm bed. Tonight he settled for the crunch of clean carrots and cold splash of water on his tongue. He'd have to nick a flint and pot for a hot meal with the potaotes tomorrow night.

Restless energy surged through him once he had a little food in his system. He removed his cloak, found a broken branch as wide as Ms. Pennyfold's muscle-laden forearms, and beat the blanket until the dust stopped puffing from it in cough-inducing plumes. Then he took another long drink and washed the dirt from his head and arms. The nip in the late-autumn air turned downright frigid, so he bundled up and jogged up and down the bank of the stream, well away from the campers, his cloak streaming out behind him. He would definitely need a fire at night, not only for cooking but to stay warm. He sat on the ground, back against a tree trunk and the blanket wrapped tightly around him.

The cold seeped into his bones, but it was better than having to spend the night in the wagon; in order to survive the trip with his sanity intact, his nights would have to be his own.

He threw off the blanket and did another jog along the stream. He ran until he started to sweat and then turned around and headed back. It was dark along the river, and he kept his gaze low to avoid tripping over any errant sticks or tree roots. He nimbly dodged a fallen branch and smacked hard into a solid form.

A grunt ripped from his throat and he stumbled backward, his heels hitting the very branch he had been trying to avoid. It tripped him and he slammed down on his butt. A splash of water soaked the front of his pants.

"Watch it!" The person moved out of the deep shadows of the trees, and Devon recognized Emmaline Tine, his siblings' former baby-sitter. She carried a large bucket, water dripping down the sides. He thought of the poem he had penned for her and left in his bedroom back home.

Em's short black hair stuck out in all directions but in an organized way that suggested she had styled it purposefully. It framed her round cheeks and sparkling eyes in a way that struck Devon speechless, though he couldn't speak anyway because the impact with the ground had knocked the wind out of him. New lines of poetry stirred in his mind, and his hand itched for a pen and paper.

"Devon Kase!" Em set down the bucket and wiped at her wet shirt. "What in the Great Mother's name are you doing out here?"

Hiding would have been the correct answer—which seemed to be all he had been doing of late—but all he said was "exercising."

"In the middle of the night?" She reached out to help him up. Her hand was cold and wet, but the contact made his stomach squeeze in a pleasant way. "Does your mom and grandfather know you're out here?"

Devon ducked his head. "Not exactly."

"You should get back to camp." She clearly didn't know the true extent of what his mom and Pop Pop didn't know.

He picked up the bucket and headed back along the river to where he had left his things, and Em followed. "You see," he began. "It's not just that they don't know that I'm out here. It's…"

The gurgling river filled the silence until Em spoke again, "I have no worldly idea what you're going on about."

"They don't know I'm out here away from camp because they don't know I'm here at all."

She grabbed his arm and they stopped walking. "You mean they think you're home, in Tussar?"

"Yes," Devon said quietly.

"Oh. Well that's something."

They resumed walking at a slower pace than before, soon arriving at the spot where Devon had eaten. He set the bucket down and pulled the blanket from the ground where he had left it. Em grabbed one end and they folded it, their breaths releasing in one big puff when they got close to hold the edges of the blanket together. It felt oddly intimate. They stayed close for longer than strictly necessary, Devon noticing he had grown a touch taller than Em. The copse was quiet at this hour, only the occasional hoot of an owl piercing through the silence.

"When are you going to tell them?" Em asked, taking a step back and taking up the bottom of the blanket.

"I don't know," Devon admitted. "Long enough into the journey where they won't send me back."

"If you don't do it soon, I'm going to have to tell them." Their knuckles touched and stayed together over the last fold.

"No!" The word echoed loudly, startling a sleeping crow, who took off in agitated flight with a loud caw.

"We're headed to war, Devon." Em's face was hooded by shadows, a faint glint of moonlight reflecting in her eyes. "This isn't a game of bagball where the winners cheer and the losers go home to try again next time. The losers in war don't get to come home. It's no place for a youngyear."

A moment ago, the feel of her fingertips on his knuckles had been affectionate in a mutual way, but now it felt condescending, the touch of someone older who thinks she knows better. He pulled his hands away, clutching the blanket to his chest.

"I'm only a youngyear until the winter solstice. Once school ends next summer, I'll be starting my primeyear life."

"But that's the point," Em said. He couldn't read her expression in the dark, but the earnestness came across in her voice. "You should have a chance to finish school before you worry about things like war."

"From what I hear, if Fyren wins, I'll be talking about war no matter what." Fire rose in his cheeks, and he hoped she couldn't see the blush on his face. "It's life and death on the battlefield and at home. We need everyone who can fight out there...or no one will have a chance to finish school."

Em let out a sigh and shivered. Devon gripped the blanket harder to keep himself from reaching out to her.

"You're right," she said. "You should be able to fight."

He took a step closer, close enough to lean forward and kiss her if he dared to. The brown of her eyes was visible now, her forehead knit in what Devon could only assume was confusion. Over war or over him? He wondered what she saw in his blue eyes, perhaps more than the boy whose siblings she used to baby-sit.

Then she leaned away a half-step and the magic of the moment was gone. "You have to promise me one thing."

"What?" he said when he really meant *anything*.

"Reveal yourself to your mom before we get to Drim. Don't throw that surprise on her when we're about to go to battle."

"I will." He had always planned on doing it before then, so long as he was far enough away from home not to be sent back.

Sensing there was something more Em wanted to say, Devon prompted, "And?"

"Respect your limits." She said it in a rush, and his confidence deflated. Here he had thought they were finally on equal ground, and all she was thinking about was his condition. He was tired of things always coming back to that.

"Sure," he mumbled and turned away.

She touched his shoulder. "Not just because of your breathing. There are a lot of Tussarians with no weapons training,

269

no battle experience. We all need to remember our limits."

An animal rustled in the nearby bushes, making both of them jump. Em immediately took a defensive stance, and it gave Devon an idea.

"You have training, though, right?"

"Of course. My fathers make weapons and they know how to wield them, and they taught me, too." The pride was clear in the firm set of her jaw.

"Can you teach me?" he asked.

"I can." Her eyes widened. "I can teach others, too. And have Da help. We can do lessons the whole way to Drim." She hugged him, though the blanket was between them, so Devon didn't get the full effect. It was enough to make the heat rise in his cheeks again. "What a great idea, Devon."

It was a great idea, even if it wouldn't help him much. He wouldn't be able to train with everyone else until he told his mom he was there, and then there wouldn't be time to do it fully.

As if sensing his disappointment, Em said, "I can train you at night...in secret. Until you're ready to show yourself."

"Yes." He tried to keep his voice from cracking. It was hard to keep his excitement in check over the thought of spending nights with Em engaged in battle preparations.

"I should get this water back to camp," she said. "I'll find you tomorrow night."

"Wait!" Devon said as she walked away. "Can you bring me a pot and flint?"

"I'll look for them tomorrow. Don't hide too deep into the woods from me, okay." She hurried off and disappeared into the dark.

It was colder than ever with her gone, and Devon's stomach rumbled with hunger. He drank some water and went back to exercising the long night away. The prospect of seeing Em the next night made it a little more bearable.

Chapter Fifty

By day, Devon rode in Ms. Pennyfold's wagon, concealed under the blanket, which only made him cough occasionally now that most of the dust had been beaten off. By night, Em would come and find him when camp was quiet. They would stay far away from any prying Tussarians on watch. She had come through with not only a pot and a flint but with seasonings and bread. With those and the root vegetables from the wagon, Devon ate regularly and heartily.

They used sticks to practice swordplay, on Emmaline's insistence. "You'll hurt yourself with a real sword. Plus they'd be too loud."

In the light of the small fire, Em taught him the proper way to hold a sword and how important footwork was, though she admitted that in battle, sheer brute force and determination could go a long way to cutting down the enemy.

"But learning the technique will help when it comes to the real thing," she had insisted, and Devon didn't argue that point. "With repetition and training your body will remember and react when your mind is frightened or distracted. The muscles remember."

It was a phrase she often said, like a mantra for every time Devon stepped the wrong way or attacked when he should have parried, earning him a rap on the chest from Em's branch. *The muscles remember.*

The nights grew colder, some bringing flurries of snow—a sure sign of magic—but Devon and Em stayed warm in heated battle, often sloughing off layers of clothing as the night turned late. Devon found himself sore in places that had never ached before, but his body grew used to holding his stick, his hands calloused in places where they had once been soft. Em warned him it would be harder with real swords, but she didn't let him try one.

One such night when they were at least halfway to Skimere, they faced each other for another bout. Em wore a sleeveless shirt and breeches, her arm muscles rippling and her brow glistening with sweat. Her hair was spikier than usual from running her sweaty palms through it. Her body and muscles were lean and long, where Devon's were thicker but not necessarily stronger.

In the cold night air, Devon removed his shirt and mist rose from his warm body. He came at her with a blow to the right. She dodged it easily and mounted her own attack. His footwork had improved greatly, and they shuffled and leaped across the leaf-strewn ground in a dance of feigned menace. Finally, Em landed a hit to his thigh that ended the match with a win for her—she always won. Though Devon had recently given her a few close calls, and she seemed pleased with his progress. They fell in a heap next to the fire, big grins on their faces.

"Nicely done." She was breathing hard, though not as heavily as Devon.

The air felt too cold as he sucked it in through his nose and mouth, his chest rattling as though full of fluid.

"One more," he wheezed. "I think I can beat you now that you're tired."

She gave him a sideways glance. "You sure you're up for it?"

He shouldered her playfully. "Definitely. Are you?"

To answer, she leaped to her feet and pointed her stick at his temple. He heaved himself up and they faced each other. He hadn't quite caught his breath from their last bout, but he refused to show any sign of weakness. He thought about putting his shirt back on to protect his chest from the cold, but it was too late as Em advanced.

The confines of the tree-covered area, the limited lighting, and the uneven ground proved tricky obstacles, but they had grown used to that. On the first night they had fought, Devon had kept tripping and Em pointed out that any real battle would have less than ideal conditions. The rough terrain was good practice at being aware of his surroundings. *The muscles remember.*

This bout started off intense, having left off where their last one ended, and only grew in fervency. She pushed him back toward a large pine tree, which he narrowly avoided. The trunk proved a good block when it took a hard blow from Em's branch. A loud crack rang out. Em twirled around the tree and pointed her branch at Devon; it was snapped nearly in half, the top part hanging on by the bark.

Devon's chest heaved for air and spots crossed his vision. Broken stick and all, Em kept coming for him. He blocked a strike, and the top half of her stick flew off into the darkness. Her eyes widened and she burst out laughing. The sound was lovely and Devon would have joined her, but he was having trouble getting air into his lungs. He coughed, expelling oxygen he couldn't afford to lose. Black spots swarmed his vision, and a whooshing sound filled his ears, blocking out her laughter. He heard Em scream his name, but it sounded muffled and far away, like she was on the far side of a long tunnel. Then his vision blacked out completely and he knew no more.

* * * *

"I can't believe you told my mom," Devon said to Emmaline as they sat together in the back of Pop Pop's wagon a day later.

"I can't believe you passed out during my lesson," she said.

Their shoulders bumped together as the wagon hit a rut in the road. Devon's mom had insisted he ride with Pop Pop, a slightly better alternative to riding with his mom and Aunt Lili. He couldn't bear to see his mother's lips pursed in disappointment the rest of the way to Skimere.

"What happened to respecting your limits?" Em asked.

He folded his arms across his chest and stared out the opposite side of the wagon, the brown grass of the endless plains rolling out in all directions until it reached a dull, gray sky.

Em continued, "You said you were going to tell her soon anyway. It's not like they're sending you back to Tussar."

"I guess." He had hoped to have more time before revealing himself, and now he wasn't allowed to practice sword work with Em anymore. He would never convince his mother to let him battle against Fyren's army. Devon sighed and leaned his head against

273

the back of the front bench. It wasn't Em's fault, and there was no sense in blaming her for calling attention to his body's failure. He pushed his shoulder against hers, even though this part of the road was smooth. "I should thank you for helping me."

"So do it," she challenged, pushing back with her shoulder. "I got an earful from my Da about the responsibilities of being a primeyear. How we're supposed to take care of youngeryears. As if I haven't been doing that in my spare time all these years. I know practically every youngeryear's favorite food and what story will lull them to sleep." She punched a fist into her open palm. "Now I'm stuck baby-sitting you when I thought I was done with all of that."

Heat rose up the back of his neck. "Baby-sitting me?"

"It's my punishment—to keep you out of trouble for the rest of the trip. When the pastyears decided to let you stay on the journey, they appointed me as your watcher."

So much for thinking they were equals. He leaned away, removing any contact between the two of them, and swallowed through a thick throat. "Thanks for saving my sorry lungs the other night. Sorry it's such a drag for you now." Then his body chose that moment to have a coughing fit.

When it was over, Em asked, "Are you okay? Do you need more medicine?"

"No!" he shouted.

"Is there a problem back there," Pop Pop asked from his seat up front.

"No," Devon repeated. "Everything's fine."

He looked out over the rest of the caravan. They were toward the front and had a good view at how many Tussarians were taking the journey to war. The line of wagons snaked down the road, too numerous to count.

After a few minutes, Em said to him quietly, "Hey." The intensity of it forced him to look at her, dark brown eyes staring into his blue ones. "I would've kept your secret if I could have. It was so scary," her voice caught, "seeing you like that. Your lips turned blue, and your chest looked like it was caving in. I thought you were going to die. Whatever it was that Pop gave you was some serious stuff. Your color came right back, and your breathing evened out."

He didn't know what to say to that. He had never seen what it looked like when he had a bad fit, only ever felt the crushing emptiness of not being able to breathe before passing out. "It's fine," he said, though it wasn't. "Pop Pop's with me so you can go off and do whatever you want. You don't have to baby-sit me."

She squeezed his upper arm. "I'll stay if you don't mind."

"I don't mind," he said, and that was the truth.

Chapter Fifty-One

After a night of restless sleep over what answer the queens would give, Kylene was the last human to come to breakfast. Tarq sat at the near end of the table and, blissfully, ignored her. Katora and Hirsten sat close, heads dipped toward each other. Neither was eating as they were engaged in an ardent conversation, so Kylene skirted past them without interrupting.

She chose a seat next to Bhar and served herself oatmeal with fresh fruit on the side. Bhar waved a piece of bacon in the air as if it would entice her to break her vegetarian ways. It had only been a few years since she had changed her diet, so she knew how delicious bacon was, but that didn't keep the pungent smell of the meat from stirring up sour juices in her stomach. She sipped her tea and forced down a small bite of oatmeal. Bhar crunched his bacon and smiled.

A wave of warm air rushed in as the door to the garden opened and Odeletta's retinue of queens waltzed in, led by none other than the witch of Faway Forest, Yeselda. Her black cloak was in stark contrast to the brightly colored gowns of the queens, who all together looked like a vibrant bouquet.

Katora pushed out of her chair so hard that it fell over. Her eyes flashed in a frightening way. She looked intimidating, all five feet of her. Kylene merely clenched her spoon harder and swallowed the lump of oatmeal stuck in her throat. Kylene had no love for the the witch of Faway either. Angry, regretful feelings surfaced as she thought about Yeselda forcing an army of animals to attack Kylene and her family in Faway Forest. Kylene had killed those helpless creatures to save herself, and Zelenka had been badly injured. Kylene clenched her fists and forced herself to breathe calmly. It wasn't likely that Yeselda would attempt any such thing here in Kristalis. They were on the same side...this time anyway.

As the queens filed in behind the witch, Kylene's hope that Odeletta might join them dwindled with each new face. The last queen entered and shut the door. Kylene sank deeper into her seat and dropped her spoon on the table with a clatter, her appetite completely gone.

"Thank you for inviting me, Kase daughter, guardian of the Elixir." Yeselda swept her hand toward Katora, managing to make the title sound like a joke. "My sister, the great Ice Queen," Yeselda gave that title more respect, "sends her best wishes. She does not feel she is fit to fight in a battle at this time. I, on the other hand, am always ready for a fight." She winked at Hirsten, and Katora's face turned scarlet. "And my sister's queens have decided to join me and you—my little humans—in this battle against Fyren."

Yeselda paused as if waiting for a reaction, perhaps applause, over the proclamation, but none came. Katora stared icily at the witch, while Hirsten looked poised to jump up to intervene in case Katora lost her temper and attacked, which wouldn't be the first time Katora went after Yeselda. Kylene's stomach twisted.

"Are you joining us for breakfast?" Bhar asked with a lazy grin. He leaned back in his chair, his hands resting behind his head, the picture of calm. Kylene wished she found the situation amusing. "Should we have more food brought out?"

Yeselda turned a red-lipped smile on Bhar. "No thank you, dear. As delicious as that sounds, I have many matters to attend to before we leave for Drim. I have brought my horsemen along to help transport you all, so there is no reason to wait for the storm to clear. We will leave once the Watcher arrives, a matter of days."

"That's too bad," Bhar said. "I was getting used to being waited on by the queens. No rest for the divine. Isn't that right, Yeselda?"

The witch sauntered over to Bhar. "Cheeky boy." She ran a blood-red fingernail from his temple to his lips. He kept his relaxed pose, but his jawline went rigid at her touch. Yeselda bent over to adjust her considerable height to match Bhar's seated level. She pulled the fingernail away from Bhar's face and rested it on her lips. "No rest indeed."

Kylene's heart pumped double-time at the intense exchange, but all Yeselda did was stand, spin around toward an interior door, and gesture for the queens to follow.

Katora, who had remained standing this whole time, shouted, "Wait! I...Hirsten and I have an announcement of our own. We have decided to, well..." She looked down at Hirsten, two radiant smiles beaming from their faces, and pulled him up to stand next to her.

Yeselda rolled her hand around in impatience. "Get on with it. I am a busy being."

"We've decided to marry," Katora declared. "We want to do it before we set off for Drim, so tomorrow, I guess?" She glanced at Hirsten, who nodded. "Tomorrow then. It will be in the garden, and Odeletta has agreed to officiate. We want all of you to come."

Now the room burst out in applause, starting with Bhar and spreading to Tarq, the queens, and a bored-looking Yeselda. Kylene's already taxed heart skipped a beat, and she was late to clap. She covered it up by coughing and then slapping her hands together as loudly as she could. While the spotlight was on the engaged couple, Kylene took a moment to sip her tea, which had gone cold. From behind her cup, she noticed a single set of eyes upon her. Tarq clapped along with the others, but his gaze was fixed on her, and it was not a friendly one. His lips were set in a stern line and his eyes were tight around the edges.

Kylene fixed her own gaze upon a beaming Katora and Hirsten. Of the two sisters, Kylene was normally the romantic, tears of joy ready for any occasion of love, while Katora usually had a more jaded opinion. Yet her sister had never looked happier, and as a lump formed in Kylene's throat, she found the tears in her eyes were not ones of joy.

It was a silly crush, Kylene chided herself. She had never really loved Hirsten, and he certainly didn't love her, not in any capacity beyond brotherly affection. He was not hers to covet, and she refused to let any jealous feelings get in the way of Katora's moment.

Kylene swallowed down another sip of tea; set her cup down rather clumsily, spilling liquid on the tablecloth; and rushed to the other end of the table to hug her sister. She felt Tarq's stare follow her and hoped her true feelings weren't as transparent as thin river ice.

"Congratulations," Yeselda said dismissively. "Now, my queens, we must prepare for battle."

Yeselda whipped her black cloak around and left the dining room to head deeper into the palace. The queens shuffled off after her. Instead of being full of bodies, the room teemed with tension. Katora picked up her chair and banged her fist against the table, disturbing the cups and platters, joy replaced with anger.

Bhar traded in his grin for a grimace. "She's so smug! Always ready for a battle, yeah right. Then why did she send her lackey animals after us in the forest?"

"Too bad Zelenka isn't here," Katora said. "I'd hold down that witch and let Zelenka beat her with a stick."

"I'd pay to see that," Bhar said, the grin back.

Tarq's head bounced back and forth between the siblings. "Did I miss something? Yeselda seems like a solid ally."

"We have a bit of a history with her," Hirsten said.

Katora turned on her heel to face Hirsten. Ky couldn't see her sister's face, but she could hear the fury in her voice as she said, "If by a bit of a history, you mean having her horsemen stun Bhar into unconsciousness, using animals of the forest to fight her battles against us, and trying to steal the Elixir from me, then, yes, we have a *bit* of a history."

Hirsten glared at Katora, all their loving feelings from a moment ago erased. "Don't snap at me! I'm not the one who did those things."

"No," said Katora in a dangerous voice. As if it were the seats that were upsetting Katora, she knocked Hirsten's to the ground. "You're only downplaying how horrible she is. What are you going to tell me next—that none of it was that bad after all?"

Hirsten stood in an eerily calm way, though his clenched jaw showed how much emotion he was holding back. "Come and find me when you've cooled off. I'm not planning a wedding with you like this." He left the room without another word.

Katora swore and slammed her fist on the table. "Great Mother! Damn that witch for ruining this moment. I hope Fyren shoots an arrow into her black heart."

"Katora!" Kylene admonished. It was a strong oath for an ally, albeit a contentious one.

"Oh, grow up," Katora replied. "We don't need to pretend to be nice to everyone all the time, especially not to creatures like Yeselda." She sighed and seemed to deflate. "I've gotta talk to Hirsten and figure out if we're having this wedding or not."

As the door shut behind Katora, Kylene asked, "Should I go after her?"

"Leave it to the lovers," said Bhar. "They'll sort it out and we'll be celebrating tomorrow. And you can bet on it that I won't let that witch ruin my sister's wedding day."

Yeselda showing up, the wedding announcement, the fighting, it all would have been so much more bearable if Kylene had a good strong drink, but there wasn't a drop stronger than black tea at the table. And with Tarq glowering over his breakfast, Kylene wasn't about to ask for something stronger. The sting of Tarq catching her drinking the other morning was too fresh.

"Tarq and I are going hunting in Blanchardwood today," Bhar said. "Maybe we'll catch something worthy of a wedding feast. Want to come along, Ky?" She had been staring at her bowl full of congealed oatmeal but looked up sharply at Bhar's offer. He winked. "Just kidding. I know you don't."

But that wasn't her concern. "You're going into the woods?"

"Don't worry, a few of the queens are coming with us. We'll be safe."

And she'd be alone in the palace while Katora and Hirsten planned their wedding. She excused herself and went to her room to sort through her complicated feelings.

Chapter Fifty-Two

It took one day for Katora and Hirsten to put together the wedding...with a little help from the Ice Queen herself. Odeletta pulled out all the stops for the couple.

Kylene had mixed feelings, but she swallowed back her resentment. Weddings were about the beauty of love and joy and commitment. Even if Kylene never found those things in her life, she would not begrudge Katora and Hirsten for them. A glass of spiked essence helped dampen the parts of Kylene she wasn't proud of, so she took another sip as she helped Katora into her wedding dress.

It was a thing of beauty, as was Katora. The pale blue color brought out the blue in Katora's eyes. The top fit tight to her chest and flowed out in light layers below an empire waist. The back was cinched tight by silk ribbons, which Kylene stood back to check once she was done lacing them up. She fluffed up the modest train that stretched out a few feet behind Katora. The sleeves were sheer, studded with sparkling diamonds, and stopped at the elbow. Rainbow-colored flowers capped off the sleeves, as well as the neckline, waistline, and bottom of the dress. Odeletta had outdone herself in creating it.

Kylene took a few steps back to take it in, all her previous feelings muted by the wide smile on her sister's face. She thought it a shame Katora so rarely wore dresses because she was simply breath-taking in this one.

"I've never seen a more beautiful bride," Kylene said.

"What about Lili or Ariana?" Katora's eyes sparkled with the joke, but it hit a nerve with Kylene.

Tears pricked her eyes and her cheeks warmed. She blinked away the hurt. "I didn't mean it that way."

Katora squeezed her arm. "I know. We're all beautiful in our own way, aren't we?" Katora twirled her around and they stood arm in arm, Kylene being careful not to crunch the flowers. "It's not too much, the dress? I want to look like myself." Katora's right eyebrow quirked up in her characteristic way.

Kylene laughed. "Nope. You definitely look like you."

Together they stared at their reflections in the mirror. The pale yellow dress Kylene wore made her hair shine golden. The top was strapless and the body was long and fitted, the silky material clinging to her slim frame, accentuating her height. Standing next to Katora, Kylene looked like a long, shiny stalk of wheat. She forced a smile that turned real as she switched her gaze to her sister.

"Now for your hair." She flicked a few strands of Katora's stick-straight hair.

Katora turned away from the mirror. "It's hopeless."

"Lili would know what to do," Kylene said quietly.

Katora sniffled at the floor and then looked up with a wistful smile. "They should be here." She didn't have to say who; Kylene knew she meant the whole family and their friends back in Tussar.

"We should be *there*," Kylene corrected. "At the farm with the essenberry fields as a backdrop for when you and Hirsten's hands are bound."

"With Ma's lasagna for dinner," Katora said. "And fresh strawberries and cream for dessert."

Kylene's voice turned bitter, "Stupid Fyren."

"Stupid Fyren," Katora agreed as she took Ky's hands. "I'm glad you're here."

"Me too." She kissed Katora's cheek and tried not to soak their dresses in tears.

In the absence of their sisters, Kylene did the best she could with Katora's hair. She brushed it until the strands shone golden. Then she braided it in two sections that joined at the end, weaving a light-blue ribbon through it. They looked into the mirror one more time.

"You look amazing," Kylene said, believing it had little to do with her handiwork and everything to do with the woman about to be married.

"We both look amazing."

They hugged, managing to not to totally crush the flowers on Katora's dress. A tear slid down Ky's cheek, and Katora, dry-faced as always, wiped it away and pinched her cheek.

"I guess I go get married now," Katora said.

"I guess so," Ky said with only a touch of sadness.

* * * *

The ceremony was a simple affair in the garden. The couple stood in front of an arbor full of honeysuckle with cherry blossoms to the sides. Everything was in full bloom. With the cloying sweetness of the flowers tickling her nose, Kylene stood at Katora's side and Bhar at Hirsten's, representing both families that could not be there. Odeletta's retinue of queens showed up in force in their finest white dresses.

The men wore long tartan jackets over white linen shirts and pants. As was customary, everyone was barefoot—to connect directly to Mother Nature.

Odeletta herself presided over the ceremony. "With the spirit of the Great Mother in us all, we pay witness to the joining of Kase daughter Katora and Gerblecki son Hirsten, who are here to show their mutual respect and love for one another. They join in marriage willingly and with the seriousness required of the commitment. To show their dedication to each other, Katora and Hirsten have decided to partake in a hand binding ritual."

That was Kylene's cue to step up to the couple and wrap a honeysuckle vine around their wrists, binding Katora's left hand to Hirsten's right one. They would stay like that for the entirety of the ceremony. She couldn't help but take one good look at Hirsten and found his focus all on Katora. He looked so happy, his smile big and wide instead of the usual close-mouthed one.

Kylene made the mistake of glancing at Tarq just before making the first wrap. He was actually smiling as he gazed at the happy couple, but it quickly turned to a subtle glare when he caught Kylene's eyes. Her hands shook as she placed the center of the vine on their joined hands and twisted it up each side to their wrists. They joined their other hands together and faced one another as Odeletta continued with the vows.

"With these hands, you will now walk the world together, even when you are apart. With these hands, you will become a family to grow and learn together, even when you disagree. With these hands, you show the witnesses here today your commitment to each other, even as you recognize you remain individuals."

Kylene stared at her own hands as Katora and Hirsten spoke their vows. It hurt too much to watch their happiest moment when Kylene feared she would never have her own. She swallowed through the lump in her throat, full of so many conflicting emotions. There was an ache in her heart for a love she could never have that matched the one in her arm from a wound that would never heal.

Her feelings for Hirsten had been a crush—not true love. It wasn't the loss of him, but the loss of a unknown future love that tore at Kylene's heart and left her shaking.

As the ceremony ended, a gust of wind shook the cherry blossoms and hundreds of tiny petals snowed down on them. A whirling gust swirled the petals around the couple before whisking them away into the sky. The guests sat as if frozen, mesmerized by the spectacle.

Katora and Hirsten kissed to break the spell, and Bhar shouted a great "whoop." Then the couple practically danced down the aisle as the queens of Kristalis sung in a language Kylene didn't know. She held her emotions back for as long as she could and darted down the aisle right behind the newly married couple. She fled the garden to find a quiet corner of the palace.

Breathing in great heaves, Kylene sank to the frigid stone floor and pressed her cheek to the wall in an effort to cool her skin. She closed her eyes and heard Odeletta's message over and over in her head. Even after talking with Odeletta, Kylene had no idea when the message would come to fruition. Her stomach twisted in agony, a physical manifestation of the torment she felt over what was to become of her.

A not-so-subtle cough startled her to her feet, which were bare and cold. Tarq's brooding face stared down with his typical condescension. She inelegantly wiped her nose with the back of her hand. He offered her a handkerchief.

She accepted it with a hoarse, "Thank you."

"Bhar asked me to come look for you," he said in an even tone. "The banquet is about to start."

After blowing her nose, she stood and a faintness overtook her. Leaning heavily against the wall, she closed her eyes until she felt the world settle. Tarq peered at her curiously, giving her a look that wasn't entirely unfriendly, though she couldn't parse out what he was feeling based on his expression alone.

"I'll get cleaned up and be along to the banquet in a few minutes." She pushed off the wall and found her legs steady, much to her relief.

Tarq wavered, as if about to speak, but then he walked back toward the garden. He stopped after a few steps. "Are you okay, Kylene?"

"I'm fine." She managed a half-hearted smile. "A little tired after all the excitement of the morning, that's all."

"Mmmhmm," he mumbled in response. Kylene waited for more, wondering if maybe she had finally broken through whatever barrier was between them, only to have her hopes dashed when he turned on his heel and stalked away.

Afraid she'd never figure him out, she pushed his behavior to the back of her mind. There were plenty of other things to worry about. Determined to enjoy her sister's wedding, Kylene took large, half-running steps to her room to throw a dash of water on her face and run a brush through her messy hair.

She returned to the garden, a smile planted on her face, and settled across from Bhar in the first seat at the long dining table. Luckily, Tarq was several seats down on the same side. Next to each other, Katora and Hirsten presided over the head of the table. Odeletta was at the far end, and offered Kylene a rare smile when she looked her way. The queens of Blanchardwood and Yeselda filled the other seats. Sumptuous platters of food and drinks sat on the table.

Roasted duck and rabbit sat on beds of greens; grilled fish, eyes bulging out of their intact heads, filled one platter; some kind of wild game that Kylene couldn't identify was on another; cheese and exotic fruit were on a silver platter; and piles and piles of vegetables of all colors were mounded on top of hearty grains.

Her stomach rolled at the assault of scents. She took a sip of essence and found it was spiked. A few sips later, her stomach settled and she accepted a serving of vegetables and grains. The grass under her feet was warm and soft. She nibbled on the food, requesting the decanter of essence to be passed down the table. She refilled her glass and took a big gulp, ignoring Tarq's heated glare. She forced a few more bites down and listened to snippets of conversation floating around.

Evening settled in over the garden, warm and heady. Her own head felt lost in a haze; she smiled and offered a few words to those around her but couldn't find her place in the moment. She took another sip of essence, forced herself to taste the sweet tang, feel the bubbles on her tongue, and linger over the bitter aftertaste of the alcohol before taking another sip.

It's your sister's wedding, she told herself. Be here, enjoy it.

But she couldn't. It was like being in a bubble, one that she couldn't pop no matter how hard she prodded. Platters were passed. Odeletta and her companions came and went from the table. Deep in conversation with a queen, Bhar disappeared down a garden pathway with her.

Ky reached for the decanter to find it empty. Shaking it in the air, she called, "Another!"

Tarq marched from his spot and grabbed the empty container. He unceremoniously slammed it on the table, the metal pinging loudly. A hush fell over the party. Katora's head was cocked to the side and her right eyebrow was raised in careful consideration of them. Hirsten's fork hovered midway between his mouth and the table. A red-faced Bhar popped out from behind a flowering bush, his hand clutching the queen's, which would have been worthy of attention if not for the scene Tarq was making.

Kylene was fully present for the first time since stepping into the garden, her cheeks and neck ablaze under everyone's scrutiny.

She took in all their faces, finally arriving at Tarq's. He had the good sense to at least appear embarrassed with flushed cheeks himself.

"What are you doing?" Ky whispered, though everyone could plainly hear.

Tarq cleared his throat. His head swiveled to glance at the newlyweds and then back to Kylene. "Uh, nothing. It's empty." He gestured toward the decanter.

Bhar detached himself from the queen and hustled over. On the way, he grabbed a full decanter. He filled Kylene's glass. "All right then?"

"Yes." Her throat was tight, so it came out squeaky and quiet.

Bhar slapped Tarq on the back hard enough to push him forward. "Thanks for taking care of my sister."

"Ah, yes," Tarq stammered. "You're welcome."

Katora stood and announced, "I think we're ready for cake."

On that signal, everyone began clearing away the near-empty plates of food and the attention turned away from Kylene and Tarq. Once clean up was done, she found herself next to Bhar with Tarq hovering nearby.

She asked her brother, "You didn't want to spend more time with the queen?"

"I'm not one to miss cake." He poured himself a glass of essence and held it out for a toast. "To the lovely bride and her groom."

Kylene held up her glass. "To Katora and Hirsten. May their love be everlasting." They clinked glasses. Aware of Tarq's presence brooding over her, Kylene took one sip before setting it down.

"Why don't you sit, Tarq?" she said. "Have some cake."

The cake was covered in white frosting, all the better to showcase the real flowers that cascaded down the layers in bursts of color. Katora and Hirsten stood to make the first cut together, and soon everyone had a piece. Kylene took a bite, but it tasted bitter and she found herself back in her bubble.

Once everyone was done eating, Ky stood off the to side as the queens cleared away everything on the table, as well as the table itself. Several of them set up with instruments in front of the arbor. If anything could entice Kylene out of her despondent mood, it was music.

The queens' opening song was a flower growing, the early notes the first green shoots emerging from the soil. As a queen drew the bow across a violin, the stalk lengthened and sprouted leaves. The bass thumped in, the popping of tiny green buds. A drumbeat burst open the buds in a riot of color.

Kylene had never had music conjure such vivid images. The song was beautiful, heartbreaking in its perfection. This was not the music of mortals.

She found herself swept up in it. Her heart pumped in rhythm with the drumbeat. The movement spread to her shoulders and then to her hips. The music thrummed in her feet and head, and the dance grew increasingly frantic. She closed her eyes and let the song take her where it would, leaving all inhibitions behind. It went beyond the physical and into a higher realm. She had felt this way one other time, in the Golden City that shone like rainbows and emanated divine music.

Nothing could touch her. The heartache, the pain from her wound were blissfully absent. The song crashed to a stop, and her high crashed along with it. She heaved in deep breaths and came back to reality. All the hurts of life returned, and she found it hard to stand, so she leaned against a tree.

The garden came into sharp focus. Bhar lay on the ground among a group of queens, a sappy smile upon his face. Katora and Hirsten embraced among some bushes, caught up in each other as if the rest of the world didn't exist. From across the grass, Tarq glared at her.

It figured that he would be the only one not caught up in the euphoria. What was his problem? Couldn't he have fun?

The thoughts left her as the music started up again. She lost herself to the beat and didn't care if she ever came back. Then she danced the night away.

Chapter Fifty-Three

To their credit, the high priestesses merely clucked motherly at Zelenka as they exited through a trapdoor cleverly hidden beneath a rug behind the high priestesses' thrones. The seams of the floorboards lined up perfectly with the opening, so even without the rug, it would be difficult to detect.

The flaxen-haired priestess went last and placed a warm hand on Zelenka's shoulder. "Sister Maran can take you to see our doctor, Sister Rumie." She swept her robes close to her body to avoid the mess on the floor and was gone through the hole.

Zelenka swayed, too weak on her feet to feel the full weight of having vomited in front of the high priestesses.

Then Palafair was there by her side, a strong arm around her midsection. "Lead the way, Sister Maran."

He guided Zelenka away from the embarrassment that should have been making her cheeks flare. Instead, her body felt chilled and she shivered. A raw sensation gnawed at her stomach.

"All of you may follow me," Maran said. "We have a meal prepared for you in the dining room."

Palafair kept an arm snaked around Zelenka's waist as they slowly navigated the stone stairs that spiraled down in a dizzying fashion, candlelight dancing in their wake. At the small landing at the bottom, Maran pushed open a thick wooden door. Zelenka squinted against the brightness of sunshine pouring in. They emerged into a long, narrow courtyard hemmed in by a metal wall. Outside the courtyard, layers of tall beach grass sprouted up, obscuring the wall from outside view.

The courtyard floor was in a natural state, made of the same sand-colored stone as the meetinghouse, moss growing around the edges. At the far end of the courtyard, instead of more wall, the rock rose into a cavelike dome, also concealed from outside by grass. As they approached, a small opening in the base of the cave became visible. Zelenka never would have guessed anything lay beyond the ornate meetinghouse, never mind such a hidden place. Perhaps Zelenka's instincts about the priestesses fortifying their meetinghouse had been right.

Maran led them through the cave entrance into a surprisingly cozy space with a fireplace, the warm firelight bouncing off the stone walls and ceiling. Three hallways branched off, and Maran gestured down the center one. "The dining room is the first room on the right." Nemez and the others headed down that way, while Palafair stayed with Zelenka. Maran headed to the smaller passageway to the right. "This way to the infirmary."

Zelenka slipped out of Palafair's comforting embrace. "Go eat."

"Are you sure?" Lines of concern etched Palafair's face. It was all for naught because Zelenka was finally starting to accept what was making her ill, and there wasn't anything Palafair could do to make her feel better.

"I am fine," Zelenka assured him. "I think it was nerves." Still Palafair stood there staring with pinched eyebrows. "Go. I will be fine."

He kissed her forehead and acquiesced.

The doctor's room was bright and airy, despite being in a cave with no windows. The texture of the walls was smoothed to the point that it hardly looked like rock. And it wasn't lit by candlelight or torches but with large chunks of glowing stones that were set into the walls and curved ceiling at regular intervals. Zelenka touched her fingertip to a glowing stone and then brought it to her mouth. Salty. Just like the glowing lughite deep in the heart of Hillock.

"Lughite," the priestess doctor said. She wore the same white robes as Maran but with red trim around the sleeves, and was the exact opposite in stature—tall and broad in the hips and shoulders. "Mined from the mountains east of the river."

"I know it," said Zelenka, as if lughite were a friend and not a natural element. "We had it in the mountain where I grew up, deep in Faway Forest on the mainland. I did not know it was here on Demick Island as well." Knowing that a piece of her childhood had something in common with her ancestors' land felt significant in a way she couldn't process right then but would be thinking about for a long time afterward.

"The high priestess tells me you have been sick," Sister Rumie said. She approached Zelenka and held out two fingers in greeting. Zelenka removed her fingers from the cool comfort of the lughite and met the greeting. They both said, "Blessing."

Zelenka avoided eye contact but felt Sister Rumie's keen assessment of her. The doctor took a small glass cup out of a drawer and handed it to Zelenka. "The privvy is next door. A sample, please, urine only."

The privvy was lit by candles, so the smell wasn't unpleasant, but Zelenka still felt a wave of nausea when she opened the lid that led to a deep hole in the ground. She peed quickly and cleaned her hands in the wash bowl. Back in the doctor's room, Sister Rumie dropped what looked like a pebble-sized salt block in the sample. It fizzed and turned the light green of spring grass.

"When have you last bled?" she asked.

Zelenka cleared her throat, not uncomfortable with the question itself but with the direction it would lead the conversation. She thought back to how long it had been since the green tilli army had left the Three River Split to find their missing comrades. "Almost two moons."

"I see. Then you know what this means." Sister Rumie held up the sample, and Zelenka nodded. The doctor indicated for her to lay on the cot on the far side of the room. "Let us have a look at how you are doing?" Zelenka sat on the cot, the hay mattress sagging under her weight. "On your back please."

Sister Rumie pulled Zelenka's shirt up to the bottom of her breasts and pulled the front of her pants down past her navel. The doctor pressed Zelenka's belly, which was a small bulge now that she dared to look at it. The doctor held a length of ribbon to it. "Your measurements are right where they should be. Any other symptoms besides vomiting?"

Zelenka stared at the lughite in the ceiling and let it spot her vision. "A little dizziness and unsteadiness, particularly with an old leg injury."

"Loose joints are common during pregnancy," Sister Rumie said. And there it was—that word Zelenka had been avoiding. She was pregnant and there was no denying it now. Zelenka's mind fell into a haze while Sister Rumie asked her questions about the nature of her injury and discussed the possible complications. "Nothing major," the doctor assured her.

Zelenka was sitting on the cot now, her legs tucked up under her, though she had no recollection of doing so. She blinked, her eyes prickly and her throat tight.

"Colonel?" Sister Rumie inquired, peering at her with concerned eyes. It was as if the doctor was speaking from the end of a long tunnel. "Are you okay?"

Zelenka cleared her throat. "Yes...no."

"Let us discuss all the options," Sister Rumie said as she went into more details, including the option to end the pregnancy.

"And if I decide to end it?" She still couldn't say the word "pregnancy" and felt a coward for it—a stupid coward for having let it happen in the first place.

"I have the medicine for it here."

"I...I had not thought..." Zelenka didn't know what to say, nor what to think. She had spent so much time denying that she was pregnant that she didn't know how to process it now that she knew she was. A firm hand squeezed Zelenka's shoulder, bringing her back to her senses a bit. "How much longer until I have to decide?"

"You should decide within the next moon. After that, the process can become more complicated, the recovery longer."

"I imagine we will be leaving in a few days anyway." There was the war to think of and so many other considerations besides. And Palafair. She had to think of him as well. "When would it happen if I did nothing?" If she had been able to think clearly, the math would have been easy, but right now nothing was easy.

"The birth, you mean?" Sister Rumie clarified, and Zelenka

nodded again. "A little more than five moons, so a spring birth."

Zelenka looked down at her stomach, which was once again covered by her clothing.

Sister Rumie handed her a small satchel. "Ginger root candies for the nausea. You can get more in any medicinal shop in town." Then she took out a small vial filled with a liquid the verdant green of magnolia leaves. "If you decide to end the pregnancy, drink this as is or combine it with tea. Bleeding will begin a few hours after taking it and should cease a few hours after that. There may be some cramping, but the medicine is designed to minimize that. There are usually no complications, but you can consult a doctor or midwife at any point in the process. A day or two of rest is recommended afterward. Do you have any questions?"

"No." Zelenka mechanically reached for the vial and tucked it into the satchel.

"Would you like some time alone?" the doctor asked. "Or to have someone come in with you?"

"A few minutes alone..." she trailed off. What did she expect to accomplish in that time? Certainly not the wisdom to figure out what to do. Zelenka had never wanted a child. She had always thought of children as a tether that would hold her back. Of course, she knew many parents who didn't feel that way; they said children brought light into their lives. But Zelenka had never thought of it that way, especially given her own relationship with her father.

Families were complicated—the world was complicated—and she preferred the duo she had with Palafair. They had talked about children before getting married, how Zelenka didn't want any. Palafair had said he was okay with that, but now she wondered if it had been a decision she had made and he had gone along with, not one they had made together. She saw the way he interacted with the Kase children and grandchildren, the joy on his face when he verbally sparred with Katora, the pride in his eyes when Devon won a bagball game. Did he ever regret the decision not to have children? And now here was another decision she had to make, one that felt almost as much Palafair's as her own. If you had asked her two months ago what she would have done, the answer would have been easy. Confronted with the reality of it now, she just didn't know.

In the past, Zelenka had taken on every decision alone. Being with Palafair had given her a strong ally, someone to share ideas and problems with, and she liked it that way. Her past self might have called it dependence and seen it as a weakness, but her relationship with Palafair made her a better person.

She would talk to him about the pregnancy—of course she would. He was her partner.

Outside Sister Rumie's cave, she was surprised to find Laurel loitering around.

"Colonel!" Laurel said. "Are you feeling better?"

"Yes, thank you," Zelenka said absentmindedly.

"Good." Laurel smiled. "You will be pleased to know I am here to make sure we have a supply of baileaf root in our medical supplies." Zelenka let out a harsh laugh that startled Laurel. "Is something the matter, Colonel?"

"No," said Zelenka. "I am fine, or I will be fine."

"Hmmm." The way Laurel pierced her lips together made her look both older and wiser, and Zelenka could almost see her doing the math in her head. "Well, if you ever need to talk about anything that might require a friend's ear, I am a good listener."

Without replying, Zelenka hurried off to the dining room to find Palafair. The tilli demicks were not dining alone. Many priestesses, the purple-robed High Priestesses among them, crowded the room. There was excited chatter all around. Zelenka limped her way through the crowd to the tilli's table. Remnants of their meal had been abandoned on the table.

"What is going on?" Zelenka had to practically shout to be heard over the din. It reminded her of Roodesh's cave and the noise of the waterfall.

"The priestesses have decided to join us." Palafair's face was flush. "They are organizing to spread the word across the whole island. We head to Bad Beach in two weeks."

It was strange to feel excited that the demicks were joining them in a battle against Fyren that would most assuredly lead some of them to death. Zelenka had only fought in minor skirmishes in her time in the tilli army, but there had been casualties. Zelenka herself had almost become one when fighting Yeselda's animal army while on the quest with Katora.

Maybe excited wasn't the word, more like hopeful. This was bringing her people together. The demicks had been separated for hundreds of years and this was cause for celebration. When the Ice Queen had sent the message that Zelenka should go home, she had assumed it meant back to the tilli. It hadn't been wrong for her to go there, but perhaps she had also meant for Zelenka to come here to Demick Island. It was time her people were united, and if it took a war against a higher being to get that done, then at least something good would come of it.

Zelenka and Palafair embraced. She would tell him about the pregnancy, but not right now when the mood was high.

Chapter Fifty-Four

The first week of preparations for the demicks flew by. With little likelihood of an invasion, the island demicks had never had an army, so the volunteers needed to be armed and trained. Messages needed to be sent to other parts of Demick Island and to the mainland to Pop—admittedly made easier with the willing help of the sciathilte. Supplies need to be gathered to be taken to Bad Beach.

For her part, Zelenka was largely in charge of the training sessions with the tilli army and the recruits. With a supply of ginger root candies at her disposal, she felt better than she had in weeks. Plus, getting to order around Gainsley, who was helping with the training, did wonderful things for her mood. She was tired by the end of each day, exhausted really, but that was to be expected after a hard day's work.

The night before they were to leave the city for the northern part of the island, picking up recruits along the way, Zelenka lay in her tent next to Palafair. A heaviness that had nothing to do with fatigue settled over her. They were on their sides, Palafair spooning her, his arm slung across her waist and his face nuzzled against her neck. Zelenka's shirt was bunched up slightly in front, and as Palafair stirred in his sleep, his fingers brushed her bare skin just below her navel. It tickled and she started, accidentally waking him.

"Bad dream?" he asked sleepily in her ear.

"No," Zelenka whispered. "A little indigestion is all."

"Want me to get you a drink?" His voice faded off as he spoke, still not really awake.

"No. It is nothing." But the pounding of her heart defied her words. "Go back to sleep."

He snuggled up closer, his hand slipping fully under her shirt to gently rub her belly. She lay very still, feeling the sensation of his hands rubbing circles on her skin. Long after Palafair had fallen asleep, Zelenka stayed awake, all her senses tuned into the one part of her body.

* * * *

The last stop on Demick Island was a small village on the northern edge of the island where the river met the Greater Ocean. It was a gray sort of place, constantly covered in a cold mist. The village itself was gray with its tiny slate houses and a rocky shore that led to turbulent, gray waters. Even the smattering of pine trees that grew thicker as one moved farther outside the town lines looked more gray than green. It was under this pallor that the sciathilte and their demick riders flew in for their final days on Demick Island. Then they would be off over the ocean on a direct path to Bad Beach.

Zelenka awkwardly climbed off Indy and limped alongside Palafair as they took shelter in the village's meetinghouse. Unlike the one in the port city, this meetinghouse was a modest building with low ceilings and a single, long room outfitted with picnic-style dining tables and benches. Zelenka was soaked to the bone and shivering, not to mention dead-tired. The excitement of training all the new recruits had worn off on the long journey across the island. It had rained most of the time, and Zelenka's whole body, especially her injured leg, ached from riding on the sciathilte for long periods of time. There was a hot meal of fish stew and fresh bread waiting for them, but the smell of it nauseated her. She had run out of ginger root candies the day before.

The makeshift living quarters of travel had been tight, and she hadn't had more than a minute or two of alone time with Palafair, and no time to discuss the pregnancy. What she had decided was to make the decision tonight once and for all. If she were to end the pregnancy, she didn't want to wait any longer in order to have time to recover before they had to be at Bad Beach.

Information from the mainland on Fyren's plans had been scarce. The sciathilte who had brought a message to Pop had returned to Demick Island without anything useful. It seemed no one knew much about Fyren except that there was great magic building at the fortress of Drim, likely from the army he was building. So all they had was a meeting place of Bad Beach in the next fortnight for all who would oppose Fyren. Pop had been gathering human allies all across the Great Peninsula but had not received a reply yet from Katora and company. With the demicks, sciathilte, and humans, it was an odd alliance of different creatures—but a strong one, especially if Katora could convince the higher beings of Blanchardwood to join them. What exactly they would be facing once they launched an attack on Drim, no one knew. It was difficult to prepare for a battle in which they knew so little about the enemy.

Until she figured out her own situation, Zelenka wouldn't properly be able to concentrate on anything else.

As she reluctantly sipped broth from the stew, she told herself she'd talk to Palafair that night. The meetinghouse offered no privacy. Gertia, the village elder, was speaking to Nemez. She was a woman fitting the environment with gray hair that stuck out in frizzy bunches. Her face was so pale, blue veins shown through her skin.

Zelenka abandoned the food and went to sit with them, politely waiting for a break in the conversation, which was mostly about the logistics of where the village recruits would meet the tilli in the morning.

She whispered something to Nemez, and he quickly granted permission for her to ask Gertia a question. She leaned in a little closer to the elderyear. "Excuse me, ma'am. With General Nemez's permission, I was hoping it would not be too much trouble to find a quiet place for a warm bath. The cold, damp weather and the long days of riding have gotten my leg in a stiff way."

Gertia's face wrinkled with a warm smile. "Of course, dearie. You can use my hut. I will have one of my girls show you the way and bring hot water around."

When one of Gertia's daughters, who was a grown woman herself, arrived, Zelenka dragged Palafair along, and she didn't care what anyone thought of it. Only a few people knew where she was going, and so be it if they thought it was weird to bring along her husband for a bath. It was a chance to have privacy where one of them wasn't half asleep.

With a suggestive wink, Gertia's daughter left them alone with a tub full of hot water. Zelenka quickly undressed and slipped in. It took up most of the tiny bathroom and was made of a dull metal that was rough on the bottom where Zelenka's feet touched, but it was blissful. She closed her eyes and sunk up to her neck in the hot water. She ducked her head all the way under and massaged her scalp, wiping away all the grit from the last few days, before resurfacing.

From close behind her, Palafair said in a playful whisper, "As much as I enjoy watching my wife bathe, I cannot imagine you would bring me with you for that sole purpose."

"There is not enough room for two, otherwise I would invite you in." This was true as the tub was higher than average but quite narrow. "I actually brought you along to have a talk." Zelenka took the bar of soap and rubbed it between her hands, watching the bubbles form rather than looking directly as her husband.

Palafair stood close by, watching silently with the patience of an elderyear waiting out a child's tantrum.

"I made an error of judgment early on in this journey," Zelenka began. "I did not realize that certain items were not regularly stocked in the army's medical supplies. I..." she trailed off, unable to get to the point.

Palafair reached out, took the soap, and let it float away while he took her hands tight in his. "My love, are you sick? I am sure we can find something to soothe you either here or on the mainland when we arrive at Bad Beach. We can send a sciathilte to Pop and have him bring whatever you need."

"No," Zelenka's voice cracked over the word. "What I needed before was baileaf root, but there is no need for it now. What I need now is help in making a decision."

Finally she looked up to see Palafair's face, to watch him take in her words and make sense of them. His expression flickered from confused to pondering and finally to understanding.

"You are pregnant," he said. Though it wasn't posed as a question, Zelenka nodded as much for herself as for him.

His face was a mask, and she couldn't read his expression. He was always so careful with her feelings, to not let his own cloud hers, but how she wished he would reveal what he was feeling now.

"That is why you have been sick. And the decision you need to make…" It was Palafair's turn to trail off.

"You know what my relationship with my father was like. You know how dedicated I am to the army. You know I have never wanted kids." They had talked about all of this when things had gotten serious between them, when they had started thinking about getting married. "Sister Rumie gave me the medicine. There is time to end it if I want to…if *we* want to." She stared down at her hands, which were getting pruney in the rapidly cooling water, and shivered.

"I—" Palafair's voice broke over the single word, his mouth hanging open with all the things he wasn't saying.

Zelenka had more she needed to say anyway. "I know you have always supported me and my decision not to have kids. Back then it was all in the theoretical. And I wish it had stayed that way, but I screwed up. It has never been my wish to keep it, but I am afraid to take this away from you."

A rush of emotions overwhelmed Zelenka, and the tears came in earnest, sobs wracking her body. Palafair stuck his arms in the water, sleeves and all, and pulled her into as much of an embrace as the tub would allow. He brought her hands to his lips and kissed each one of her wet knuckles. She sobbed for a long time until it receded to hiccups.

"Our decision, my love," he whispered into her hands.

"What?" she asked, not because she hadn't heard but because she didn't understand.

"It was not your decision alone." His warmth radiated through his clothes to her cold body. "It was always *our* decision, and I stand by that."

Zelenka let out a half-sob, half-laugh and placed a tender kiss on his lips.

"Come now." He held out a towel. "Let us get you out of that cold water."

She dried herself and dressed in clean clothes. Then they lay together on the couch in front of the fire and talked.

She rested her head on Palafair's chest. "The doctor recommended a day or two to recover. That means not leaving with the rest of the army. Do I need to tell them?"

Palafair ran his fingers through her hair and massaged her head. "It is not their business. We tell only who you want to and no one else."

After more discussion, they decided to keep the matter private. Palafair left to tell Nemez that she was sick and staying on Demick Island a few extra days.

When he came back, he joined her on the couch again and said he would stay with her. "For the rest of our days," he whispered into her hair.

She drank the medicine before falling asleep in Palafair's arms.

Chapter Fifty-Five

Devon was in agony, stuck in between his mom and Pop Pop, his butt smacking the wooden seat with every rut of the road, of which there were many. Em had been reassigned from baby-sitting him to the more important job of weapons trainer. Devon wasn't allowed to participate, so he had hardly seen her. The only time he was allowed on his own was to relieve himself, and even then someone was always hovering nearby, calling out to check on him. At night, he had to share his mother's tent, which they set up in the back of the wagon to keep off the cold ground. She slept right next to the flap, the only exit, so it was impossible to sneak out. His skin itched from the constant surveillance.

As the caravan moved through the plains south of Skimere, the day temperatures weren't much warmer than the night ones and the wind picked up. Anything that wasn't tied down was subject to being whipped up by a big gust and tumbled through the dry grass, never to be retrieved. The travelers huddled under blankets and warmed rocks at night to tuck into their beds. One day he begged to be allowed to jog alongside. His legs were twitchy and sore from disuse. Thankfully his mother relented. As he trotted at a comfortable pace, he didn't even mind how his breath hitched with the inhalation of frigid air.

The only excitement was when Nika, the brigha Pop Pop had spoken about, showed up one night. Apparently Nika had coerced his aunt Kylene into taking a blood oath to protect the brigha. Even if Devon hadn't been allowed to listen in on the conversation, he would've heard Pop Pop's explosion of anger from clear across the camp. Devon learned a few new curse words that he was itching to try out with his friends back home. The other news from Nika was bad as well. Drim was positively brimming with magic and no one could get close enough to find the source.

Nika joined their caravan the rest of the way to Skimere,

though Devon noticed she kept her distance from all the Kases, whose looks were purely murderous. They had barely reached the cobblestone streets of Skimere before a sciathilte greeted them with news from the other towns and cities. The humans stood shivering outside an inn while Pop Pop collected the letters from the sciathilte. The inn was the biggest in Skimere but not large enough to accommodate all the Tussarians. At least Em and her fathers were able to stay there with the Kases.

Devon's mom went to meet with Pop Pop about the news in the letters, and Devon was once again left out of anything important. He was too tired and dirty to care, so he cleaned up quickly in the wash bin and fell asleep on his bed fully clothed.

Once Devon had rested, he thought the pastyears would be sufficiently distracted that he might sneak off and see some of Skimere. He spotted Em reading in the corner of the dining area. Spurts of conversations about strategies and who would go where and when could be heard as he made his way to her.

He plopped down and saw she was reading a book of poetry. He blushed as it reminded him of the poem he had penned for her; that felt like a million years ago when he was a romantic youngeryear with a crush. Somehow he didn't feel that way anymore, neither like a youngeryear nor like his feelings for Em were only a crush. She ignored his presence completely.

He tipped his chair back on two legs, which got her attention enough for her to push the chair back down on all fours, her fingers brushing his leg, before going back to her book.

"Wanna get out of here?" he asked.

Em slowly finished the poem she was reading, placed a bookmark in the page, and titled her head at Devon in a way that made him think maybe she wasn't entirely annoyed with his presence. "Where would we go?"

"I figured you would know somewhere good."

Biting her bottom lip, she stared off into space, thinking. Devon's breath hitched and he played it off as a hiccup.

"I do know somewhere," she said. "C'mon." She grabbed his hand and pulled him to the exit.

"Where are you two going?" Devon's mom asked as they breezed by.

"A bunch of us are going to play cards." Em lied without a waver to her voice—unless that was what they were actually doing, which he wouldn't mind. "I'll keep him out of trouble." Then she pulled Devon along.

His mom yelled after them, "Don't stay up late!"

Devon hesitated, wanting to ask if that meant he would get to go, as there had been talk of him staying in Skimere. A sharp tug on his hand was all he needed to keep moving. They headed out the front door of the inn and into the nippy evening air, so they definitely weren't going to Em's room. The sun had sunk below the buildings of the city, plunging the streets into twilight. Despite the creeping darkness, the city was bustling with the clip clop of hooves on cobblestone, the jingle of bells on shop doors, and the conversations of passersby. Tall lanterns glowed along the main walkways, so it never got fully dark. People and a few demicks bustled about, most of them tucked into cloaks against the cold. A stiff breeze blew down the street, moaning quietly underneath the louder sounds of the city. Devon shivered. He wished they had stopped to get their cloaks; his hand grasped in Em's was the only warm part of his body.

She steered him down lit roads and then through alleyways without lights, the city darkening and getting colder with each passing minute. Devon shivered again and hoped they were almost there. They entered a tight alley formed by two brick buildings. It was littered with leaves that blew noisily in the wind. The packed dirt was sticky underneath Devon's boots, and his imagination ran wild with what might be causing it—mainly on scenarios that ended with blood being shed.

"Almost there." Em guided him deeper into the alley than Devon cared to go, but he hid his reservations as she seemed perfectly confident. She stopped so abruptly that he bumped into her. It was so dark, he hadn't seen the brick-red door amid the actual bricks of the building. There was no door handle to open it from the outside. Em rose her hand to knock but pulled it back and turned to face Devon.

"This place isn't exactly on the map," she explained. "It's best if we keep it a secret."

"Is it safe?" He hoped the trepidation didn't show in his voice.

"Sure, but it's exclusive...and for young people only—no one above primeyear allowed and even some older primeyears get turned away. Well, except for the owner, who looks ancient. She's usually around."

"But an older youngeryear is okay?"

She looked him up and down. "Yeah, you'll be fine. Maybe don't mention your age, though."

He nodded. That was not something he planned on telling anyone.

Em finally knocked, and the door slid sideways a crack, kind of like a barn door, but there was no track that he could see. Was it magic or some clever bit of hidden engineering? He was betting on the latter because it seemed a waste to use magic on such a thing. Em stuck her hand in the crack. Her wrist wiggled as she flashed a series of hand signals to whoever was inside. The door slid all the way open to reveal a room no bigger than a horse pen. And it was dark, really dark, lit only with the light of a single candle on the floor. The only other object in the room was a small stool that Devon would surely crush if he sat on it. Next to the stool stood an anni demick. He pushed open a door on the opposite end of the tiny room and said, "Have fun."

Devon wasn't sure what he had been expecting in this primeyear-only space, but as he walked over the threshold, heart pounding in his chest, it defied his expectations. Instead of something rowdy and illicit, it was serene with an air of scholarship. A long bar ran the length of the room to his left, bright bottles and glasses reflecting the flickering candlelight. A spectacularly large iron chandelier hung from the tall ceiling, which had exposed beams. Candles burned in the chandelier, and there wasn't a lantern in sight, only candles—lots of them, on tables and in small nooks in the walls—their flames like thousands of shiny moths fluttering about the room. It created a strange sense of movement.

Chairs and poofy pillows were clustered together in different configurations, some around tables and other forming circles around open spaces. A quiet violin filled the room with a melancholy melody, the kind of music that made Devon feel both a completeness and a longing in his heart. Humans and demicks were scattered throughout, some reading alone or in groups, some playing cards or other quiet games. Two women embraced in a slow dance near the violist.

A primeyear woman in a quiet corner of poofs glanced their way and did a double-take. She jumped up from her over-sized pillow and ran to them, capturing Em in a dramatic hug that included a twirl, the woman's linen trousers billowing out around her legs. She set Em down and kissed her lightly on the mouth, and Devon felt heat creeping up his cheeks. Em let out a squeal of delight.

Nearly breathless from the enthusiastic greeting, Em turned to him. "Devon, this is Veenie."

Veenie was a sight to behold. She had short, spiky hair like Em but with streaks that were an unreal shade of bright blue. It would have made the bluest of irises wilt in jealously. The rest of her hair was white-blond, and she had deep brown eyes. In addition to the linen pants, she wore a leather vest, corded in front with black ties and fringed with off-white fur at the neck and waist. On her feet were simple leather sandals, and Devon couldn't believe she wasn't freezing. His feet hadn't yet thawed out from the cold walk, and he was wearing lined boots.

"You're back so soon!" Veenie exclaimed. "I didn't expect this!" She spoke in a loud tone that drowned out the music, but no one outside their group paid her any attention.

"Me neither," said Em. Her expression went from joyous at seeing her friend to downcast, her lowered voice reflecting the somber reason for being in Skimere. "We go to war soon."

"War!" Veenie said, continuing to speak in exclamations. "Come sit and tell me all about it!"

They joined Veenie's friends in the corner, all of them

squishing together to make room for the newcomers. Most of them knew Em already, so the introductions were primarily for Devon's sake, though he forgot many of their names as soon as they were said. A heady, earthy scent filled the air and Devon noticed incense burning on the floor nearby. Cups were passed around and more pleasant greetings were exchanged as Em and Devon settled in.

They were close to a large fireplace that crackled and shot sparks. With the candles, the incense, and the blazing fire, he wondered if this establishment of primeyears was destined to burn down. At least he had finally warmed up. In fact, he was beginning to understand Veenie's light attire as sweat formed in his armpits. He took a sip from his glass and was pleased to recognize the sweet, dry taste of spiked essence.

The drinks flowed freely as did the conversation. Everyone talked all at once and in pockets of topics that filtered through smaller groups among the large one. The conversations ebbed and flowed in a chaotic but organic way. Several cups deep, Devon was trying and failing to follow a discussion on a book of poetry he had never read. Veenie and Em both chimed in an opinion before defecting to another conversation, leaving the two who had originated the topic to continue their debate.

Devon's ear caught Veenie's excited voice as she critiqued the guitar player who had taken the place of the violinist. Yet another conversation turned to gossip about people Devon didn't know and then moved on to the excellency of the essence they were drinking, a topic Devon was proud to hear. Finally Em popped in next to him. She held Veenie's hand, and they appeared to be in a heated debate.

"Odeletta and Fyren's failed love is the stuff of myth. It can't be all that serious!" Veenie said.

"Of course it's serious!" Em was the one talking in exclamation points now. "Nearly the entire town of Tussar marches to Drim. An army of tilli soldiers, accompanied by the legendary sciathilte, fly there now!"

"Very serious," said Devon, who had hardly spoken since arriving. His deep, serious tone startled himself and caught the attention of the group. "My aunts and uncle are in Blanchardwood this very moment at the Ice Queen's palace."

"Maybe she was bored after all those years of isolation with her queens," one of the poetry advocates said.

"No one could be bored with a beautiful group of queens at their side!" interjected Veenie.

"No one's heard anything from Fyren in centuries," someone else chimed in. "Nothing since the war at Drim."

"All the more reason to fear him," said Devon, his posture no longer relaxed back into the pillows. "What has he been up to all these hundreds of years? Not a word of him in all that time, and now in the last two seasons, tidings of a growing power near Drim."

"Rumors!" said Veenie. "That's all I've heard!"

Their debate had caught the attention of the rest of the room. The guitar player had fallen silent, his instrument forgotten on his lap.

"Not rumors." Devon looked to Em for support, but she shrugged and jutted out her chin as if to say "you're up." Devon took a deep breath and stood, addressing the entire room as if it was his duty. "We're all too young to remember the last war, as are our parents and our parents' parents. The oldest elderyears have spent their entire lives in peace, as have all of us for many generations. Like many of you," he glanced down at Veenie, "I thought war was an ancient, long dead threat. Surely after all these years of peace, we had evolved into a society that is beyond such atrocities."

He stepped out of the circle of pillows and poofs and moved next to the guitarist in the center of the room. "But if the higher beings can succumb to the basest of emotions, like jealousy and greed and apathy, aren't we, as mortal creatures, subject to the same fallacies? And to a higher degree. A powerful being like Fyren would count on our weaknesses—our short memories and short lives moving us to complacency—in order to outfox us and make a move back to power."

Devon's face blazed with warmth. With Em beaming up at

him, he was fully committed to convincing his captive audience. "I've heard the accounts of the growing magic from those who have seen it themselves." The word "brigha" flitted around the room, and Devon confirmed their suspicions. "Yes, a brigha has seen the magic. Odeletta, the Ice Queen, sent a lightning bolt across the Great Peninsula to summon my kin to her. She's been reading the signs, even if the likes of us haven't been. Mark my words, war is coming, whether you want to believe it or not. We can either prepare or we can let Fyren bring his wrath upon us unawares."

There was no applause of support, only Devon's footsteps echoing on the wooden floor as he returned to his poof, breathless from the effort.

Veenie had no qualms about adding her opinion. "Devon Kase, you are a fine storyteller!" She raised a glass of his family's essence. "I applaud your effort to rouse the youth! But you have not convinced me that the myths are true and that we must go to war!"

A murmur began in one corner of the room and spread as debates sprang up. The nature of those who frequented this establishment was one of discourse, not necessarily one of action. All through the night, the young citizens of Skimere debated and discussed war, calling upon Devon and Em to recount the evidence. Em made promises to train them on the sword. Devon argued his points until his voice was a croak and his breath raspy. One primeyear man confessed his mother had recently gone to Drim and never returned.

Eventually a large number of them were swayed to action. They would march on Drim with the Tussarians and fight alongside the tilli army and the sciathilte. Those who chose not to join were not judged harshly but simply accepted as having come to a different conclusion, though Devon secretly thought them fools. A few primeyears claimed to be pacifists and could not be convinced to take up arms for any cause, no matter how strong the threat of evil.

In the end, an enlivened group proceeded to the inn where Pop Pop and the other Tussarians were staying. After having declared she was skeptical but reticent to be left behind, Veenie joined the believers. Devon marched through the streets to bring his very own army to his grandfather and mother, and hopefully prove his worth to lead his own charge when the time came...or at the very least not get left behind.

Chapter Fifty-Six

Outside the inn at Skimere, the Tussarians were packing up the wagons to make the final march to Bad Beach when the snow began to fall. Much of the sky was still blue when the first flakes fell, sticking and then quickly melting on Devon's hair and cloak. He glanced at Em as they packed up the swords they had been using to help train the young Skimerians who had volunteered. They weren't totally pathetic with a weapon, though they were far from proficient. Em said she'd keep working with them on the way to Bad Beach.

A trickle of people from other cities and towns had come to join the ranks. It didn't feel like enough when they had no idea the size of the enemy they would face, but it would have to do. There was still no word from Katora in Blanchardwood, but they couldn't wait any longer to hear from her. A sciathilte had arrived the night before with news from Demick Island. The tilli and many of the island demicks would arrive at Bad Beach in a matter of days.

Em had just covered the steel with a blanket when the sky darkened and the flurries turned to heavy snow. It stuck to her head and softened the stark color of her hair. Devon shook the snow from his own head and pulled up his hood, but the wind quickly blew if off again.

"I don't like the look of this," he said.

"It's just snow." Em playfully rubbed snow off his head.

"It's never just snow," Devon muttered.

He'd learned from Pop Pop that snow in the Great Peninsula was never simply a weather phenomenon. The trick was figuring out what it meant, especially because there didn't seem to be any specific message attached to this storm as there had been with the lightning strike that had ruined Kylene's play.

His gaze was fixed on the gray clouds when a tiny figure emerged. It began as a speck that flew lower and lower until

Devon could make out the form of a sciathilte, the deep blue—almost black—of a clear sky at midnight. It took a little longer for the other Tussarians and the Skimerians to recognize the mythical creature, but once they did, a collective intake of breath rippled through the crowd. Many of the Tussarians had watched the sciathilte fly out of Faway Forest in grand fashion, but most of the Skimerians had never seen one.

It landed right in the street next to the convoy of wagons, causing a stir. The city streets suddenly swelled with bodies—humans and anni demicks alike—to get a glimpse of the creature. A couple of the primeyears from the other night sought out Devon, wide-eyed and impressed.

"Great Mother!" Veenie said. "Devon, I sincerely apologize for doubting you. I just...I never..." She seemed to be out of exclamations.

He slapped her on back and chuckled. "Yeah. It's hard to believe it until you see it."

Her hand hovered over her mouth, and she spluttered speechlessly. She and Em exchanged a look that Devon couldn't quite interpret. Then they embraced in a way that made Devon's stomach clench in jealousy. He looked away as they kissed.

"I know others who will come!" Veenie declared.

"Let's go," said Em.

"We leave soon," Devon reminded them as they were swallowed by the swirling snow.

With a frown, Devon climbed up into the seat of the weapons wagon for a better view. The snow was falling hard and the wind was whipping it into the air, but he could make out the sciathilte, Pop Pop, his mom, and several other Tussarians conversing. The buzz of the crowd and the drone of the wind drowned out what they were saying. Devon jumped from the wagon and fought his way over.

"So they're coming?" Pop Pop was saying.

"Yes," replied the sciathilte in its weird, buzzing voice. "They were seeking the assistance of the witch of Faway to expedite their arrival from Blanchardwood."

Devon assumed the sciathilte was speaking of Katora's group, and that would be good news that they were coming, but Pop Pop's forehead was creased in concern. Pop Pop glanced around at the faces looking to him for guidance, and he quickly smoothed the lines of his face and offered a more hopeful expression. "We must make haste to reach Bad Beach ourselves. This weather is a bad omen and will be a hindrance to our progress."

"I seek out my swarm." Without any preamble, the sciathilte took to the sky and disappeared into the swirl of snow.

"Finish packing and we leave before the hour's out!" Pop Pop yelled.

Devon grabbed his grandfather's elbow, startling him. "There are others who will join us now that they've seen the sciathilte. We must wait for them."

Pop Pop's gaze turned once more to the sky, or rather the torrent of snow that was obscuring it. "One hour. That's how long we wait. The citizens of Skimere had their chance. I hope they come now that indisputable proof is before their eyes, but we can't delay. This snow is worrisome, very worrisome."

Devon dashed off to alert as many people as he could of the news. Once he was out of the crowd—as no one there needed convincing of what had come to Skimere—he skidded to a stop at a crossroads and blankly stared down one direction and then the other. Luckily Em emerged from around a corner.

"Veenie has already spread the word among those who didn't want to come the other night," she said. "It's the older folks who need to know. We'll stop at every public gathering place until we run out of time."

Em led them to a busy street with restaurants and shops. They each took a different side and started alerting anyone who would listen to head to the inn. Devon ran in through the door of a shop—a clothing one a quick glimpse showed—and shouted, "Sciathilte at the inn! War is upon the Great Peninsula! Pack your bags and march to Drim!"

He was more concerned about stirring up people's interest

than being completely accurate. Once people got to the inn, the witnesses to the sciathilte's existence would fill in the details. He dashed down several busy blocks, making as many stops as he could. His lungs pinched uncomfortably as he rounded another turn. The snow had lured many people outside to take in the rare sight. Devon was running out of time, so he made one last announcement, "War is upon us! To the inn! Head to the inn!"

He tried retracing his path, but the snow continued to increase in intensity and he lost his way. But then he came upon a group of citizens running toward him, faces flush and eyes alight with excitement. One woman punched her fist in the air and called, "C'mon. Magic has come to the inn!"

It wasn't the message he had thought to spread, and perhaps Em's efforts had incited these people to action, but it was the excitement he had been going for—and at least he knew which way to go. The crowd thickened as he neared the inn, which slowed his pace. Then it was a fight to get through the crowd to find Pop Pop standing atop his wagon seat, eyes agog. He caught a glimpse of Devon and offered a quick smile, his eyes never losing their sense of awe. Devon's mom, Em, and Veenie were among those near the wagon. Em's cheeks were flush; she caught Devon's eyes and shook her hands in triumph.

Pop Pop raised his arms above his head to try and quiet those who could see him through the snowstorm. "Everyone, please, can I have your attention?"

The hush started with the pocket of people closest to the wagon and spread throughout the crowd that had grown so large much of it was lost in the thicket of snowfall. Even the wind hushed as if waiting to hear what Pop Pop had to say.

"Those of you who can hear me, please spread the word once I am done talking," he said in a loud voice that carried through the whisper of snowflakes. "As I steel my heart to head off in a snowstorm to war against the fallen higher being Fyren, I find it warming to see all of you here in support. In light of new evidence, which those of you who were here to witness the sciathilte's arrival can attest to, I hope more of you are ready to join our cause. My daughter is on her way to Bad Beach with the queens of Blanchardwood and the witch of Faway Forest."

His deep voice carried far and wide on the still air. "All I have been saying, and all that my grandson has been saying," he shot a quirked eyebrow in Devon's direction, "about Fyren and war is true. I'm afraid we cannot delay our departure any longer. I encourage those of you who are ready to go today to pack your supplies and join our march. If you need more time, your fellow citizen Veenie," at that, the primeyear woman climbed up next to Pop Pop, "will lead a second march in three days time."

The wind chose that moment to pick up and break the careful lull of both the weather and the people. Pop Pop tried to shout out a few last words, but they were lost in the storm.

Em's hand found Devon's. "We must get to our wagon!" she shouted. "We're leaving!"

They pushed through what was now becoming a blizzard. Em's Da instructed them to sit in the back of the wagon and cover themselves with blankets. Then they were off, rocking their way over cobblestones in a whirl of white, but it was cozy under the blankets with Em's warm hand still in Devon's and Veenie staying in Skimere for a few more days.

Chapter Fifty-Seven

The day after the wedding, the blustery storm continued in Blanchardwood. Despite the weather, the Watcher arrived from Faway Forest, the bird form flying high above the worst of the blizzard until it reached Kristalis.

The bird flew into the dining room during dinner, landed on the table, and shook off the snow that had gathered on its small body. Yeselda gave him a pointed look that was inscrutable to Kylene, but clearly the Watcher understood because it shook its head with a small no.

"Very well," Yeselda said quietly before addressing everyone at the table loudly. "We leave tomorrow at dawn."

It had been decided that Yeselda's three horsemen would transport the humans so they could keep up with the higher beings and arrive at Bad Beach in a matter of days. There was no word from Odeletta about joining them, but Kylene tucked a sliver of hope away that she would change her mind before dawn.

Once Yeselda swept out of the room, the bird flying behind her, Tarq asked, "What was that about?"

"No idea," said Katora. "I guess we should all get to bed."

* * * *

It was cold and dark when Kylene came down to breakfast the next morning. She covered a long yawn before resting her head on her palms, both elbows on the table. Bhar sleepily made his way through an impossibly large pile of eggs, a dozen strips of bacon, and a heap of toast, plus a whole pot of tea. Tarq was not only aloof with Kylene but avoided eye contact with everyone. Katora and Hirsten were the last to arrive, both looking rather disheveled. They should have been heading out on their honeymoon and touring the Great Peninsula for pleasure, rather than racing across it to go to battle.

Collectively, the queens were a stoic group—the wedding

being a notable exception—but this morning, their stern faces seemed extra impassive. The Watcher startled the humans, except for Katora, who merely glanced up when it arrived in griffin form instead of the bird one. The only one who seemed her usual self was Yeselda. Her dark hair, not a strand out of place, perfectly framed her luminous eyes and deep-red lips. Kylene supposed it was easy to look perfect when one could use magic to change their appearance.

For her part, Kylene slipped a nip of alcohol she had saved from the wedding into her tea and felt a little more human after finishing her first cup. She would be content with that and leave greater being status to the likes of Yeselda.

When the sun lightened the horizon to a pale pink, the travelers were ready, their lower halves freezing as they stood in two feet of snow, waiting for their rides. Yeselda's henchmen led their steads through the snow to the front of the ice palace. Kylene and Bhar mounted the white horseman's steed, whose blindingly white coat blended in with the snow. In an unusual configuration, which Katora insisted upon, Hirsten and Tarq rode together on the crimson horse and Katora alone took the black one. Kylene saw Katora shiver as she mounted, not from the frigid air but from the cold fear that arose from contact with Ebony Knight's horse.

Odeletta remained noticeably absent.

Kylene looked back at the palace as the horses cantered away with unnerving speed. Yeselda, the horsemen, the Watcher, and the queens led the way on foot in a blur of motion. Kylene caught a glimpse of a face in a window high up in one of the turrets. She blinked and the ground in front of the palace changed almost imperceptibly. Green peeked up underneath the snow. Kylene thought that couldn't be possible as it had been several feet deep moments ago. But sure enough, underneath the horse's hooves was a path of snowdrop flowers that led all the way to the frozen river. They were present in such abundance that the white petals kept most of the green stalks from view, so it looked like snow from afar. Kylene knew the flowers were a final farewell from Odeletta; the Ice Queen would not be joining them in the battle against her old lover and foe Fyren.

The horses were astonishingly swift, and soon the evergreen trees were a blur as the travelers whipped past them. They were out of Blanchardwood and halfway through the first stretch of grasslands when they stopped for the night.

"Of course, we could keep moving," Yeselda said smugly as Katora started a fire to cook a meal and keep warm overnight, "but I understand you humans have baser needs to attend to."

"You can go on without us," Katora retorted, flames reflected in her blue eyes. "I'm sure the horses know the way to Bad Beach."

"If only I could." Yeselda fluttered blood-red nails in Katora's direction. "But Fyren is intent on making things difficult, and I doubt you would make it without my assistance."

Kylene and Hirsten both reached for Katora and held her at bay. Kylene was close enough to hear Hirsten whisper in Katora's ear, "Peace, my firecracker." Heat crept up Kylene's neck and she retreated to the other side of the fire to eat her supper.

* * * *

The higher beings and the humans upon the horses traveled so fast across the plains that the journey took on an unreal quality. The constant wind brought tears to her eyes and muted her hearing, so that she felt like she was in a sped-up fever dream. By the end of the second day, they were skirting north of Hirithor Woods.

Riding behind her, Bhar said, "I'm glad we're not going through those woods. I hear the trees are ancient and vengeful. And that's the least of its horrors."

Bhar was always teasing her about scary things, but as she stared at the impossibly tall trees, their canopies haphazardly waving in different directions instead of flowing with the wind as normal trees did, a chill crept up her spine. One would blow about and then fall still. Then a second would blow before stilling, only to have the first one start up again, as if they were communicating with one another. At one point, Kylene thought she saw one uproot itself to jump in front of another, or perhaps it was a trick of the waning light. Whether Bhar was serious or not, Ky was relieved to leave Hirithor Woods behind.

They stopped shortly after to camp near Whitewater River, and all the humans were as cranky as a tired youngeryear. Katora and Hirsten were arguing, Bhar was sniping about the meager portions, and Tarq was more ornery than usual. His brooding figure cast a large shadow over the fire as if marking it his territory.

Kylene decided to go for a walk along the river, Yeselda yelling after her, "Do not go too far! We would not want to lose one of our precious humans."

She was sore from riding, her muscles cramped and achy, and her arm was feeling worse than it had in a long time. She found a quiet spot near the river and leaned against a small tree. The night was clear, and the stars were popping out one at a time. She tucked her knees in close and wrapped the cloak around them to keep warm. A rustle of the grass nearby caught her attention. The fox stepped out.

It opened its mouth, the tongue gem-free for once, as if to speak. Finally, thought Kylene, hoping the mystery of this creature was going to be solved. Instead of words, it let out a whine and took a few tentative steps closer. It flopped onto its back and rolled around, sending up puffs of dry dirt. Then it lay still on its back, tongue lolling out the side of its snout. The compulsion to pet the pretty thing, to feel its soft fur, overtook her. She knelt down and reached out.

"Stop!" The warning cry came from behind.

She whipped her head around to find Tarq. The path his gaze followed told her he had not only seen the fox but scared it off as well. Sure enough when she turned back around, the animal was a speck in the distance, and after a moment, she lost sight of it entirely in the dark.

"Why would you do that?" Tears of frustration pricked her eyes—more than frustration. The lost opportunity of making a connection with the fox left her feeling hollowed out.

"I...uh," he stammered. "You shouldn't touch wild animals."

Any relief over the fact that he had seen the fox too, thereby proving it wasn't a figment of her imagination, was overshadowed by rage. The anger rushed through her chest and made her light-headed. She had put up with his rude and standoffish attitude, but this affront into business that wasn't his put her over the edge.

"How dare you?" she accused, poking a finger into his chest. He didn't wince at her touch, as she thought he might, but stood and took it. "I was about to—" she hesitated, not sure how to explain the true circumstances of her relationship with the fox, and not really wanting to explain it to him of all people. "This has nothing to do with you."

"What exactly is this?" He gestured off in the distance where the fox had disappeared.

"None of your concern." The tears were falling freely now. To have missed out learning more about the fox reminded her of having to leave the Golden City. This hollowness in her chest was only a hint of how she had felt upon being pulled out of that magical place.

"Please tell me."

All she saw in his face was honest pleading, but it wasn't enough to convince her to spill her secret. "Never."

"Kylene." He reached out and gently touched her arm. He looked her in the eyes as he had never done before. Her muscles twitched under his touch. "That..." he hesitated over the next word, "fox is not to be trusted."

"What would you know of it?" She sniffled and the tears kept silently falling, but he had her attention.

Tarq began to pace. Hair fell past his eyebrows, so she couldn't get a good look at his eyes, and he was back to avoiding eye contact. "Can you just trust that I know?"

"Why would I?" she said quietly. Was he really so unaware of the way he had treated her and why that might not lend itself to trust?

"Of course you wouldn't." He blew out a frustrated breath. "Will you trust me enough to stay away from that fox if you should see it again?"

He was the opposite of his usual aloof self, darting back and forth and trampling down the grass. He was distressed, but until he could give her more than a generic warning, Kylene saw no reason to heed his advice.

"I told you this doesn't concern you."

"Gah!" He threw up his hands amid all the pacing. Then the mumbling began, and lots of hand waving—a conversation of one that Kylene wasn't invited to. Finally he stood still, seemingly having come to some conclusion. "Okay, I'm just gonna tell you." But then he was quiet.

Kylene waited a beat before saying, "Tell me what."

"I sense magic." He pressed his hands to his cheeks and pinned his gaze to the ground. "If I'm at the right angle, I can sometimes see it on a person or object, like when the sun hits the raindrops in just the right way to make a rainbow." He resumed pacing, kicking up dust. "When I see Katora's magic, it's the deep green of pine trees speckled with white. It's a visible aura all around her body. Bhar's looks the same but is more compact. Hirsten's is the color of parchment with streaks of dark brown. His is concentrated mostly around his hands. The liquid of the Elixir itself sparkles with gold." He paused but didn't seem done, so Kylene waited patiently.

He stopped moving and finally looked right at her. "Have you ever noticed I pretty much only guide people to places of magic, places others can't find? That's because I feel magic, too." He shivered slightly and wrapped his arms around his body protectively. "Like a tingle of goose bumps but inside my body. The stronger the magic, the farther away I can feel it. Exposure to too much magic does weird things to me. It can make me nauseous or too cold or too hot." He pinned his gaze on her. "And you—"

"Me?" Kylene interrupted. "What about me?"

"What do you mean *what about you*?" There was an accusation in the question, but of what she had no idea. "Kylene, you're so full of magic, it's hard to be around you, never mind look at you."

The hot flow of tears that minutes ago had been for losing her connection to the fox were replaced by ones of humiliation. It was hard enough being in the same family as Katora and Bhar, who were celebrated—albeit secretly—for their magical connection to the Elixir, and being around Hirsten, with his ability to create images on maps with a touch of his fingers. Kylene had learned to be humbled by being around those blessed with magic when she had none herself, but this declaration by Tarq was a blow to her insecurities.

"You're cruel to mock me." She flashed him a dangerous glare.

"Mock you?" He looked her directly in the eyes. "Do you truly not understand how much magic you possess? It practically burns me to touch you. That's why that oath business with Nika is so disturbing, because it's all tied up with your magic. If that oath is real, someone can make you use it for their own will."

"No, you're wrong." She looked at her boots, not able to face the earnestness in Tarq's expression. "And Odeletta said the oath was taken in bad faith. She said the best thing to do was not dwell on it and make my own choices with a strong heart. That's what I've been doing, or trying to do, ever since I heard those terrible words she whispered in my ear. 'You will make the ultimate sacrifice.' That's what Odeletta's message was to me." It felt good to finally have the truth out there, even though she wished she had made her confession to someone—anyone—else. "She said nothing about me having magic. I trust her to tell me the truth, so you must be wrong." Yet as she said it, she thought of the circular way Odeletta, and all the higher beings, had of speaking. The Ice Queen might not have lied to Kylene, but that didn't mean she spoke the whole truth.

Tarq took a step closer, and she couldn't help but look him in the face. "It's the purest gold I've ever seen. It surrounds you, pulsing around you all the time. You glow with it. It's like you're the sun."

Kylene held her breath. There was only truth in his eyes. She let out a long sigh.

"That's why you don't look at me, or touch me."

"Yes." He hung his head. "I'm sorry I didn't tell you sooner.

322

It's dangerous for people to know what I can do, as it's dangerous for people to know about powerful magic like the Elixir...like you. I hoped you of all people would understand why I've kept my ability a secret because I thought you were keeping yours a secret. But I see now that you had no idea of your magic." He peered at her in a sideways kind of way. "How can you not know?"

"I don't know," Kylene whispered. She wasn't sure she believed him. She had never had any reason to believe she possessed magic. On the contrary, the fact that she had chronic pain from the poisoned spear solidified the idea that she wasn't magical, didn't it? Surely a person who glowed with magic would be able to heal her own body. Tarq may have believed his words, but Kylene knew better. He was mistaken; whatever he saw in her wasn't magic.

She marched back to camp, determined never to speak of the matter again.

Chapter Fifty-Eight

As expected, the snow worsened as Devon and the Tussarians traveled northwest from Skimere to Bad Beach, meaning the travel was slow and treacherous. Devon might have been mad about this if it hadn't meant snuggling up in a blanket with Em in the back of Pop Pop's wagon. Sure he was cold and wet most of the trip, but it was hard to be upset about the weather when it was the reason for the snug conditions with the girl of his dreams. The only problem was that he wasn't sure if he was the boy of *her* dreams, or if her dreams were about boys at all.

That kiss between Em and Veenie burned in Devon's mind, and he would find himself replaying it at the most inopportune times. Like at breakfast when Em would bring a piece of food to her mouth, or when Devon would make a joke and her lips would lift in laughter, or when a snowflake would hang for a moment on her eyelashes before melting. So pretty much anytime he looked or thought about Em, which was most of the day because there wasn't much else to keep his mind busy while on the road.

Finally, one afternoon as the horse fought to pull the wagon through the ever-thickening snow and Devon and Em were underneath a blanket to escape the furious flakes, Devon broached the topic. "So...you and Veenie are a thing?"

Em furrowed her eyebrows. "A thing?" Her breath rose in a mist and filled the tiny, darkish space they shared.

"Yeah." Devon shrugged. "Like a couple."

Now it was Em's turn to shrug, which Devon felt more than saw. "We've been together, but nothing official."

"So you're into girls?" It was an intrusive question, but he wasn't sure how else to discuss the topic; subtlety was not one of his strong suits. Heat crept up his cheeks as he felt her stare, but he was too embarrassed to meet her gaze.

"What business is it of yours who I like?"

Devon cleared his throat. "I'd like it to be my business, who you like. I mean, if there's chance it *could* be my business." The heat crept from his cheeks to the back of his neck and down to his armpits as he blathered on. "I know you used to baby-sit my brother and sister and mostly know me as a youngeryear, but I'm days away from being a primeyear, and I'll be done with school in a few months. And if you and Veenie are a thing, I totally respect that and will let you be. And if you're only into girls, that's cool, too. But if the age thing, and the Veenie thing, and the fact that I'm a boy aren't issues, then I was wondering if maybe *we* could ever be a thing. Because I'd really like that."

It was one of the least eloquent speeches in the history of the Great Peninsula, but Devon was glad he had said it, even if he ended up spontaneously combusting from embarrassment. So far Em hadn't thrown the blanket off the two of them and jumped off the wagon, so Devon took that as a good sign.

"Veenie and I aren't a thing, not really. We hang out when we're in the same place, but it's not like we're in love. I like to have fun, so I guess I'm into whoever I have a good time with."

"Fun," Devon murmured. "I can be fun."

Em faced him, the blanket shifting to force them closer together, her gaze more serious than he had expected. "You don't scream fun to me."

"Oh." His shoulders sagged as his hopes deflated.

She placed a gloved hand on his arm and he wished there weren't so many layers between them. "It's just that you can be kind of intense...in a good way. I mean, you think deeply about things. You work at stuff over and over again until you get it right. And that's all good." The way she said it didn't make Devon feel like any of it was good; all it made him think was that he and Em would never be a thing.

"It's all right. I know who I am and that's okay if that's not what you want."

"But what if it is," Em whispered. Then she chewed on her lip, and Devon's heart just about exploded it was beating so hard. His breath caught in his throat in a way that had nothing to do with his condition. "Great Mother, it scares me. I've never wanted intensity in a relationship, but I'm not sure I could do it any other way with you."

"I wouldn't want it any other way."

"I know."

He pulled his glove off and touched her cheek. Her skin was warm despite the frigid weather outside the blanket. Right now all that existed was the heat between them in their tiny, shared space. He leaned forward, his lips close to brushing hers, when the wagon came to an abrupt stop. Their foreheads thumped together, and the blanket fell from their heads. Devon braced himself against the wagon floor, and Em scooted backward.

Pop Pop looked over the back of his seat at them. "The snow's too thick. We're stopping to figure out a way to continue."

Em hopped over the side of the wagon. The snow came up to the tops of her boots. "I need to find Da." Then she trudged away from Devon, abandoning their almost kiss.

* * * *

Kylene and her companions waited along the Sombre River for word from the higher beings that it was safe to continue on to Bad Beach. Kylene had never felt so restless in all her life. She wandered away from her companions, who remained testy, down the river where it turned marshy before opening up to the inlet. A pair of white birds with great long necks waded in the muddy waters. Ky found a dry spot among the reeds to hide away from the others. They hadn't encountered any snow since leaving Blanchardwood, but it was cold, and the wind off the water bit her cheeks.

The dash across the Great Peninsula had kept her mind tired enough not to worry, but in the stillness of waiting, all the anxiety came rushing back. Odeletta's message ran through her head over and over again. *You will make the ultimate sacrifice.* Talking with the Ice Queen had assuaged her fears for a time, but no matter how often she assured herself that making the ultimate sacrifice could play out in any number of ways—not all of which were worst-case scenarios—the fact remained that Kylene would fulfill the message in one way or another. She clasped her hands together to keep them from shaking. But nothing kept the tears at bay. She hid her face in her hands and let the tears fall through her fingers.

A gentle breeze rustled her hair, and she looked up. The wind swirled in a circle around her remote space, the reeds bending in turn with the wind. When they stilled, the fox was there.

Kylene's breathing steadied as she stared into the fox's gold eyes. "I've been told you're dangerous."

The fox stayed perfectly still, meeting her gaze. It opened its mouth to reveal a tongue laden with perfectly rounded gemstones. They were yellow with a bright streak of gold in the center, like a cat's-eye.

Kylene let out a slightly hysterical sounding "ha!" and then sat up straighter. "But how am I to know what's dangerous and what's not when it seems no one will give me a straightforward answer about anything? Or they downright lie to me." She narrowed her eyes at the enigmatic creature. "What are you doing here? Why do you keep bugging me?" After a pause, she slowly asked, "What are you?"

The fox snapped its tongue back into its mouth, jewels and all. It turned toward the marsh but looked back at Kylene in an imploring way as if to say "come find out."

"You know what?" Kylene stood and brushed off her backside. "Maybe I will." Her fear was replaced with a reckless anger as she removed her fur coat and boots to follow the fox into the muddy waters.

The white birds squawked, the feathers on the back of the their necks ruffled in agitation, and they flew off into the blue sky. Kylene could have taken the birds' actions as a warning, but instead, she ignored them, trudged along after the fox, and dove into the cold, brackish water.

* * * *

Several days after the tilli and sciathilte left the demick village for Bad Beach, Zelenka and Palafair rode Indy over the dangerous open waters of the Greater Ocean. Zelenka had almost told Palafair she didn't need the extra days for recovery, but she was glad to have a few days together to sort through their feelings and to rest. She hadn't told anyone else about the pregnancy or her decision to end it, though she was considering talking to Laurel about it, not as a fellow soldier but as a friend. That would have to wait until after whatever happened at Drim came to pass.

When she arrived, Zelenka was pleased to see the tilli were settled at Bad Beach. They had set up camp behind a long row of sand dunes that were tall enough to offer a buffer from the icy ocean breeze. The training of the new soldiers under the leadership of the old ones was turning the formerly ragtag bunch into a real army.

She and Palafair had barely had time to get their tent set up when Ronan came running through the open flap. "Allies arriving, Colonel...with a whole band of greater beings."

"Katora!" Palafair said with a barely contained grin.

They rushed out of the tent and followed Ronan to the east side of camp. The first thing Zelenka saw among the crowd of newcomers was the cruel red lips of the witch of Faway; she was flanked by her henchmen.

"What is she doing here?" Zelenka hissed quietly to Palafair.

"Peace, my love," he said. "She is on our side."

Katora, Bhar, Hirsten, and a human Zelenka didn't recognize dismounted from the horsemen's steeds. It was only then that Zelenka began to take in the rest of the group. It was an impressive entourage of higher beings who towered over not only the demicks but the humans as well. They all wore dresses of pure white that rivaled the freshest of snows. They had to be the queens of Blanchardwood. Then there was the Watcher in its bird form, hovering above the crowd with wings flapping in the ocean breeze.

Katora rushed to Palafair's side, the other humans in tow. Her expression was pensive where Zelenka had expected it to be relieved, or at the very least curious, given the presence of the sciathilte in the camp.

"Kylene," Katora said in a rush, "has she arrived? Have you seen her?"

Palafair looked from Katora to Zelenka and back again, his

eyebrows furrowed. "We have not seen her. Why is she not with you?"

"She went for a walk earlier today while Yeselda, the Watcher, and the queens came to scout the area. She never came back. We thought—hoped—she saw the camp and decided to stay."

With a look from Palafair, Zelenka immediately pulled Nemez from his conversation with the higher beings and brought him to Katora. "General, the humans are missing one of their own. Did she come here to camp?"

Katora was pacing over a small stretch of sand, and Bhar was wringing his hands. Hirsten and the other primeyear man were slightly off to the side, looking as if they didn't know what to do.

"Is she here?" demanded Katora. "Did my sister come to camp?"

"We have seen no humans since our arrival several days ago," Nemez said.

"She's not here. Great Mother, she's not here!" Katora's voice rose several pitches as she spoke.

Hirsten grabbed her by the hand and held her close to him. "We'll find her," Zelenka heard him say into the top of Katora's head.

The witch stalked over, and Zelenka felt Palafair's steady hand on her shoulder.

"I see the Kase daughter has not been found," Yeselda said. "Pity."

Despite her complicated relationship with the Kases, Zelenka found the witch's comment to be harsh. She was inclined to stomp on the witch's foot and remind her to have some compassion, but Bhar beat her to the punch...literally. He marched up to Yeselda, swung his arm back, and punched her across the face. The sharp smack of knuckles on flesh hushed everyone, except for the sciathilte who buzzed quietly among themselves. Hirsten held tight to Katora, probably to keep her from attacking the witch as well. The Watcher quickly flew over, transforming into a griffin mid-flight and landing quietly in the sand next to Bhar. Palafair had let go of Zelenka in order to position himself between the witch and Bhar, though Zelenka wasn't sure Yeselda even noticed him as small as he was.

For her part, Yeselda merely curled her lips in a vicious smile and stared at Bhar with venom in her eyes. "That was unwise, Kase son."

"You evil witch!" yelled Bhar, his face getting redder by the second.

The tension crackled around them like cloud-to-cloud lightning.

"Peace," said Palafair, his arms spread out in a conciliatory way.

The griffin grumbled in his deep voice, "The demick speaks wisely. We are not enemies here. The enemy lies across the inlet."

"Very well," said Yeselda, her expression changing to one of indifference. "Humans are so very volatile. I do hope you find your sister," she said to Bhar before walking back to her horsemen.

"Let us deal with the matter at hand," Nemez said. "When exactly did you last see the girl?"

"This morning," said Katora. "She headed to the river for a walk, and we haven't seen her since."

The whooshing of air accompanied the arrival of a very tall woman. Her dark wind-swept hair fell past her waist and her long dress was impractical for any kind of physical activity, though that didn't seem to impede her in the least. Based on the unnatural speed with which the woman entered the camp, Zelenka realized she was not a woman at all but another queen.

She held a bundle of gray fur in her arms. "I found these on the shore where the river turns to marsh." She unfolded the fur coat to reveal a pair of muddy boots.

"Those are Kylene's," Katora said in a quiet voice. The humans wore coats similar to the one the queen held. Then Katora did something Zelenka had never before seen; she burst into tears. Hirsten wrapped her in a hug, and Bhar joined them in the embrace. "I have to go find her."

"No!" Palafair said. He had tears in his eyes, too. The Kases were Palafair's family long before Zelenka was, and she wrapped a comforting arm around his shoulders.

"Palafair is right," said Nemez. "The area beyond the dunes is unchartered. We cannot assume it is safe."

"We can send scouts to look for her," Zelenka said. "We should scout the area anyway, General, and it can have the dual purpose of a search party." Katora looked up from her cocoon of support, but Zelenka didn't let her offer up herself. "Not you. Sciathilte and higher beings only. It is too dangerous for us mortal creatures."

"Agreed, Colonel," said Nemez.

"I will lead the search party for the human girl," offered Indy, who had been listening nearby. The use of the singular pronoun was not lost on Zelenka, nor was the influence of all these different species on each other as they came together for a noble cause.

Palafair bowed. "Thank you. She is dear to many of us."

Indy buzzed off to the higher beings' area of camp, followed by Nemez, the queen who had found Kylene's clothes, and the Watcher in his griffin form.

"What do we do now?" Katora asked, her eyes rimmed in red.

Palafair reached up for her hand and gave it a squeeze. "Eat and rest."

Katora quirked her right eyebrow. "Impossible."

"We'll play cards," said Bhar.

"Cards?" asked Hirsten. "I don't think Katora wants to do that."

"No." Katora's face had a determined air. "That's exactly what I want to do."

"I know a few soldiers who would be eager to join you," Zelenka said, thinking of Palafair's card buddies.

"Yes." Palafair nodded. "I will get the officers and meet you outside our tent."

"Do you play?" Zelenka asked the primeyear man she didn't know, who had been keeping to the side, out of the family drama. He wore a hooded expression, but she felt a particular kinship to him, knowing what it was like to be outside looking in on the Kase family.

"Yes," he said, "but I don't think—"

"Of course Tarq will play," Katora interrupted. "Tarq, this is Zelenka, Colonel of the tilli army. She's married to Palafair, who has worked with our family for longer than I've been alive." Tarq nodded to Zelenka. "Tarq was our guide in Blanchardwood."

A flurry of wings caught their attention as several sciathilte took flight, heading off in different directions. Several of the queens and the Watcher also headed over the dunes.

Zelenka caught the sweet gesture of Hirsten squeezing Katora's hand and whispering, "They'll find her."

"Let's go," Katora said as she stalked off. It seemed her bout of sentimentality had worn off to be replaced by her usual gruffness. It was the same way Zelenka dealt with vulnerability.

As she showed the humans the way to the tent, she marveled at how it was probably one of the reasons she didn't get along with Katora; Katora's actions were a mirror into her own, and it wasn't always a pretty reflection.

Chapter Fifty-Nine

Devon felt days late to his own birthday party when the wagon finally trudged into the camp at Bad Beach. With the incessant snow, it had taken ages to travel from Skimere. Using the tracks the first group had left behind, Veenie's group had caught up to them long before they reached their destination. The entire convoy had cheered when the snow had abruptly stopped the day before, confirmation of it being a magical storm. One minute, they were in whiteout conditions, slowly moving and barely able to see a foot ahead; the next, they were in clear blue skies, the only trace of the storm the several feet of snow left on the ground behind them. They made good time the rest of the way, and now they were at Bad Beach at last.

Devon jumped out of the back of Pop Pop's wagon and stretched. Behind the tall dunes was an impressive military operation. Tents dotted the sand as far as the eye could see. Demicks practiced sword fighting and archery in the open spaces. A few sciathilte were among the demicks, but most of the mythical creatures were gathered in a reedy area of the camp, the tips of their wings poking out of the blades and a constant buzzing emanating from them. Pop Pop instructed everyone to set up an adjacent camp.

Devon had expected their arrival to stir up some sort of reaction, but the camp was all business as if hundreds of wagons hadn't just ridden in. Then he saw Katora and Bhar running through the maze of tents, Palafair in their wake.

"Pop!" Katora cried and wrapped him in a big hug around the waist. Bhar embraced both his father and Katora, making a sandwich of his sister. Pop placed one hand on his daughter's face and one around Bhar's shoulder and grinned so wide that it made Devon's face hurt to watch. Devon's mother came around from another wagon and kissed both her siblings on the cheeks.

"I'm so glad to see you," Pop Pop said. He noticed Palafair patiently standing nearby. "And you, too, Palafair." He looked around as if expecting to see someone else. "Where's Kylene?"

Katora's expression darkened, and a silent tear slipped down Bhar's face. "Oh, Pop, she's missing." Katora's voice broke over the admission, and Devon's heart skipped a beat.

Pop Pop stumbled back a step and leaned against the wagon. "Missing?"

Devon almost ran to his side, but even though this was a family moment, he somehow felt out of place. Then Katora explained about how Kylene had gone missing the previous day, just before Katora and the others arrived at camp. Pop Pop's face turned paler the more Katora talked.

"Odeletta's queens, who left Blanchardwood with us, and several sciathilte are out looking for her," Katora said. "They'll find her, Pop. I know they will."

"I don't think they will," said a dark-haired primeyear who stood next to Hirsten. So consumed by the drama unfolding, Devon hadn't noticed either of them arrive.

Katora's head whipped around. "What do you mean, Tarq?"

"I think your sister is in trouble," Tarq said. "Out in the plains on the way here, I saw her talking with a creature. It looked like a fox, but I don't think that's what it truly was. I saw...uh, sensed something sinister about it. I tried to warn Kylene, but I don't think she believed me. I think the fox was Fyren in disguise. I think he has taken Kylene."

Katora and Ariana both rushed at Tarq. That finally spurred Devon into action. He tore his mother off the primeyear man as Hirsten did the same with Katora, but not before both the women got in a few blows.

Bhar, looking murderous, stood over Tarq, who had a bloody lip and was rubbing his arm where it had been punched.

"And what do you think he did with her?" Bhar demanded.

"I-I don't know. But I don't think he'd hurt her. He probably has her at Drim." Tarq hesitated before saying, "There's more. She told me she got a message from the Ice Queen when the lightning struck."

Katora held her hand to her chest. "Ky got a message, too."

Devon had loosened his hold on his mother, but he kept a hand on her shoulder. "What would Fyren want with Ky?" she asked quietly.

"Her magic," Tarq blurted out. "I think he's been stealing her magic and wants the rest of it to fight against us."

"Kylene has magic?" Devon said. How many secrets was his family keeping from him?

"No," Katora said, "she doesn't." She turned to Pop Pop. "Does she?"

Pop Pop opened his mouth, but no sound came out. His eyes rolled into the back of his head, and he inelegantly slid down the side of the wagon and passed out.

* * * *

Halfway across the marsh, Kylene's clothes grew heavy and the cold water sent shivers through her body. The fox was nearly to the other side when Kylene's muscles started to seize up and her face dipped under the water. Earthy, salty water shot up her nose. The water was murky and her body heavy as she sank. She fought to swim up toward the brighter water. She floundered but kept moving her arms and legs against the pull of the water and managed to push her way back above the surface.

A surge of adrenaline warmed her body and gave her the energy to stay afloat until she felt mud beneath her feet. She trudged her way to the edge.

As soon as she stepped out of the water, bootless and coatless, goose bumps prickled her skin like a premonition. A winter wind slapped her face with her own wet hair, and she couldn't stop shivering as she followed the fox through the reeds.

The creature dried itself with one good shake and moved on, but Kylene dripped like she had been caught in a downpour and no amount of shivering would dry her. The fox looked back as if to urge her along. Behind the fox, the landscape was nothing but sand. It was then that she had a sudden urge to turn around and swim back across the marsh.

The fox's black eyes didn't sparkle in the bright sun but seemed to suck in the light. Kylene remembered Tarq saying the fox wasn't to be trusted. The revelation of Tarq being able to sense magic and his declaration of Kylene possessing it had overshadowed his warning, but it stuck with her now. She cast her gaze back to the river, dotted with friendly willow trees on the other side. Then she looked at the fox and the vast, desolate beach; she knew which way her heart wanted to go.

The fog of anger she had felt on the far side of the marsh cleared away and left a knot of fear in her stomach. The fox yipped impatiently and jerked its snout toward the endless sand.

"I made a mistake," Kylene shouted against the wind. "I should go back. My family will be worried."

The fox gave her a baleful look before turning away and stalking across the beach, leaving no footprints behind. It was the lack of footprints more than the dangerous look that made her certain she was in over her head and dealing with a very powerful being.

She bolted upriver, hoping to find a narrow place to swim across the water. Ahead of her, purple flames shot ten feet into the air with enough force to whip her back a few feet. She swung around and found two lines of flames in the sand, forming a narrow path of the fox trotted along. There was nothing to do but follow...or perhaps there was another option.

Kylene faced the wall of flames and held her hand as close to the fire as she dared. She felt no heat, though the sizzling sound in her ears made one sense belie the other. She stole a glance at the fox to find it far in the distance, the path of fire extending along with the creature.

If she had kept her coat, she could have used it as a shield and her boots would have protected her feet, but those were both on the other bank and no use to her now. Her clothes were soaked, so that would help protect her against burns. She could use her outer shirt to cover her face and hair. It was a desperate plan, but what other choice did she have? The fox was too far ahead for her to see it anymore, but she was certain it meant to harm her or use her for nefarious purposes. She had a suspicion about its identity but wasn't arrogant enough to think she was important enough for a powerful being to bother with her.

A lick of flame wavered close, but still she felt no heat. Emboldened by this, Kylene poked the tip of her finger into the purple blaze. It was ice-cold, and her finger instantly went numb. She pulled back her hand as the biting cold crept through her hand and up her arm, which fell uselessly to the side. The numbness spread. When it reached her chest, Kylene clutched at it with the hand that still worked. Pins and needles prickled her stomach and stretched down her legs before they were taken over by the icy numbness.

She fell to the sand face-up, her mouth stuck slightly open in shock. Her eyes—the only thing she could move—darted back and forth across her narrow view of blue sky. She could breathe, but it felt thin and strained.

A man's face appeared before her, gleaming gold eyes taking in her precarious situation. Russet hair hung low to the sides of his face, and his nose was thin and long like a snout…like a fox.

"You" she wanted to accuse, but all that came out of her slightly open mouth was a weak exhalation.

He said nothing, simply grabbed her hood and pulled her immobile body through the sand. The flames were gone, but Kylene was more trapped than ever. And she couldn't even scream for help, not that there was any help to be found on the desolate beach.

Chapter Sixty

Outside her tent, Zelenka gathered Palafair, Nemez, all the Kases who had made the journey to Bad Beach, Tarq, Indy, Yeselda, the Watcher, and the queens. Not one of the scouts had found any sign of the young woman. All the higher beings saw was a lot of dark magic coming from Drim.

Night was approaching and a cold wind was blowing sand in their faces, but there was no covered location where they could all fit, so they stood around a fire, shivering in the bitter winter air. Tarq recounted his theory about Fyren capturing Kylene so he could use her magic against them.

"It doesn't make sense," Katora said. "Kylene doesn't have magic."

"She does," insisted Tarq. "A lot of it."

They continued arguing over the point, much to the amusement of Yeselda if her wry grin was any indication of her feelings. Zelenka noticed Pop watching carefully, his face pale, but with no comment.

"How can you know this when we—her own family—didn't?" asked Katora.

"I just do," Tarq said, gaze pinned on the fire.

"It's because he's a brigha," said a voice outside of the circle of brightness cast by the flames, "like me."

A dark-haired human stepped into the light, the many jeweled rings on her fingers sparkling in the firelight. She was flanked by two enormous men, their bushy faces making them look more like bears than humans. Zelenka poised her hand over the dagger at her belt and wished there was a spear nearby, but the tilli weapons had all been collected to be cleaned and sharpened. Aside from Yeselda's amused smile, the higher beings all seemed rather indifferent to the new arrival. The humans and demicks edged on nervous.

"You!" Katora shouted, brandishing her own dagger. It seemed the guardian of the Elixir was ready to pick a fight with everyone today; Zelenka admired that kind of spunk and was glad not to be on the receiving end of it.

The brigha gave a showy bow. "Nika at your service."

"You knew Kylene had magic." Katora's voice was steel. "That's why made her take the blood oath. I will kill you!" It was once again left to Hirsten and Bhar to hold back the impetuous primeyear woman.

"I don't think you want to tangle with me tonight," Nika said. "Not if you want help finding your sister."

"Enough!" said Pop, his cheeks finally showing a bit of color. "Settle down, Katora." She sheathed her dagger, and Zelenka relaxed a little. "Tarq, are you a brigha?"

Tarq swallowed before whispering "yes," the word hissing like flames on a wet log.

"And you and Nika both saw Kylene's magic?" Pop asked.

Tarq nodded, while Nika said, "She positively dripped with it, an ostentatious gold exuding from her."

"And this fox, Tarq, what made you think it was Fyren?" asked Pop.

The primeyear glared at his fellow brigha and said in a slightly sarcastic tone, "He positively dripped with dark magic."

"Great Mother!" exclaimed Katora.

Yeselda cackled. "Your sister had little enough when I ran into your lot in Faway Forest. So little I barely noticed it among all the mortal magic. Clearly I would have shown more interest in her if I had known."

"And you didn't notice it at Kristalis or while we traveled here?" asked Katora.

"I was not looking for it," Yeselda said lazily. "And I had other concerns on my mind."

"So what changed?" asked Zelenka. She had never cared much for magic, not with her father's obsession with the Elixir looming over most of her life. "Something must have brought it out of her."

"The Golden City," piped in Palafair. Zelenka remembered that Kylene had claimed to be transported to a Golden City while on Katora's quest in Faway Forest. The city had been the inspiration for her play that had been ruined by the Ice Queen's lightning bolt. Zelenka had known of the city as a tilli legend, a place where a demick alchemist lived. When the people of the city grew too greedy, the alchemist had turned himself into a golden statue. Zelenka hadn't believed that Kylene had actually visited the city; she thought it had been some kind of hallucination or delusion. But now Zelenka wondered if Kylene had actually visited the city and it had imbued her with magic.

"Yes," said the Watcher, who had turned back into a small bird after returning from the search for Kylene. "Katora told me her sister had gone to the Golden City. It was another task for another time, and it seems that time is upon us."

"We cannot let Fyren attain her magic," said Yeselda.

"I agree," said the Watcher.

"Forget Fyren." Katora's fists were clenched at her sides. "We have to save Kylene."

"I shouldn't have let her mix with that fox in the first place," Tarq said, and Katora shot death glare at him. "I'll be able to recognize her magic. I can find her."

Zelenka's head was beginning to spin with all the information and opinions going around, but if her opinion counted, she thought they should save Kylene *and* keep Fyren from using her magic. Nemez, who had the most military experience among the mortals, was uncharacteristically quiet, so Zelenka asked, "Will a sciathilte be willing to fly Tarq out to Drim to see if there is any trace of Kylene's magic?"

The reliable buzz of Indy vibrated through the night. "I will do it."

Darkness was fully upon them, the stars twinkling merrily with no indication of the turmoil on the dunes. But as Indy had told them once before, darkness was no hindrance to the sciathilte.

"Can you see magic in the dark?" Zelenka asked Tarq, who merely nodded.

"Nika should go, too," Pop said, not asking her for permission. The brigha didn't protest. She didn't seem the philanthropic type, so Zelenka wondered what her motives were, but all Nika revealed was a poisonous smile.

"Are any of the sciathilte willing to take her?" Zelenka asked.

Unlike the demicks, the humans were too large to fit two on a single sciathilte. Indy relayed the message and found another volunteer.

"I will go as well," boomed the deep voice of the Watcher. "We will leave at once. It might be easier to find a trace of gold in the dark, especially now that we know what to look for." If a bird could glare that was what the Watcher's squinting eyes were doing at Tarq. Zelenka didn't blame the higher being; if they had known about Kylene's magic sooner, they might have found her on the first try.

Yeselda let out an exaggerated sigh. "I am bored by this. Do let me know if the girl is found." She wandered off and the queens followed her.

"I hate her!" Katora said. She narrowed her gaze on Tarq and Nika. "Come to me the minute you're back..and you better have my little sister."

Katora's sister Ariana put an arm around her as all the Kases retired to their wagons, probably not to sleep but to worriedly pass the time as they waited to hear about Kylene.

"We will!" Tarq called after them, but they were already swallowed up by the darkness.

"Let's get this over with," Nika said. They mounted the sciathilte and took off into the sky and out of sight, the Watcher along with them in his bird form.

"We should rest," Palafair pointedly said to Zelenka.

She waved him off. "I am fine. General Nemez, may I speak with you privately?"

As Palafair retired to the tent, Zelenka and Nemez walked through the demick camp at a slow pace.

Nemez surprised her by speaking first. "If this is about why you stayed an extra few days on Demick Island, I will tell you this,

341

it is none of my business, but I am happy to talk with you about it if that is what you desire."

"Oh," Zelenka said, taken aback at his candor. "Thank you for the offer...and for respecting my privacy. But it is another matter entirely that I wish to discuss." He gave her a curious glance that encouraged her to continue, "I wondered your thoughts about the future of the tilli now that we have reunited with the island demicks...and given that we survive whatever is to come in this fight against Fyren."

"I have been giving this very topic much thought."

They came to a fire where a group of island demicks were brewing tea. The islanders smiled shyly and offered them a cup. Nemez held back and let Zelenka take the lead on how to respond. She accepted and they sat for a few minutes, talking quietly with the islanders, before continuing their walk.

When they found themselves in relative solitude on the edge of the camp, Zelenka asked, "And what conclusion have you come to on the matter?"

"I have decided that it does not matter what I think about the future of the tilli." He stared up at the sky as if the moon held the answers before turning his gaze back to her. "What matters is you, Zelenka."

"What about me matters?"

She suspected where his line of thought was going before he even said, "Whether or not you want to lead us."

"What if I do not want to lead? Will you take that role?" She scuffed her foot in the sand, creating a small imprint.

"I am your military leader, your general. That is all. I could never fill the role that you are meant to have...that your father wanted you to have." His face was open and earnest; it unnerved her. "I know I said we could hold an election for a new leader, but I think you should be our leader. You are good at it. That is why I had you speak to the priestesses on Demick Island and why I put you in charge of training the soldiers. Great Mother, you found the missing army and convinced them to follow you home when they believed you were responsible for their predicament. You have proven yourself in so many ways as leader of the tilli, and I will call you my leader no matter what name you choose to go by."

A tightness of anxiety filled Zelenka's chest, but her heart was pounding at what this could mean. But there was something she had to get off her chest first. "You treated me like a criminal when I came back to the Three River Split. I have thought that way about myself since the moment I pushed Roodesh to his death. He may have wanted me to succeed him, but I killed him, and those two things do not work together. Perhaps the madness of Roodesh was already taking hold of me."

"Zelenka," Nemez said quietly, his voice thick with emotion, "I regret the way I treated you. I thought..." His breath hitched. "I thought you had done something to the army. Even as my conscious reminded me of your loyalty and that you would never do anything to hurt them, the evidence suggested otherwise. Once I knew the truth, it made so much more sense, and I knew I had made an error."

"But I am a murderer." Zelenka lost the fight against the sob that made its way up her throat. She bent over, hands on her knees, and cried, "I murdered the man who was my father!"

"No." Nemez gently rubbed her back. "No, my dear Zelenka, you are not a murderer, nor are you mad. It was an act of mercy what you did. He was taking us down a path of destruction. All the leaders in the army saw this, but we did not know how to stop it. Even then you were fighting for our people. I did not understand it then, but I do now. We all do now. I have spoken with the older army leaders, and no one thinks you a murderer. You did a desperate, hard thing. You saved us."

Wiping the tears from her cheeks, she stood and let the wind dry her face. "I have tried to tell myself that very thing, but it never feels any better."

"I would be worried if you felt okay about it."

Zelenka let out a bitter laugh. Maybe that was why she had never been able to fully reconcile her feelings about Roodesh's death; she had thought that doing something for the greater good should have felt good. She was never going to feel good about it, and that was a feeling she could accept. "I still do not know if I want to be the tilli leader."

Nemez's expression turned grim. "First we have to make it through whatever battle is coming. Then you can make a decision whether to accept the role or pass it on to someone else. And now you know my opinion on the matter, if that is worth anything to you."

"It is."

Several shadows crossed over the moon, further darkening the night landscape for a moment before heading into camp. The sciathilte and the brighas had returned. Zelenka and Nemez rushed back to the heart of camp to find out what news they brought.

Chapter Sixty-One

When Kylene's body regained feeling, it was an abrupt change from numbness to experiencing every sensation in almost excruciating clarity. She wondered whether it had been better to be numb and not feel the grit of sand rubbing places that were hard to clean or the throb of bruises forming down her spine from being dragged. Was it better not to have the ability to wipe away the warm slice of tears down her cheeks?

Even though she could move again, there was little hope of escape as she was locked in a dark cell with only a small window to let in the moonlight. The fox had dragged her across the sand, into a stone building, and left her in this dungeon. She suspected she was being held at Drim, the stronghold of Fyren and the only building near Bad Beach, though it had been impossible to see much of it in her immobile state.

She was beginning to believe she did in fact possess magic. And that the fox was Fyren and he wanted to steal it from her, or rather steal *more* of it. The threads of her memory were coming together to weave a disturbing pattern. The songs and stories of how Fyren had stolen Odeletta's power with true love's kiss. The fox showing up when Kylene had been crying. The gems on its tongue. Nika forcing Kylene to take the blood oath. Odeletta whisking a tear turned diamond into her mouth. Tarq telling Ky she glowed like the sun.

And always, always Odeletta's message rang in her ears. *You will make the ultimate sacrifice.*

She wiped the tears from her cheeks, even as more flowed down her face. She stood and screamed through the bars of the small opening in the cell door, "Fyren! Come here and face me in your true form, you fox!"

If she was going to make the ultimate sacrifice, she would do it fighting for something good, not numb on the floor.

***

The air changed when the Watcher and the sciathilte with the brighas flew back into camp. Devon felt it like a vibration through his body.

With his family, he gathered around those who had returned. He had been a silent witness to the whole conversation about his aunt Kylene and her magic. It was unnerving to see Pop Pop, who always had things under control back at the farm, so upset. The situation was starting to feel bigger than Devon could handle. He had sought out Em while they waited for news about Kylene, and she was there, the solid presence of her body pressed against his, their hands entwined.

Pop Pop was the first to speak before the brighas had a chance to dismount. "Did you find her?"

A few demicks joined the group, as well as the witch of Faway and the queens from Blanchardwood.

"We found her golden thread," the Watcher said. The higher being was back in its griffin form, but its voice was always the same no matter what shape it took.

"But you haven't brought her back," Katora said with a glare at Tarq and Nika.

"She is deep within Drim," the Watcher explained. "There was no way for us to retrieve her."

The vibration started up in Devon's body again, and he realized it was coming from Indy, who was communicating the conversation to the rest of the sciathilte.

"It was a stroke of luck we were able to detect her magic at all," said Nika. Her bearded bodyguards were back at her side and looking formidable but grumpy. Devon covered a yawn with his free hand; maybe they were as tired as he was. "At first it was only Fyren's dark cloud surrounding the fortress. We were about to return when there was a spike of golden color deep in the center of Drim that faded to thin threads of gold spread throughout the black."

"And you're sure it was Kylene's magic?" asked Pop Pop.

"It was hers." Tarq's voice was hoarse. The firelight

accentuated the dark bags under his eyes. With so many higher beings in close proximity, Devon wondered what it was like for the brighas to be able to sense the sheer amount of magic floating around. It had to be exhausting, though Nika didn't seem to be suffering. Her green eyes were as vivid as ever.

The witch, Yeselda, looked pensive for once and addressed the Watcher, "Is it dire?"

"The flash of gold was very strong and Fyren's magic was the strongest I have seen it in hundreds of years," the griffin responded. "It would be unwise to allow him to acquire any more."

"We attack at dawn then," Yeselda declared, and a collective shiver ran through those in earshot. The fact that two higher beings—creatures who did not scare easily—deemed the situation dire was alarming. Add in that dawn was only a few hours away, that many of them had not slept that night, and that many were not prepared for a battle at all, and Devon would categorize the situation as a disaster.

Zelenka's voice rose up from the group of demicks, "You do not get to decide when we attack."

"You would have us wait, and let Fyren drain the girl of her power and have the first strike?" Yeselda challenged.

"Time works in our favor as well," Zelenka said. "Gives us a chance to organize and prepare."

Yeselda let out a barking laugh. "There is no preparing for what Fyren has in store for us."

Devon was inclined to agree with Yeselda; waiting seemed like a bad idea, no matter how unprepared they might be. But there was one thing that occurred to Devon that he couldn't believe no one had addressed yet. He let go of Em's hand and raised his up, as if asking for permission to speak in class. "What about Mother Nature?"

Having the full force of Yeselda's stare on him was something Devon was not prepared for. "What about the Great Mother?" Her clipped tone indicated she wasn't to be trifled with, not that Devon would have imagined doing any such thing to a higher being.

"I only meant that," he cringed when his voice cracked and

cleared his throat, "what I mean is surely if Fyren is a threat to all of us, then Mother Nature with all her power and wisdom would not let him destroy us."

"You question the Great Mother's actions, or inactions in this case?" asked Yeselda. Her blood-red lips quirked in a menacing smile.

Pop Pop, Katora, and Devon's mom all moved closer to him, and Em gripped his forearm hard enough to hurt. He swallowed, his throat feeling like it had a lump of charcoal stuck in it.

Zelenka piped in, "The youngeryear raises a good question." Devon had to stop himself from saying he was almost a primeyear; the winter solstice was tomorrow, and it was looking more and more like the day they would go to battle against Fyren.

The Watcher intervened in a diplomatic way. "We are higher beings, but we are not Mother Nature. We trust in her to act when necessary and leave the rest to us, as you mortals should."

It was strange to hear the Watcher lump all the higher beings in with the humans and demicks, like they were the same and only Mother Nature was on a higher level of existence. Still, it hadn't completely answered his question. "So she'll come if we need her?"

"It would be wise to proceed as if the Great Mother did not intend to interfere," said the Watcher.

"But why?" Devon couldn't let it go. "Why wouldn't she help us?"

The griffin tilted its head and blinked as it said, "We are not the Great Mother, so we cannot say."

"Forget it, Devon," Katora said. "You'll never get a straight answer out of these higher beings about the way Mother Nature works." The crowd around them had grown as the discussion wore on. It seemed word of what was going on with Fyren had spread and many more humans and demicks had gathered around. "I'm all for getting this fight started and getting my sister back."

Before anyone could disagree, Katora grabbed a torch out of the sand and climbed atop a dune. "The esteemed witch of Faway Forest, Yeselda," Devon detected a hint of derision in Katora's voice, "advises us to bring the battle to Fyren at dawn before he can further strengthen his power. What do you say? Do we challenge this monster before he unleashes his evil upon us? Do we take up arms to save my sister and ourselves? Do we fight at dawn?" Her words echoed in the night and faded to silence.

Devon held his breath as he waited for chaos to break out.

Em gripped his arm tighter than ever, her face flush with the anticipation of battle. "We fight!" she yelled, and the crowd took up her cry.

"Fight! Fight! Fight!"

Devon took up the call as well, goose bumps rising on his skin. The cries roused those who had been sleeping, and soon the whole camp was a flurry of activity and planning. The higher beings took charge of organizing the humans into ranks and arming them. The sciathilte and tilli demicks prepared the rest of the demicks, a select group of them chosen to lead the first wave of the attack. Soon Devon found himself holding a sword in a group of young primeyears led by Em. They would be among the third wave of attackers if it came to that.

By the time the eastern edge of the sky had begun to lighten, the army of higher beings, sciathilte, humans, and demicks were marching out of their camp among the dunes and take on Fyren.

Chapter Sixty-Two

The fox-like face appeared in the opening of the door to Kylene's dungeon cell. It was dark, the moon having moved out of reach of the window, but she could see his features plainly, the gold eyes and long nose. He entered the cell, leaving the door open. The hall behind him was black, not a single torch or candle to light the way. He wore a long, black robe that brushed the floor when he walked. She stood and straightened to her full height, finding it almost matched his. He had appeared much taller when she had been immobile on her back being dragged through the sand.

"Fyren," she said, more sure than ever he was the fallen higher being.

He inclined his head. "Kase daughter. Or may I call you Ky?" he asked in a high, nasally voice. It was the first time she had heard him speak and she had expected something less childlike, though his reputation was enough to intimidate the bravest of creatures, childish voice or not.

"Never." The suggestion of using her nickname prompted her to give him her most-intimidating glare, which admittedly wasn't very intimidating.

He shrugged and clasped hands, touching his lips with his pointer fingers as if lost in thought.

"Whatever you have planned, you'll never get away with it," she said, channeling a bold side of herself she wasn't entirely familiar with. "My family will come for me. And Mother Nature will come for you."

"You think the Great Mother will save you all from me?"

"She's done it before."

"I have grown smarter since then." A ghost of smile played across his lips, a look that made sweat drip down Kylene's neck. "And stronger thanks to you. I took that first gem of a tear from you on a whim that proved very fruitful. One flower and many gems later, I had all I needed to contain Mother Nature and make an army."

Was it her imagination or had the cell grown warmer since he had arrived? She looked around and noticed small details about the patterns of the stones that made up the walls—subtle swirls and whorls of color—and the individual lines of scuff marks on the floor, details she hadn't been able to see in the dark only minutes before. But no new light sources had appeared, or heat sources.

She blinked, refusing to be distracted. "You're not stronger than Mother Nature."

"One does not have to be stronger than another to outwit them." He spread his lips in a full smile that revealed pointy teeth. "One must only know the other's weakness."

"Mother Nature has no weaknesses." Sweat continued to form on Kylene's skin, droplets that tickled as they slid down her chest and back. Her senses continued to sharpen, and she could smell the salt of her sweat, hear a distant, steady drip of water even as her own ragged breaths filled her ears. A bitter taste sat on her tongue, like having swallowed ashes.

"Yet she is not infallible," Fyren said in a placating tone, and Kylene had the impression of a child playing schoolteacher. "It turns out that the Great Mother, master of all the elements, can be contained."

She felt every hair on her arms prickle as goose bumps rose on her skin. "I don't believe you."

"It is not for you to believe or disbelieve. It simply is. That which we master can become master of us."

"You higher beings and your riddles." She was growing more irritable by the minute...and more sensitive. The fibers of her socks chaffed her feet, and every piece of sand that remained on her body was a needle in her flesh.

He held out his slender hand, the thinnest wrinkles and tiniest pores standing out to her. "Come. You are right about your family. They, and many others, are on their way. I want you to have a good view of what I have planned for them."

She didn't get a chance to refuse as purple flames shot up

around her. They licked dangerously close before they forced her to move into the hallway to a set of stone steps that spiraled up. Fyren followed closely behind, the flames having no effect on him. There was no gain in going numb again, so she allowed herself to be led up the stairs without protest.

Along the way they passed a small window on the east side of the fortress, and she spied a mound of sand with a lit pyre on top. The pyre's fire burned the same purple as the fire that trapped Kylene. A thin moat filled with water surrounded the mound. Flies zipped around it, and Kylene wondered if there was a dead body buried underneath. It was a curiosity that took her mind away for a moment before it settled back on the harsh reality of being trapped by a higher being. She sighed and trudged up the steps until they reached a small, circular room at the top. The flames followed her to the entrance and trapped her inside with Fyren.

* * * *

Drim sat atop a sandy hill dotted with grasses that overlooked the Greater Ocean. Below the fortress, the beach was flat and the tide low, so the shoreline stretched far toward the horizon, mostly sandbar with small pools of water in between. As the army approached, the sun rose up over the water and cast the stone fortress and tide pools in orange light. It brought to mind fire and impenetrable foes, and all that was at stake.

The truth was that Zelenka and the tilli army had thousands of hours of training, but their actual battle experience was limited to the occasional scuffle with humans who dared to travel to Faway Forest and the beasts that called the forest home. Zelenka, having fought against Yeselda's animal army during Katora's quest, was among the most experienced, and she had come away from that battle with life-threatening injuries. The humans were even less equipped to deal with battles.

A world that thrived on peace for thousands of years did not make for one that was adequately prepared for war. Even the higher beings were generally peaceful creatures, meddlesome and puzzling certainly, but not necessarily prone to violence—the witch of Faway perhaps being an exception to this at times.

Energy coursed through Zelenka's veins, masking the ache in her leg, as she led her battalion, the enormity of the moment becoming all the more real as they drew closer to their enemy.

But where was Fyren? Would it be him alone against the thousands gathered or had his magic conjured up an army of their nightmares?

Zelenka scanned the beach for any signs of life, then moved on to the water, and finally searched the fortress for their foe. All was quiet, the wind and the waves the only sounds accompanying the shuffle of marching feet across the sand. Her group included many of the experienced soldiers and was in the first wave of fighters, alongside a brave group of sciathilte volunteers who would take the fight to the air. Palafair marched next to her. She had thought about asking him to join the third wave, where several of the Kases were, but had decided against it; she was proud to march for the future of the Great Peninsula with her husband by her side.

The bird form of the Watcher flew by the ranks, having completed a flyby of Drim. His form as a small bird was a signal that there was no obvious threat, aside from the unnatural amount of magic emanating from the fortress. If the Watcher had come in griffin form, it would have signaled obvious danger. It also meant it was time to launch the first series of attacks.

The Watcher landed next Katora and both brighas. The higher being would mask them with his magic, and they would try to infiltrate the fortress to rescue Kylene. In their limited strategizing session, it had been decided that the other higher beings would lead the humans, so Yeselda, her horsemen, and Odeletta's queens were spread out among those ranks. The demicks had the sciathilte.

Zelenka mounted Indy to lead the charge, and Palafair was nearby on a bright yellow sciathilte, whom Laurel had dubbed Buttercup. It seemed a long time ago since Zelenka and Palafair had left Kase Farm on a stubborn gray pony named Captain Buttercup.

Nemez was also on the front lines, riding a sciathilte that

glinted grass green in the rising sun.

The Watcher's magic was working on Zelenka, and hopefully Fyren, because she couldn't see where the rescue party was, but hopefully they were snaking their way up the hill to enter Drim. With their metaphysical connection, the sciathilte darted and dove as one, the demicks along for the ride. Their path was erratic on purpose, so as to keep them from being an easy target while also being a diversion for the rescue party. They completed one circuit around Drim and headed back to where the humans and higher beings waited on the beach.

The idea was to draw the enemy out so the sciathilte could dive on them, attacking with their stingers while the demicks attacked with spears. Zelenka felt for the familiar shape of her weapon strapped to her back. If needed, a second wave of foot soldiers would come. Most of them had swords, though there were a few skilled with a bow that would aim for enemies up on the structure.

Just as they finished their second circuit around the fortress, a buzzing energy filled Zelenka. Though it didn't feel exactly the same, she assumed it was the sciathilte communicating with each other and continued to scrutinize Drim for the enemy. Then Indy vibrated beneath her in the distinct sensation of communication, and she realized the buzzing energy wasn't coming from the sciathilte.

She stared at Drim, and from one blink to the next, it turned fuzzy. She blinked rapidly but couldn't focus on the fortress. Looking away, she found a clear view of the ocean spread before her. A sharp pinch pierced her cheek, and she swatted at it. In her hand sat a squished bug, its thin, transparent wings and white body splayed out on her palm. There were tiny bent legs crushed up below the wings. She flicked the carcass off her hand. A second bite got her on the neck, and she slapped at it.

The sciathilte took a sudden dive, so she wasn't able to inspect the second bug. She tightened her grip on Indy as it zoomed back toward the foot soldiers. A glance back at Drim showed a cloud of white flowing from it. Soon the cloud was upon them, a giant swarm of tiny white bugs. Her spear would be about as effective against this foe as the sciathilte's stinger. She searched for the bright yellow sciathilte that held Palafair but could see nothing through the swarm of insects.

Indy abruptly changed directions, nearly unseating Zelenka. She yelped and held on tighter, no longer able to swat at the insects. Sharp bites nipped at any exposed skin. The insects reached areas of her body that were covered as they infiltrated her armor and clothing.

Indy flew them out of the thick cloud, over the sandbars, and headed to deeper waters. Zelenka could finally see clearly as the concentration of insects lessened, though many still clung to her, nipping at her raw skin. Her hands were bloody with bites. A rainbow of sciathilte were headed toward the open water, some looking diminished from the many insect bites they had suffered and barely keeping to the air. Much to Zelekna's horror, some of the sciathilte were carrying demick-shaped bones on their backs or no one at all.

"Hold on," buzzed Indy, and Zelenka's stomach lurched as they dove toward the ocean.

She held her breath and closed her eyes as they plunged into the salty water, but the cold shock wasn't enough to erase the image of those bones from her mind. They surfaced, and she had enough time to take one big breath before Indy dove back down below the surface. They continued to drop in and out of the water until most of the insects had moved on to attack the humans on the beach. They hovered above the water, the sciathilte dripping and Zelenka shivering, the skin under her fingernails blue from cold instead of red from blood.

A streak of yellow flew by. Zelenka wiped the salt water from her eyes and spotted Buttercup. Palafair was slumped on the sciathilte's back, his arms and legs hanging limply at his sides. Buttercup took a deep dive downward. Zelenka screamed as it hit the water and Palafair tipped off into the choppy waves.

She didn't have to say a word; Indy shot straight for the lifeless body of Palafair. It scooped up the demick in its front legs and carried him to a sandbar. Zelenka jumped down, ignoring the jolt of pain in her leg and pressed her hand to his chest to find a heartbeat. A little blood had been washed away from his dip in the water, but more was oozing from the insect bites. His eyes were closed and his lips were purple. He was barely breathing, the shallow rise and fall of his chest far too slow.

Zelenka choked back a sob and thought of the small vial of Elixir she had given back to Pop when they stopped over in Tussar. Why hadn't she kept it? "We have to get him to Katora."

Indy's many eyes, usually so inscrutable, were shiny with thousands of tiny tears. It nodded and scooped up Palafair once more as Zelenka climbed on its back. They flew toward Drim and back into the heart of the insect swarm.

* * * *

Devon had never seen anything in his life that could be described as horror. He had read stories with violence and had a big imagination, but nothing could have prepared him for seeing something that was a true horror. And now he was living it.

He watched the white cloud pour from every opening in Drim and head straight for the sciathilte carrying the demicks. It devoured demicks right down to the bone and damaged the seemingly impenetrable exoskeletons of the sciathilte. When the insect cloud turned toward the human battalions, the horror weakened his knees and it took a stern yell of "stay strong" from Em to prevent him from running away. Not that running would do any good. There was nowhere to go on this desolate beach to protect them from this enemy.

The sciathilte flew to the ocean and were attempting to use repeated dunks into the water to thwart the insects. Any humans who made a run for the water were cut down to the bone by insects before they made it past the mud flats. Devon saw several demicks fall off the sciathilte and disappear under the waves before his attention was diverted back to Em, leader of his group.

The first insect bite to his cheek came with a sharp pinch. Of all the foes Devon had imagined Fyren's army to be, ravenous bugs were not among them.

"Fire!" she shouted. "We need a smoky fire to keep them at bay!"

The fire starting supplies were back at camp, so they had to make do with the materials at hand. The groups that had been formed broke down as people scrambled for anything flammable. Some went for the reeds on the hill to Drim, while others tore the clothes off their backs, exposing themselves to more insect bites for the greater good.

The few queens who were able to conjure flames set to work, but they weren't quick enough to keep the bugs from doing serious damage. People were falling to the sand, clutching at their faces and writhing. Katora had gone off with the Watcher to find Kylene, so there was no Elixir to help anyone. Not that it would have been safe to administer it with the enemy buzzing all around them.

Finally enough fires were lit to produce smoke. Devon kept close to Em as they ran through the sand, up and down the hill with armfuls of tall grass. Several queens were using strong puffs of magical breath to fan the flames and urge the smoke to spread. Devon's breathing felt slow and sluggish as he inhaled smoke, and he stopped and bent at the waist to try and catch his breath.

None of it was enough to quell the enemy. The bites kept coming and people kept falling.

Devon straightened and caught Em's attention with a frantic waving of his hands. Her hair stuck out wilder than ever, her cheeks were red and angry, and her eyes were bloodshot.

"We have to do something," he wheezed.

"What?" she yelled, looking around desperately. She slapped her own face, leaving a smear of blood behind.

"Get to Fyren. Injure him or distract him or something." He could no longer see out to the ocean through the thick, black smoke that curled out of the fires. Screams could be heard over the rushing sound of the flames. Figures scrambled around them, but it was hard to tell who anyone was or where they were going. The rank of soldiers had deteriorated into chaos. A bug bit Devon's neck, but he ignored it.

Em patted the sword at her side—useless against the insects

but maybe not so useless against Fyren—and nodded. He grabbed her hand to keep from losing her and headed in the direction of the fortress past where people were gathering what was left of the grass for the fires. The smoke wasn't as thick here and the insects were more concentrated. Devon ripped two sections from his cloak, and they wrapped them around their heads and neck, covering everything but their eyes.

A shadow fell over the stone steps as they reached them. "Where are you young humans going?"

Devon looked straight into the face of the witch of Faway. She looked beautiful as always, her black hair tidy and her lips full and red, not a bite or blemish on her perfect skin, as if she hadn't been involved in the battle at all. His breath caught and he coughed so long that Em answered for them, "To find Fyren. We stop him, we stop the bugs."

Yeselda quirked an eyebrow. "You will never succeed."

Em pushed passed the witch, pulling Devon along. "You can't stop us from trying."

She followed them up the stone stairs. "Dear mortals, I would not keep you from your bad decision. But I will come with you. I have a few choice words for my brother."

Without asking for permission, Yeselda cloaked them with magic, a warm, almost wet sensation washing over Devon. Everything outside their magical bubble took on a slightly distorted appearance, and the insects could not penetrate it.

"Why don't you put everyone under the bubble?" Devon accused.

"That would be a lot of hearts to conceal," answered Yeselda as her face took on a strained look, a single bead of sweat forming on her forehead. "It would require more magic than I possess."

Devon didn't understand what laws of magic Yeselda was referring to, but at least he and Em were shielded from the insects. He grabbed Em's hand once more, though there was no chance in losing her as the only creature with them was the witch. Then they entered the infamous fortress of Drim.

Chapter Sixty-Three

If Kylene had been at a play, her spot from the tower window of Drim would have been the perfect view of all the action. With her heightened senses, it would have been a glorious scene. But what was unfolding below was no staged drama; it was a massacre.

She watched through vision blurred from the tears she held back with all her might—lest she give Fyren more power—as the swarm moved from one area to the next, leaving behind devastation.

The window held no glass and was open to the air, so she heard the screams of the demicks and the unnatural buzz of the sciathilte swarm. The sharp white of demick bones against the colorful sciathilte twisted her stomach. When the sciathilte retreated to the ocean that sparkled gold and amber in the rising sun, the swarm moved on to the humans on the beach. Having a little more time to prepare, they were able stoke up smoky fires and disorientate the insects.

Kylene felt a spark of hope in the heat of desperation.

All the while, Fyren in the form of a man watched from behind. He seemed deep in concentration, his brows knitted, a smile playing on his lips on occasion. Magic washed off him in waves. Kylene thought to knock him over and break his concentration, but when she tried to touch him, she found herself blocked by an invisible shield. It had to require a whole lot of energy to maintain the shield and keep control over the insect army, but he showed no signs of strain.

The spark of hope began to wither.

A tear finally broke from her eye, the salt of it burning her hypersensitive skin. Fyren reached out to snap it away before Kylene could stop him. Several more tears slipped out and were stolen before she contained them. Feeling suddenly weak, she reached out and held herself up against the stone window frame.

Those purple flames blocked the only exit, except for the window. It was large and open, a long way down, but a way out all the same. What would Fyren do if she jumped?

He must have seen her staring and guessed what she was thinking, or maybe he could read minds, because he said, "You could jump."

"You wouldn't stop me?"

"I would cushion the fall, so it would not kill you." His gaze continued to follow the battle outside.

"But I'd be broken, and then you could use me as you wished." No, jumping wasn't the solution. But she had an idea about what had happened to Mother Nature, and if her hunch was correct, it might turn the tide of this one-sided battle.

A commotion outside the tower door stole Fyren's attention. Kylene couldn't see who was behind the purple flames, but she guessed they were on her side because Fyren turned away from the window, though one of his hands remained pointed in the direction of the insect army.

"Kylene!" shouted Katora from the other side of the flames.

It was easy for Kylene to recognize that voice with her heightened sense of hearing. "Don't touch the fire!"

"It's all right," said Katora, and Kylene couldn't help but think that her sister always had to be contrary. "We have the Watcher."

Katora, the Watcher in griffin form, and Tarq stepped one by one over the threshold, the flames distorting around them as they entered. Katora held her dagger and Tarq's bow was at his side, but Kylene doubted that either would do much to subdue Fyren. Last to enter was Nika of all people. When Kylene saw Nika's messy curls and green eyes, her blood ran cold. Her finger throbbed where Nika had pricked it for the blood oath.

The Watcher, whose lion body and eagle wings took up a quarter of the room, stalked to Fyren. "Why do you do this, brother?"

"Boredom," Fyren quipped, his one hand still orchestrating whatever was going on outside. Kylene could no longer see through the window as she had crept closer to the door.

"Remember how this turned out last time," boomed the Watcher. "How many lives will be wasted before our Great Mother decides to intervene?"

"I am willing to wait and see," said Fyren.

"You will never have what our Great Mother has." The Watcher was careful with its movements, keeping some distance from Fyren, but not with its words. "She guides the world with love, where you guide with hatred. This will not end well."

"Not for the mortals, but it may yet work out for me." Fyren's wry smile was more foxlike than when he was actually in animal form.

A new set of voices came from the doorway. This time the flames moved aside for Devon, a primeyear woman who looked vaguely familiar to Kylene, and the witch of Faway. The room was very crowded now. Kylene could have slipped out unnoticed if not for the problem of going numb when she touched the fire. The higher beings were able to use magic to get through the flames and that gave Ky an idea for an escape plan.

Yeselda was watching her brothers carefully. Kylene sidled up next to her and subtly nudged the witch's hip. With a sharp look, Yeselda glared at her. Sweat beaded on the witch's forehead as if she were under great strain.

Kylene tried mouthing what she wanted, so as not to attract attention, but Yeselda, who was distracted by the Watcher and Fyren, wasn't getting it. Devon had been watching them and nodded, his eyes wide and bright.

Kylene pointed to the east and mouthed, "Outside."

Devon nodded again. He inched closer to Fyren until he was right behind him. "Hey, fox face!"

When Fryen turned, Devon clocked him on the nose, a loud crack of fist on jaw echoing off the stone walls. It set off a chain reaction of motion. Fyren reached with both hands for Devon, while the Watcher roared and leaped between the two of them. Katora screamed and grabbed her nephew, positioning him behind her. Yeselda stood there and laughed.

It was the distraction Kylene needed. She reached deep inside herself to picture the shining gold buildings and hear the bittersweet music of the Golden City. She imagined a feeling of safety wrapping around her body, and an emanating warmth convinced her it was working. She opened her eyes to find golden flames surrounding her, warm to the touch but not scalding. With a quick inhalation, she ran for the doorway.

The purple flames were no match for her golden ones. After crossing the barrier, she let the fire around her burn out to save energy as she ran down the spiraling stone steps and burst out of a door at the bottom. She barely felt the sea breeze as she raced across the sand to the mound with the pyre. She heard the singing of the arrow a second before it pierced her back. A white hot pain spread all throughout the left side of her body. Then came a wet warmth across her chest. A buzzing numbness overtook her as she fell to the sand.

* * * *

The flurry of activity was what Devon had wanted when he punched the greater being. With Katora and the Watcher between him and Fyren, the rush of excitement was wearing off and Devon's hand began to hurt...badly. He tried to shake off the pain, but his knuckles were already swelling with purple bruises.

The fact that he understood what Kylene needed when the witch of Faway didn't was consolation for the pain. If Ky was right about the Great Mother, what his aunt was about to do could turn this battle into a winning one. It was a good thing he had run off to the temple on Capdon Mountain and learned about elemental magic, otherwise he never would have been able to help.

The distraction didn't last long because all of a sudden bright flames engulfed Kylene, catching everyone's attention. The flames were so bright, Devon couldn't look directly at them, though the higher beings didn't seem to have that problem. Before anyone could react, the ball of fire flew out of the tower room and disappeared down the stairs, disintegrating the purple flames in the doorway.

Fyren cried out, "No!"

He yanked the bow out of Tarq's hands, whipped an arrow from the quiver, and ran for the stairs, his motions so quick, they were blurred. Everyone ran after him, Devon in the lead and the griffin form of the Watcher creating a bottleneck behind it. The twisting stairs brought Devon around a turn and almost into the back of Fyren, who stood on a landing in front of an arched window. The bow and arrow were drawn, pointing out the small opening.

Behind Devon, the Watcher let out a throaty growl. "Do not." The threat came too late as Fyren loosed the arrow.

From his vantage point, Devon watched the arrow fly straight and true through the air right into Kylene's back. The impact jerked her forward, before sending her to the ground, her arms splayed out above her body. The moment Kylene was struck, Fyren also fell, his posture on the stone landing mirroring his victim's in the sand below.

Katora let out a shriek and raced past the window, everyone but Fyren and Devon following behind. The shock of seeing his aunt shot drew the breath out of Devon; his lungs heaved and he gasped for air. He clutched at the stone wall, trying to keep himself upright, but he went down on his knees, his vision spotting.

No one else knew what Kylene had meant to do, so he had to finish what she started. With blackness overcoming his vision, he searched for a calm center within himself. He took a deep breath; so much air filled him, it made him dizzy. But he also felt strong in a way he never had before. He stood and dashed down the stairs to have his heroic moment at last.

* * * *

The strangest thing happened as Indy flew back over the smoke and mayhem of the battle. One moment Fyren's insects were zipping around, attacking everything in sight, and the next they were perfectly still, statues frozen in midair. With their wings immobilized, they began to drop, flies raining down on the sand. Zelenka saw all this in a detached kind of shock. Despite her army training, she found it hard to care about the greater battle, her sole focus the battle against death that Palafair was losing. Splayed out over Indy's front legs, he looked dead already. Zelenka could see the slight rise and fall of his chest, so she knew she hadn't lost him yet.

Indy directed them past the battlefield and flew over Drim. Zelenka prayed to the Great Mother that Katora had found Kylene and was no longer invisible under the Watcher's magic. She was about to direct Indy to land on an open battlement when she spotted movement on the opposite side of Drim. Kylene's white-blond hair flew out behind her as she ran across the sand. Zelenka knew that wherever Kylene was, Katora was sure to follow.

"That way!" Zelenka yelled, pointing.

Indy zoomed down to the primeyear girl. Zelenka never saw anything strike Kylene. What she did see was Kylene lurching forward and dropping to the ground, her arms reaching out but falling short of a hill that held a purple-flamed pyre. The fletchings of an arrow stuck out of Ky's back.

Indy slowed to a hover and buzzed, "What now?"

No more arrows came. Zelenka was debating whether or not it was safe to land when more people burst out of the fortress and ran for Kylene, Katora among them. Indy didn't have to be told to fly down and land next to the Kase sisters. Indy held onto Palafair, while Zelenka jumped down. There were others who had rushed out to the scene, among them Yeselda and the Watcher, but all they did was stand in witness.

"Katora!" Zelenka yelled.

"Hang on." Katora fell to her knees and reached out to her sister but pulled back before touching her. Blood stained the sand around Kylene. Katora scrambled for her pack and pulled out a small vial. "Should I take the arrow out?"

The brigha Tarq said, "No!"

Without touching the arrow shaft protruding from Kylene's back, Katora dripped Elixir onto the wound. "I need to get some in her mouth."

"Katora!" Zelenka shouted again. "Palafair needs the Elixir."

Katora shot a glare in Zelenka's direction, but then she

spotted Palafair, taking in the limp form of his body, and her expression turned desperate. "Bring him here," she said as she continued to tend to her sister. "Tarq, help me."

Indy set Palafair down next to Kylene. Zelenka limped over to him, having aggravated her old injury somewhere along the way, and caressed her husband's hand. It was sticky with blood and cold...too cold. "Katora," she said, her voice a croak.

Tarq was holding Kylene on her side, the girl's eyes were closed and her face was unnaturally pale. Katora forced some Elixir beyond the pale lips and into her sister's mouth, then she dripped some on her chest where the tip of the arrow poked out. There was blood everywhere.

Tarq finally said what everyone around them already knew, "Katora, she's gone."

"No!" Katora screamed. "Try to stop the blood flow, give the Elixir time to work." She touched Kylene's face with the gentleness of butterfly wings and cried. The vial of Elixir fell from her hand onto the sand. Tarq ripped off his cloak and pressed it to the wound.

Zelenka's heart was in her throat as Katora sobbed over her sister, but Zelenka had Palafair think about. She snatched up the vial before all the precious Elixir spilled into the sand and began applying it to his many wounds.

A figure sped past them all and jumped over the water surrounding the hill with the pyre, his feet kicking up sand as he ran to the top.

Chapter Sixty-Four

"Devon!" Em yelled as he reached the top of the hill, the purple pyre in front of him.

Even after running down the stairs, across the sand, and up the hill, Devon barely felt winded. He stood and surveyed the elements. The first three were obvious: the pyre was fire, the sand was earth, and the moat around the hill was water. The tricky one was air, but he figured it out when a fly buzzed by his ear. He spotted two more flying around the mound of sand. It was subtle, but the disturbance of air from the flies' wings was enough.

Fyren the Fallen had ensnared Mother Nature with the four elements. It was why she hadn't been able to interfere in the battle, or likely why she hadn't interfered before then. Not many believed in elemental magic anymore, but the priestesses at the temple on Capdon Mountain did, and Devon had learned just enough from them to put the pieces together as Kylene had done before him.

Kylene's bloody body and Katora's sobs were an exclamation on how he had to succeed where his aunt had failed. Shooting Kylene with the arrow seemed to have backfired on Fyren because it had also incapacitated him, but higher beings were immortal and Devon had no idea how long it would be before Fyren was working against them again. He had to release Mother Nature now. He started with the mound of sand, pushing it down over the moat to take care of water and earth.

"What are you doing?" Em was at his side, staring at him incredulously. "This isn't helping your aunts."

"It's not about them," he grunted. He would think about his aunts later; he had to save the world first. "The Great Mother. Bound by the elements." He felt strong enough to move the entire Great Peninsula and continued to shove sand onto the water. Em moved out of his way, understanding his need to do this if not the reason for it.

Yeselda finally caught on to what Kylene had been trying to convey in the tower and swatted one of the flies. It dropped to the ground, dead. The Watcher transformed into its bird form and grabbed a second fly in its mouth, swallowing it down. The two higher beings reached the third fly at the same time. Yeselda held out her hand and the Watcher slapped it with a wing, crushing the last fly between then.

Working at a speed he had never imagined possible, Devon leveled most of the mound, completely covering the water in the process. He continued to sift through the sand until he unearthed a plant with tiny blue flowers. Now crumpled and browned from being buried, it had once been the true blue of a clear autumn sky. Forget-me-nots, a symbol of true love, the kind Mother Nature had for the world she nurtured.

The only thing left to do in order to unbind the Great Mother was to destroy the fire.

The wind picked up and whipped the flames higher, forcing Devon to move away. Katora and Tarq were still tending to Kylene, and Zelenka to Palafair. Em, Nika, and a midnight blue sciathilte stood by and watched. Yeselda had her hands up and appeared to be using her magic to fight the purple fire but with little impact. The Watcher in its griffin form attempted to use its wings to blow out the flame, but it only stoked it further. Devon was about to suggest finding a bucket and going to the ocean for water when the higher beings' heads turned toward Drim.

Devon sucked in a breath as he watched Fyren step out of the fortress and stride across the beach.

"Brother," the Watcher growled. "Enough of this. Stand down."

Fyren laughed. "My fire too much for you?"

"You coward!" Yeselda shouted. "Release our mother and let her settle this."

"Ha" was all Fyren said.

Devon took in the stricken faces of those around him and the lifeless bodies of Kylene and Palafair, and then his gaze fell on

Fyren's sneer. Images of Fyren's insects decimating the sciathilte and demicks and then turning on the humans were seared into his memory forever. A bubble of energy filled him, fueled by his anger. He stepped up to the purple pyre and blew out every bit of searing anger he harbored for the fallen higher being. A great gust of wind burst from his mouth and blasted the fire into oblivion.

All the strength Devon had felt a moment ago deflated when the air left him. He had done what he had come to do, and now he couldn't breathe.

* * * *

Kylene couldn't breathe but found she didn't need to. Her eyes opened to a dark sky filled with stars, but not like any stars she had seen before. They were more brilliant than the ones in the night sky on the Great Peninsula and in multitudes she couldn't have imagined. Some shot across the sky, their tails burning behind them, while others cluster together in great spiraling masses.

Kylene, not feeling entirely solid herself, floated among wispy clouds. A sweet, quiet music filled the air...and filled her heart, a heart that no longer thumped in her chest, but it was there and feeling every emotion to near bursting. Had it really been pierced clean through by an arrow moments ago?

There was no pain in her body. Her arm, the one that had been hurting her for years, was strong, limber, and injury free.

I must be dead.

The thought didn't scare her, but it should have. Then again she had glimpsed the afterlife once, when she had been transported away to the Golden City. All this time she had thought she had gone to another part of the corporeal world, but the Golden City was more like this place than the world of the Great Peninsula. The hold of the city lifted, and she realized the weight of it had been nearly as agonizing as the chronic pain.

And now there was this world of stars and music, and it was so peaceful, tears threatened to burst out and never stop. The details of her old life were there but smudged, like looking at a reflection in a puddle of muddy water. The faces of her family were faded, but the love shone through, each person a flower blossoming in her heart. Thinking of her home and the farm in Tussar was more a mood than an image. The impressions remained, but the finer points were muted.

Her emotions, which had always run high, were stronger than ever. Love was the most obvious one as it was all-encompassing, filling her to the brim. Beneath it, other feelings forced their way up. The positive ones—joy, kindness, wonder— were keener than before. The negative ones—fear, resentment, anger—washed over her too, but she understood them like she never had and found she could bear them. They balanced out the overwhelming euphoria of the positive emotions.

"Welcome, Kylene Kase." The voice filled her head. It was a kind, motherly voice, one she had never heard but knew all the same. Mother Nature, the Great Mother herself.

Kylene looked around and saw no corporeal being among stars and clouds. But there was a presence, a light in the sky. Not the soft yellow of a summer afternoon, but the sharp slice of winter sun reflected off the snow—a hint of warmth with the wrath of winter beneath it. "You have been longing for this place. What do you think now that you are here?"

Kylene had trouble finding the words to describe her feelings but found she didn't need words. The emotions poured out of her and she said, "Home. It feels like home."

"You are home...for now." There was no threat there, but Kylene wasn't sure she liked the sound of it. "You may go on toward the stars. Or you may go back."

Kylene would have sucked in a breath if she had any. "Go back? You mean to the Great Peninsula, to my family, back," the word no longer felt right but she used it anyway, "home?"

"Yes." The simple, yet incomprehensible, word echoed in Kylene's head.

"But I am dead," she said, feeling like she was stating the obvious and by doing so insulting the Great Mother. "Even the Elixir cannot bring people back people from the dead. That is what Katora told me. So how can I go back?"

"Tell me this. Why are you here?"

"I was shot in the heart with an arrow," Kylene said, feeling once again that pointing out the obvious was somehow disrespectful.

"And how did you come to be in that situation?"

Kylene made a lamenting groan in her throat, reliving the battle in her mind. Humans and demicks alike falling at the hands of Fyren's insect army. Realizing that Fyren had bound the Great Mother by the four elements. There was the slice of pain in her chest, the warm blood seeping out too fast to stop, her life draining away. Someone sobbing against her chest before it all went dark. Those details were sharp, clearer than any others she had from her life. There were no tears here, so she choked back a sob and found she couldn't speak. She had failed to save Mother Nature.

But the Great Mother was here, in her mind if not in the flesh. Kylene didn't have to speak her story for Mother Nature to know it.

Kylene found her voice, "You are no longer bound to Fyren."

"No," said Mother Nature.

"How?" A wind rustled her hair, and she saw what had happened after she was shot, how Devon had figured out how to free Mother Nature. "What happened to Fyren?"

Another image came on a breeze, this one of green shoots bursting up from the sand where Fyren stood and wrapping around him. The plants forced the fallen higher being to the ground and consumed his form. Tiny blue forget-me-not flowers blossomed into a riotous patch.

"Oh," she said. As the stars swirled above her, a memory from her life came back. "I thought I was to make the ultimate sacrifice to save Nika."

"You did." Mother Nature's voice was somber. "You saved Nika and many others when I could not."

"So I fulfilled my blood oath and Odeletta's message." It was indeed as Odeletta had said, it had come to pass but not in the way she had expected. "So I can go back?"

"There is time," the Great Mother said. "I can do what the

Elixir cannot. I can save your life...if you want me to."

She dared to ask, "If I go back, will the pain come back?"

"I will restore you the way you were."

The answer made the decision feel impossible. Here, she was free in a way she had never been in life, and the promise of those stars showed her she could fly if she moved on. To think of going back to her life of constant pain made her feel heavy. But there was more to her old life than pain.

Her heart filled with moments. Sitting next to Ma in the living room of the old wooden house on Kase Farm, Pop strumming the guitar while Kylene sang. Her sisters' laughter as they dressed and prepared for Ariana's wedding, all of them together and joyous. Bhar running through the outskirts of Faway Forest when they were youngeryears, his mischievous face grinning. Hirsten's brown eyes so close to hers in the back of the wagon.

It wasn't only things from the past, either. All the hopes and dreams she had for the future washed over her. They made her want to scream, "Yes! Send me back!" The pain would be worth all the moments to come, the bitter and the sweet.

She didn't need to say a word; Mother Nature saw it all in her unbeating heart. The breeze turned to a whirlwind. A force pulled at Kylene. The stars rushed away in a blur as she shut her eyes and was sucked back down to her body.

An instinct, like a prickle underneath her skin, forced her eyes open.

Chapter Sixty-Five

Puffy white clouds floated above Kylene, and for a moment she thought she was back with Mother Nature in the space between life and death. Then the clouds fluttered in a fresh ocean breeze, and she realized it was not clouds but a canopy above the four-poster bed where she rested. Bright sunlight from huge open windows spilled through an opening in the sheer curtains surrounding the bed. A blazing fire in a stone fireplace kept the winter chill from the room.

She moved slightly and a wave of pain rolled through her chest where the arrow had struck. Underneath the white hot pain, the old familiar ache of her arm was back, the enemy she had to learn to live with rather than letting it get the best of her. She let out a soft moan.

"You're awake," said a gruff voice.

With difficulty and more pain, Kylene propped herself up on the pillows. Tarq sat on a cushioned settee at the far end of the bed, looking bleary-eyed and sleepy, but he rose quickly and moved away from the bed.

"Where are we?" Ky asked.

"Drim," Tarq said.

"Impossible." Drim was as dark and cold as the higher being who had commandeered the fortress. There was no version of Fyren that would have decorated a room like this.

"Odeletta arrived shortly after the battle ended. She has been redecorating and providing supplies and small comforts for all us who fought. I think she feels guilty for not coming sooner, or as guilty as a higher being can be."

The shock of being in this bright room instead of the starry sky with Mother Nature's voice in her head was beginning to wear off, but it would take a long time to process all that had happened in the battle...and all that had happened since lightning had ruined her Golden City play. The longing for the city had left.

She found she lacked the strength to speak and let Tarq fill the silence as he saw fit.

He stood with his hands behind his back, shuffling his feet nervously. "Katora and Pop have been by your side non-stop. With Bhar and Hirsten's help, I finally convinced them to get some sleep. They'll be mad they weren't here when you woke up. Everyone else has been popping in to check on you."

Kylene found her voice to ask, "Everyone?"

"Yeah, everyone," he said. "The higher beings, the general of the tilli army, everyone from Tussar who came to fight, even that other brigha, Nika. All of your family that's here, of course, except for your nephew."

Kylene sat up straighter at the mention of Devon, and she gasped at the throbbing pain in her chest.

"He's okay," Tarq clarified. "He's been confined to bed rest since he blew out Fyren's pyre."

During all this talk, Tarq hadn't made eye contact with Kylene until he mentioned Fyren, and even then his gaze was wary.

"It's okay," she said. "The name doesn't bother me, so long as he can no longer hurt anyone. He's much more beautiful as a plant than he ever was as a fox." She smiled at her own joke, though she didn't go so far as to laugh; that would have hurt too much.

"So you saw that," Tarq said. In a way she had, but she didn't expect him to understand what had happened under the stars with Mother Nature, so she remained silent. "What happened? I thought for sure you were gone from this world. The arrow went right through your heart. Your body was cold, and there was no breath in you. Katora says it was the Elixir that saved you, but it can't bring people back from the dead."

"No," Kylene agreed. "It can't." That was all she said on the matter; she didn't owe Tarq any of her secrets. "Do you still see my magic?"

"Yes, brighter than ever."

His gaze was fixed on her as if her sunny glow didn't bother him, but she believed her magic was there. She could feel it coursing through her veins. How she hadn't been able to feel it before, she didn't know, but each beat of her heart brought a pulsing energy through her body. It didn't negate the pain of her old injury or her new ones, rather it was a new sensation on top of the others.

"What will you do now?" asked Tarq.

"Go home and recover." She longed for time away from the road and riding on horses, for time to read a book and take a bath, for time to walk along the river and dream. "What about you?"

"I'm never content to stay in one place for very long. Maybe I'll head to Skimere and see if anyone needs my services." He stared out the window as if he wasn't sure what he wanted to do next, and Kylene wondered if his life was a lonely one and whether he liked it that way.

"You're welcome at Kase Farm if you find yourself in Tussar. I will need a guide when I return to Kristalis."

That got his attention, and he pierced her with his unreadable gaze. "So you plan on going back."

She nodded and decided to throw him a little tidbit. "I do. I have much to learn from Odeletta."

He narrowed his eyes but not in an unfriendly way. "I bet you do."

They sat in amicable silence for a few minutes until Kylene could wait no longer. She had to know the cost of the battle.

"How many casualties?" she whispered.

"Fewer than it could have been if not for you and Devon figuring out how to unbind Mother Nature." Kylene sensed Tarq's response was meant to soften the blow of her culpability in the deaths. It was her power that had fueled Fyren and allowed him to control the insect army, and there was no denying that.

"How many?" Kylene insisted.

"Twenty-two humans, forty-seven demicks, and nine sciathilte."

Seventy-eight lives on her conscious, a burden no one would be able to convince her was not hers...at least in part.

"And Palafair?" She didn't have to say more for Tarq to understand what she was asking. He shook his head, a mournful expression overtaking his face.

In the vision from Mother Nature, Ky had seen his lifeless body, but she had harbored a spark of hope that the Elixir had been able to save him. The spark in her heart died, and she laid her head back. The tears fell hot and fast into the fluffy pillows. A hand closed around hers and the bed shifted as Tarq sat next to her.

When she felt drained and couldn't have possibly squeezed another tear out, though she was sure there would be more later, she sat up once again. She gritted her teeth through the pain. "I must see Zelenka."

"You need to rest," Tarq said. He was no longer touching her hand, but he maintained eye contact.

"No." She was done being told what to do. This was her life, and she refused to simply go along for the ride on everyone else's adventures.

"Katora will kill me if I let you out of bed. Your father, too."

Kylene smiled as she slipped her legs over the side of the bed and found a pair of fuzzy slippers waiting for her on the floor. It never failed to amuse her how everyone was cowed by Katora, her small but formidable sister.

"Tell them you couldn't stop me. That I was a force of nature," Kylene quipped in a joke that only she understood.

For his part, Tarq held open the door as she achingly made her way out of the comforts of her sick room.

"Send my condolences to Zelenka," he said.

She nodded and headed off to find the demick whose husband died because of Ky's magic.

* * * *

Zelenka was packing when she sensed a presence in the room. She looked up to find Kylene, appearing very much like a ghost with her pale face and flowing white nightgown.

"Zelenka," Kylene said in a whispery voice that added to the ghostly illusion. She moved in a stilted way that showed she was in pain and not, in fact, a ghost. She knelt in front of Zelenka and offered up an embrace, which Zelenka accepted. "I'm so sorry about Palafair."

"Thank you," Zelenka mumbled. All the platitudes were blurred in a haze of mourning. She was too numb to process Palafair's death and needed to be away from this fortress. No amount of sprucing up by the Ice Queen could erase the pallor of death that hung over it.

Kylene recovered herself and looked around. "You're leaving. Where will you go?"

"Demick Island. I need a fresh start, and it felt like home from the moment I arrived. There is a village on the north coast with giant pine trees and misty mornings. It suits me." Zelenka wasn't sure why she was telling Kylene all of this, except for maybe the earnest expression on the human's face—an earnestness that couldn't entirely mask the guilt.

Zelenka patted her hand. "I do not blame you, you know." She meant it, too. She didn't blame Kylene for the deaths any more than she blamed herself. She realized now she shouldn't have blamed Katora either for using the Elixir to save her life.

Life played out in strange ways with demicks, humans, higher beings, and other creatures all playing their parts and contributing to different outcomes. Zelenka had learned that Kylene's magic had aided Fyren, but it was magic stolen. Magic was an entirely different player in the world, and one that was fickle to control at best. "I was unable to protect Palafair, and you were unable to prevent Fyren from taking advantage of you."

Kylene burst out into tears. In between sobs, she said, "How could you tell? I wasn't going to say anything…I didn't want to make you feel like you had to ease my guilt, to put that burden on you."

"Dear, Kylene," Zelenka patted her hand again, "you are terrible at hiding your feelings." Kylene looked like she was about to apologize, but Zelenka shushed her. "It is refreshing. I always know where I stand with you."

"Please don't try to make me feel better. Unless that is what you need to do. Do whatever you need to do right now."

Zelenka smiled around the deep sadness she feared would never go away, while at the same time fearing it would one day fade away and with it the memory of Palafair. "That is what I am doing by leaving."

"Good." Kylene's lip trembled, but no more tears came. "I will do my part to keep Palafair's memory alive back in Tussar. Everyone loved him. He was part of my family, if only temporarily until he found a family in you."

Zelenka's eyes stung. "Say good-bye to your family for me, will you?"

"Of course." Kylene gathered her in for one more hug. She stood awkwardly and slipped away as quietly as she had slipped in. Zelenka wished that whatever part of Kylene had been lost in the ordeal would be renewed with time, stronger than before... though she held no such wish for herself.

There was one more stop to make before she left. She knocked on a thick wooden door in the lower floors of the fortress where the demicks had taken up residence. There were none among them would hadn't suffered a loss, and the hallways were quiet.

Laurel opened the door and said in a hoarse voice, "Colonel."

"Please, call me Zelenka." She entered the dark room, the west facing windows not catching much of the morning light. "I have come to say good-bye."

"Hmmm," Laurel said. After a beat of silence that felt like judgment, she continued, "And what of the tilli you leave behind?"

"The sciathilte will take you back to Faway Forest...or to wherever you would like to go. Nemez will continue to be your leader until you choose a new one." Zelenka had already spoken to the general and told him to hold an election for the new tilli leader without her.

She noticed Laurel's things were all packed up, the bags neatly arranged on the bed. "I see you are ready to go."

The young captain looked down at the ground, rubbing the tips of her boots together nervously. "I am, but not to Faway

Forest."

"Where will you go?"

"I had hoped to go with you to Demick Island." A blushing Laurel stared her straight in the eyes. "Colonel...Zelenka... whatever you want to be called, you are my leader. And my friend. I follow you."

"As do the rest of the tilli," Nemez said from the doorway that had been left open.

"All of you?" asked Zelenka.

"Yes," said Nemez, "and a fair few of the anni as well. The threat of Fyren is gone, but I would like to keep the army strong, with you as our leader."

It wasn't the quiet retreat Zelenka had in mind, but maybe an army was what she needed instead of solitude.

Laurel placed a hand on her shoulder. "This is what we want, but only if it is what you want. And we understand you need time to mourn Palafair." Laurel let out a soft sob. "We all loved him, you know."

"I do." Tears stung the back of Zelenka's eyes. She had never embraced her right to lead the tilli, but the idea had grown on her lately. Palafair's death had obscured the desire to lead, but she felt it there in her gut. "I would be honored to have you along on my new journey."

Laurel clapped her hands once, loudly, before looking sheepish. "Sorry. It is wrong to be excited."

Zelenka touched her cheek. "No, sorrow should not diminish all other feelings. If anything, it should be a reminder of how to fall deep into a feeling—the good and the bad." She hoisted her bags back up on her shoulders. "I should talk to Indy and see if more sciathilte are willing to take us across the ocean." Indy had become more than an ally in their time together and had expressed an interest in staying on Demick Island, and then perhaps traveling to see more of the Great Peninsula in time.

"I already did," said Nemez. "Many of the sciathilte were eager to return to their seclusion in the forest, but some were not. They will take us to Demick Island, though we will not all be able to travel at the same time. I had hoped you could find us a place to set up a village."

"I know just the place." There were lots of unclaimed lands on the north shore of Demick Island. With permission from the islanders, that would be where the tilli settled. "I will visit the priestesses and make plans."

"We can go with you," said Laurel. "The Ice Queen welcomed us to stay as long as we needed, but I am eager to leave this place behind."

"I am, too." A ghost of a smile played at Zelenka's lips. The prospect of being alone to mourn had seemed ideal, but now with a plan in front of her, she was beginning to see a hint of the future, and though it didn't include Palafair, it was something. With the promise of feeling the salty ocean air on her face again, she went in search of Indy to set off for her new home.

* * * *

Devon thought he would go mad with boredom before they let him out of bed. Since blowing out the pyre trapping Mother Nature, his breathing had been better than ever, but there was no convincing his mother or Pop Pop to end his respite. Em came by to update him on the goings on since Fyren's demise. He found himself staring at her lips as she described the transformation the fortress had undergone with the Ice Queen's magic.

"The inside is beautiful now, though the outside is as grim as ever." She sat on the foot of the bed, looking out the window. He wished she would move closer, but they hadn't been alone since before arriving at Drim when they had almost kissed in the back of the wagon. Someone from Devon's family had been with him the entire time; he wasn't sure if they were afraid he would suddenly drop dead or try to escape.

Bhar was on watch now, and he sat in the corner of the room, the front of his chair tipped up as he played a solitary game of cards. Slamming down the chair legs, he glanced at Devon and Em. His eyebrows rose ever so slightly, and he cleared his throat. "I'm going to get something to eat. You two want anything?"

"No," they said in unison.

"Don't let him get in any trouble," Bhar said to Em with a wink.

Em stayed on the end of the bed when the door closed, so Devon stretched his legs and went to sit beside her. He was a little worried about the state of his hair, but he pushed that embarrassment aside with the chance to be close to her.

She continued to stare out the window. "I suppose a 'thank you' is in order. You saved us all."

Heat rose in his cheeks, and he dared to place his hand atop hers. "We all played a role. I thought I wanted to be a hero, but I now realize in order to be a hero, lives must be in danger. And not everyone can be saved." Em grunted, and he longed to hear her laugh. He waggled his pointer finger in front of her face. "What's this?" She gave him a quizzical look, but at least she was looking at him, so he did it again with his finger. "I don't know, but here it comes again."

There a was a pause in time as she stared at him, mouth agape. But then she busted out in a hearty laugh, and he followed. Soon he was lying on top of the bed next to her, trying to catch his breath. He stared at her profile and longed to reach out to her as much as he was afraid to. He had made her laugh, but he would always be an intense person...that was who he was.

She turned to face him. "That felt good." Then she leaned in and kissed him. His lips met hers in intensity, and they didn't stop kissing for a long time.

When they finally pulled away from each other, Devon was once again breathless, but not in a scary, gasping for air kind of way. They stared into each other's eyes for awhile, foreheads gently resting together.

"I think I'm ready for something a little more intense than what I've had in the past," she said.

Devon caught his breath enough to say, "I'll make sure to tell you one stupid joke a day, so things don't get too heavy. Deal?"

"Deal."

And then they were kissing again, until someone loudly knocked on the door. They were able to separate and sit up before

Bhar came in. He gave them a knowing smile and clapped his hands. "Good news. You're free to leave this room, Devon."

Devon jumped off the end of the bed. "Really? I can go outside."

"You're gonna have to. You need to get ready." Bhar grinned, but Devon shook his head, not understanding where this was going. "We're headed home tomorrow."

Now that Devon had finally gone on an adventure, he found the thought of home to be a welcome one. He'd be ready for another adventure one day, but for now, he itched for his notebook back in his attic bedroom because he found he was bursting with poetry.

Epilogue

Odeletta was no longer the Ice Queen as the cold bitterness that had gripped her for centuries had finally thawed. She supposed the moniker would linger, though she had little care for how mortals regarded her. Her new title Queen of Spring would catch on in the next generation.

The woods immediately surrounding Kristalis had thawed into spring at last. The rest of Blanchardwood was another story. It remained a snowy domain, infused with too many years of frozen magic to find another season. Perhaps one day winter would loose its icy fingers on the forest.

Fyren, once again the Fallen, was concealed in a fragrant patch of forget-me-nots as blue as the sky on a clear winter day. He would not be forgotten—her heart wouldn't allow it—nor was he truly gone. The bonds of a lover crossed remained unbreakable. She felt his presence, albeit diminished to a trace, in the stones of Drim and in the sands of Bad Beach. She would feel it in the flowers of her home, this she knew without having to be there.

Higher beings couldn't die any more than mortals could live forever. The loophole was in the transformation of one to the other, and Fyren was still very much a higher being.

Kylene Kase was another story. Once mortal, she was something else now...not a full-fledged higher being, but on her way to becoming one if she chose that path. So far it had proved an irresistible one; Odeletta's queens could attest to that. Each had been human at one time and had faced a similar decision.

Immortality always won out. So far. Perhaps Ky would be different.

The Queen of Spring stood in the very tower where Fyren had held Kylene captive. Odeletta's mistake in thinking herself weak had led to the present circumstances where she was too late to offer more than creature comforts to the battle weary.

The stone window ledge beneath her fingers crumbled as she tested the strength she now knew she possessed. A strength that would not fail her the next time Fyren decided to make a play for power. Because he would make another play, but not before all these mortals had long perished.

Odeletta watched as several sciathilte carried demicks up over the ocean, their exoskeletons glinting like beacons in the fading sunlight. The rest of the demicks would stay awhile, and Odeletta found herself pleased to be able to help them, a new emotion for her. Then again all emotions, save heartache, were foreign. They were like burrs stuck to a sweater, an annoyance that needed to be plucked away. Soft hearts were not for higher beings, but she supposed hers would harden enough to find an equilibrium suited to her status.

The humans were next to leave with their horses and carts of supplies; humans required a great many things to survive. Ky rode toward the back on a light brown horse, her golden magic brighter than the sun. It wouldn't be long—not by Odeletta's measure of time—before she saw her pupil again.

Then the Queen of Spring would show the budding queen what true power was.

ACKNOWLEDGMENTS

Once again it has taken me an incredibly long time to write an Elixir book, so long that it's hard to remember all the people who have helped me along the way. If I've known you in any kind of meaningful way in the last ten years, you've probably had some kind of impact on this book.

Thank you so much to the readers who have trusted me with their time and imaginations by picking up one of my stories and thanks to all the parents, librarians, and teachers who help young readers find books they love. Big thanks to the librarians at my local library for all their support and to the folks at the Indie Author Project for recognizing the important stories self-published authors are telling.

Parts of this story have been churning in my mind for a long time, ever since my dad gave me the idea of writing a book for my sister Kylene. She deserves not only the dedication in this book but also a prime spot in the acknowledgments. The first book, *Elixir Bound*, ended up being more about me than about Kylene; it was my way of mourning her death. This book, *Elixir Saved*, was a way to celebrate her life. Though the Kylene in the book is just a character, not really my sister, I do hope an essence of her real spirit is captured within these pages. It is yet one more ripple she is continuing to make on this Earthly realm.

While writing is a solitary endeavor, making a story into a book is not. A huge thanks to my critique partners Katlyn Duncan, Kai Strand, and Mary Waibel for their keen reads of this beast of a book and to Debby Carroll for her sharp copy-editing skills. As always, all mistakes are mine, but these women have helped to shine my words into something I can be proud of. Thanks to the Weston Writers Group for taking a look at the early chapters and for keeping my spot at the critique table warm. One of my first writing buddies is my nephew and thinking of our old writing sessions helps keep me motivated today. Self-publishing is its own crazy adventure, so I want to thank a couple of fellow indie authors who are examples of the best of this community S. Usher Evans and S.J. Pajonas.

A book cover is one of the most important parts of introducing readers to a story and setting the tone for a book. The talented Susan Tait Porcaro has outdone herself with this magical cover. Thank you so much for creating images that represent my books so beautifully...and for taking the extra time for all the little things I've asked of you.

Family is very important to me as you can probably tell from reading the Elixir stories. To my other siblings—Kelly, Kerrie, and Billy—you have indelibly contributed to my stories and to the person I am today—both good and bad. ;) Thanks to my parents for their support and raising all of us crazy kids. And finally to Batman and the boys, you are the most important parts of my universe and you each shine brighter than the biggest supernova.

About the Author

Award-winning author Katie L. Carroll always says she began writing at a very sad time in her life after her sister Kylene unexpectedly passed away. The truth is Katie has been writing her whole life, and it was only after Kylene's death that she realized she wanted to pursue writing for kids and teens as a career. Since then writing has taken her to many wonderful places, real and imagined. She has had many jobs in her lifetime, including newspaper deliverer, hardware store cashier, physical therapy assistant, and puzzle magazine editor. She works from her home in Connecticut that is filled with the love and laughter of her sons and husband.

Elixir Saved is the much-anticipated sequel to the YA fantasy *Elixir Bound*, winner of Best YA Book for the 2019 Connecticut Author Project. In addition to the Elixir series, Katie is the author of the middle grade adventure *Pirate Island*. For more about Katie and her books, visit her website at katielcarroll.com.

CPSIA information can be obtained
* www.ICGtesting.com
ited in the USA
V021119130520
'S